CONWICK UNIVERSITY

COGNITIO PRO COPIIS

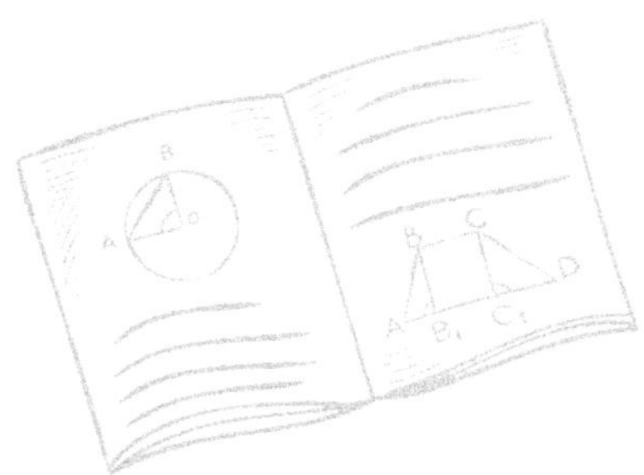

CONWICK U

Book One - Lexi's Story
THE GIRLFRIEND AGREEMENT

Book Two - Ronnie's Story
THE BOYFRIEND VENDETTA

Book Three - Andie's Story
THE EX FACTOR

the GIRLFRIEND agreement

ROWAN CROFT

THE GIRLFRIEND AGREEMENT

CONWICK U BOOK ONE

ARTIST CREDITS:

Fae Quin | @fae.loves.art

Matty Snizhniy | @matty_snizhniy_art

Christine Ledbetter | @capt.christine

Cover and Interior Design by We Got You Covered Book Design

WWW.WEGOTYOUCOVEREDBOOKDESIGN.COM

SHIRE-HILL

PUBLICATIONS

UNITED KINGDOM

ISBN: 978-1-914483-31-8

CONTENT WARNING

This story contains the following themes: a family member with chronic illness, familial loss, grief, abandonment, financial anxiety, explicit language (including frequent strong profanity), a scene involving sex while intoxicated (dubious consent), explicit sexual content, alcohol as a coping mechanism in times of emotional distress, references to past promiscuity and emotionally immature and inappropriate behavior, a scene of mild violence (someone may or may not get kicked where it hurts), and more *Twilight* jokes than is probably reasonable (but hey, loving *Twilight* while also roasting it is a time-honored pastime, so enjoy.)

LEXI

Age: 19

• literal genius
• has number–form synesthesia
• on a full scholarship to Conwick
• runs on caffeine, existential dread,
  and poor impulse control
• loves true crime and math
• allergic to bullshit

CONWICK UNIVERSITY

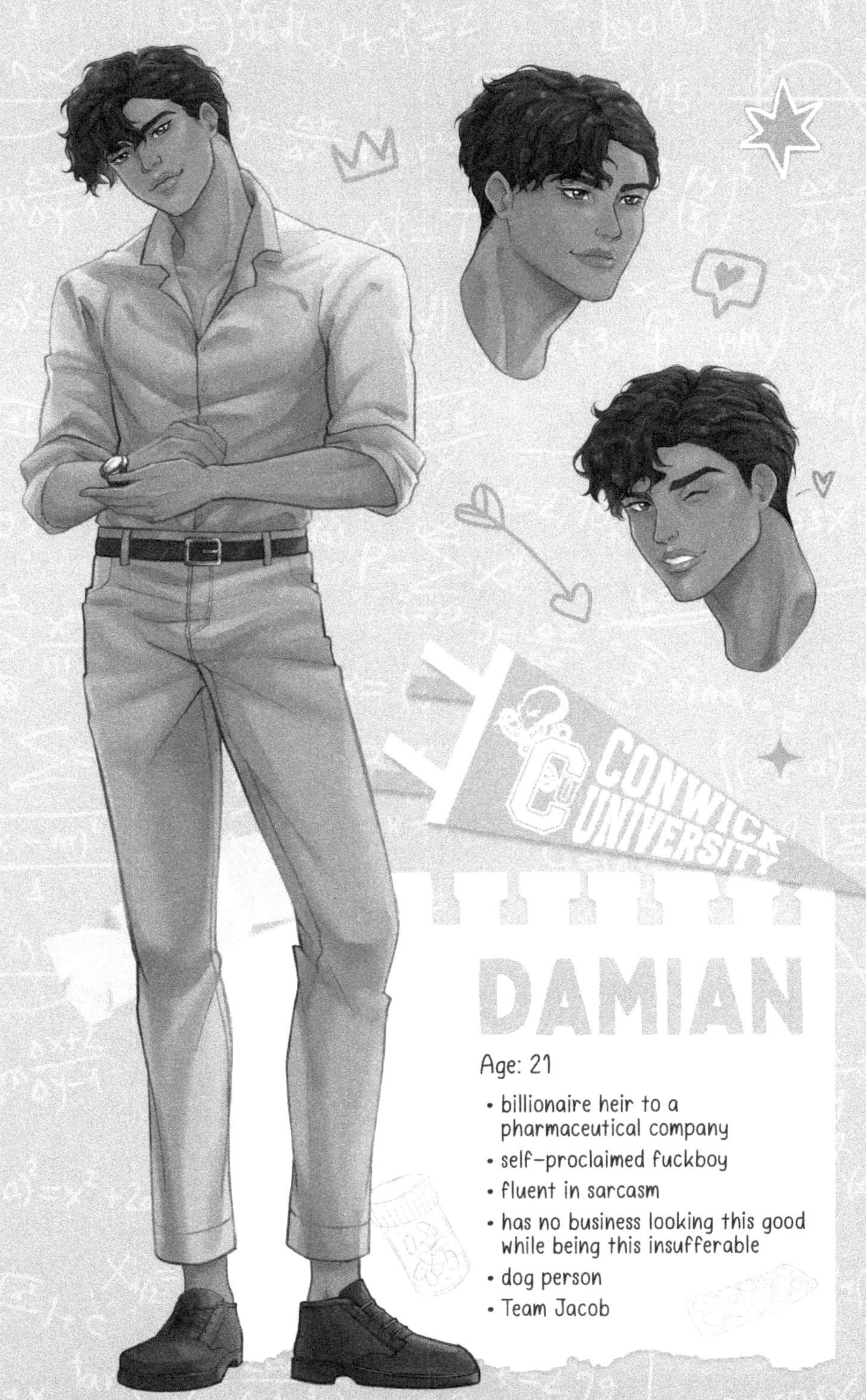

CONWICK UNIVERSITY

DAMIAN

Age: 21

• billionaire heir to a pharmaceutical company
• self-proclaimed fuckboy
• fluent in sarcasm
• has no business looking this good while being this insufferable
• dog person
• Team Jacob

CHAPTER ONE

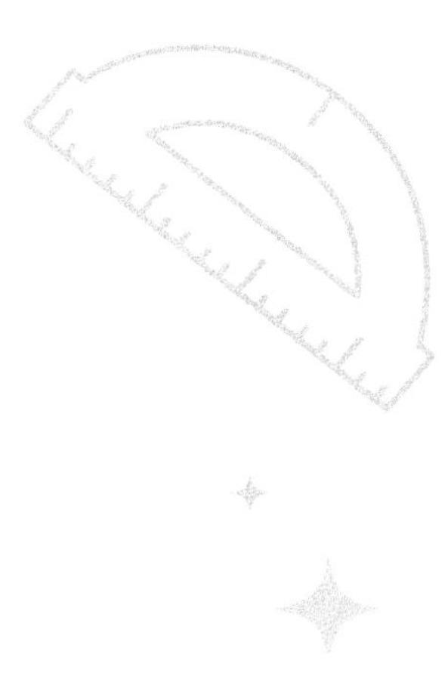

✦ *Lexi* ✦

**Poor impulse control + alcohol =
life choices I'll regret in the morning.**

SEPTEMBER

My back slams into the hard wooden door, and I expel a sound that's half gasp and half moan against soft lips that remind me of velvet. An unbidden giggle escapes me in my drunken stupor as warm hands slide across my thighs and pull my legs tighter around the muscled waist belonging to the tall, blurred figure before me. I wish I could see his face more clearly, but I took out my contacts since they were irritating my eyes (I was starting to resemble someone with hay fever who just snorted several lines of pollen), and I don't have my glasses on hand. I might make it a point to pick outfits with pockets, but no pocket in the world—at least where women's clothes are concerned—will comfortably fit a glasses case. Plus, the copious amount of alcohol I ingested earlier is making everything extra fuzzy. As such, all I can really make out is that kissable mouth, which pulls away now, leaving me hungry—*so* damn hungry—for more.

Suddenly, the world tilts and I'm on my feet instead of where I want to be, which is wrapped around him…whoever *he* is.

I pout as the lips I was devouring only seconds ago twist into what I assume is a smirk.

"Someone's eager," it says, but the liquid courage flooding my body wipes away any embarrassment I might feel at those words.

With a confidence Sober Me would die to possess, I answer with a nonchalant, one-shouldered shrug. "Well, I won't be if you keep me standing out here all night."

My mystery man—the owner of that perfect mouth I desperately want to kiss again—lets out a low, throaty chuckle that sends an arc of electricity racing through me. It's an entirely new kind of buzz, and I wobble, a little unsteady on my feet.

My gaze drifts down the hallway over the course of the moment I wait for him to unlock the door. Although I can't see the details, I know all too well where I am. I've never been in this dorm before; only select students at the university are invited to reside in this particular building, which was donated by some rich douchebag's daddy a few decades ago to probably buy their kid's way into school. The rest of us are either townies, like me, who live in Newport and travel to campus for classes, or are residents in the lesser dorms, like my best friend, Ronnie, who isn't *quite* at one-percenter level of wealth but isn't exactly scraping the bottom of the barrel. Her cousin, Andie—my other best friend—is her roommate (and the third leg to our little tripod), and while she doesn't technically come from money herself, she benefits from having two very doting uncles who have plenty to spare. Ronnie's dads have ensured they have every advantage in life, even paying for Andie's and her little sister Sammy's education.

Aside from the small number of us who earned our way into Conwick solely with our brains—and, in my case, an extremely generous scholarship awarded by the school—the majority of those in attendance are rich, many of them disgustingly so, earning the institution its elitist reputation as a prestigious private university. It's not Ivy League, but in terms of academic expectations and student selectivity, it's definitely close, though it's obvious Conwick favors the affluent and powerful over people like me, who are only here to fill a quota. The dormitories are just one aspect of the college that reflects the obscene wealth polluting the campus, with Leeland Hall being the most exclusive and desired by students, reserved only for those families with cash to burn who are willing to pay a king's ransom in room and board for their child.

Having never seen the inside of any of the dorms aside from Garfield Hall where Ronnie and Andie live, I can only stare in wonder as the guy beside me—whose name I'm blanking on, assuming I ever learned it at all—pushes open the door and leads me into what is less of a dorm room and more of a lavish apartment.

I freeze mid-step, floored by the extravagance of my surroundings and the sheer size of the space, which I can grasp with ease even if it's all pretty distorted. Garfield Hall—lovingly nicknamed "the Orange Pussy" by the residents there—is practically a five-star hotel, and yet, next to this place, it might as well be a dumpster. No, not a dumpster. A dumpster *fire*. Damn, no wonder none of the truly wealthy students bother renting real estate in town. Why would they when they have their own high-end apartment building at their disposal here on campus?

My jaw drops as I step into the living room, my eyes springing wide as I take in the well-styled, modern decor, which makes my own house seem paltry by comparison. A sectional sofa and glass table stand opposite a black rectangle on the wall that is either the world's most boring painting or an obnoxiously large TV, the layout accented by side tables, plants, and other furnishings that—even obscured by my inadequate sense of vision—make the room look like the set for a Pottery Barn photo shoot. It even *smells* expensive in here, and I can't help wondering if this all came with the space or if some interior decorator was brought in by my mystery man or his rich parents to decorate.

I shake my head, ignoring the way my surroundings spin with the movement. This can't *really* be a dorm room, can it? I haven't stepped through a portal into a parallel universe? Maybe I'm asleep and this is the beginning of a dream where I'm the love interest in a billionaire romance. Or a porno.

Yeah, that last option definitely seems the most plausible of the two.

Well, if this *is* a sex dream, I'm here for it.

Drawn into the fantasy, I inch forward a few more steps, peering through decorative archways into an open plan kitchen and dining area on my left, and then over at a bedroom with a huge four-poster bed on my right. My focus clings to the otherwise indiscernible black bedspread, which hugs what must be a king-size mattress from the size of it, maybe larger. The material gleams beneath the overhead spotlights, which come on suddenly as if in response to my perusal.

I startle at the touch of a hand on my wrist, and shifting my eyes upward, meet the gaze of the owner of that luscious mouth, offering him a smile as he guides me into the bedroom with a devious grin. As if under a spell, I giggle again and bite down coyly on my bottom lip—a poor, drunken attempt at flirting that I would *never* dare commit the crime of while sober, and which I'm sure I'll die of shame over tomorrow.

For now, though, my inhibitions are gone, and all I care about is letting loose and enjoying this moment for what it is. The fall semester has only just begun and already I need relief from the constant stress that plagues my day-to-day life. Although Ronnie was the one who encouraged me to go to the party—who said I should blow off some steam and start sophomore year off on the right foot…or at least on a more *relaxed* foot—it hadn't taken much convincing to get me to go despite my usual distaste for crowds and loud music. I just didn't realize at the time that *this* was what I really needed, not a game of beer pong with a bunch of random frat boys.

As if determined to satisfy my unspoken needs, Mystery Man pulls me close with large, firm hands. Then he's kissing me again, those soft lips traveling down to my throat, every scrape of his teeth on my skin doing things to my insides that definitely shouldn't be legal.

"Can I?" he whispers against my neck, and I nod, not even sure what he's asking permission for, but willing to let him do anything if it will mean he keeps touching me. If it means he touches me *more*.

Warmth pools in my belly when our lips meet again, and I sigh into his mouth the moment his hand moves lower, stealthily slipping between my legs. A shiver follows the light graze of his fingertips as they carefully slide up under my skirt, but to my dismay, they linger there, teasing the sensitive skin of my inner thighs—inching closer to where the heat inside me is strongest but not close enough to alleviate the ache building there, as if intent on holding back. On letting the anticipation build. Each brush of his fingers feels electric, sparking a slow burn that spreads through my body until every touch, no matter how light, has me squirming.

Breath shaky, I urge him on, pressing my chest flush to his. It's been a while—*too* long, really—since I last had sex, and all my body parts seem to respond to that nagging desire inside me as if they have a mind of their own. My tongue sweeps deeper into his mouth as I fumble clumsily with the buttons on his shirt, the pounding of my heart just as frantic as my unsteady hands. It's pale blue, I can make out that much. Gucci, probably.

I snort.

"What's so funny?" he purrs in my ear, nipping my lobe with teeth that I'm sure are blindingly white, perfectly straight, and likely cost a small fortune in dental care.

Before I can answer, he puts me out of my misery, an obscene moan parting my lips as he skillfully pushes my underwear to one side, and dips his hand between my thighs in the most perfect form of torture. When he sweeps a finger through my folds, I practically melt at his touch.

"You're so fucking wet," he whispers in my ear. He gently bites my earlobe again, and I gasp when he sinks one finger into my heat. Spurred on by my cry, he moves his hand faster, another finger joining the first, and as he plays with me, his fingers dipping in and out, his palm smacks repeatedly against my clit in a way that'll have me coming before he's even inside me. I'm so pent-up, I won't last long at this rate.

I grab his wrist to still his hand, and he studies me, confusion ablaze in hazy but stunning eyes the color of dark chocolate swirled with honey. Shaking my head, I push Mr. Probably Too Rich For His Own Good back onto the bed, running my palms over his deeply tanned—and *very* defined— abs as I crawl over him and straddle his pelvis, kicking off my red heels in the process. With a pleased hum, I trace the ridges of his muscles, the skin unyielding beneath my fingers.

Someone goes to the gym, I muse, worshiping the firm planes of his body.

As I touch him, his hands cup my ass, and he pulls me downward, grinding his length against me. I can feel the heat radiating from him, can *feel* just how hard he is through his jeans, and every movement as he guides my hips is a delicious friction, sending shock waves of warmth rippling through me, making my very soul hum with need.

"Do you have a condom?" I ask, my breath hitching as my fingertips continue their keen exploration.

"Top drawer. Nightstand." He grunts out each word, then bites down on his plump bottom lip as he rolls our hips together again.

Panting, I extricate myself from his grasp and lunge forward onto my stomach, reaching for the table beside the bed…but in my inebriated horniness, I miscalculate the distance and tug the drawer in question open with far more force than is actually required.

Eager, indeed, I chide myself as the compartment comes loose and at least a hundred shiny square packets in varying colors explode into view. A handful even spill over onto the floor.

Raising a brow, I glance over my shoulder, my eyes landing once more on Mystery Man, his features frustratingly vague. My focus strays to his hand as he impatiently palms himself through his jeans, that syrupy heat stirring in my lower belly again at the sight. Swallowing, I force my gaze back to the treasure trove of contraceptives. The foil seems to glisten and glow, illuminated under the spotlights like I've discovered some kind of sexual Atlantis.

For a beat, I simply stare in amazement at the blurry but unmistakable contents of the drawer. Just how much sex does this guy have to warrant stockpiling this many condoms?

Enough that I think I can safely assume he's not interested in anything serious.

I let out a breath of relief. At least I won't have to worry about him chasing me for my number after this. I don't have the time or energy for more than a senseless hook-up right now. Not with my school work, my scholarship requirements, and taking care of Mom. I have way too much on my plate as it is. I don't have the mental bandwidth for a guy, no matter how hot he is…I think…or how completely *insane* his touch might make me feel.

As if aware of my thoughts, Mystery Man mutters something unintelligible, then his hand brushes my leg, jerking me back to the here and now. A shiver of awareness surges through my body, his fingers like brands on my skin that instantly ease me, helping to push all outside worries away and bury them down deep where they won't be able to impede on this moment. I need to stop thinking before I inadvertently cockblock myself and ruin my night.

Clearing my head, I reach out toward the nightstand and pluck a dark purple foil from the pile, then sit up, ready to give Mystery Man my undivided attention. As I move, my hair shifts in front of my face, and though I shove it back behind my ears, the silky texture is unforgiving and just slips back into whatever inconvenient position it wants. I am *so* not used to straightened hair, but Ronnie had wanted to see what it would look like, and if there's one thing that girl is a pro at, it's getting her way. My makeup, my hair— that was *all* her. Not that I can't pull in my natural state if I wanted to…or ever bothered to try (I've noticed men really aren't that picky if sex is on the table), but considering I'm about to get dicked down when I would normally be playing the role of hermit at home, I suppose I should thank her.

Straddling Mystery Man's legs, I pick up where we left off, rising onto my knees to give myself some needed clearance as I yank down his jeans. As they slip down his thighs, my eyes dip to the generous bulge that greets me in anticipation. I might be half blind, but I can tell he's big. *Really* big. The thin fabric of my panties grows damp from just imagining what it will feel like to have him inside me.

Eager to start, I skim my fingertips along the waistband of his briefs, then pause when I catch a glimpse of the name printed there. The letters are indistinct, melting together into an amoebas blob, but I would swear it says Versace.

I snort again. This pair of underwear alone probably costs more than my entire wardrobe combined.

"God, you're so sexy," Mystery Man mutters, sitting upright. With a warm hand, he pushes my hair over my shoulder, then cups his fingers around the back of my neck to pull me in for a kiss that would leave me weak-kneed if I was still on my feet. His tongue plunges into my mouth, colliding with mine in a dance that increases in pace and intensity until I only seem to exist in this kiss. He tastes like mint and gin and something so profoundly intoxicating I can barely think straight. Hell, I can barely breathe.

I rake my fingers through his thick umber hair, ravenous for those perfect lips and for everything he has to offer under his tight, overpriced briefs. Oh, my sweet little rich boy. I sincerely hope your dick is at least half as impressive as your trust fund.

We part just long enough for him to kick off his jeans and underwear, and for me to wrestle my top over my head and unhook my bra. His undivided attention is on my chest as soon as it's bare, and I relish the feel of each wet sweep of his tongue as he licks and flicks the tip of it across my nipples, his hands squeezing my breasts as he alternates between fondling and then drawing them into the scorching heat of his mouth. His touch is so warm and his lips are the sun as he drags them over my skin, burning me with every caress.

Grabbing Mystery Man by the chin, I tilt his head back and chase his lips, desperate to taste him again, kissing him deeply once more as he pulls me into his lap, his hard-on rigid against my stomach. It seems to beg for my attention from where it stands wedged between us, and pre-cum leaks onto my fingers as my nails carefully graze over the head and then slide downward along the smooth skin of his shaft. He seems even bigger than he had looked with his underwear on, and I'm hungrier than ever to feel the fullness of another human inside me again. Now that I think about it, I haven't experienced such intense physical attraction to someone since I lost my mind and spread my legs for one particular fuckboy my freshman year. It's not that I haven't *wanted* that connection, I just haven't been able to bring myself to let a guy touch me or even get close on an emotional level after the havoc that asshole wreaked on my life.

But that happened to Past Lexi, and I'm done letting her mistakes control me. As I learned the hard way, sometimes, sex is just sex, and it doesn't always mean something to both involved parties…even if the participating male member makes you think otherwise. Often, it doesn't mean *anything* to the other person, which I'm certain is the case with this guy if the volume of condoms in his bedside drawer is any indication of how commitment-phobic I'd wager he is. I doubt he even knows my name. I sure as hell don't know his.

And it's going to stay that way because names lead to familiarity, and I need that distance between us to keep feelings out of the equation. I don't have time for feelings. I don't *want* feelings. I just want my lady cave to get plundered and to have a mind-shattering orgasm that isn't caused by something with batteries for once.

I can have meaningless sex, I assure my dubious conscience.

I can do this, and not expect anything to come of it or for him to give a damn about me after. I *can* allow myself just one night of pleasure and then move on, no strings attached. No nuclear fallout. In and out. One and done.

With that little mental pep talk out of the way, I break the kiss and hold up the packet still clutched in my hand, tearing the foil open and deftly removing the condom inside before I can change my mind. Mystery Man offers me a crooked smile, then exhales a stilted breath when I stroke him again, a long groan parting those gorgeous full lips when I slowly roll on the rubber sheathing. When he's covered, I lift my hips and position myself over his cock, ready. *So* fucking ready. He carefully shifts my panties aside, and this time, I'm the one who groans when his thumb teases over my swollen bud, pulling a startled whimper from me. Every touch feels so damn good, I can't take it anymore. I can't wait. I need him—I need *this*—like I need air to breathe.

"Are you good?" he asks, his voice husky.

"Yeah," I manage in a panting breath. I am *more* than good.

Licking my lips, I lower my body until his head is snug against my entrance, and we both exhale trembling breaths at the same time as I sink into his lap, taking him in an inch at a time. As he enters me, his erection pulsates, and I swear I can feel his heart racing inside me. Or maybe that's my own heartbeat I sense. Either way, this feels so damn good and we haven't even started moving yet.

Mystery Man smiles into my neck, placing a sucking kiss on the dip at my collarbone, allowing a moment for me to adjust to the welcome invasion. As soon as he's fully seated, he looks at me, and I become aware of a question in the silence between us. He wants my permission again—this time to start, to fuck me into oblivion—and I nod once more, all too happy to grant it. With another kiss at the base of my throat, he lifts me up by my hips, pulling out just a little, and then thrusts back into me with enough force to make me cry out.

"Again," I breathe, my tone pleading.

With a guttural growl, he loops one arm around my back, and flips me over onto the mattress so he's kneeling between my open legs. The sudden shift catches me off guard, but before I can process what's happening, he pulls out in one smooth motion and peels off my panties with a swift tug, tossing them carelessly behind him. Then, hooking one of my knees over his shoulder, he plunges into me again, deeper, *harder*—moving in an almost desperate rhythm that makes me tremble beneath him. My gasp of shock quickly turns into a wail of pure bliss, my back arching as I grasp at the sheets. His fingernails dig into my hip bones, holding me still as he drives into my core over and over again, his movements fast and unwavering, hitting all the right places. I'm dizzy with desire, my arousal building, my whole body quivering as he guides me toward the edge.

"You feel amazing," he says, one hand squeezing my breast, and the ego boost combined with the touch of his magic fingers is all it takes. When my orgasm hits, I scream so loudly I wouldn't be surprised if someone heard me on the other side of campus.

Thankfully, I'm far too intoxicated to care, my focus centered on the shiver of pleasure rippling over my skin and on the wave of ecstasy I'm joyfully riding, like a high I never want to end. As it fades, I go limp in my rich stranger's arms, and after a few more pumps, he, too, reaches the brink.

"Fuck," he snarls, clamping those dark eyes shut. He then drops his face into the crook of my neck as his hips shudder, convulsing once…twice… three times against mine.

Fuck, indeed. Exhausted and sated, I melt into a puddle on the bedspread beneath me, more content than I've felt in a really long time. Or at least since January, which was when I last had sex. Was it only eight months ago? It feels more like years. God, I needed this.

Neither one of us says another word as he pulls out—disentangling himself from my jelly-like limbs—discards the condom, and then flops onto the pillow beside me, exhaling a heavy but satisfied breath. I consider getting up and removing myself from the room for all of five seconds, then decide I'm too drunk (and definitely way too blind) to entertain the notion of stumbling home at this hour, even if it means doing the walk of shame in the morning. Deciding that's Tomorrow Lexi's problem, I let my eyes drift closed and fall into the sweet embrace of sleep…

Only a few minutes seem to pass before a buzzing against my thigh is wrenching my eyes open again. Light floods in through a window to my right, and I wince as my head throbs relentlessly, each beat of pain keeping in perfect time with my pulse.

Pushing a tangled mess of hair off my face, I press the heels of my hands into my eye sockets, and reach for my phone, tugging it free from the hidden pocket Andie (using her superhuman sewing skills) graciously sewn into my skirt, which now sits crooked on my waist. I blink the sleep from my eyes to find Ronnie's name flashing almost aggressively across the screen.

I swipe to answer and bring the device to my ear.

"Hello?" I barely recognize my voice when I speak. My throat is raw and dry, as if I've been gargling sand…or a whole lot of dick. My memory of last night is so spotty, it honestly could be either.

"Lex?" I yank the phone away from my face, flinching at the high-pitched screech emitting from my best friend that seems intense enough to crack glass. "Where the *hell* are you? I've been calling you for hours."

"Sorry." A yawn swells in my chest before I can get the full word out. "I was sleeping. What time is it?"

"Nearly ten," she answers, her tone scolding. "Where'd you run off to last night? I would've sworn I saw you disappear with Damian Navarro, but I know you would sooner huff glue than go anywhere with that unapologetic bag of dicks."

All the blood drains from my face as I'm struck by a chill and a sense of bone-deep dread. For the first time since waking, I take stock of my surroundings, finally seeing them a bit more clearly without the bleariness of alcohol adding an extra layer of obscurity to my vision and severely impacting my judgment. It takes Ronnie repeating my name several times for me to snap out of my stupor and grasp what in the drunken hell I've done.

Bracing myself, I roll over and risk a reluctant glance at the now slightly less blurry face of my one-night stand, praying to any god that will listen that it be anyone but *him*…before realizing almost immediately that there is no god. Or at least none who are on Team Lexi.

"Fuck my life," I breathe into the phone as I stare in horror at the fuckboy who ruined my freshman year where he sleeps soundly beside me.

LEX!
LEX!
LEX!!
FUCK MY LIFE.

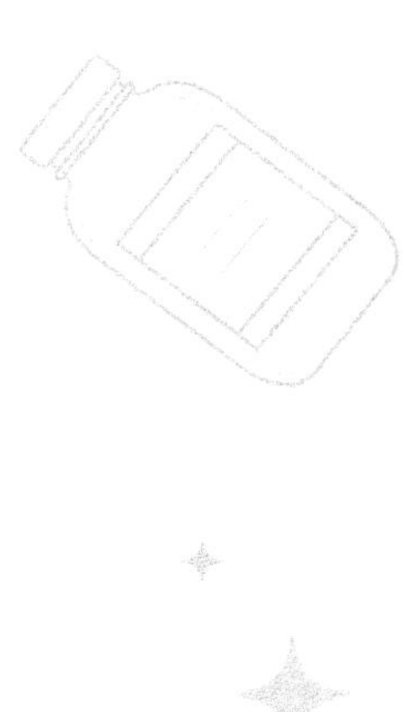

CHAPTER
TWO

✦ *Damian* ✦

Año nuevo, vida nueva - New year, new life

Translation: New year, new me...or maybe not.

My eyes blink open, my vision bleary as I try to pull the room around me into focus. The ceiling spins in protest, the whirling movement churning my stomach, threatening to bring up whatever concoction of spirits that Yesterday Damian thought wise to drink last night.

Christ, I really hate hangovers.

For a long moment, I don't move—partially because I'm hoping I'll fall back asleep, but mostly out of fear I might end up vomiting all over the 1020 thread count. Not that I particularly give a damn about bed sheets. I can always buy more. But buying more means getting up, and right now, all I want is to stay horizontal.

"Fuck my life," a voice whispers beside me.

Oh. I'm not alone. Interesting. I guess I'm experiencing a bit of sex amnesia this morning.

Curious about the identity of my guest, I turn my head, taking in the half-naked blonde lying on the other side of my mattress, unable to keep my gaze from straying down to her exposed chest. Goosebumps pimple her bare breasts, and her nipples are erect, not unlike my cock, which immediately tents the blanket. She clutches an older model iPhone to her ear and is staring at me like I'm the Ghost of Christmas Yet to Come and I've just told her Tiny Tim is dead. Mascara is smeared under her eyes, and a slightly frizzy golden lock sticks to her cheek, her hair bedraggled—but by no means unattractive—from a night of heavy drinking…or fucking. Based on my own state of undress and the headache currently splitting my skull in half, I'm guessing we partook of both.

"Not quite the reaction I'm used to," I murmur, propping myself up on one elbow to get a better look at her, my queasiness and desire to sleep for the next several hours quelled by the rush of horniness sweeping through me. She's hot. Nice hair, long legs, stunning eyes. Basically everything I look for in a woman. Not that I'm exactly picky. Anything with female anatomy is my type.

"I need to call you back," she grumbles into her phone before sliding off the mattress and jumping to her feet like she would rather be anywhere else on the planet than here in bed with me.

I can't help the frown that takes shape on my lips. "Leaving so soon?"

Ignoring me, she scoops a skimpy black top and bra off the floor near the foot of the bed, hastily putting on both and straightening her sexy pleated red skirt, the hem of which barely brushes the middle of her thighs. I don't tell her that her shirt is on backward; something tells me she wouldn't take too kindly to me pointing it out.

Once she's dressed, she glances around for a moment, panic streaking her face, and I follow her wandering gaze, curious what has her so riled up. As the seconds tick by, she looks more and more flustered, and it's only when I spot the panties dangling off the edge of the bed that I realize what she's searching for.

Sitting up, I reach over and gently pinch the lacy fabric between two of my fingers.

"Looking for these?" I ask, flashing her a coquettish grin.

A crimson blush stains her cheeks that would be positively adorable if she didn't look like she was going to kill me. Rushing forward, she snatches the underwear from my grasp, clumsily stepping into them and then adjusting them under that sexy short skirt. Although it's brief, I'm awarded an enticing glimpse at what's underneath, and I berate my brain for not remembering the events of last night in detail.

Avoiding my gaze, my taciturn guest steps into a pair of red heels, then flings her hair up into a messy bun before finally deigning to look at me. Her expression is sullen. Unimpressed, almost, which can't be right. I am nothing if not impressive.

"*Yeah*…this was a mistake," she says.

Ouch. I've never heard that one before. Maybe she really is unimpressed. Then again, even wasted, I'd bet I'm still more skilled in bed than at least half the other guys at this school. This can't be about the sex.

Which means it can only be about me.

Surely, she isn't a Repeat, although that would certainly explain the hostility radiating off her like heat, the visible tension in her shoulders, and the hatred burning in her stunning green eyes. I hope I'm wrong. Drunk Me knows better than to make the amateur mistake of fucking the same woman twice. Repeat sex leads to feelings (on their part), and feelings always lead to someone getting hurt (again, on their part), and I don't have the time or patience for that bullshit drama in my life. I have zero interest in being tied down by a girlfriend, and just want to enjoy my senior year at Conwick before I swap campus life for a corporate one.

Can't a guy just want some meaningless sex without the expectation of commitment?

Besides, why would I want a girlfriend when there are so many tempting fish in the sea? Tempting fish like Blondie, who blows out a loud breath through her nose and plants her hands on her hips, giving me a sour look that one could easily mistake for disgust. Maybe she's nauseated? She *does* look a little pale.

Yeah, I've definitely never gotten *that* look before.

"I think it would be best if we just pretend this never happened, and go our separate ways," she states in a matter-of-fact tone, then adds with an almost impressive malevolence, "That shouldn't be too hard for you." She glares at me, her gaze molten, a scowl on her lips, and it takes all the self-restraint I have not to laugh.

Usually, I'm the one giving this talk to whatever unsuspecting lady Drunk Me brought home so they don't try to make me breakfast in bed and corner me into becoming their boyfriend—an all-too-frequent occurrence since the day I first set foot on this campus. It's tiring fending off such advances at times, but necessary; I'm in no state for commitment at the moment, and if

I do ever settle down, it certainly won't be with some money-hungry college chick looking for a rich future husband.

But this? This is a first. No one has ever tried to blow *me* off before, and I'm not sure if I should be relieved or insulted.

I give her a quick once-over with narrowed, roaming eyes.

Blondie, you have piqued my interest.

"Sure thing, random girl I just met. Although"—I tap a finger against my bottom lip—"can you technically forget something you don't remember? I had a *lot* to drink last night. Or maybe…you just weren't very memorable?" With a playful grin, I pat the soft mattress beside me, tracing inviting circles on the sheet with my palm. "Care to come back to bed and help me figure out which it is?"

Hey, it's not really a repeat hook-up if she hasn't even left my place yet, right? A second round would just be part two of what we already started.

My cock takes notice of the attractive flush painting her skin and the way she chews her bottom lip, as if to hold back some biting comment. Fuck, she's incredibly sexy when angry.

She sneers. "Wow, calm down, Rico Suave. Jesus, you're an even bigger asshole than I thought."

I snort. "*I'm* the asshole? You're the one lumping all Latinos together. All Spanish-speaking people aren't the same, you know."

"I…what?" She blinks, those beautiful eyes growing round with confusion. "I didn't—I mean, I wasn't…"

A smirk tugs at the edges of my lips as she fumbles her words. "Rico Suave? The guy who sang that song is Ecuadorian, whereas *I'm* Mexican. Well, half Mexican if we're being exact, but that's beside the point. Anyway, I'm going to go out on a limb and assume you were referring to my sexual prowess with that reference and not my ethnicity, in which case"—my mouth curls into a smug Cheshire cat grin—"thanks for the compliment."

Contempt wipes the shock from her face, and the muscle in her jaw pops when she clenches her teeth. Chuckling softly, I sink back into my pillow, hiding my disappointment behind an all-too-familiar wall of indifference. And here I was really hoping for a little morning pick-me-up. Ghost of Christmas Yet to Come? More like Ghost of Christmas Enjoy The Blue Balls.

Oh, well. I'll just have to jerk off in the shower after she leaves. "Hey, you're the one who said this was a mistake. You can't fault me for proving you right."

Scoffing, Blondie turns on her heel and struts off, stalking toward the apartment door with fury dominating her steps…though not before bumping into the door frame on her way out of the bedroom, tripping, and nearly falling flat on her face. A startled expression warps her features as she catches herself, transforming into another glare when she straightens and glowers at the wall as if it somehow jumped in her way. When I fail to stifle my laugh at her reaction, she turns that glare back on me, huffing like an angry bull, then resumes her forward march.

This time, I can't hold back my laughter. Is she still drunk, or is she normally this gravitationally impaired?

Usually, I wouldn't chase after a woman. No one is worth the time or energy needed to pursue them, not when anger is involved and said anger is directed at me. And especially when there will always be another, more amiable conquest waiting to replace them. But this one…there's something about her negative reaction to fucking me that has me intrigued. And I suppose I'm a little concerned about her ability to get home unharmed if she can't even safely make it out of this bedroom. When it comes to human decency, I'm roughly ten percent gentleman, but on the sex side, I'm one hundred percent generous lover, and call it market research or masochism, but I need to know what I did wrong, and I can't find that out if she trips and plummets down the stairs to her untimely death on her way out of the building. Plus, I can't risk her ruining my reputation with the entire school year still before me. Think of all the one-night stands I'd miss out on.

"Whoa, whoa, hey, wait a minute."

As I leap up from the bed, the sheet and blanket both slip away, exposing me in all my naked glory. I don't stop to grab my underwear or anything to cover myself, instead racing bare-assed toward the door, jumping in front of my sexy stranger, and blocking the exit like a petulant child. She stops mid-step, and another exasperated huff slips past her lips, but her attention betrays her interest as it focuses on my still erect cock, as if she can't resist a final glance. Maybe she's even thinking about the way I was buried inside her last night.

I grin when her cheeks burn apple red.

Meeting my gaze, she sneers at me before averting her eyes again. "Get out of my way, Damian."

"So, you *do* know me." Then again, who at this school doesn't? As the eldest son of a billionaire CEO and heir to the country's largest pharmaceutical company, it would almost be harder to *not* know who I am. My face has graced tabloid covers and internet gossip pages since I was fifteen years old—or maybe that's just when I first began to notice it—with articles ranging from what I'll do with my birthright to who I'm supposedly dating, like I'm a Kardashian or one of David Beckham's kids or something. I'm what you'd call a "catch," especially now that I'm old enough to be classed as an eligible bachelor, which has pretty much turned everyone around me into a hungry piranha. Women. The paparazzi. They devour any scrap of news they can get about me. I'm this generation's Paris Hilton or, in terms of media interest and scrutiny in regard to my love life, Leonardo DiCaprio—minus the acting career and respectable boner for global warming. We're hot and rich, and the fact is that hot, rich people tend to get lots of attention.

And yet, something tells me my family's wealth and status isn't how Blondie here knows me. I don't even think she's interested in my bachelorhood since, at the moment, she looks to be anything other than hungry. She actually appears a bit queasy.

When she doesn't respond, I continue to prod her. "The better question is: how do I know you? Other than from last night." I flash her a salacious smile.

"You are *unbelievable*," Blondie mutters. "You know, maybe if you weren't always getting drunk with your frat buddies, you might retain the brain cells needed to form long-term memories."

Chuckling, I lean back against the closed door. My, my, she's feisty. "I'm going to take that as a yes. You know, now that you mention it, you look kind of familiar… Did I fuck your best friend or something? You girls do tend to travel in packs."

She crosses her arms over perky breasts I'd pay good money to press my face into. God, I hope Drunk Me took the time to enjoy them properly last night.

"Nope." She lifts one slender shoulder, then lowers it in a lazy shrug. "I'm afraid the idiot you fucked was me."

When I don't respond, opting instead to gape at her like some kind of brainless dumbass, she sighs, and grips the bridge of her nose between her thumb and forefinger. "We met last school year. I was the naive freshman"—she gestures to herself before jabbing an accusatory finger in my direction—"and *you* were the fuckboy junior. Ring any bells?"

My stomach churns again at her words, which are all it takes to kill my morning boner. So, Blondie *is* a Repeat. Shit.

Way to go, Drunk Me, you dick.

I try and fail to swallow down the surge of bile rushing up my throat. Fuck. I think I'm going to be sick.

"I meet a lot of girls," I counter. "At this point, you sort of blur together. I'm a busy guy. I can't possibly remember you all."

Blondie nods, and an empathetic look crosses her face as she takes a step toward me, closing the distance between us with a seductive glint to her eye that has my cock twitching and attempting to rally despite the nausea gripping my stomach that's giving me flashbacks to the spinning teacups at Disney. She places warm hands on my shoulders and brings her lips to my ear, our cheeks brushing.

"Well, then maybe this will jog your memory."

A choked cry tears from my lungs at the shock of the sudden impact of her knee with my crotch. Darkness washes over my vision, and as I fall to the hardwood floor, instinctively curling into the fetal position, I can just make out Blondie stepping over me like I'm a piece of shit she's wiped off her shoe. She fumbles with the doorknob for a moment, then yanks the door open and storms out into the hallway.

She pauses only long enough to look back at where I lie on the ground, cupping my throbbing dick and balls, unable to move from the debilitating cramps spreading into my abdomen.

A menacing smile hitches up one side of her mouth. "Tick the box for this on your bucket list, jackass."

Groaning, I tilt my head back until it touches the floor as a vague memory flickers to life in my brain. It slowly takes shape in my thoughts, growing clearer, forcing its way past the incoherence of my pain.

My eyes bolt wide as I manage a single word. "Fuck."

And just like that, I remember where I know Blondie from.

The severity of my hangover combined with the shame of my actions is directly proportional to how much caffeine I'll need to make it through this conversation.

Rage burns through me hot and fast, like a shot of liquor injected into the vein, as I race through the unfamiliar corridors of Leeland Hall as quickly as my stilettos will carry me. Despite my current visual impairment, I only trip once on my way through the building, but something in the universe must be looking out for me—though definitely not God or I wouldn't be in this mess—because I catch myself before I fall and destroy what little shred of dignity I have left.

A comforting warmth caresses my bare arms and legs the moment I step outside. It's only early September, so we still have the summer heat, which I'm thankful for given the skimpy outfit Ronnie insisted I wear to the party, but *not* so thankful for when the sun overhead beams straight into my face, searing my retinas and blinding me even more than I already am. I wince, sensitive to the light, my skull pounding. Punishment, probably, for the events of last night.

To my extreme annoyance, the quad beside the building is populated with dozens of fuzzy forms. Students, no doubt, which I should have been prepared for since their presence here is typical for a Friday morning. Masses of incoherent blobs are situated on the ground, likely studying on blankets, while others amble along in small groups, heading to class or to their respective dorms with their friends. I keep my gaze fixed ahead as I walk, my pace brisk, but even blind—even trying my best to ignore them—I can feel the way they all shower me with their judgmental gazes, as if they can see the evidence of what I did like a visible brand on my skin.

The anger in my chest swells with each step I take, and my hands curl into fists at my sides as I suppress the banshee-like scream rising up in my throat. The motherfucker didn't remember me. Why, oh *why*, am I so surprised?

Of course, he didn't, Lex! I was nothing to that manwhore freshman year, and I'm nothing to him now except another stupid notch he can add to his overpriced belt. Another tick on his fucking list. From the day we met— regardless of how hot and intense our hook-up might have been—I was nothing but a mere blip on Damian Navarro's sex radar.

A rogue lock comes loose from my bun—my hair reverting to its naturally curly state thanks to the humidity in the air—and brushing the sweaty strands away, I tug my phone free of my pocket and scroll through the contacts until I find Ronnie's name. Her voice blares in my ear after just one ring.

"Okay, bitch. What the hell?"

"Sorry. I couldn't talk before. Jesus, my head is *literally* throbbing."

"Um, yeah." She huffs, and I can practically hear her rolling her eyes at me. "I'm not surprised considering the way you were pounding drinks like a British sailor last night. You ready to tell me where you ran off to?"

An icy shudder rolls over my skin as disjointed memories of the frat party and the mistake that followed pop into my head as if to torment me. Every time I dare to blink, Damian is all I can see, his smug smile haunting my thoughts. A smile I would pay good money to slap right off his face.

"I really don't think I can have that conversation without caffeine," I grumble. "Meet me at Izzy's in ten? Oh, and do me a favor and bring my glasses with you? I left them in your room last night when we were getting ready."

Ronnie lets out a long-suffering sigh. "Fine, but this better be juicy. I'm not facing the assholes on this campus bare-faced for nothing."

"Don't worry," I assure her, groaning internally. "This is so juicy you'll be able to drink it."

Izzy's, Conwick's own independent coffee shop, is one of those artisanal rustic kiosks, with warm wood walls, chalkboard menus, and amber-tinted vintage filament bulbs hanging along the front edge of the awning. It's centrally located, positioned at the northeast side of the main quad right next to the student center as if it's an extension of the building itself, but it has plenty of outdoor seating so customers can enjoy their drinks outside, come rain or shine—or even snow, for those willing to brave the New England winters, and who are too stubborn to get their order to go when space within the center is limited. Which is almost always. Izzy's makes the best coffee around and is popular with not only the students but with faculty, too. I swear I've even seen the odd local sneaking onto campus to partake of its greatness.

Not wanting to contend with the near constant crowds, Ronnie, Andie, and I usually skip Izzy's when the cold weather hits, and just opt for one of the inferior chains in town so we can sit inside and keep warm while we discuss that week's latest gossip—or rather, while Ronnie and Andie discuss said gossip and I listen to their prattle intently, pretending to be interested in people I don't know. The coffee is never as good as Izzy's, but nothing on earth is good enough to warrant freezing to death or losing a finger to frostbite. At this time of year, though, we're all too happy to soak up the fresh air, which means I get to enjoy Izzy's caramel macchiato for a while longer before succumbing to the local Newport variation.

Ronnie is already waiting for me at one of the tables when I arrive—even as a blur, I'd recognize her anywhere, her mane of vibrant copper hair like a beacon that guides me to her through the crowd. She bolts up from her chair at my approach and gasps like someone auditioning for a telenovela.

Rushing over to me, she presses my glasses into my hand, and I quickly push them onto my nose, sighing when the world around me slides into sharp focus. I blink a few times, then glance at Ronnie, who gapes at me with shocked doe eyes.

"Did you trip on your skank heels on the way over here? You are a hot mess minus the hot," she says, her upper lip curling. "Here, take my sunglasses before somebody sees you."

She pries a pair of designer shades off the top of her head—the tortoiseshell frames are so obnoxiously huge Audrey Hepburn would be impressed by their size—and shoves them onto my face before I can protest, pushing them right in front of my glasses. I'm sure I look absolutely ridiculous wearing both, but I'm so grateful for the relief from the scorching sunlight that I decide to leave them in place.

"You know," she says offhandedly, giving my shoulder a light, sympathetic pat, "it's a good thing we aren't around any elementary schools. I'd be sincerely worried you might frighten the children."

I scowl at her, but she just brushes me off with a flick of her hand, gesturing for me to go sit down before prancing over to the counter to order.

My thoughts are a tidal wave of nausea, pain, and regret as I collapse at the first table that crosses my path. My vision is glassy as I wait, and I stare blankly ahead, seeing but not truly processing my surroundings. I'm so out of it I could be sleeping with my eyes open. Either that or fucking Damian Navarro again has shaken me far more than I thought.

The tinkling sound of Ronnie laughing is like a defibrillator to my heart, and I glance at where she stands at the outdoor counter, looking as glamorous as always despite her comment on the phone about being bare-faced in public. If anything, she looks like she just walked off a movie set for a romcom, confidently donning a flowy knee-length skirt, heeled sandals, and a pink bralette as she talks up the cute barista. He grins at her over the register, dimples for days in each cheek, and when she giggles at something he says—tossing her perfect curtain of hair over her shoulder—little cartoon hearts seem to explode from his eyeballs.

"I'll have a vanilla latte with a sprinkle of cinnamon," I hear her say with a flirty wink at Dimple Boy. She then glances over at me, a worried frown tugging down the corners of her mouth. "For that one, a caramel macchiato with *several* extra shots of espresso. The largest size humanly possible. Do you do buckets? Make it a bucket if you have one."

Ronnie plops down in the metal chair opposite me a few minutes later, our drinks secured in a recyclable tray in one hand, and the barista's number scribbled across a brown napkin clutched like a trophy in the other.

"Sorry." She offers me a gentle smile, slipping my coffee free of the cardboard holder. "They don't sell it by the bucket. The largest I could get was a venti."

I make grabby hands at her. "I don't care. Gimme."

She slides the cup over with an appraising tilt of her head, and I lift it to my lips, moaning like a porn star faking the world's biggest orgasm as the warm, soothing liquid coats my tongue. As I swallow, an unsettling thought crosses my mind.

Did I moan like that last night for Damian?

Nope. We're going to nip that in the bud right now, thank you very much.

Desperate to put off the topic of my terrible life choices for as long as humanly possible—or as long as Ronnie will allow me to—I jerk my chin toward the napkin still clamped in her hand. "I see the barista gave you his number. Does this mean you're officially over Jay?"

An air of hostility overtakes Ronnie's serene summer glow, and she shoots daggers out of her eyes at me, their russet depths borderline homicidal. "I thought we agreed to *never* speak of that lying sack of shit again." When I lift a brow, she leans back in her chair and crosses her arms. "As *if* I would still have feelings for Jay…assuming that's even his real name." She scoffs. "No. Nope. I am setting my sights on greener pastures. More *available* pastures."

"Like Dimple Boy over there?" I quip.

Ronnie bobs her head. "Exactly."

Yeah, I believe that about as much as I believe Damian will ever stop being an entitled prick. The only way Ronnie is dating again anytime soon is if Timothée Chalamet and his chiseled jawline ask her out.

"I see." I nod slowly, then shoot my free hand out across the table with far more speed than I would expect myself capable of in my hungover state, successfully grabbing her phone before she can intercept me. "Then you won't mind if I check to see if you really deleted his number?"

"Hey!" She scrambles to retrieve the device, but fails, reluctantly falling back into her seat. She gives me an affronted look when I turn the screen toward her face to unlock it.

As I scroll through her contacts, I think back to freshman year when Ronnie all but dragged me and Andie to her home in Santa Cruz, California, where we then met Jay, who was also staying in the area for spring break. At the time, Andie and I had both felt so certain he was *the one* for Ronnie. And it wasn't because he was almost disturbingly handsome or English, a lethal combination—not that the latter would have affected her too much seeing as one of her dads is Scottish—but it was the *way* he had looked at my best friend, like he was Icarus and she was the sun, and he would happily let himself get burned just for the chance, however brief, to be near her.

It's not unusual for people to be attracted to Ronnie, like Barista Boy with his little heart eyes or the model-pretty retail assistant who helped us pick out some clothes when we went shopping earlier this week just before the new semester started. She's gorgeous, after all, inside and out, with a personality as charming and bold as her looks. But prior to meeting Jay, it seemed like any connection she made only ever scratched the surface, and was always limited to the physical. And it's for that reason her relationships never last. Ronnie dates for the *person*, for the sincerity of their soul, not their gender, and yet, despite always seeing who they are deep down, those same people never seem to see the real her. They never bother to dig deeper, to try to look past the aesthetically-pleasing exterior.

But with Jay, it was different. From the moment their paths crossed one sunny afternoon on a beach near the Santa Cruz Boardwalk, he looked at her as if he could see past her pretty face to who Ronnie was on the inside. You had to be blind not to notice it, not to perceive how he hung onto each word she said, like he needed every last one to survive. Frankly, it *looked* like love, even though they had only just met.

They spent almost the entire spring break together, and then, at the end of that week, he ghosted her. No goodbye. No nothing. Not even a break-up message over text or voicemail. Although she denied it, I knew my horoscope-loving best friend—who believes in fate, and true love, and was so excited by their astrological compatibility—was completely heartbroken and is *still* torn up about it six months later. She doesn't hide it well, and her persistent anger at the mere mention of his name only makes her actual feelings more obvious. I think it's the lack of closure that bothers her most. A feeling I understand too well.

Just as I knew I would, I find Jay's number in her phone—not because I know it, but because I can't think of anyone else Ronnie would have listed in her contacts as **PRINCE DICKFACE** followed by seven puking emojis, a Union Jack flag, and a tiny crown.

"Okay, this doesn't seem healthy," I mutter as Ronnie stands up, and haughtily snatches the device from my fingers.

"It's a process," she retorts, returning to her seat with a huff. "I am *healing*."

"And rage-texting Prince Dickface when you're drunk is part of that process?"

Ronnie gives me a dubious look. "I'm sorry, aren't we meeting because *you* just did the walk of shame?"

I open my mouth to deny it but can't.

"That's what I thought," Ronnie says with a victorious smirk. "Nice attempt at deflection, though. Now, spill."

Grimacing, I set my macchiato down on the table. "What's the rush? Andie isn't even here yet, and I know you texted her about this." That, and I don't feel like repeating this more times than I physically have to.

Ronnie purses her lips. "She has class right now, actually, which we both know you were already aware of. Stop stalling."

I shake my head, my efforts to delay my shameful revelation thwarted. "I can't say it, Ronnie. I'm too embarrassed."

Her tone is reproachful when she snaps, "You are *not* withholding on me. Don't make me unfollow you on TikTok."

"I don't have a TikTok," I remind her. Or an Instagram. Or any social media at all, for that matter. I'm not necessarily against it, it's just not for me.

Ronnie snorts. "Well, if you did, your attitude would make me unfollow you." When I still don't say anything, she prods, "Well? Are you going to tell me, or do I need to torture it out of you?"

Groaning, I cover my face with my hands. The truth is torture enough. *Just say it,* I tell myself. *Rip off the Band-Aid.*

"I had sex with Damian again," I admit, the words tumbling out in a rush.

The confession leaves my lips just as Ronnie takes a sip of her drink, and she sputters, choking on her latte. She slams the cup down, rattling the tiny, round table, and coughs a few times to clear her throat. I spread my fingers and peek at her sheepishly through the gaps. Behind her, I glimpse the barista staring at us, and I briefly wonder if he's going to jump over the counter and come offer to give her CPR or, perhaps, a moist towelette, like something out of the bodice-ripping Regency romance novels she adores so much.

"I'm...sorry?" she says once she's composed herself. "I think I just had an aneurysm because I *thought* I heard you say you had sex with Damian Navarro."

My hands slide down to cover my mouth, as if doing so will mask my shame.

Gasping, she points an accusatory finger at me. "I fucking knew it. I *knew* I saw you two together at the party last night." She leans back in her chair, her tongue pressing against the inside of her bottom lip, jutting it out in an adorable pout. After stewing for a few seconds, she asks, "What the actual fuck, Lex? How can someone with such a big brain be so stupid?"

Ronnie was raised here in the States, and she sounds it. But every once in a while—usually, when she's angry—a tiny twang comes out, compliments of her father, who was born and bred in Glasgow, and the summers she would spend in Scotland visiting her grandparents as a child. Her dad—a well-known TV chef—moved to the U.S. in his early thirties after falling head over heels for an American stunt double who could be Pedro Pascal's twin, and together, they settled in California where they then got married, and had Ronnie via surrogate. Having parents with that kind of story, it's no wonder Ronnie is such a firm believer in true love.

I, on the other hand, never had a relationship like that to look up to. My dad was, and always will be, a deadbeat.

"Trust me," I say, sinking low into my seat in the hope the ground will open and swallow me whole, "I'm judging myself enough for the both of us. No extra criticism needed."

"I just… I don't understand," she stammers. "After what he did freshman year, how could you let that asswipe touch you again? What, did you trip and land on his dick?"

I reach for my coffee, taking another tentative sip. "I had a lot to drink. And my contacts were bugging me, so I took them out. You know how blind I am. I couldn't exactly see him clearly." I wince at how bad that sounds, but try my best to appear indifferent, as if this whole ordeal is no big thing and not the worst mistake I could've possibly made right at the start of sophomore year. "I honestly didn't know who I was going home with."

"Wow." Ronnie arches a disapproving brow. "Drunk You is kind of a slut."

"Hey," I scold, "that's not very uplifting of you. I thought you were all about female empowerment?"

"I apologize," she says, pressing a hand to her chest in mock deference. "Of course, you are not a slut. Damian is the slut. And on any other day, under any other circumstance, I would be thrilled that you got out there, and experienced a sexual awakening after all these months of self-inflicted abstinence. I'd love that for you. Really. I am here for that journey. But *Damian?*" She shakes her head, her pink lips pursing. "I mean, yeah, he's super hot and all, so Drunk You can be forgiven for your lapse in judgment on that particular front, but aside from the *obvious* reason this was a terrible idea, he's fucked, like, every girl at this school, Lex. I'm honestly surprised he doesn't have the clap." Then, as if coming to some terrible realization, she mutters, "That we know of. Maybe get tested just to be safe. Who knows, he might be clean, but his dickhead personality could be contagious."

I groan again, scrubbing a hand over my face. "That's not helping."

"I'm sorry"—Ronnie shrugs as if she isn't really sorry at all—"but Drunk You has hit a new low, babe. I'm just glad Andie isn't here to witness this. We both know she'd have a lot to say on the matter of your very misguided vagina."

"Which is exactly why we shouldn't tell her."

Ronnie barks out a laugh. "I can't keep something this good from her. She's family, bitch. And family spills the tea."

Hard to argue with that logic. Besides, it would've been difficult to withhold this from Andie with the way the three of us are almost always together…and especially given how active the rumor mill is here on campus. Sometimes, I feel like I'm in high school again and not college.

Still, at least if Ronnie tells her, I won't have to.

A sudden panic washes over my best friend's face, and she reaches across the table, anxiously grabbing my hand. "Wait. I haven't asked the obvious question. Did you consent? Do I need to go have words with that bastard?"

I wave my free hand dismissively at her. "Poor life choices aside, I consented."

She releases me and sits back, her expression contemplative. "Can you really consent if you were wasted?"

"We were *both* drunk," I point out, "and trust me…we both wanted it. Not saying that makes it okay, I'm just pointing out that it was as much my fault as it was his, so I don't think you can hold that over him."

Ronnie offers a noncommittal "Mm," but looks unconvinced.

Leaning forward, I prop my elbows on the table and grip my head in my hands. "God, I am so pathetic. I'm officially never drinking again if these are the kinds of decisions I make when I surpass a 0.08 blood alcohol level."

Ronnie giggles. "You're such a nerd." When I glower at her, she reaches across the table again, and lovingly pats my cheek. "Maybe we should just get you a collar that shocks you if Damian gets too close."

"Ha. Ha." I cross my eyes at her behind her gargantuan sunglasses, pulling a face.

"This isn't a cry for help, right?" she asks after a moment, her tone and expression now apprehensive.

"What?"

"You aren't, like, rehashing your fling with Damian for attention, or because you have PTSD or something, are you?" she clarifies.

While I do feel fairly traumatized by the events of last night, I don't know if I would call it PTSD.

"I think that's a little dramat—"

"Post traumatic sex disorder," Ronnie interrupts. "I promise you, Lexi, it's a thing."

Scoffing, I slump forward, dropping my head to the table, wishing for a swift death or, barring that, some Aspirin. "I don't have post traumatic sex disorder, Ronnie. I'm just an idiot."

"Well, yeah, you're right about that. Was it at least good?"

I lift my head just enough to peek up at her. "Was what good? The sex?"

"No, your last gynecology appointment," she deadpans. "Of course, the sex, you dummy! Was it worth knowing you sold your soul for a good dicking?"

"Classy." I sit up, ignoring the throbbing in my temples when I reach for my coffee again. I nurse it for a beat before willing myself to answer. "Honestly, I don't remember a lot of it. If it was anything like last time, well…" I bring one fist to the side of my head and thrust my fingers outward, making an exploding sound with my mouth.

Her face lights up with immediate understanding. "Mind-blowing. Typical."

"Why are the assholes always so good at sex?" I whine. "It hardly seems fair."

Ronnie clicks her tongue and tuts. "Because they get a lot of practice, duh. These frat jerks are vagina magnets, and our darling Damian is no exception. Did you at least manage to give him the slip before he woke up?"

My cheeks burn as I recall our interaction this morning and what I did prior to storming out of his dorm. I'm pretty sure I bruised my kneecap. "Not exactly…"

"Alexandria Renée Dornan," Ronnie shrieks, "you did *not* fuck him again, did you?"

The other patrons sitting within earshot shoot us curious looks, some laughing at Ronnie's outburst, while others whisper behind their hands as they take in my disheveled appearance.

"No way in hell," I growl. "And keep your voice down."

She exhales a quiet *hmph*. "Okay, then what *did* happen?"

A grin hitches up the right side of my mouth that quickly drops into a frown. I replay my final few moments with Damian, but instead of the triumphant fury that consumed me earlier, now, I feel kind of bad about what I did. I wouldn't normally react to any situation with physical violence. Internal rage, yes, but violence? No. Though, maybe that's not actually true considering this is the second time I've done this to him. Maybe Damian's crappy personality and overall douchey demeanor simply bring out my inner lunatic. Or maybe I just wanted to hurt him as badly as he hurt me, and a kick to the sack is the closest comparative pain to what I experienced. Past Lexi certainly seemed to think so.

The worst part is I thought I was over it—over everything that happened between us. But seeing him this morning, and having my naivety thrust in my face *again*…it just brought me right back to last spring. And now, I just feel like an idiot.

I guess I'm not over it after all.

"I…" I swallow thickly, then clear my throat. "I kneed him in the dick."

"Oh, honey." Ronnie's tone oozes with pity. "Assault is not a good look on anyone. You really are just trying to relive all your worst choices from freshman year, aren't you? At this rate, you might sterilize the poor boy." She hesitates for a few seconds, then adds, "We're sure this isn't a cry for help?"

Rolling my eyes, I bend forward again until my forehead is touching the table…then proceed to bang my skull against it despite my splitting headache. Once, twice, three times.

"Hey!" Ronnie reaches out to stop me. "First, these are Chanel. Be careful." She plucks the sunglasses from my face and pushes them onto the perch of her own nose. "Second, what are you doing, you maniac?"

"Trying to give myself amnesia so I can forget this ever happened." I turn my head and press my cheek flat to the metal surface. My forehead aches; I may have actually killed a few brain cells with that final impact, assuming I have any left after last night since I *clearly* lost my mind when I chose to sleep with Damian again. God, anyone listening to this would never believe my IQ is 212—higher than Einstein's, not that it shows with the decisions I've made this past year. Hell, I can practically feel him condemning me from beyond the grave.

I guess it just goes to show that a high IQ doesn't guarantee common sense…or good judgment.

Ronnie considers me for a moment. "I think you're going to need to give me a full play by play if I'm to properly assess the situation. Don't leave out a single detail. No matter how sordid, I want to hear it."

Lacking the will to fight her any longer, I relive the horror of the previous night and this morning, while Ronnie gasps every five seconds, doing her best impersonation of an actor practicing for their Oscar win. By the time I've finished recounting my tale of woe, she seems to have run out of air, and reacts only with a hand pressed to her lips.

"He didn't even remember who I was," I finish.

"What a tool." She shakes her head, her loose locks fanning over her shoulders. Her expression intensifies as she lowers her sunglasses and meets my gaze over the top of the frames. "What did he say when you mentioned the bucket list?"

"I didn't stick around long enough to find out." One, because I had just assaulted the man, and two, to spare myself further embarrassment.

Ronnie frowns and reaches for my hands, cupping them in both of hers. "Oh, sweetie, want me to gouge out his eyes with hot pokers? We can go to prison together. We'd look cute in matching jumpsuits."

I bite back a grin. "Thanks, but I think he's been punished enough for one day."

My phone buzzes, vibrating across the table, as Ronnie pats my arm with one hand and blows me a silent kiss with the other. I catch it and bring it to my chest as I peer down at the screen. "Hang on, it's my mom."

My finger swipes the answer button as Ronnie sings, "Tell Carol I said hi!"

"Hey, Mom," I say, bringing the phone to my ear. "How are you—" Before I can get the full thought out and ask how she's feeling—the first day post-treatment is always the worst—the crying on the other side of the line makes me go silent.

"Lexi, I—"

Panic ignites inside me like fire, and I can feel my heartbeat in my veins as I bolt upright, standing so quickly I nearly knock over my chair.

"Mom? Are you okay?" I breathe, even though I'm terrified of the answer.

Ronnie shoots me a worried look, mouthing, *What's wrong?*

I hold up a finger and stare down at the pavement underfoot.

"I just…" Mom's voice breaks on those words, and she sniffles loudly. "I need you to come home."

A chill of fear creeps up my spine, and I shiver despite the sun beating down on my skin. Something isn't right. I mean, it's normal for Mom to not feel great after one of her infusions, but she's never called me crying before. Besides, my aunt should be with her today, and since she's a nurse, she has any sickness-related side effects handled.

Which means this is about something else.

A terrible thought takes shape in my brain, but I shake it away. I can't let myself go to the worst case scenario. Not yet.

"Okay…I'm on my way. I'll see you soon."

Mom abruptly disconnects the call, which isn't like her at all. She'd never hang up without telling me she loves me or saying something maternal like, "Be safe! Call me when you get there!" regardless of how awful she's feeling.

"What's up?" Ronnie touches my hand, and I jump at the contact.

"I don't know, but Mom's upset. I gotta go," I say, shoving my phone back into my pocket.

"Okay, girl." Ronnie stands and gives me a one-armed hug, planting a soft kiss on my cheek. "Call if you need me."

"Yeah." I offer her a forced smile. Then, adjusting my glasses with trembling fingers, I turn and sidestep the table, walking as fast as my trusty heels can manage, leaving Izzy's, Ronnie, and my horrible choices of the last twenty-four hours behind me.

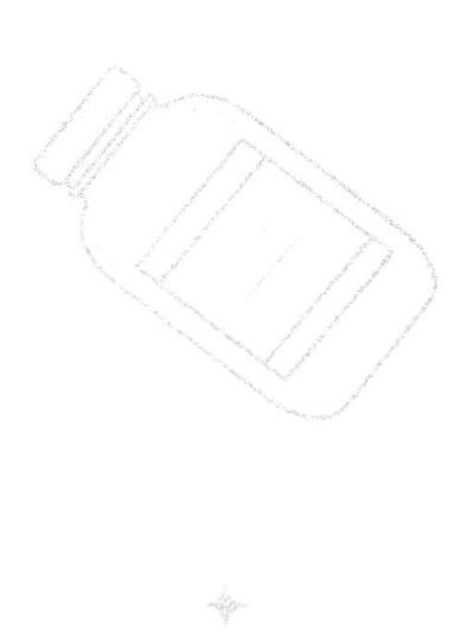

CHAPTER
FOUR

✦ Damian ✦

"Fuck." I suck in a sharp breath through my teeth as a shudder rockets through my body—not so much from the pain, but from the cold of the ice pressed to my crotch. My fingers curl around the plastic bag, but I don't move it away despite my discomfort. As if being hungover wasn't bad enough, now I have to deal with the relentless ache of taking a knee to the prized family jewels.

Irritation courses through me. Sure, I might've been a bit of a dick to that girl, but my asshole behavior in no way warranted *that* reaction. It's not like I forced her to have sex with me. We might have both been drunk, but even Drunk Me knows to ask for consent, and call me old-fashioned, but I like my sexual partners to be willing participants. Therefore, our anonymous encounter was as much on her as it was on me. It's not my fault she regretted it after…though, to be fair, I'm definitely regretting it, too. In my defense, if I *had* realized who I was taking home, I would've run in the opposite direction with my dick tucked firmly between my legs.

Closing my eyes, I push out a strained breath. This shit is exactly why I avoid Repeats.

The most annoying part is, even if I had been at least partially sober last night, I'm not sure I would've known who Blondie was. I certainly didn't this morning. It's weird. Usually, I'm a pro at committing all my hook-ups to memory, providing an endless stream of fresh material for the ol' spank bank on the rare occasion I need it. But for some reason—and despite being *super* hot—I didn't recognize her at all. She looked different than how I remember. Was it the hair? Hers was curly if I'm recalling correctly, but I don't think that's entirely it.

I snap my fingers and let out a loud "A-ha!" in triumph. Glasses! Yeah, that's it—she was wearing glasses when we hooked up last school year. *Shit.* I slump back in my chair, mortified. Am I really that blind? Wait…is *she* blind? She didn't have her glasses on last night or this morning… Could she even see me clearly? Suddenly, her bumping into the door frame and fumbling on her way out of my dorm room makes a lot more sense. It also explains why on earth she would sleep with me again given our less-than-savory history. As for me, I don't have any excuse except that I'm obviously as dumb as all the fictional people of Metropolis who can't tell the difference between Clark Kent and Superman. Because Blondie Superman'd me *hard.* Shit, if she hadn't mentioned the bucket list, I still probably wouldn't have a single fucking clue who she is.

I mean, yeah, *now* I remember her—thanks hindsight, you bitch—but that doesn't help Damian from half an hour ago or my still throbbing cock, which can't seem to decide whether it wants to be erect or limp, caught somewhere in-between in my pain. Grimacing, I shift the bag of ice, and pull at the waistband of my shorts, peeking down at my sad-looking semi.

You deserve this, my conscience whispers.

I release a loud, aggravated huff. *Shut up, you.*

A knock at the door draws my gaze over my shoulder, but before I can tell whoever's there to go the hell away, it creaks open and a familiar voice calls out, "Yo, Navarro."

Ugh. I am *so* not in the mood for visitors right now. Especially when that visitor is Mason.

Suppressing a groan, I call back, "In here," not daring to move from my seat at the table, partially out of fear of unsettling my half-hard cock, but also because I might puke from the pain if I attempt to stand up.

I meet Mason's gaze as he steps into the kitchen. "Whoa." He stops short, his pale eyes widening at the sight of me in all my pathetic post-coital glory, my normally bronze skin tinged an unappealing gray from the nausea. I must be a real striking vision right now. His eyes dip to the pack of ice balanced on my crotch. "What happened to you? You're not jerking off, are you?"

I scoff. "The better question would be *who* happened…and no, I don't typically jerk off at the kitchen table using a bag of frozen water." Obviously. As if the bag on my dick wasn't a clear enough indicator of what the fuck I'm doing. I hiss again when the ice shifts a little. "Shit, that hurts."

Mason arches a thick brunette brow at me. "They have medication for that, you know. I don't think ice will help."

"It's not an STI, you dumbass."

"You certain about that, D?" Mason counters. "You've been balls deep in a *lot* of pussy. You can't always be sure what you're taking home."

Well, he's right about that last part at least.

He shoots me a doubtful look, but I don't have the strength or patience needed to argue with him. Drunk or not, I wrap my tool. The used condom in the trash beside my bed is proof enough that Drunk Damian always uses the head on his shoulders before charging in with the head in his pants. If only I'd had the same foresight to stop and think for a second about who I was fucking.

A headache forms behind my eyes, and wincing, I dig my fingers into my temples, hoping the pressure will counterbalance the pain. Mason pulls out the chair next to mine and spins it around, straddling the seat and clapping me hard on the shoulder. The impact seems to jostle my brain, making me want to throttle him. "Not up for round two tonight, then, I take it?"

I press the heels of my hands into my eye sockets, then drop one hand and peek open one lid just enough to glare at his smug, punchable face. I'd like to see if he still has any desire to party after taking a knee to the junk. Luckily for him, I'm in too much pain to move, so I just scowl at him like he's an idiot. Which he is.

Unfortunately, I don't think he gets the message.

"After last night? Yeah, that's a hard pass." I don't bother mentioning that I can only handle so many consecutive nights of Mason's douchey frat brothers. Or of Mason, for that matter.

He holds up his hands. "Your loss, man."

Pushing to his feet, he claps me again on the shoulder and offers me a pitying smile before turning to leave.

"Hey, you know the bet we made last year?" I blurt out against my better judgment. I don't know why I'm bringing this up. I want nothing more than to forget the embarrassment of this morning, but I just can't seem to let it go. Blondie has haunted every moment of my day, her presence lingering like a damn poltergeist.

Mason pauses with one foot in the hallway and spins around, inching back into the kitchen, crossing his lanky arms over his chest, which makes him look about as tough as a Twizzler. "Oh, you mean the one where I said I would give you my Maserati if you completed a sex bucket list of my choosing?" The grin slips from his face, and he glares at me. "Yes, I know the one. The video did go viral after all."

The video. As if I needed reminding of that. Our bet was definitely not the most mature move on my end, but we had agreed to keep it between us. Sure, that was mainly to avoid skewing the results in either of our favors, but still, it was meant to stay on the down-low. That was until Mason—possessing a whopping two brain cells—decided to post a livestream on social media of him handing over his Maserati when I won. A video in which he divulged exactly *why* he was giving me his car because the part of him that wasn't livid he lost the bet thought the whole thing was funny.

To say the video unleashed pure chaos on my life would be an understatement.

"I still miss that fucking car," Mason whines. "You better be treating her well."

I shrug. "You shouldn't have bet against me."

A skeptical look creases his features as he plops back down on the chair beside mine, staring at me like my face is one of those crowded pictures in a *Where's Waldo?* book. "What made you bring that up? I thought you said, 'We need to forget this ever happened,'" he says in a poor imitation of my voice, hooking his fingers into air quotes.

Ugh. Doomsday. Time to be judged.

"I accidentally brought home a Repeat last night."

"*Dude.*" Mason reels back, wrinkling his thin, pointed nose. "Rookie mistake."

My lips twist into a grimace as I glance down at my shorts. *Yeah, tell that to my bruised dick and balls.*

A hollow laugh fills the silence between us, and I internally chastise myself for divulging this information to anyone, especially Mason of all people. I've known the guy for seven years—we went to the same private high school and now attend the same prestigious university, mostly because our daddies were rich enough to buy our admission—but I'd hardly call him my best friend. I'd barely even call him a friend. He lives for the drama and is about as loyal as Judas.

Still, I don't really trust anyone else at this college either, leaving me with few other options when it comes to venting my frustrations. A less wealthy person wouldn't hesitate to sell my secrets to TMZ, and after the fallout from the video last spring, I have to believe Mason will think twice before doing something so stupid again. Or at least he'll have the sense to ask me first. I hope.

But dumbass or not, the reality is, Mason is one of the only people at this school who gets me. When you come from an affluent family, it's hard to know who your friends are and who's just getting close to you for your money, which can make life really lonely. Mason might be a grade-A ass, but with him, I know my family's net worth has zero bearing on why he talks to me. He sticks around because we entertain one another, and for now, that's good enough for me.

"So, who was it?" he asks.

I shake my head. "That's the thing. I can't remember her name. I only remember who she was on the list."

I conjure a mental picture of the bucket list Mason created last fall and silently tick the box next to each line. *Theater girl. Check. Another guy's girlfriend. Check. Two sorority girls at the same time. Check. Check. Professor*—oh, that one was fun. *Check. Bonus points for twins. Check. Check. Check. Check.* The list goes on and on in my head until we get to Blondie.

"By all means, keep me in suspense," Mason deadpans.

I hesitate for a moment, then push out a breath through my nose before muttering, "Poor Girl."

His brow furrows, and I can practically see the cogs turning in his tiny brain as he funnels back through whatever memories he retains from last year, assuming he still has any brain cells at all. God, that first semester was such a shitshow.

He blinks a few times as if the mere process of thinking is painful. "The scholarship freshman?" he finally works out.

"Well, she's a sophomore now, but—"

"Now that you mention it, I do remember you talking to some random blonde last night. I didn't recognize her. Not that I would," he adds with a derisive chuckle.

Hunching over the table, I lean my weight on my elbows and roughly comb my hands through my hair. "Yeah, I didn't either."

Come to think of it, I can't recall ever seeing her in passing on campus or at Phi Sigma's parties aside from last night's. Other than the handful of times we met in the university library my junior year, there was only one other instance I saw her, and that particular interaction was as memorable and painful as this morning's. Maybe she doesn't live in the dorms? If she's a townie, that would explain why we haven't crossed paths on a social level since we hooked up.

As for school, I don't think we share any classes, and it's unlikely we'd spend our spare time the same way or even in the same places. Scholarship students like her are usually working in the administrative office or library during their free periods and evenings, or doing whatever else it is that poor people do for fun. We might as well occupy different hemispheres for how much separates the two worlds we live in.

Huh, I guess it really is true what they say: out of sight equals out of mind. The last time I saw Blondie was shortly after Mason's video went viral. After that, I didn't see her again, so I never spared her a second thought.

Except…I'm thinking about her now. She isn't out of my mind anymore. And I have no fucking clue why.

Getting kicked in the junk has clearly rattled my senses, I tell myself. Yeah. That must be it.

"You don't remember her name by any chance, do you?" I ask, failing to achieve the air of nonchalance I was trying for.

Mason shoots me a stupefied look. "No. Why would I? And why the hell do you care?"

I don't. Not really. It's not like I plan on asking her out or ever seeing her again if I can help it. If anything, I want to avoid her at all costs. And after this morning, I'm pretty sure she wouldn't want to see me.

Besides, I don't think my dick would survive another beating. Not the variation she dishes out, anyway.

"I don't really," I protest. "I just—"

"Are you icing your junk because Poor Girl broke your dick or something?" Mason interrupts. "How kinky is the sex you have? Damn."

He reaches for the bag of ice to assess the damage underneath, but I swat his hand away.

"Damian Jr. is *not* broken," I grumble. "He's just sore. And it wasn't from the sex…" An embarrassed flush creeps up my neck. "Poor Girl kneed me in the boys."

Just like she did last spring when she confronted me about the list.

Mason blanches, his hand dropping to cup his own testicles in solidarity with my pain. "What a psycho bitch. Wait, is this the same chick who kicked you in the dick that first week back at school after spring break?"

I nod as a dull ache throbs along my hairline, letting my eyes flutter closed. "Yep." But even as I say it, there's no heat behind the word.

"Oof." Mason shakes his head. "Maybe you should start IDing your hook-ups."

I snort. "Yeah, you might be right about that."

Beside me, my phone buzzes, trembling with enough force to send it skipping across the table. Only mildly curious, I turn it over and glance down at the screen.

Mein Führer

Your mother and I need to speak with you.

We'll meet you at Fernando's for lunch at midday.

Of course, my dad chooses *now* of all times, when I'm hungover and stinking of sex, to demand my presence. Dread spreads through my insides like a rush of cold water. Shivering, I push the phone away from me. "Shit. I gotta go. My parents want to meet me for lunch."

Mason's dad is also a tightass, so he doesn't need me to tell him twice to fuck off. Rising, he holds out a hand to fist-bump me. "All right, man. I'll catch you later." As he struts out of the kitchen, he throws over his shoulder, "Thoughts and prayers for your disfigured dick. Maybe you'll get lucky and it won't be permanent."

When I flip him off, Mason flashes me a wounded look, holding a hand to his heart. With a demented cackle, he finally leaves, and I exhale a breath of relief once I'm alone again. Unfortunately, that relief is short-lived, blasted into oblivion when my phone buzzes once more.

Swallowing, I pull it toward me, scowling down at the message.

Mein Führer

Don't be late.

I roll my eyes. "Whatever you say, Hitler."

One phone call multiplied by the number of steps it takes me to get home = the amount of time I have to panic about what could be wrong with Mom.

I'm out of breath by the time I step through the front door. Conwick's campus is only a stone's throw away, but my legs are aching after speed-walking in heels for four blocks, and my hangover is somehow getting worse despite the caffeine weaving its way through my veins like a drug. My head aches, and a stitch forms in my left side as my body mistakes my rush to get home as exercise.

"Mom?" I push the door shut and kick off my shoes, throwing my head back and sighing at the soothing sensation of my bare feet on the worn floorboards. God only knows what I look like right now, but I feel like day-old reheated trash. Thankfully, Mom's never been one to shame.

"In here, Lex."

At the sound of her voice, my heart jumps into my throat. Despite how she was on the phone, I'm still taken aback by her tone, which is fraught and wavers, holding none of its usual steadiness. Okay, something is *definitely* wrong. Even in her darkest hours, Mom has always kept her cool. Nothing ever fazes her, which is why she's the perfect relaxed yin to my somewhat—who am I kidding, *very*—uptight yang. My person I go to for everything.

My rock.

The fear that propelled me here sloshes in my stomach like acid, and my mouth is unbearably dry as I shuffle into the living room, like an inmate on death row being escorted to their execution. Mom sits on the mustard-yellow three-seater sofa, her back as stiff and straight as a board, her hands clamped together in her lap like a triggered bear trap. She's unnaturally still, and her knuckles are milk white from how tightly her fingers are straining as they cling to each other.

She doesn't look great, but she also doesn't look any sicker than usual, though the relief I expect to feel at that observation never comes. Swallowing, I pause a few feet away, maintaining some distance between us, as if doing so will somehow keep the bad news I sense coming at bay.

"Hey," I hedge, fidgeting with my glasses like I always do whenever I'm worried. I cast a quick glance to my left through the archway into the seemingly empty kitchen before letting my attention stray back to Mom. I've never once been afraid to look my mother in the eye, and yet, in this moment, I'm terrified. "Where's Gina?"

"Hospital," Mom mutters absentmindedly, her usually bright gaze dull, the skin around her eyes red from crying, though her tears have dried up since we spoke on the phone. "She had to cover someone's shift at work. Family emergency."

I bob my head, even as I feel a slight tug of resentment. Post-treatment days might not be medical emergencies, but I still wish Gina hadn't left Mom on her own. Or that she had at least called me first so I could've come home sooner to be here in her stead. But that's Gina for you. My larger-than-life aunt has a heart of gold that must be four sizes too big for her body, like some sort of reverse Grinch. She's a sucker for sob stories and is always the first in line whenever anyone needs a helping hand, launching herself into action without hesitation or a second thought on the matter, like she's trying to be the next Mother Theresa, even if it sometimes means she stretches herself a bit thin.

Still, despite often going out of her way to help others, Gina *always* puts her family first, and it's for that reason I can't be mad at her; I know she wouldn't have left today unless my mom had insisted. Plus, she's earned a lifetime of good grace in my book. After all, she's been our greatest asset over the last eighteen months, through "the Dark Days" as I've come to call them, and not just because of her invaluable nursing experience but because of her giving nature and optimistic attitude—a trait she shares with my mom that clearly didn't pass down to me. She's incredibly spirited with the most infectious laugh, able to light up the largest room with her presence, which has helped to keep Mom's spirits up when the optimism runs low—which is vital for anyone battling cancer. Plus, Gina is so loud that if she were here, everyone within three blocks would know it.

"Oh." I tug on a loose thread dangling from the hem of my shirt, stalling for time to delay whatever world-shattering news Mom has in store for me. "When did she leave? You weren't here on your own all night, were you?"

A chuckle breaks through my mother's solemn exterior, and for a moment, I think she's back to normal. Happy, like she always is. But then the clouds darkening her expression return, overwhelming the brief break in the storm. "Believe it or not, Lexi, I am capable of being on my own for more than five minutes."

I roll my eyes, ignoring the sudden prick of heat in the corners. I can feel the moisture building there, threatening to blur my vision, waiting to overwhelm me. Even my tear ducts know what's coming.

Diversion, I tell myself. I need a diversion—to drive the conversation elsewhere. What better way to escape bad news? Avoidance is a proven technique. I would know, I learned it from my dad. Avoidance is his middle name.

If I don't hear it then it won't be real.

I glance in the direction of the kitchen again. "How are you feeling? Are you hungry? Do you want me to make you something?"

In my peripheral vision, I catch Mom shaking her head. "I'm fine. Come sit with me." When our eyes meet, she loosens the death grip her hands have on each other and gently pats the cushion beside her.

Bracing myself, I trudge toward the sofa and plop down, still making it a point to keep some space between us so I can breathe without having a panic attack or worse, word-vomiting all my worst fears, which would definitely do neither of us any good. We sit for a few moments in a strained, uncomfortable silence, and as the seconds tick by, I almost feel like I'm in first grade again and I've just been caught putting glue in Jennifer Harbottle's hair in retaliation for her drawing with bright orange Sharpie all over the back of my favorite shirt (a vintage Trolls tee with a giant rhinestone belly button). I expect Mom to say something—to tell me what's wrong so I can help fix the problem—but she doesn't. Her mouth is a steel trap, offering nothing.

I stare at her, wordlessly pleading for answers, but she just stares straight ahead, avoiding my gaze.

When I can't take the suspense any longer—when I'm literally about to explode from the nerves rioting under my skin—I snap, "Are we going to just sit here all day, or are you going to tell me what's wrong?"

I don't have time to feel bad about raising my voice. Her eyes shift to mine, and my stomach instantly sours with a fresh bout of nausea. "These arrived today," she murmurs, retrieving two pieces of paper from the coffee table and handing them to me.

As I frantically skim the paperwork, all the air rushes out of my lungs. It's like I've just been slammed in the chest by a wrecking ball. Was this feeling what Miley Cyrus was singing about? Because everything hurts, and I can't seem to breathe.

With shaking hands, I blink twice, forcing myself to focus on the pages in front of me; both are letters from our health insurance provider, which my mom gets through her job. The first warns of a raise to our yearly deductible, while the second informs us of a change to the formulary, indicating what services and medications are covered under my mom's policy as of the upcoming calendar year...

As well as what they're no longer willing to pay for.

"Wh...what does this mean?" I ask, my voice barely a whisper, even though I already know the answer.

I just can't process it at the moment.

Mom lets out a tired sigh, and her shoulders slump, revealing the prominent notches in her spine through her T-shirt. She's gotten so thin recently. "If we want to continue receiving healthcare, we'll have to pay a lot more money out of pocket...and figure out a way to afford my medication since, come January, it's no longer covered."

At her words, my eyes dip back to the formulary as if pulled there by magnetic force. Sure enough, the Tier 5 meds that my mom's life *literally* depends on—

and which were previously covered—are now noticeably absent.

I blanch, and it takes all the willpower I have to find the strength to speak. "Well, how much is it likely to be? And what about your treatments?"

"Still covered. For now. But they won't pay for anything starting in January until the deductible is paid in full, and it's just…it's too much, Lex. And that's without the added cost of my meds." She runs a shaking hand over her head, and for a split second, I envision what she looked like before the cancer. When she still had hair, it was blonde, just like mine. "I called the pharmacy earlier and it's…not good. Without insurance, we're looking at about sixteen thousand dollars a month for my prescription."

"Sixteen *thousand* dollars?" I screech.

My eyes water as they drop to the papers still clenched in my hands, and I once again scan the letter informing us about the upcoming change to the deductible, reading and re-reading the words typed there until they finally sink in.

The five-digit number explodes in my mind—a tower of teetering red, green, and yellow blocks that slot into place one after another, stacking higher with every subsequent zero until they threaten to topple over and crush me. No matter how I mentally shift the pieces, there's no way to push them away…or tear down the towering weight of what they represent.

"Plus another twelve thousand dollars for the deductible?" I croak, my disbelief strangling the words.

Anger rockets through me, and as I jump to my feet, my fingers slacken, dropping the pages to the floor. Between this news and my run-in with Damian earlier, I'm more than ready to punch something.

"But you're sick. You *need* that medication. You *need* that treatment! Have you called Tim? Maybe it's a mistake or he can fix it somehow. Surely, he knows we can't afford this."

My mom is a bookkeeper for a small, local construction company, and her boss, Tim, is quite possibly the nicest man alive. He's been so accommodating with her treatments, always giving her time off when she needs it and going out of his way to make her comfortable in the office. Hell, if he didn't rely on her to keep his employees paid—Mom included—I'm certain he would have granted her indefinite paid time off until she was better.

If there's anything he can do to help, I know he would.

Mom shoots me an exasperated look. "There's nothing he can do, Lex. This was the insurance company's decision, not his, and I'm not about to go stirring the pot when I'm lucky I even still have a job at all considering how much work I've missed. A lot of people in my situation aren't so fortunate."

I glare at her. How can she consider herself lucky right now when our world, which was already flipped upside down by her cancer, has now been torn apart from the inside out, ripped into pieces that we might never be able to put back together again? How much more heartache can one family take?

"What about Gina? Can she do anything?" I pause as another thought occurs to me. "Does she even know about this?" I stare at my mom with pleading eyes, trying to ignore the elevated pitch to my voice, which has gone up several octaves, inching closer to hysteria.

Mom frowns and gives a slight shake of her head. "I didn't want to distract her when she's working, so I'll tell her this evening. Not that it would matter, though. It's not like she can claim me as a dependent, which is the only way she could get me on her insurance, and then there's you to think of, so no. Even if getting on her plan *was* an option, I wouldn't do it if it meant leaving you without healthcare."

"That's such bullshit!" I shout. I start to pace the length of the room because, if I stand still any longer, I might scream or try to break down a wall, like in that old movie my film-obsessed aunt made me watch where some half-naked Spartan dude chest-kicked another guy into a pit. "Without treatment, you could—" Silence swallows the rest of my words. I can't say it. If I say it, it becomes a real possibility, and that is an outcome I can't bear to face.

A groan escapes my lips as I push the locks that have escaped my bun off my forehead and hunch over, planting my hands on my knees. Is this some sort of karmic punishment for fucking Damian again? Have I been cursed? I swear to god, it's like his dick is bad luck.

My teeth sink into my bottom lip, and I bite down hard, fighting back my impending tears. I can't cry in front of Mom. If I cry, she'll cry again, and then neither of us will find a way through this.

Think, Lex. Think. What are your options?

I bolt upright, resolved. "I'll get a job. I'll pay for your prescription myself."

Mom scoffs and leans back against the sofa cushions, which seem to swallow her frail figure whole. "A part-time wage wouldn't come close to covering this, sweetie. You know that."

"Who said anything about part-time? I'll drop out. I'll get multiple jobs if I have to. I'll start an OnlyFans. Whatever it takes." Plopping back down onto the couch beside her, I clasp her hands firmly in mine. "You're more important to me than an education."

"Like hell you will." Sitting up straight, she pulls her fingers free to cup my face. "I did not work my ass off for years to ensure you had every possible opportunity for you to drop out this close to the finish line. *You* have worked too hard for this. I know it's not MIT, but a degree from Conwick will still open doors, and you will *not* squander your future on my behalf. I just—" She falters, swallowing loudly. "I just wanted you to know about this so we can prepare ourselves."

I flinch at her words. She isn't saying what I think she is…is she? "Prepare ourselves for what?" I manage to ask, but my voice is meek.

Mom sighs, and it's the sad heave of a woman giving up. "The alternative to me continuing treatment."

A traitorous tear slides down my cheek, which I quickly wipe away before more can follow. "Fuck that," I tell her, grabbing her hands again. "We'll figure something out. We always do."

She doesn't argue, offering me a tender, reassuring smile, but I can see the doubt behind it.

Though I try hard not to, I frown. If my mother, the eternal optimist, doesn't have faith that everything will work out…

How can I?

CHAPTER
SIX

✦ *Damian* ✦

Donde hay confianza, da asco - Where there is trust, there is disgust

Translation: Familiarity breeds contempt. Yeah, you can say that again.

Fernando's is a high-end, award-winning Mexican restaurant about a ten-minute drive from campus. Another twenty minutes beyond that and I'd be back at home, which I've made it a point to return to as little as possible since I enrolled at Conwick. I had hoped to study abroad for college, desperate for some space between me and my parents, but they refused to fund my "international shenanigans" as my father so lovingly put it. The bastard wouldn't even let me go farther afield within the borders of the U.S., claiming he needed me close by for the sake of the family company. He might have been telling the truth, but it's equally likely he just wanted to punish me for not being a perfect, obedient son. "Why can't you take advantage of the opportunities here? Don't you know how many people would kill to be in your shoes?" he once asked me during our umpteenth argument on the matter, his mouth pulled down into his signature grimace that always makes it clear what a disappointment I am to him.

I picture that look on his face at this moment as I step out of my blue Maserati MC20 Cielo—the car I won from Mason this past spring—into the blazing sun beating down on the Fernando's parking lot. To the unsuspecting eye, I appear calm and collected, but unease rolls over my skin as I cross the tarmac, making me shudder despite the heat. My parents might have excellent poker faces, but their one tell is they only ever take me to eat at Fernando's— or bother to meet with me at all these days—when I'm in trouble or they have bad news to impart. Probably because the menu here reminds my father of my abuela's cooking, stirring memories of his childhood in Guadalajara, and nothing boosts the spirit for a little soul-crushing quite like comfort food.

I frown, tossing my car keys to the valet, then strut through the doors into the air-conditioned restaurant, trying my best to ignore the anxiety gripping my chest, and failing miserably. I make it a point to avoid Fernando's even more than I avoid going home. Call me superstitious, but my parents have tarnished every dining experience I've ever had here, and I can't help feeling like the place is cursed. The last time I stepped foot in Fernando's was when they gave me the worst news of my life.

I can only imagine what shit they're about to drop on me now.

A pretty hostess welcomes me, and while her tone is professional, her wandering gaze betrays her attempt at formality. I flash her a flirty grin, and inform her I'm meeting someone, not clarifying who to gauge her interest. Her disappointment is instantly clear on her face, though she tries to hide it behind a veneer of politeness. My smile deepens. Depending on what mood I'm in when this is over, I might ask for her number.

With a quick goodbye, I proceed into the dining area, where a familiar melody stops me dead in my tracks. My chest tightens at the sight of the balding man playing an arpa jarocha on the small wooden stage to my right, and I watch his fingers pluck the strings of the harp as if lost in a trance. The song he's playing—"Besame Mucho" by Consuelo Velázquez—is one I often hear whenever I visit my abuela. It was her and my abuelo's favorite song, and every time I catch her humming or singing it, I know she's thinking of the great love they shared and missing him just as much as I do.

Hearing it now makes me want to flee to her home in Mexico, even though I know there's no escaping the impending confrontation with my parents. What I wouldn't give to have my abuela with me now or to at least possess a fraction of her fearlessness. *She* never tolerated my dad's bullshit.

Swallowing, I tear my gaze from the musician, and turn my focus to my parents, who are sitting exactly where I expected to find them: on the left side of the room at their favorite table by the large windows overlooking the marina next door. My Connecticut-bred mother—looking gloriously dewy this morning like she just came from a facial—sips out of a small china tea cup as my Mexican father scowls beside her over his daily horchata. He looks almost as amused as I feel about being here.

With a heavy sigh, I straighten my back and begin my approach. My mother notices me first. She places her dainty cup down on its saucer and rises when I reach their table, giving me a quick kiss on the cheek. My father acknowledges me with a sidelong glance and a grunt.

"Lenore, Hector," I say with mock tenderness, as if I'm genuinely happy to see them. Spoiler alert: I'm not and they know it. "To what do I owe the pleasure of your company this fine afternoon?"

Tsking, my mother holds me back at arm's length. "Must you do this every time, Damian? You know I hate it when you call me by my name."

I offer her an apologetic smile. "Forgive me, Mother. You look lovely. How are you?"

"Enough of the pleasantries," my father barks. "Take a seat, hijo."

My blood runs cold at his icy tone. He's in a chipper mood today. Not.

Tensing, I sink into one of the two available chairs at the round table (opting for the one beside my mother, leaving an empty seat between me and my dad) as my mom returns to her own chair, perching on the edge like a bird on a tree branch. I expect my dad to begin berating me as soon as I sit down, but instead, a disquieting silence stretches in the space where I expect his reprimand, with only the backdrop of hushed chatter, soothing music, and the clatter of utensils to break it.

Every unspoken moment is more unnerving than the last. I can't take it. We've been together for barely two minutes and my nerves are already completely fried.

"Excuse me." I signal to a passing server, who pauses beside our table, her face taut with a very obvious disdain as she regards me. I don't think we've met before, so she can't be a past hook-up—though my certainty about that wavers when I think of Blondie and our run-in this morning. That whole situation is making me paranoid.

Waving that thought away, I assure myself that this lady probably just loathes rich snobs like my parents. And by extension, me. Can't say I blame her—as someone who has spent my entire life around extreme wealth, I know from experience that most people with money are assholes.

"Can I get a glass of the Balché Cero?" I ask.

"It's a bit early to be drinking, darling," Mom murmurs, touching a hand to my forearm.

I shrug. "Hey, it's five o'clock somewhere, right?"

"He'll have water," Dad interjects, his authoritative voice just loud enough to make everyone present go silent. When the server's gaze dances between us, her expression no longer antagonistic but uncertain, he curtly adds a dismissive, "Thank you." She immediately scurries away like a cat that's been shooed.

Crossing my arms, I slump in my seat. Sure, it's childish to sulk, but if my father doesn't want me to act like a child then maybe he shouldn't treat me like one. "Buzz kill," I grumble under my breath, throwing a dirty look in his direction.

With a deflated sigh, he shakes his head. Ah, there's that disappointment I'm so used to seeing. "From the looks of it, you don't need any more alcohol, hijo. Are you still drunk from last night, or are you merely hungover this time?"

I scoff. "Shit, I wish I was still drunk for this. Why do you think I ordered the wine?"

"Enough," he chides. He doesn't raise his voice; we are in public, after all, and god forbid we make a scene.

It's all about public perception, Damian. That's the excuse my parents have always used whenever I react with "too much" emotion. That's why they always bring me here when it's time to kick my ass with their latest dose of bad news. If other people are watching, I won't have a meltdown, and they won't have to deal with the fallout.

Do they even care that this smokescreen we hide behind is only pushing me away?

"I think you know why we called you here."

I meet my father's stern gaze across the table, swallowing the sudden lump in my throat. "Haven't the foggiest," I admit. It's the truth. I don't know why they wanted to see me, though that's only because the list of what I could have done to offend them is nearly endless. Without details, how am I supposed to narrow it down?

He cocks a wiry eyebrow. "No? Lenore, would you care to enlighten him?"

Dread pools in my stomach when I look at my mother, who hesitates a moment before reaching into her purse, retrieving a folded-up piece of paper, which she gingerly hands to me. Taking it from her, I smooth it out on the table to find it's the cover to a trashy magazine…and not one of the good ones.

My smiling face stares back at me right under the headline:

PRESCRIPTION FOR SCANDAL!
PHARMA HEIR'S SEX BET SENDS SHOCK WAVES THROUGH ELITE CIRCLES

"Seriously?" I push the paper away. "Why are you rehashing this? It happened *months* ago. It's old news! And I already made a public apology about it. What more do you want?"

Not that the bet should have warranted an apology since I hadn't planned on it becoming common knowledge. Stupid Mason and his stupid livestream, though the video itself wasn't even the worst part. Don't get me wrong, it was *bad*—there's really no way to make a sex bet look good—but it was what he posted in the comments after that blew everything up.

It was a scandal of epic proportions, and to say my parents ripped me a new asshole would be putting it lightly. The story graced the pages of tabloids and was a prominent talking point on social media for weeks, but that was ages ago. The world has long since moved on.

Besides, as I already told my parents, it was Mason who made the list public, not me. I never intended for anyone to find out about it…especially the girls who were on it. Okay, yes, it was *kind of* a shitty move to make the list in the first place, I admit that. Though, technically speaking, the list was Mason's brainchild, not mine. Besides, it wasn't like my behavior during the bet was any different than how I normally act in my pursuit of the opposite sex. I was simply hooking up with whoever fit the specific criteria instead of anything with a vagina and a pulse. I never led any of my hook-ups into believing we could be something more—by now, everyone at Conwick is aware I don't date—and I definitely never went into it with the intention of hurting or embarrassing anyone. Again, that was all on Mason.

But then…I should have anticipated his almost impressive inability to keep his fucking mouth shut. And for that, I suppose I *am* at fault—not only for trusting him but for thinking it wise to take him up on the bet to begin with. As fun as it was, if I hadn't agreed to the bucket list, then Mason wouldn't have livestreamed the outcome…or felt compelled to respond to the comments, revealing the identities of all the women I slept with.

Like Blondie…or my freshman year psych professor, who only kept her job because she was no longer my teacher at the time we had sex.

Dad huffs out a humorless laugh. "Yes, your three-line Instagram apology was very compelling." Holding my gaze, he leans forward, tapping a finger against the crinkled tabloid cover. "Look at the date, hijo."

Fisting my hands in my lap, I glance down at the date printed just above the barcode. September 6th.

Wait. That's today's date.

Why would tabloids be printing stories about this again? News of it ran dry months ago. The video no longer exists—it was deleted within hours of Mason going live—and we destroyed every shred of evidence related to the list, including the names that were on it. There is quite literally nothing left for anyone to hang over my head.

"Your"—Mom clears her throat, and I glance up, noting how uncomfortable she looks—"wager you made with your friend has certain investors feeling… *unconvinced* about your future involvement with the company. At least one has gone on the record about it that we know of. Hence why news of your little stunt has resurfaced despite our best efforts to quash it."

Okay, I was wrong. My mother's words don't just hang over my head. They're a goddamn guillotine.

"Do you understand the severity of the situation you have put us in, hijo? Without those investors, we could crumble." My father shakes his head, and for the first time since I sat down at this table, I notice the fresh worry lines creasing his face.

My parents both stare at me in silent anticipation, but I don't know what they expect me to say or what they want me to do. What *can* I do? It's not like I can turn back time. What's done is done.

"Then find new investors?" I suggest, even though I know it's the wrong thing to say.

Dad exhales through his nose like an angry bull, while Mom lets out a delicate tut. "It's not just the investors, Damian," she says. "The board isn't convinced either."

I snort. "Who cares what those dinosaurs think? If it's mediocre old guys you need, this country is full of them."

"Damian." My father's tone holds a sharp, warning edge.

"What?" I fire back, feeling increasingly defensive with every word out of my parents' mouths. My patience with this conversation is exhausted. "*You* own the company. Tell them all to take their opinions and go fu—"

"Enough!" He slams his palm down on the table, and the whole restaurant instantly goes silent.

So much for not making a scene. Dad must be furious to allow his composure to slip like that.

For a moment, he glowers at me, only looking away to cast a knowing glance at Mom. Then, with a deep, calming breath, he drops his voice and growls, "I will do no such thing."

"Why?" I press, even as my brain tells me to shut the hell up.

His responding glare is scathing. "Because I agree with them."

This admission takes a few seconds to penetrate my thoughts, during which time I just stare at my dad, open-mouthed. "What?" is all I can manage to say.

A tired sigh escapes him as he rubs a weathered hand across his face. "I've had enough, hijo. *We've* had enough."

A pang strikes me square in the chest, and I swing my startled gaze toward my mother. "Mom?"

But she just shakes her head. "The partying. The bets. The skipping classes… This has gone on long enough. It ends now, Damian."

Okay, the bet they knew about. Singular. But bets? *Plural*? Partying? Missing classes? I flash them each a scornful look. "What the fuck? Have you been spying on me?"

Dad rolls his eyes at my offended tone. "We wouldn't have to spy on you if you would learn to behave."

I choke out a disdainful laugh. "Well, if you've been spying on me then you know I've already completed almost every required course for my major and minor, and only have bullshit core curriculum classes this semester—which only started four days ago, I might add. And those lectures are full of useless information I'm never going to actually use, and which do nothing but force us to pump out more time and money for a degree. A degree I'm sure Dad can just buy me if need be considering he bought my way into that school."

I know the exact moment I've crossed a line by the way my father's face scrunches with rage and my mother's complexion goes from a glowy uses-the-sunbed-at-least-once-a-week beige to owns-every-Celine-Dion-album-in-existence white. At the same instant she says my name, scolding me for my impertinence, Dad hisses, "How ungrateful can you be? I worked hard to get where I am, and we have provided you with every possible opportunity to better yourself and set you up for the future. A *good* future. All we have ever asked is that you show a little incentive, but instead, you've squandered these past four years with embarrassing behavior befitting a toddler." He shakes his head, his expression darkening. "The first year we could understand, but the last three?" He clicks his tongue, but doesn't say anything more, and the lump growing in my throat is too thick for me to find the words to respond.

Sometimes, I think my father's real middle name must be Irony. Worked hard to get where he is? I don't think so. My grandfather was the hard worker in our family. He was the one who founded a pharmaceutical company in Mexico that started from nothing and went on to make millions, allowing him to move to the States and expand his business here, where it continued to thrive until he was one of the richest men in the world. He then moved his family to New England, away from their home in Guadalajara, though my abuela returned there after his death since that was where he wished to be buried.

As for Dad, he was in his late teens when he relocated to the U.S. with my grandparents—still young enough to be a dependent for visa purposes—and a few years later, after Hallazgo really began to take off, he met my mother, who comes from old money, and whose lineage can be traced back to the Pilgrims who first settled in Massachusetts. She's always insisted she loves my father for his "wonderful personality," but that's hard to believe considering the guy acts like he has a giant foot up his ass ninety percent of the time. In reality, I'm sure him being the heir to a billion-dollar company is what drew her eye. My ma is nothing if not a gold digger, and my pops was all too happy to accept her family's connections, of which there were many. Any love between the two is manufactured bullshit.

My father continues, his voice terse, "We're fed up with your nonsense, hijo. If it wasn't for your mother's repeated pleas on your behalf, I would've pulled the plug sooner."

Now, *that* catches my attention. "Pulled the plug?"

He leans back in his seat, nostrils flared, and his dark eyes—so like my own—glint in the afternoon light flooding in through the window. "Cut off."

My pulse quickens as the meaning behind those words sinks in, weighing in my bones like lead.

For several seconds, I stare at Dad in shock, blinking like an idiot. "Come on. You can't be serious." When he says nothing else, I look at my mother again. "Mom?"

She doesn't meet my gaze. "All you had to do was get an education and behave. Why was that so difficult?"

My mouth goes dry. "You're acting like I'm flunking out of school when I'm not. I'm doing fine. And might I remind you, *everyone* parties in college. It's practically a requirement." The words come out barely louder than a whisper rather than as the forceful protest I intend.

A sneer disfigures my father's features. "*Fine* is not CEO material. Nor is this."

Placing his phone on the table, he spins the screen to face me, revealing a post on his X feed with the hashtag **#hardonforHallazgo** and a picture of me outside a busy Providence nightclub sporting a very conspicuous boner. I don't normally walk around with raging erections, but I lost a bet, and I am nothing if not true to my word. You win some, you lose some, and I definitely lost that one, especially now that I'm banned from at least seven different Rhode Island nightclubs for life.

Still, I can't deny it was funny.

My parents, however, looked unamused.

"Okay, first, that was just harmless fun. Hardly newsworthy. Second, you should be thanking me for the free promotion. I was simply proving our new erectile dysfunction drug really does wor—"

"Do you think this is all a game?" Dad interrupts, his facade of calm on the brink of cracking once more. "*You* are the future of Hallazgo, Damian. Everything you do, no matter how harmless you think it may be, reflects on the company and on its perceived stability. Those dinosaurs you mentioned? Our board of directors? They, our shareholders, and any future investors are already forming opinions about you, which could very well affect what role you play in the years to come, if any." *If any.* Those words ping around in my brain like a warning bell as he frowns at me, the disappointment in his gaze clearer than ever. "Your abuelo would turn over in his grave if he could see what you've become, and I refuse to leave the legacy of his life's work in the hands of a…" He falters as if he can't find a strong enough word for what he wants to say, then gestures to literally all of me before finally spitting out, "pendejo."

Frankly, I'm not sure whether to laugh out of surprise or to feel deeply insulted given the offensive nature of the term. It's not every day my old man calls me a moron, and he's called me a lot of things over the years. While it might not seem that harsh by American standards, if we were in Mexico, his word choice would've raised some brows.

I've definitely struck a nerve this time.

"So, that's it?" I retort, unable to keep my rising panic from my voice. "You're cutting me off without any warning? No 'three strikes, you're out' or anything?"

In truth, if I were to tally up everything I've ever done to piss off my parents, I'd probably realize I've had way more than three strikes. They just never reacted so conclusively to my behavior before. They always let me off easy—a slap on the wrist here, a few choice words there. They never threatened to kick me out of the family, and because of that, I thought they never would, especially after what we've been through. But it's been four years now since the Day We Don't Speak Of, and I guess they're tired of waiting for me to get over it. To stop acting out. But the thing is, I feel like I have to hang on. I have to act out to remind them. I *have* to care the most because, if I don't, it seems like no one cares at all.

"You misunderstand me, hijo." My father's tone takes on a cajoling croon, making this conversation all the more ominous. "This *is* your warning. You have until graduation to prove to not only your mother and me, but to the entire board, that you're serious about your role in this family and at Hallazgo. Failure will not be tolerated. There will be a vote, and if we do not believe you're mature enough to start work at the company as of this coming summer, you won't step into a position there at all, and you will officially be on your own. No more handouts. No more excuses. It's time for you to grow up." My dad raises a finger and makes a clicking sound with his tongue as if he just remembered something. "Oh, and if you think you can just keep coasting, and fall back on some cushy trust fund like the other fresas at your school, you're sorely mistaken."

I bristle at the way he says fresas—at the clear implication in his tone that I, too, am one of these privileged, spoiled brats he's referring to.

His gaze hardens as he hammers the final nail in the coffin that is my shattering future. "Your abuelo didn't believe in silver spoons. And neither do we."

My jaw tenses. My abuelo believed in earning your keep, and detested when people raised their kids without an appreciation for hard work. I've always known that about my family, and yet, I never imagined myself losing the privilege I grew up with. Just as I never considered what I might do if I lost it.

But in my family, an inheritance is only bequeathed one way, and that inheritance is tied to Hallazgo. It's conditional. Earned. And in my father's eyes, I haven't earned a fucking thing.

"I'm well aware," I mutter, tight-lipped.

My mother takes hold of my father's hand where it rests on the table, and together, they stare at me with piercing eyes, a force to be reckoned with. As for me, I just see them as heartless puppeteers pulling the strings controlling my life.

As I glance between them, I gradually begin to comprehend just what it is they're asking of me. They want me to show them I can act like an adult… but what do adults do that I don't? Have money? Technically, it's family money, but that's got to count. Check. Have sex? Check. Have a job? Well, that one's all lined up, assuming I can prove I've changed, both to them and to a room full of stuffy old dudes who don't even know me beyond my name.

Changed… The word settles on my skin like dried sweat, making me itch.

How the hell can I prove to them I've changed when I don't have any inclination or desire to do so? When I don't want to be a carbon copy of my father or miserable like my emotionally-constipated mother? Okay, sure, I can start attending my classes more often, but something tells me that won't be enough to sway them. Not this time.

No, they want something else. Something to show them I can really be serious…

My mother squeezes my father's hand in hers, and that slight public display of affection draws my focus, giving me a brilliant idea.

A grin slowly forms on my lips. They want me to demonstrate stability? To prove I can be serious? To convince them I'm no longer an immature playboy?

Well, challenge accepted, assholes. Because I think I know just the way to do that.

Now, I just need a willing participant.

CHAPTER
SEVEN

**Statistically, the odds are I will grow a third boob
before I find a legal way out of this crisis.**

After a much-needed shower to wash the shame of screwing Damian
off my skin, I spend the rest of the day on the sofa in my comfiest
sweats, watching trashy television with Mom. Normally, we'd
binge-watch *Cold Case Files* or some other show or film about crime and
murder, but I don't think either of us can stomach anything having to do
with death at the moment. So, we settle for an old sitcom where the worst
that happens in the characters' fictional world is cheating. A shit scenario for
the wounded party, but not quite as shit as cancer.

Once seven o'clock hits, Mom can barely keep her eyes open, and I help
her to bed before settling back on the couch, those damning letters from the
insurance company taunting me from where they lay less than two feet away.
I sit with my elbows on my knees, hands steepled in front of my face like I'm
a villain plotting the downfall of my nemesis. In reality, my mind is blank as
I burn holes in the coffee table with my stare.

I thought finding out my mom has cancer was the worst news I would ever
get. But this—hearing there's nothing we can do to battle it because of our
financial situation—is worse. Way worse. And the crazy thing is our finances
aren't even bad. I mean, we're hardly destitute. We get by just fine. But even
if we didn't, something like this shouldn't happen to anyone.

I can't accept it. I won't. I'll find the money one way or another. Hell, I'll rob a fucking bank if I have to. Or failing that, there's always the option of selling pictures of my feet on the internet.

A sharp knock on the front door startles me out of my daze, and I jump off the sofa, dashing to answer it before whoever's on the other side does it again and inadvertently wakes up Mom. She needs her rest. She needs to keep up her strength until I figure out what to do.

"Coming," I hiss, unlocking the deadbolt, pausing for only a split second to wonder who it could be. It won't be Gina—she's working the night shift tonight—and I'm not expecting anyone. I suppose it could be a serial killer; I've watched enough documentaries to know rocking up to an unsuspecting victim's door could totally be their MO. At this point, I might actually welcome one. Getting stabbed to death would certainly be one solution to my problems.

Unfazed by the thought of my potential demise at the hands of some Ted Bundy wannabe, I pull open the door, and to my surprise, I find my two best friends smiling back at me from the other side of the threshold. Ronnie offers me a tiny wave, clutching a large Louis Vuitton bag to her chest, while Andie stands beside her in all her 5'10" glory, looking like the latest cover model for Sports Illustrated. Between Ronnie, with her flawless babydoll skin and gorgeous auburn hair, and Andie, who stands a whole head taller than her cousin with her swimsuit-ready body, shining mahogany mane, and the enviable perma-tan she inherited from her Chilean father, it's easy to see why people stare when they walk into a room. As for me, given how little I care about makeup and clothes, I sometimes joke that I'm the "before" picture in a makeover montage.

Unsurprisingly, the cousins are dressed in pajamas, which just goes to show that one can be rich and still be your typical college student at heart.

"Hey," I mutter, confusion pinching my brow. "What are you guys doing here?"

Ronnie shoots me a stupefied look. "Moral support. Duh."

Andie's mouth quirks into a timid smile, and I glimpse the apology in her chestnut eyes before she says it. "Sorry for barging in on you, Lex. Ronnie and I just wanted to pop by to make sure you're okay."

A chill passes through my body at her words. *Am* I okay? I was just contemplating committing a crime or selling pics to foot fetishizers for money, but that doesn't mean I'm *not* okay…does it?

When I don't say anything, Ronnie frowns and gestures past me into the hallway. "Well, are you going to let us in?"

I hesitate, not because Mom is asleep, but because I'm so close to losing my cool that if I invite them in, there's a good chance I'll fall apart, and I don't want to put that burden on anyone. This introvert keeps her wallowing to herself.

Averting my gaze, I cup my hand over my mouth and fake the world's most unconvincing yawn. "I would, but I'm literally about to pass ou—"

"Cut the crap," Ronnie interrupts. "First off, it's still light outside. You aren't going to bed unless you're secretly eighty-seven years old, so we all know that's a bald-faced lie. Second, I know you better than you think, Lexi Dornan, and it's obvious you're in emotional peril. What kind of friends would we be if we left you alone in such a vulnerable state?"

Bemused by Ronnie's outburst, I glance at Andie, who mimes pushing invisible glasses up her nose. *Ugh.* I didn't even realize I'd done that. Stupid anxiety and its control on my stupid fidgeting hand.

"*Well?* Am I right?" Ronnie presses.

I shift my weight from one foot to the other, my hands clasped together to keep from touching my glasses again—from revealing the one telltale sign that always indicates to anyone who knows me well that something is wrong. That I'm not okay.

I'm tempted to lie, to tell her I'm fine and to insist they go home, but I don't. I'm not sure why. Maybe, deep down, I do want to talk, or at the very least, not be alone right now. Or maybe Ronnie has finally mastered the art of mind manipulation.

Either way, the admission tumbles from my lips as if beyond my control. "Maybe."

Sometimes, I think Ronnie should reconsider her plans for after college. She wants to be an actor—specifically, a star on West End or Broadway before eventually moving to TV or film—but her talents would be much better utilized as an interrogator working for the FBI or even the military, as absurd as the notion may seem. My dainty BFF might not look the part, but she has this intensity about her that is borderline terrifying, and people generally have a tough time saying no to her because of this almost hypnotic effect she has on them. I once saw her make a grown man full on weep in less than thirty seconds of talking to him. I have no doubt that, if she really wanted to, she could pull out just about anyone's deepest, darkest secrets.

She certainly never has to work hard for mine.

Her lips curl into a triumphant smirk. "That's what I thought. Well, we come bearing four listening ears and two pairs of shoulders for you to cry on should you need them. Oh"—she unzips her bag, allowing me a quick peek inside—"and several bottles of wine. Assuming you aren't too hungover, that is."

"It's the good stuff," Andie adds, as if I really needed further convincing.

Although I roll my eyes, I can't hide the grateful smile spreading over my face. "Come on in," I say, moving to one side of the entryway. "I'll go get some glasses. But we have to keep the noise down. Mom is asleep."

Ronnie flounces into the hallway wearing a shit-eating grin, as if she knew she'd get her way all along, and plants a kiss on my cheek before skipping up the stairs to my bedroom with her cousin in tow. No one can ever claim the woman doesn't have confidence, that's for damn sure.

I wander into the kitchen and grab the pink and teal tumblers Gina got me for my birthday last year—each one labeled with a cheesy drinking-related pun, like *I make pour choices*, *Wine about it*, and *Sip, sip, hooray!*—then make my way up to my room where my friends wait for me, checking their phones while lying on their stomachs side by side on my bed. Andie's cheeks are slightly flushed, which tells me she's texting her boyfriend, Eli. They've been dating since March and are still very much in the honeymoon phase of their relationship, though it's entirely possible this is just how they'll always be considering how nauseatingly cute and in love with each other they are. Even the story of how they met is adorable, as if they were unconsciously channeling that Tom Hanks movie about the two bookstore owners who fall in love over email. Except, instead of owning a bookstore, Eli is a local radio DJ and Andie his devoted listener who would frequently text requests to his show. They then began chatting online, neither aware of the other's identity, only to bump into each other completely by chance when we were in Santa Cruz for spring break this past March. It was an eerie coincidence, as if some invisible force had dragged him those three thousand miles from Rhode Island and physically put him in her path so they would meet.

Ronnie says the whole thing was kismet. Especially since, to top it all off, Eli is also a student at Conwick. She wouldn't shut up about Andie's horoscope for weeks after that.

As for Ronnie…who can really say what she's doing. She could be swiping right on Tinder, stalking Timothée Chalamet on Instagram, or quite literally hiring a private investigator—or hitman—to hunt down Jay for all I know. With her, the options are nearly endless.

When I close the door behind me, they immediately stash their phones, giving me their undivided attention. Ronnie then bolts upright, grabs her bag off the floor, and pulls out two bottles of wine, holding both up for me to choose. Without hesitation, I point to the Chardonnay.

They make room for me on the bed, and we sit in silence as Ronnie uncorks the bottle and carefully fills the glasses halfway. She then examines each of the tumblers before purposely handing me the one printed with the words *Wine about it*, as if that will somehow make me talk. For a moment, I expect her to say something first, but she doesn't, waiting patiently. I'm grateful she doesn't bring up the Damian-shaped elephant in the room.

"So, what's going on, Lex?" Andie finally asks in a gentle voice when I don't, in fact, whine about it, opting instead to quietly sip from my glass. "Is your mom okay?"

There's no hiding the grimace that pulls at my lips.

Part of me really doesn't want to get into it. I've held the tears in all day for Mom's sake (except for that one little bastard that managed to slip free), and I'm afraid that if I open the flood gates and let them loose now, they might never stop. Another part of me wants to spill my guts, and weep as they hold my hands and tell me that everything will be okay. Even though it won't.

Not unless I find us a way out of this nightmare.

"The insurance company raised our deductible and, come January, won't cover her oral chemo meds anymore." My voice breaks on that last word, and I pause, drawing in a breath and taking a few seconds to steady myself. Once I'm certain my composure won't crumble, I add, "Her treatments are still covered, but when the new year hits…well, it won't matter. They won't continue paying for her infusions until that deductible is paid in full, and as for the meds themselves…" I scoff. "They cost a fortune on their own. So, no. I don't think she will be."

Ronnie presses one hand to her mouth, her eyes practically bulging out of their sockets. Clearly, she didn't expect my news to be this bad. She flounders, quickly downing her wine, then gasps out the only response that suits the situation. "Shit. That's beyond fucked up."

I nod as my gaze drifts down to the quote staring back at me from the front of her glass—*I make pour choices*—and for a moment, I find myself thinking of Damian again. Poor choices, indeed. I bet that asshole has never worried about money a single day in his life.

"Yup," I grumble, chugging the rest of my drink, and hold my tumbler out for a refill.

Once my glass is topped off, Ronnie sets her own empty cup down on my bedside table, and takes my free hand in hers, rubbing her thumbs over my skin in slow, soothing circles. Her cousin mimics the motion on my back, her palm warm through the fabric of my T-shirt.

"What are you guys going to do?" Andie asks.

I shrug. "I mean, I told her I'd drop out of Conwick and get a job, but she wasn't really fond of that idea."

Ronnie snorts. "What kind of job do you think you'd get as a college dropout, smarty pants? Probably not one that would pay anything close to what you need." She releases my hand and taps a manicured nail against the middle of my forehead.

A frown twists my lips and tugs at my brow. I hadn't thought that far ahead, but she's right. I can't rely on a perfect SAT score and a college scholarship to get me a job with a high enough salary. Or at least a job with good benefits, not that I could claim Mom as a dependent. Which would mean paying for everything she needs treatment-wise out of pocket. Without a degree or sufficient experience in the field, my options are limited. Still…

"I don't know what other choice I have." A lump swells in my throat, and I force myself to swallow. "If I don't, she might…" But I can't finish that sentence. I can't even finish that thought.

"What about crowdfunding or something?" Andie suggests. "A lot of people do that these days to pay their medical bills."

"Which is *so* sad," Ronnie laments. "The system is well and truly fucked."

I exhale a wheezy, mirthless laugh. "Agreed, but I don't think my mom would want me asking a bunch of strangers for the money. She'd see it as charity and find a way to feel guilty about it until it eats her alive. Which we can all agree is ridiculous, but I think it's because we've had to do things on our own for so long that she sees this as just another problem for us to bear the weight of alone. Gina might be able to talk some sense into her, but I don't see that happening. My mother is nothing if not stubborn."

Not that I've entirely discounted the charity route. It would just have to be through some official channel for Mom to accept it.

"I could ask my dads to pay for it," Ronnie says, as plainly as if we were just discussing the weather. "God knows they have more than enough money."

My heart falters, but though my chest warms at her offer, I adamantly shake my head. "I can't let them do that, not with the kind of money we'd need. Besides, we all know there's no way in hell Mom would agree to take it. Plus, your dads are paying three tuitions right now between you two and Sammy, and Conwick isn't exactly a state college." Samantha—Andie's younger sister—isn't in college yet, but she goes to a swanky private high school which costs nearly as much as Conwick. I can't even imagine trying to afford one tuition let alone three. Thank god for my scholarship or we'd really be screwed. "They have enough to pay for."

And as much as I wish I could accept Ronnie's offer, this isn't their problem.

Andie makes a pensive humming sound. "Well, there must be something out there that can help without turning you into a charity case. Or a stripper." She drums her fingers on her chin before rolling off the bed, a devious smile forming on her face as she prances over to my desk and sinks down into the spinning gray chair. "Let's have a little look, shall we?" She opens my laptop, brings up the browser, and starts typing in the search bar. When she hits enter, a website pops up, and I sneer.

"Craigslist? *Seriously?*"

She looks at me and cocks a brow. "Hey, this site has been known to have some quality shit on it. Besides, despite that incredible brain of yours, you have no qualifications, mi amiga, and minimum wage will not help you with your current predicament. Therefore, in the immortal words of Leia Organa, Craigslist is your only hope."

"*Ugh*, are you quoting *Star Trek* again?" Ronnie asks, not bothering to mask her disdain. Unlike her nerd-culture loving, D&D-playing, cosplay-enthusiast cousin, Ronnie loves the classics, period dramas, and all things smutty romance. When it comes to sci-fi and fantasy, though…well, let's just say we could only convince her to watch the *Lord of the Rings* movies because of Orlando Bloom.

Andie spins the chair around and gapes at her cousin. "*Star Wars*. My god, how are we even related?"

I don't point out the obvious—that because they aren't biologically related, the odds of them sharing any traits, including non-hereditary ones like taste in film genre, are slim. In fact, the two cousins are about as polar opposite as you can get despite being the children of twins, but that's only because Marco isn't Ronnie's biological father. When he and Simon—Ronnie's other dad—hired a surrogate to help them have a baby, they both decided to throw their special sauce into the mix and never find out which swimmer was fastest. But the moment Ronnie was born with that porcelain skin and red hair, it was evident whose sperm had won that particular race.

Still, as Ronnie said this morning at Izzy's, genetics aside, Andie is family. Just as these two bickering morons are *my* family.

Blood doesn't mean a damn thing.

Sliding off the bed, I crouch beside Andie at my desk and wave a hand at the screen. "That's definitely *not* what Leia said, but start scrolling." Not that I actually believe Craigslist is the answer, but at this point, I'm willing to try anything.

Ronnie joins us, resting her chin on Andie's left shoulder while I hover behind the other, watching with carefully contained interest as she presses on the trackpad with her thumb and swipes down, down, down with her index finger, coaxing listing after listing to inch up into view. My eyes scan over every job title that floats into my eyeline, and as the seconds creep by, whatever flicker of optimism I felt at this plan withers and dies.

"Professional pancake flipper? These are ridiculous."

"Ohhhh, this one's looking for female social drinkers." Ronnie thrusts her arm out, pointing at one of the ads. "I could do that. So could you, even if you are a bit of a lightweight." When I give her an *Excuse me?* look, she blows me a kiss.

Curiosity piqued, I urge Andie to click on the listing and then scan the description. Drink to pay the bills? Don't mind if I do. But when we reach the bottom where payment is mentioned, reality knocks some of the sense back into me. "They're paying in IHOP gift cards. Pass."

"But…pancakes!" Ronnie whines.

I throw a sidelong glance in her direction. Ronnie could literally buy an IHOP if she wanted. She doesn't need to be paid in gift cards. Then again, I know all too well what she's like when she's hungover. Pancakes are her Kryptonite. Alcohol and pancakes? A dangerous combination. Temptation personified.

"Pass," I repeat. At my command, Andie clicks the back button and returns to scrolling the listings.

"Let's see…" She mutters absently to herself as we continue scanning. "Sandwich artist. No. Experienced bra fitter. Interesting, but no. Beard mentor?" She peers up at me over her shoulder. "What the fuck is a beard mentor?"

I shake my head. "Why are you asking me?"

Blinking, I fix my gaze back on the laptop, taking note of the bottom-most listing visible on the screen. The payment amount is posted just under the title, and the number of zeros following the dollar sign immediately catches my eye, forming a string of red and yellow blocks in my mind. But this time, instead of a tower that threatens to crush me, the numbers seem to form a bridge to my possible salvation.

"Hey, what about this one?"

I reach around Andie and press my finger to the trackpad, clicking on the link in question. When the screen changes, she begins to read aloud, "'Wanted: Fake Girlfriend.' Okay, that is just sad. The poor guy must really be desperate. I mean, who goes to Craigslist looking for a girlfriend? And not even a real one at that?"

"Knowing nothing about him, it's hard to say, but I'm sure he has his reasons," I murmur.

"Or maybe he's a *murderer*," Ronnie states, drawing out the word for emphasis.

A huff breaks through my lips—half laughter, half exasperation. "A definite possibility. But look what he's willing to pay."

Ten thousand a month might not be as much as I need, but it's close, and far more than I would get elsewhere, making it worth the risk of getting unalived in my book. And if I can get a part-time job on the side, then maybe, between the two, I'll have the cash to keep Mom going to the end of her treatment. Or long enough to figure something else out.

Ronnie gives the ad another skeptical glance over Andie's shoulder. "Yeah, that's how I know it isn't legit, babe. Even *I* would suck a stranger's dick for that kind of cash and I have an AmEx Black Card."

Well, that's saying something. Ronnie might be a relentless flirt, but she has high standards, and would never fool around with someone unless they'd managed to earn her respect…especially after Jay. She would certainly never be caught dead having a one-night stand with a person she didn't know or like, no matter how hot they are. Unlike my train-wreck self.

Damian's face floats into my thoughts again, but I swat it away. Buzz off, asshole.

"What about the time frame?" Andie asks, pointing to the part of the listing where the poster very specifically mentions needing a willing female to pretend to be his girlfriend for a nine-month period. It's pretty weird, but ten grand over nine months? That's potentially life-saving money. Besides, how hard can it be? As long as he doesn't expect anything more than the odd fake date and nothing creepy, I'm game. "And the age?" she continues. "He says early to mid-twenties in the ad, not nineteen."

I shake my head at that. It's a petty distinction; I'll be twenty in the spring, so it's close enough. Besides, I highly doubt the guy is going to ID whoever answers the listing.

"Pretty sure he just wants someone legal," I counter. "And technically, I *will* enter my early twenties before the nine months are over."

Andie pushes out her lips. "Good point." Her eyes then flash to her cousin. "It's probably fine. I mean, why would he put all that if he was just looking to murder whoever answers the ad?"

Ronnie gapes at her cousin in disbelief. "You just answered your own question, dummy. To get people to answer the ad, *obviously*."

"Or to perv on them," Andie muses, as if the idea just occurred to her. "Or maybe it's just a joke."

I worry my bottom lip between my teeth, deliberating. Sure, the ad seems too good to be true, but it could also be a lifeline—a sole buoy in the middle of a raging ocean that might be the only thing to save me from drowning.

Andie might be right—the job could very well be a joke—but if it isn't? If it *is* legit, and that kind of money is actually in arm's reach? Well, then I would be an idiot not to grab it while I have the chance.

I jolt when Andie's hand brushes my arm, and I meet her gaze, mystified by the look of concern I find spreading across her face. "Lex, all jokes aside, you can't seriously be considering this. I know I'm the one who suggested Craigslist, but really, I was just trying to take your mind off the shit with your mom."

"It's ten grand a month," I say slowly, keeping my voice steady so I won't break into tears. "That's almost enough to help Mom complete her treatment, or at least get us most of the way to the finish line. Besides, nothing else on here comes close to offering that kind of money." I throw a weighted glance at Ronnie. "Maybe it's fate."

"Oh, boy." Ronnie plops down on her cousin's lap, and props an elbow on my desk, looking up at me hard as if trying to read my thoughts. "How dare you use the undeniable power of the universe against me." She pauses for a moment, studying my face. "We're not going to talk you out of this, are we?"

When have either of you ever talked me out of anything? I almost ask. For a scholarship student at one of the best colleges in the country, I'm a bit of a chaotic mess. Instead, I say, "It's at least worth investigating to see if the job is legit. Plus, if it is, I won't have to drop out of school."

It's a win-win for everyone then. Mom gets her treatment, and I get my elite education that we both busted our asses so hard for. That outcome is worth sacrificing some of my time and dignity. Well, a lot of my dignity. But who knows? Maybe I'll get lucky and the guy will be cute.

Yeah, right, a voice says in the back of my head. *Because cute, available, sane guys totally need to post wanted ads for girlfriends online.*

I shudder. Ronnie's right. Maybe not about the murderer part, but the guy's probably a total creep. Regardless, this might be the only option I have. I can handle a creep for ten grand a month.

"Just promise us, if you won't take my dads' money, that you'll at least look into the charity route first," Ronnie begs.

I offer her an endearing smile and nod. "Of course." I already planned on doing just that, but having this in my back pocket won't hurt. A girl always needs a back-up plan.

All I can hope now is that I won't need it.

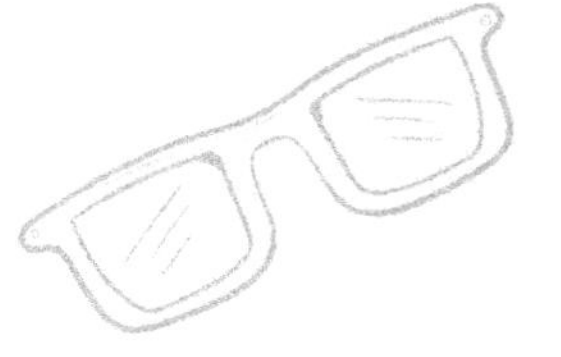

CHAPTER
EIGHT

Damian

*La paciencia es la madre de la ciencia - Patience
is the mother of science*

**Translation: Patience leads to success...
or maybe I need a new plan.**

WANTED: Fake Girlfriend (Newport area)
Compensation: $10,000 a month
Employment type: part-time
Job title: Lifesaver

Seeking laid-back female in early to mid-twenties (though will consider older, within reason) to pretend to be my girlfriend for a period of nine months, starting immediately. Willing to pay $10,000 a month to the right candidate. Due to privacy concerns, further information is only available upon interview.

Serious inquiries only.

The mattress shifts beneath my weight as I flop backward onto my bed and comb a hand through my water-soaked hair before propping my arm behind my head. I lift my hips slightly to adjust the towel at my waist, then reach for my phone where it lies on the blanket beside me, holding it up roughly two inches above my face as I open my email. Again. This must be the thirtieth time I've checked it since I woke up an hour ago, and my disappointment weighs just as heavily as it did the first time my mail app declared I have no new unread messages. Or at least any that aren't spam or some sus "company" trying to sell me a penis enlarger. I don't need any help in that department, thank you very much.

I blow out a loud, exasperated breath through my nose. After lunch with my parents on Friday, I thought for sure that a girlfriend would be the perfect way to prove to them I can be serious about…well, life in general, I guess. But seeing as I'm not interested in dating, I figured that, by hiring a stranger to pretend to be said girlfriend, I would have the *appearance* of commitment without needlessly tying myself down to a relationship I don't actually want. And since all I need is to make it to graduation, it would be easy enough to stage an amicable break-up once my dad is appeased and my future at my abuelo's company is secured.

At the time, it seemed like an ingenious plan with all the reward and none of the risk. After all, it's not like I would really have to worry about anyone at Conwick stumbling across the ad by accident—not when the majority of the student body has money to spare and are as likely to look at local job listings as they are to take public transport. Sure, there might be some exceptions to that, but the odds are mostly in my favor. And I don't think my parents even know what Craigslist is, nor would they have cause or reason to check it.

But it's been nearly two days since I put up the listing, and reality is starting to crush me with doubt. I don't get it. I'm offering a small fortune in exchange for what should be a simple job, and I haven't had a single response. How can that be? I mean, I know this is a nice area, but there are plenty who don't come from wealth who live locally—like a server who's grown tired of living off tips or a bartender who's fed up with handsy drunks. Surely, my offer is better than either of those scenarios.

No, it can't be the money that's putting people off…so maybe it's the wording? I know I was vague on the details, but that's only because the last thing I need right now is another scandal blowing up in my face. If word were to get out about this and reach my father, this would definitely be the final straw. He'd cut me off faster than I can say Hallazgo.

I swipe my finger across the phone screen, pulling up my internet browser and re-reading the listing, which I've kept open in one of a small handful of tabs. The others vary from creative ideas for public dates to the tip-line numbers for different tabloids (I'll need to be seen with my future fake girlfriend if this is ever going to work). I even have a template for a non-disclosure agreement ready and waiting. It's not like I can use the family lawyer for this, but I also can't very well have whoever responds to the ad running their mouth as soon as the nine months is over…or the interview, for that matter.

Assuming anyone answers the listing at all.

My phone starts vibrating in my hand, and my abuela's smiling face pops up in place of the browser as if she can sense my distress all the way from Guadalajara. Pushing myself upright, I tap a finger against the green answer button, then toss the device screen-down onto the bedspread.

"¡Hola!" my abuela says as I stand and cross the few feet to my dresser, unhooking my towel and dropping it in a heap to the floor. "Damian? Am I doing the FaceTime correctly? I can't see you."

With a snort, I call back, "It's just FaceTime, abuela. And you're doing it right. Just give me a minute to get dressed." Quickly drying myself off from my shower, I pull on some briefs and throw on the first T-shirt I grab, then walk back to the bed, pick up my phone, flip it over so the screen is facing me, and wave to my grandmother, who beams back.

"Ah! There you are," she coos. "Now, I can see you."

"Hi, abuelita."

The smile slips from her face, and she lifts a wry, disapproving brow at me. "Why weren't you dressed? You're not still in bed, are you?"

"It's Sunday," I retort, my tone defensive, as I turn and plop back down on my mattress. "There's literally nothing else to do in this town."

That, and I need to be on my best behavior right now if I'm to avoid my dear papi's wrath, which means no more public displays of drunkenness or weekend hangovers. So much for a fun senior year.

My abuela clicks her tongue, shaking her head. "Los jóvenes de hoy en día," she mutters under her breath, then waves a dismissive hand at me. "Anyway, how are you, mi cielo? I miss you."

"I'm okay." Well, that's not entirely true, but I don't elaborate any further, instead saying, "I miss you, too," which is a fact. So, at least I'm being fifty percent honest with her. "How are things?"

She tosses what looks to be a kitchen towel over her shoulder, and I realize she must have taken a break from her daily baking session to call me. As a Roman Catholic, her Sunday mornings are typically spent at church, but she doesn't publicly observe the religion as often as she used to since my abuelo passed away, opting instead to pass that time at home, embracing her own quiet form of reflection. Still, she must've missed the memo that Sunday is supposed to be for rest. One of these days, I should really order her Uber Eats.

Despite our family being literal billionaires, my abuela has always refused to hire a cook, insisting the kitchen is her domain and she will not tolerate any strangers there. And she's the best there is—her food is second to none. Her tres leches cake in particular could seriously win awards. Just thinking about it now has me salivating.

And to top it all off, she's a freaking saint. Since my abuelo died and she's been living on her own, my abuela spends her time cooking for local shelters and food banks to help those less fortunate, as if the millions she already donates to charity every single year isn't enough. Truth be told, I idolize her just as much as I idolized my grandfather, and yet…I know I can never live up to either of them. They both always had hearts of gold whereas mine is shriveled and dry, like an old prune. Sometimes, I wonder how my abuela can love me—dumbass, disappointing shit that I am.

"Oh, you know, same old, same old," she answers. "But you don't want to hear about a boring old lady. Tell me what's new with you. How's school? Have you found yourself a girlfriend? Or"—she pauses, flashing curious eyes at me—"a boyfriend, perhaps? I don't mind either way, you know. I'm very—what do the kids call it? Awake?"

I bark out a laugh. She really is the best. Somehow, I doubt Lenore and Hector would be quite so accepting. "The term you're looking for is woke. And no, I don't have a girlfriend."

Yet.

"And school?"

That arching eyebrow that always informs me she can see through my bullshit is back.

Not in the mood for a second lecture in the span of two days, I slap on my most deceptive smile. "School is fine. Honestly, it's the same old here for me, too."

No need to go into detail or inform her that her son is an asshole. I'm sure, deep down, she already knows.

"¡Ay, dios mío!" she cries dramatically, pressing the back of her hand to her forehead. "I cannot believe you're in your last year of college. Time goes by so fast."

Too fast.

The thought springs to the front of my mind unbidden and hits me like a punch to the gut. I deepen my smile to hide my wince.

"Yeah, but that's not necessarily a bad thing," I say to soothe her, even though I don't mean it. Such a sentiment might be true for most people, but not me. *I* don't want time to keep ticking forward. If anything, I want to turn back the clock, to rewind and try to prevent the event that veered my life so far off course. Or at the very least, just have a few extra days—

I clench my jaw and shake that silent wish away before it can form. Daydreaming about rewriting the past or even reliving part of it won't change a damn thing. Besides, I have plenty to worry about in the present.

"And just think," I continue, easing the pain in my chest with a thought that actually brings me joy, "I can come visit you more often once I graduate."

The handful of times a year I do manage to get down to Mexico really aren't enough. Not when I know how finite our lives truly are. And my abuela isn't exactly getting any younger. I should probably make it a point to go see her more frequently.

"*Pfft*, sure," my abuela says, rolling her eyes. "Assuming your father doesn't work you to the bone the moment you start at Hallazgo."

For the first time since lunch with my parents on Friday, I feel the sharp, unrelenting sting of fear. Doubt was already setting in, but hearing my abuela speak so casually about my future at the very company she helped my grandfather build has the reality of my situation crashing down on my skull like an anvil. But unlike in the cartoons I watched growing up, there are no little yellow birdies looping over my head. For me, that anvil is a killing blow.

Was my dad being serious? Would he really cut me off from the family?

Worse still…would my abuela let him?

"Damian?" my abuela prompts when I've been quiet too long.

"I'm here," I murmur, but my voice is small.

"What's with that look? Are you okay? You're not sick, are you?"

I give a shaky jerk of my head and force my smile—which had slipped in my sudden burst of panic—back into place. I don't want to talk about my dad right now. Or my future at Hallazgo. One, because I may lose my cool and I don't want to drag my abuela into my mess, and two, because I can't be one hundred percent sure she won't take his side. This *is* the company her darling deceased husband built from nothing that we're talking about, and while my abuela might love and adore me, if she had to choose…well, I can't say with absolute certainty that she'd choose me.

"I'm just fine. Don't you worry about me," I assure her, searching my brain for a change in subject. "How's Xolo doing? Can I see him?"

Xolo, my abuela's dog, is a Xoloitzcuintli—a Mexican hairless dog— and he is quite possibly the coolest fucking thing in the world. He looks intimidating as shit, like he could guard the gates of Hell, but in reality, he's a huge softie, who lives for belly rubs and treats.

I blink at my abuela, waiting for her to call for Xolo, but she just stares at me, looking unconvinced.

"Hm," she grunts after a moment. "Fighting with your father again, I take it?"

Welp. So much for avoiding *that* topic.

"Sooo, does this mean I *can't* see Xolo?" I ask, but my grandmother, ever the bullshit detector, just lifts her brow again.

"Damian." Unlike my father, she doesn't have to raise her voice to get my attention. Just from her tone, I know she means business.

For half a second, I consider ending the call if it will allow me to escape this conversation. But I can't do that to her—not because I love her, and she's the sweetest person in the world, but because if I do, there's the very real possibility she'll fly here just to whoop my ass for being disrespectful.

Man, this weekend blows.

I scoff. "I'm surprised you can't hear his disdain for me from all the way in Mexico."

My abuela flinches at my tone, and her face immediately softens. "You don't mean that, mi nieto."

Oh, but I do.

"Hey, maybe I'll move down to you once I graduate. That would be nice, wouldn't it?" My mission: distract her with the idea of seeing her only grandchild more often—every grandparent's dream. Although, at this rate, it's more of a reality than a dream since I'll probably *have* to move in with her as I won't have anywhere else to go. "Then you could see me every day."

She clicks her tongue. "Don't even joke about such a thing. Le vas a romper el corazón a tu abuela."

I press a hand to my chest, feigning offense. "How dare you. I would never break your heart, abuelita."

Her responding sigh makes my stomach flip. Oh, boy. I am *not* going to like what she says next.

"My door is always open to you, mi amor. You know that. But this rift with your father…" She gestures to the space just in front of the camera as if the rift in question is a physical thing we can see. "You need to fix it. Whatever the issue is now, maybe try seeing it from his perspective."

My lips press into a scowl, and in a sulking tone, I snap, "What about *my* perspective?"

She gives me a sad, pitying look. "He knows, Damian. He knows you're hurting. We all do. But at some point…necesitas seguir adelante."

You need to move on.

She's not wrong. I know it's not healthy to hold onto the past the way I've clung to it the last four years. But how do you move on when letting go means forgiving something I don't have it in me to forgive?

How do you move on when letting go is so fucking painful?

"Yeah," I mutter, lowering my eyes, unsure what else to say.

"Are you still coming to visit for Día de los Muertos?" she asks in a gentle voice after a long moment has passed.

I meet her gaze again and nod. "Of course, abuelita. I wouldn't miss it."

And then, because she knows me well enough to sense I need some space, she says, "Good. I'll see you then, mi chiquito. Te amo." She waves and blows me a kiss, and I blow one back with a tender smile.

"I love you, too. See you soon."

I stab my finger down on the red end call button, and my abuela's face vanishes, returning me to the last window I had open before she FaceTimed me. My Craigslist ad stares back in silent judgment as if taunting me for what I'm beginning to realize was a really fucking stupid idea.

I pull up my email app again, my heart pounding behind my rib cage in anticipation and hope. Hope that, for once, something will actually work out the way I want it to. But just like all the other times I checked it this morning, there are no new messages. Only more spam. Only more offers for unnecessary penis enlargers.

Jesus, I seriously need to sort out this email.

"Fuck!" I shout, throwing my phone across the room and collapsing back onto the bedspread.

I am royally screwed.

My tolerance for being placed on hold < the increasing likelihood of me murdering someone today.

By the time Monday morning rolls around, I'm in panic mode. It's like the universe purposely schedules bad shit for Fridays or weekends, so you have to suffer the anxiety of waiting until the following week when the nine-to-five businesses open again and something can finally be done about it.

Well, the new week has arrived, and here I am, attempting to sort out the shitstorm that my life has become. Normally, I would be in my Applied Discrete Mathematics lecture, but I emailed my professor an hour ago feigning illness (a *great* start to a new semester) so I could make some calls while Mom is at work. Luckily, Professor Bensen is also my advisor, and after nine months of said advising, we're well enough acquainted for him to know I wouldn't skip class this early in the school year—or at all—unless I urgently had to. And since my scholarship is based on academic performance more than attendance, missing one lesson really isn't an issue.

Besides, I couldn't do this with Mom home. Her moral compass is permanently facing due north, and seeing as she's refusing to stand up for herself, she's left me no choice but to stand up in her stead, even if that means throwing all our morals out the window. She might not want to fight the injustice of a corrupt medical system, but like hell am I going to sit back and do nothing. Especially when the matter of her *literal* life or death boils down to some greedy company, and their underhanded tactics to try to save a few bucks.

Which brings us to the task at hand. Thanks to my exceptional brain and its affinity for all things math related, I've been doing our taxes since I was thirteen, so I know both Mom's and Gina's social security numbers and all their other personal information, making it all too easy to pass myself off as either of them over the phone. It also helps that I sound like Mom, not that being able to impersonate her well makes what I'm about to do any less illegal. Identity theft is a crime, but hey, drastic times call for drastic measures, and I'd rather beg for forgiveness than ask for permission.

I make myself comfortable at the kitchen table with a steaming cup of much-needed caffeine, the paperwork we received in the mail on Friday, and a depressingly short list of phone numbers. They were the only potentially useful ones I could find over the weekend, and I take a moment to glance at them before starting at the top of the list with Mom's doctor. Since she was the one who wrote the infusion order and the prescription for her oral medication, I'm hoping she might be able to help us, either by prescribing new pills that will actually be covered on our formulary or by reaching out to the insurance company on our behalf.

As the phone rings, I pump my leg under the table, my heel tap, tap, tapping the floor as my entire body vibrates with nervous energy. One automated response and three "press one for reception" prompts later, I'm connected to the receptionist, who—in a bored drawl—informs me that, "Dr. Park isn't available right now, but can I take a message?" I try my best to stay calm while expressing how imperative it is that I speak with her as soon as humanly possible, but the receptionist merely offers to pass on my details, stating, "You can expect a call back sometime tomorrow."

When I push the issue, she begrudgingly hands me over to one of the nurses, who regrettably says he can't help me, as if I didn't already know that. Hence why I asked to talk to my mom's *doctor*. Irritation spreads through me, making me feel itchy, and I let out a loud breath through my nose as I once again ask to speak to Dr. Park. "One moment, please," the nurse insists, but instead of handing me over to the doctor per my request, the call is forwarded to yet another nurse, who repeats what the previous one said almost verbatim before directing the call back to reception.

I'm passed around this way for the better part of twenty minutes, tossed back and forth between the nurses and reception like an unwanted hacky sack, until a new voice comes on the line, and I finally hear those three glorious words I've been waiting for: "Dr. Park speaking."

I relay the problem with as much tact and poise as I can manage given the pure fury and vitriol racing through me that we're even in this situation. Dr. Park, to her credit, is empathetic, but ultimately explains there's little she can do other than appeal the insurance company's decision with something called a medical letter of need that would express why my mom requires that particular prescription. When I ask how likely it is that the appeal would be successful and our insurance company would reverse their decision, her response is a grim, "Not likely at all." Still, she offers to send it regardless, which I suppose is better than nothing.

As for switching to a different pill…well, that isn't a viable option due to the same bullshit insurance factor. Or in the case of the few drugs that *would* be covered, because of the negative reactions Mom had when she tried them prior to moving on to the current medication she's taking. Before she was switched to acalabrutinib, which is what she's on now, Dr. Park had trialed her on several lower tier drugs—the cheaper options that are, as of this moment, still covered by our insurance. Unfortunately, the side effects were too bad for her to keep taking them, which is just freaking typical. Of course, the meds Mom reacts poorly to are the only ones our insurance will actually pay for, as if they intentionally changed our cover just to punish her body for something completely out of her control. These assholes, I swear. Like she hasn't suffered enough.

I only realize I muttered that last thought aloud when Dr. Park expresses her confusion, to which I hastily thank her for the appeal, and then make an excuse to end the call before she can catch on that I'm not my mother.

My pulse beats wildly under my skin as I lean back in my chair and release a heavy breath, the wood creaking from the shift in weight. You'd think I just rode the world's fastest roller coaster the way my heart is racing from that call. I hate the feeling. Adrenaline junkie, I am not.

Pushing up my glasses, I rub at one eye, my vision bleary as I glance at the second number on my list. It slides into focus as the frames fall back into their previous place on the perch of my nose.

Next up: the bastard insurance company.

Hands shaking, I type in the digits. I know before I even hit the call button that this won't go well, and I'm proven right by the forty plus minutes they keep me on hold, each passing moment driven closer to madness by the same annoying jingle on the other end of the line that plays over and over and *over* again in my ear on a torturous loop. When the music ends and I hear the sweet, blissful sound of a human voice, I nearly shout, "Thank fuck!"

Unfortunately, that sense of relief doesn't last long, and aside from suggesting I change our insurance benefits to a more expensive tier that would actually include the drug Mom needs during the upcoming open enrollment period, the customer service rep says there's nothing they can do to help us on our existing plan. The way the guy talks, you'd think the changes to the formulary were law, and not just something the company decided on a whim to boost their profits.

With a tired sigh, I ask for the difference in cost between our current plan and the upgraded option, and as the man regurgitates the numbers his computer spits out, I see them build up before me like a clusterfuck of LEGO blocks, each one a different color and shape. They slide together in sync with my brain as it makes the calculation against our existing monthly expenses, but the picture they form isn't pretty. Or remotely affordable.

When I end the call, it takes all my self-restraint to not throw my phone across the room.

"What a waste of time." Groaning, I press my fingertips into my aching temples and glance down at the screen.

An hour and a half has already elapsed, and I'm no closer to a solution than I was when I first started making these calls. I'm at zero for two, and while I still have a handful of numbers on my list to try, this whole situation is really starting to feel hopeless.

"Stop it, Lex," I growl, slapping myself hard on the cheek. "Your momma didn't raise no quitter."

And right now, that same momma needs me.

Finding my resolve, I move on to the next call. The remaining numbers on my list are all for cancer charities and patient assistance programs, and I decide to start with the charities first since I know the odds of PAP helping us are slim to none. A quick Google search was all I needed to learn that, regardless of our circumstances, it's likely we'll be denied because Mom doesn't meet any of the prerequisites for cover. She won't qualify, even if rejecting her means she could die. It's as simple and cut-throat as that.

Unfortunately, the charities aren't much help either. After spending an ungodly amount of time on hold with each one, I'm told all the grants for chronic lymphocytic leukemia are closed at the moment, and the best they can offer is to put me (aka my mom) on a waitlist to potentially receive a portion of funding when the grants eventually open again. But there's no saying when that would be, and since these things are first come, first served—and the representatives can't divulge how many other people are ahead of us on the list—there's no guarantee Mom would receive anything at all, let alone the staggering amount we need.

"So much for that idea." I sigh, crossing off yet another number on my list. Yup, this is definitely hopeless.

I end my losing streak with two different assistance programs, and those calls turn out exactly as I expect. One of the reps even goes so far as to scoff when I give him my mom's salary information, as if it was stupid of me to think for just one second that we might be worthy of help.

With the last number crossed off my list, and my patience one fraying thread away from snapping, I rise from the kitchen table and storm over to the sofa, grabbing the first cushion I can get my hands on and pressing it so hard to my face I struggle to breathe. Then I scream as loudly as I can into the fabric since suffocating myself against the polyester blend seems like a smarter decision than homicide, not that I've entirely ruled out the latter. That last rep in particular better hope he never crosses my path.

I scream until my voice is hoarse and a headache throbs behind my eyes, then drop the pillow, and flop down on the sofa, feeling even more despondent than I did at the end of the previous week when this crapfest began.

Planting my elbows on my knees, I lean forward and smooth my curls away from my face. "What the hell am I going to do?"

I don't really know who I'm asking. The universe, maybe? God? Buddha? Satan? Our lord and savior, Ruth Bader Ginsburg, who is surely smiling down on all feminists from Heaven? But if any of them are listening, they don't respond. Clearly, my life is a punchline, and I'm the only one not in on the joke.

I glance in the direction of the kitchen table as if I'll magically find an answer there, and that's when I spot the wine tumblers from Friday night on the counter where I left them out to dry on the drainboard. Although they're upside down, I can easily read the words *I make pour choices* on the glass in the middle. The bold magenta letters seem to judge me.

My eyes never leave the glitter-stamped pun as I push to my feet, and walk back to the kitchen as if drawn there like a marionette pulled by its strings, my fingers clumsily retrieving my phone from where it lay on the table. Ronnie would kill me if she knew I was considering this, but what other option is there? I have quite literally exhausted every avenue. Surrendering my dignity is all I have left.

Besides, my recent coitus session with Damian has proven that I am a natural at making terrible, impulsive decisions. What's the harm in one more?

I don't even bother to sit as I tap the app icon for my phone's browser and type in the web address for Craigslist. The page load time is agonizingly slow (I really need to talk to Mom about upgrading our internet sometime this century), and when it finally pops up, I hastily jab at the screen with my fingertip, scrolling the local listings like a woman possessed until I find the one I'm looking for.

It's still there. The panic in my chest eases a little, though behind it, there's a nagging apprehension I can't shake. I guess part of me was hoping the listing would be gone so I would have a perfectly good excuse not to go through with this. But now, I don't have an excuse. And if I *don't* go through with this, I would be purposely turning my nose up at the one possible solution I have left to help Mom.

Shoving my reservations aside, I tap out of the browser and pull up iMessage, selecting my existing chat with Ronnie.

Me

I tried but nothing panned out

I know you don't approve but I'm answering that ad

Her response comes a few moments later.

Ronnie

You better not die on me bitch x

"No promises," I mutter under my breath. I've answered a grand total of zero online ads in my life, so I can't really say what the typical creep to normal ratio is.

Me

I'll bring my rape whistle and pepper spray. Promise 🖤

Or failing that, I can always just knee my future fake boyfriend in the balls. What works on fuckboy assholes is certainly also likely to work on scumbags. I'm about to swipe out of our chat when Ronnie texts me again.

Ronnie

If you insist on meeting up with this guy let me know when it's happening so I can track you

That way I can call Liam Neeson when this weirdo inevitably kidnaps you and tries to sell your ass for cash

I snort. I'm starting to regret sharing my location with Ronnie on my phone's tracking app.

Me

Your confidence is so reassuring. Btw I'm not a missing iphone, I'm a human

Ronnie

Hey you've seen Taken. I'm just looking out for you girl x

Rolling my eyes, I fire back:

Me

I know. And I love you for it 😘

Now cross your fingers that this guy is at least somewhat normal

I don't wait for her response, swiping out of our chat, and returning to the browser where Craigslist waits, ready and eager, like a horny date. Biting on the tip of my thumbnail, I read the listing over one final time, and then, before I can talk myself out of it, I hit the reply button at the top of the screen.

A link to a random email address pops up, which opens in my mail app as soon as I tap it. I hesitate, unsure what to say, then settle on the straightforward approach. Plain and simple. Though, Ronnie may just call it blunt.

To my surprise, the poster responds almost immediately with a suggested time and place for us to meet tomorrow afternoon, which I double-check against this semester's class schedule before shooting back an answer, confirming that I'll be there.

My inbox dings again two minutes later.

Are you comfortable signing an NDA?

I mull this over for a moment. Given the privacy concerns mentioned in the ad, I'm not surprised he'd want a non-disclosure agreement. Hell, he'd be stupid not to pursue one since this whole fake girlfriend charade won't mean a damn thing if he goes around revealing his identity to anyone and everyone who responds to the listing. There's also the possibility the woman he ends up hiring could write a tell-all book about it at the end of the nine months, or they could blast the details of the arrangement on social media just for the chance to go viral and have their five minutes of fame. If this guy was smart, he wouldn't risk either outcome, and the fact that he's asking at all tells me that he has at least a modicum of sense.

Still, there are the downsides to consider. If this person, whoever they are, does turn out to be a creep, would that mean I couldn't report him to the police if he tried anything? Then again, if something feels off when we meet, or I get bad vibes, I can always just bust out what seems to be my signature move, and deliver a swift, debilitating kick to the dick and run before I sign the NDA in the first place. My slimeball radar is at least somewhat reliable even if my asshole sensor can't be trusted.

A sudden worry grips my stomach and twists it at the thought of this guy turning out to be a carbon copy of Damian. Or worse, a douchier version of Damian. A douchier douche…if such an abomination is even possible.

Deciding it's worth the risk, I message him back, agreeing to the NDA.

"*Ugh*, fingers crossed you aren't anything like *that* asshole," I grumble as Damian's smug face fills my head as if to warn me this is a horrible idea.

CHAPTER
TEN
✦ Damian ✦

**Hoy por ti, mañana por mí - Today for you,
tomorrow for me**

**Translation: Scratch my back, and I'll scratch yours...
unless you kill me first.**

"This is the greatest idea I've ever had," I say to myself, chuckling under my breath and rubbing my hands together in my best impersonation of a Bond villain. All I'm missing is the cat. I glance at my watch—it's 4:14. She should be here any minute now. Anticipation grips my chest as my gaze strays to the passing faces around me, wondering which one, if any, is my mystery lady and soon-to-be fake girlfriend.

In one of my emails to **pilover2005@icloud.com** yesterday, I suggested Touro Park for our meeting because it's centrally located and small enough that our interaction would be public. No shady dark corners or cliff edges that might make a potential business associate think I'm a pervert or a murderer. Plus, it's a popular spot, so it wouldn't stand out as a strange place to meet, or lead to us attracting any unwanted attention. To the unsuspecting eye, I'm just a guy on a bench enjoying a sunny day with a to-go cup of coffee. Nothing unusual or suspicious about that. And when my mystery lady arrives, whoever she is, we'll be just another couple on an afternoon stroll in the charming heart of Newport.

No one will ever suspect the truth.

I lift the disposable cardboard cup from where I placed it on the seat beside me, and bring it to my lips, taking a sip of the soothing, warm liquid. With nothing else to do but wait, I pass the time by counting the stones in the round wall of the structure marking our agreed-upon meeting place. Newport Tower, or the Old Stone Mill as it's also commonly known, is a well-preserved ruin and focal point of Touro Park, so it's pretty hard to miss. According to the accompanying placard (which I was driven to read out of boredom), one rumor is the mill was built by Vikings, though I struggle to see how the tiny construction of rock got its name. Our garage is taller than this so-called tower.

I check my watch again. 4:21. My mystery lady is late, which doesn't say a lot for her dependability or punctuality—the latter of which will drive my mother crazy—but I don't let myself discount her completely just yet. There could be a perfectly logical explanation for the delay, like traffic. Or spontaneous combustion.

Or maybe she just isn't coming, remarks a snide voice in my head.

Pushing out a sharp breath through my nose, I rise to my feet and turn in a circle, examining my surroundings to get a proper lay of the land, even though I've been here dozens of times. The temperature has dipped today, but the summer sunshine is determinedly hanging on, so the park is alive with people going for runs or simply taking the time to have a nice walk outside before the season changes and the cold front hits.

Despite the sun and the coffee warming my insides, I shiver, rocked by a chill of apprehension that seeps deep into my bones. My eyes rake over every nearby female face, then dart away again before anyone notices to avoid me giving off creeper vibes. The girl who answered my ad said she'd be wearing a butter yellow hoodie, but so far, all the ladies in the park today have blended into a boring beige mold of near identical jackets, jeans, and boots, creating a basic bitch collage the likes of which I've only seen on Pinterest. No butter yellow hoodie in sight.

I tug my phone free of my pocket and pull up my email, checking to see if she's messaged me to tell me why she's running late, or maybe just to say she's changed her mind. Genius plan or not, I wouldn't blame her if she did. My own mind is teetering on the see-saw of indecision, and even I'm starting to think this whole idea is absurd.

Upon discovering my inbox is empty, I stow my phone, and move to take another drag of my coffee only to find the damn cup is empty, too. With an annoyed huff, I turn in place, this time on the hunt for a trash can, and that's when I glimpse it out of the corner of my eye.

A butter yellow hoodie.

I pause and raise my gaze to the face just above it, noting the large green eyes gaping at me from behind larger glasses and the wild blonde curls that serve as the frame to a picture that looks vaguely familiar.

I glance at her hoodie again to be certain of the color, then ask, "Pill lover 2005?"

She winces—at the question or my voice, I'm not sure—then sputters, "You have *got* to be shitting me." Her expression instantly darkens as she scowls at me. "Also, it's not *pill* lover, it's *pi* lover."

My brow furrows. "Pie? Like the dessert?"

She lets out a disdainful sigh. "*No*, like the mathematical constant."

The furrow deepens. "Well, that's…needlessly confusing."

Pinching the bridge of her nose, she snaps, "It's not *confusing*, it's a play on words, you illiterate jackass."

I knew she looked familiar—and give or take another moment, I might've put two and two together—but it's the way the word "jackass" falls from that now very recognizable mouth that turns the light bulb on in my head. The epiphany hits me like a brick wall, and just like that, it's Friday morning again and she's storming out of my dorm room, the picture of fury. The recollection is fleeting, changing into something else, and now, it's Thursday night after the Phi Sigma party and I'm fucking her into my mattress. That particular flashback is more of a vague interpretation of what I imagine happened versus an actual memory thanks to the insane amount of alcohol I ingested that evening, but it, too, flicks past quickly, and next, I'm transported to the campus library eight months ago, to the first time we had sex. Two months before she found out about the list. I remember that moment vividly—the way my hips snapped into hers as I drove her up against the book stacks, and the heat of her breath on the palm of my hand

BUTTER-YELLOW HOODIE
PILL LOVER 2005?
YOU HAVE GOT TO BE SHITTING ME.

as I covered her mouth to keep her quiet.

Funny, how the only fuzzy part of that memory is her face. A face, which, yet again, makes me realize just how fucking stupid and inattentive to detail I am. Only a matter of days ago, I was dwelling on how I didn't recognize her the last time we fucked, and now, here I am, making the same mistake once more. I'm starting to think I need to make a murder board of my conquests seeing as I've clearly developed face blindness. I mean, Christ, she's even wearing her glasses this time, and I still somehow didn't make the connection.

To say Clark Kent looks less than pleased about it would be an understatement.

"Poor Girl?" I blurt out when nothing else comes to mind since I apparently have a death wish.

She places an indignant hand on her hip, and I swear I see her left eye actually twitch. "I have a name, asshole."

"Right. Uh…" Shit. And here I thought I couldn't seem like any more of a twat.

"Lexi. Dornan," she growls through clenched teeth. "Not that I expect you to remember that since you obviously didn't the last time."

"You got me there," I say with a forced laugh before my brain circles back to why she's standing in front of me in the first place. "Are you seriously the chick who answered my ad?" Then another thought occurs to me, and I take a step back. "You aren't, like…*stalking* me, are you?" Just in case this woman is as deranged as I'm beginning to fear, I cup a hand over my crotch to protect Damian Jr. and his two friends.

"Stalking you!" Her eyes bug out, and she huffs an incredulous breath. "As if I would waste my time stalking you when I have zero interest in being on the same *planet* as you!" Her chest heaves, and an outrage that would impress even my father ignites in her gaze, like a wildfire intent on consuming me, flesh and bone. I take another cautious step back, eager to escape the searing heat of her glare.

I imagine this must be what it's like to be trapped in a cage with a hungry lion.

Lioness, I correct myself. They're the real hunters in the animal kingdom, and to Poor Girl, right now, I probably look like a gazelle.

I resist the urge to give her a thumbs up—or my personal favorite, the finger gun—in a misguided attempt to lighten the mood. From the way she's looking at me, I have a feeling that would only piss her off more than my mere existence is already accomplishing on its own. Instead, I shove my free hand in my pocket where it can't antagonize her further, while the other restlessly grips the empty coffee cup. She glares at it, and I can't help wondering if she's imagining her own hand strangling my neck.

"So, if you're not stalking me, why are you here?" I ask when she doesn't move closer, and I'm no longer in immediate fear of her kicking the balls off my body.

At my question, her face turns ashen, and she clutches her stomach as if she's about to throw up. She swallows loudly. "Please tell me I'm hallucinating and you aren't really the one who posted the…" She hesitates, taking a moment to glance around to make sure no one in the general vicinity is listening, then hisses in a whispered rush, "Fake girlfriend job on Craigslist."

I gape at her, unable to mask my surprise. "Wait, you're seriously here about the job, and not because…" I trail off.

Because what? Because she's obsessed with me? Because she wants to cut off my dick and feed it to her eighteen cats? As a dog person, I *know* an enemy when I see one. And she looks like a cat lover.

I suppress a grimace. As hard as it is to believe, I have to remind myself the world does not, in fact, revolve around me, and this could just be a very weird, very unlikely coincidence.

My concentration drifts as I consider the probability of that. I mean, really, how could this even happen? What are the fucking odds? I chose Craigslist of all places to specifically avoid the possibility of anyone from our college stumbling across the listing by accident. It's not like Conwick students need jobs when they have trust funds and Daddy's credit card to burn a hole in their pockets.

Then again…I'm guessing Poor Girl doesn't have a trust fund. She's one of a very small number of students at Conwick on a scholarship, and based on what little I learned about her when we first met—and what I've deduced about her since our paths crossed again—I can say with absolute certainty she doesn't come from the same financial background as most of the other students at our university. She definitely isn't due to inherit a billionaire dollar corporation, like me.

Hm. Maybe she's worse off than I thought.

Poor Girl scoffs, and my attention snaps back to her. "I am such a moron." There's a slight wobble to her voice, which is a barely-there breath now, only just perceptible past the late summer breeze. She shakes her head, lowering those gorgeous green eyes that bore into me with intense hatred only seconds ago. "I should've known something like this would happen."

Before I can fully process the situation, or summon up the brain cells to remember the NDA, Poor Girl turns on her heel and walks off, just like she stormed out of my dorm room last week. Except, unlike the vengeful rage that encompassed her then, this time, she only exudes a deep shame.

I stare at her back, noting the way her shoulders hunch as she wraps her arms around her torso, like the restraints of a straitjacket. Hit by an unexpected sympathy—and because I need to stop her before she runs off and tells someone about this—I surge forward, trailing after her like I'm her shadow. "Where are you going?"

She glares at me over her shoulder, alarmed, like an animal that knows it's being hunted. "Leaving," she replies in a curt breath, quickening her pace.

"Hey, wait." When she doesn't, I break into a jog. Though she's fairly tall herself, my long legs catch up to hers with ease. "Hey, hold up."

Without thinking, I place a hand on her back, and she immediately whirls around and slaps it away, stopping us both in our tracks. "What do you want, Damian?"

Holding up my hands in surrender, I take a step back, expanding the berth between us to give her some space…and so I'm out of reach in case her knee starts feeling twitchy again. "Just wait a minute. Please."

"You have five seconds," she grumbles, crossing her arms.

I'm about to remind her of the non-disclosure agreement—the words are literally on the tip of my tongue—when another light bulb blinks on in my head. It's crazy, but what about this entire situation isn't completely bananas?

"Four seconds," she says.

I breathe out. Here goes. "You answered my ad, which means one of two things." I hold up a finger. "One, you have a strange fetish for role play, and get off on pretending to be a complete stranger's girlfriend. Or two"—her scowl turns into a death glare when I extend another finger—"you need the money. I'm going to guess from your rather aggressive reaction to the question of you stalking me that the answer is two."

Her eyes widen for all of two seconds before her face hardens into a menacing glower. "Why did you post the job, anyway? As a joke? To humiliate the idiots who answer it?"

"I wouldn't do that," I counter, but my protest sounds weak and unconvincing. Given what happened between us last spring, I suppose I can't blame her for thinking I would stoop to that level. After all, isn't that exactly what I did to her? By reducing her to a checkbox on a bucket list, I made it abundantly clear to her, and to everyone else involved or watching, that I have zero qualms about hurting another person for my own entertainment.

I never really viewed myself that way until now, and this realization makes me wonder if this is what my parents were so worried about. If they saw this reckless selfishness in me, and feared it might take hold in a more permanent way, the same way the can—

"One second," Poor Girl barks, disrupting my thoughts.

Clearing my throat, I push the memories away before I can go too far down that particular path, shoving them back into the mental box marked "Do Not Open" where they belong, then I open my mouth to give her some bullshit excuse about why I posted the ad. Something to convince her I'm not the asshole she thinks I am. But nothing comes out because I *am* an asshole. And only the truth will redeem me, if anything can redeem me in her eyes at all.

I don't need her to like me. Shit, this will honestly work better if she doesn't. But I do need her to at least not despise me so much that she won't agree to go along with my scheme. Eighty percent hatred, twenty percent cooperation. That's all I require.

"If you must know, I posted the job because I want to get my overbearing parents off my back—well, my dad, really. Hiring someone to be my fake girlfriend seemed like the most straightforward way to do that."

She stares at me in disbelief as if trying to work out whether or not I'm joking. "I…don't understand."

I sigh. "They want me to prove to them I'm 'Hallazgo material,'" I say in a voice mocking my father's, hooking the fingers of my free hand into air quotes. When Poor Girl doesn't respond, I add, "My literal livelihood is on the line here. They'll disown me if I can't show them that I'm capable of committing to something."

Her frown returns, wiping the surprise from her features. "Here's a thought: why not just get a real girlfriend? Or you could try not being the world's biggest dick, and then maybe your dad wouldn't wish he'd pulled out."

Well, damn. I press a hand to my chest. "Ouch. Harsh snipe, Dornan."

She purses her lips, her unblinking stare pressing me to elaborate, and even starts tapping her foot for good measure. Her expression practically screams, *Why the hell am I wasting my time talking to you?*

I have to admit, she's a positively adorable bundle of rage, and I'm unable to resist poking the bear just a little. "Wait, was there a question in there? All I heard were the insults."

"Why don't you get a *real* girlfriend?" she asks again, enunciating each word. Well, snarling them more like.

Another exasperated sigh parts my lips. "Look, if you must know, I don't want the messiness that comes with a real relationship. You women get all clingy, and emotional, and"—I wave a hand at her, my grimace growing with every word—"irrational, and I just don't want to deal with that. It's why I never sleep with the same woman twice. On purpose."

"I'm starting to see why you'd need to pay someone," she deadpans.

I snort. Why can't she see how ideal this plan is…and why am I even pressing the matter? This arrangement would work best with a stranger I can silence with a gag order, not a Repeat who knows way too much about me for comfort. I'd be better off finding a more accommodating lady who doesn't hold a potentially homicidal grudge against me. Though, at this point, I'm not even sure if "grudge" is a strong enough word. This girl is a ticking time bomb, and I am the detonator about to set her off.

But with no other options and a looming deadline, I can't afford to be picky.

"I know you don't like me, but what I'm offering is a simple business transaction that would mutually benefit both parties. You'd help get my parents off my back, and in return, you'd get to enjoy the pleasure of my company while getting paid handsomely." When her expression doesn't change, I slap on the biggest, smarmiest smile I can muster and blurt out the first likeness that comes to mind. "You know, kind of like an escort."

Her brows shoot up, reaching for her hairline. Then her eyes flash with what looks a lot like murderous intent. "Wow. You are an even bigger douche than I thought. And that's saying something."

Shit. That didn't work. Bad comparison. Retreat, Damian. Retreat!

"Don't be like that, Lucy," I plead, trying to salvage the situation.

"Lexi," she corrects me, her tone unforgiving.

I nod several times like a bobblehead. "Right. Sorry. *Lexi*. Listen, the truth is, you're the only one who answered the ad. Sure, I could wait around for someone else, someone who *doesn't* hate my guts, but I'm short on time, and honestly, I'm desperate, and something tells me that you must be, too. Plus, you clearly despise me, so I don't need to worry about you catching the feels."

I just have to hope that same loathing she harbors for me won't urge her to set my plan on fire. Here's to hoping money is a big enough motivator for her to work *with* me, not against me.

"What makes you say that?" There's a wariness in her voice as her eyes narrow into slits, as if she's trying to see past the protective shell of my skin and weed out all my secrets. Or figure out if I'm bluffing.

Well, Poor Girl, I assure you, I'm not.

"That you won't catch the feels?" I ask, unsure what she means.

She rolls her eyes. "That I'm desperate," she clarifies.

I shrug. "Well, it's kind of obvious you must need the money. Otherwise, you would've left the second you saw it was me you were meeting."

She doesn't object to this statement. She doesn't say anything at all. She won't even look at me, and for a moment, I wonder if I've broken her. If I've pissed her off so much that her hatred for me has somehow pushed her over the edge into catatonia.

When I can't bear the silence any longer, I murmur, "Come on, Dornan, we can help each other. You scratch my back, and I'll scratch yours."

Her eyes snap to mine again, hard and cutting, like diamonds. Or like a knife in the hand of someone far too eager to stab me. Holding my gaze, she raises one finger, and steps forward, shoving it under my nose. "There will be no back scratching, *got it?*"

Flinching, I inch away a step and nod. "So…does this mean we have a deal?" I dare to ask.

An eternity seems to pass in the ten seconds it takes for her to respond. Retracting her hand, she grunts out, "Fine. But I want fifteen grand a month, not ten. I want to be paid for my time upfront. And we need to set some boundaries. Some rules, if you will…assuming you know what those are."

A smirk plays at the edges of my lips at the stony look in her eyes. This might end up being more fun than I thought. I thrust out my arm. "You drive a hard bargain, Blondie, but I accept your terms. You won't regret this."

She reluctantly takes my hand with a deflated laugh. "Yeah. Sure. We'll see about that."

The contact of Damian's hand around mine sends a jolt of electricity racing through me. And not in a cute, romance book kind of way where the spark between two characters is a literal shock that manifests when they touch for the first time. No, this is definitely more of a I-feel-like-I've-just-been-tased-by-a-cattle-prod kind of way, and it causes a crippling anxiety that ignites in my blood and consumes me until all I can think about is getting as far away from Damian "Fuckboy" Navarro as humanly possible. I need space. I need to think about what I've just agreed to…preferably someplace quiet and dark where alcohol is available. That compulsion gnaws at me hungrily, taking control of my body as my mind takes the passenger seat to my panic, which wrenches my hand free of his and has me bolting from Touro Park like I'm the goddamn Road Runner and that jackass—who is apparently harder to get rid of than herpes—is my nemesis, Wile E. Coyote. Well, meep, meep, motherfucker. If only I'd had an anvil handy to drop on his head.

I don't stop running until sufficient distance has been put between us and I'm safely in the warm embrace of one of my few places of sanctuary, though I wish it was a cozy dark hole I could crawl inside and die in. I hate that the reality of what I'm about to get into overshadows my relief at knowing

I'll have the money to take care of Mom, but foreboding chokes me when I think about having to spend any length of time with that asshole.

I grimace at the thought. I really don't know what the hell I was thinking agreeing to this stupid arrangement. Me…pretend to be Damian's girlfriend? I snort, shaking my head, and spin the highball glass on the table as I sink deeper into the cushions of the farthest back booth of my favorite Newport bar, Grape Expectations. It's one of those rustic gastropubs with lots of wood and exposed brick that serves local draft beer, spirits, and cocktails, with all the drink names inspired by books. Plus, it has minimal lighting so I can easily hide my shame in peace as I nurse my drink, pretending I didn't just agree to sign my soul away to the freaking devil.

Technically, I'm not old enough to drink in a place like this, let alone legally drink at all, but with Newport being a college town (and Conwick students having *very* deep pockets), the bartenders tend to look the other way. And for the few who don't, I have my handy-dandy fake ID, compliments of one of the guys in Andie's local D&D group, who is a townie like me, and makes cash on the side forging government documents and selling painted Warhammer figures on Etsy. You know, whatever pays the bills.

While a public space probably isn't the best place to have a quarter-life crisis, I couldn't go home—Mom and Gina would've noticed something was wrong and pulled the truth out of me, which I definitely couldn't let happen. Not when everything hinges on this arrangement playing out exactly as Damian plans. Not when I urgently need the money he's offering. So, instead, I came here. Where there's alcohol to drown my sorrows, and no one will judge me so long as I keep my tab open.

My eyes dip to my phone, checking the time, then swing in the direction of the door when it opens, the hum of the outside world popping my little bubble of quiet. It's early—the bar only just opened for happy hour—so there aren't many people here yet, which makes me look a bit like a day drinker, but is definitely for the best as far as my dwindling sanity is concerned. I need to process what in Satan's fucked-up playground I'm about to submit myself to, and it would be nice to have as few witnesses as possible when I tell Ronnie and Andie what I've done.

My stomach flips when the cousins storm into the bar like a S.W.A.T.

team busting up a drug ring, figurative guns blazing, ready to whoop some criminal ass. Except, the only ass that needs whooping in this scenario is mine. Embarrassed, I give a little wave to get their attention, and when their eyes shift to where I sit slumped in the corner with a drink in hand, I can't mistake the worry that stretches across their faces. I had warned Ronnie that I was going to meet the "Craigslist Guy," so I can only imagine what she must be thinking right now, especially after the S.O.S. text I sent them after fleeing the park. I typed it up in a frenzy on my way here, and while I usually love me some autocorrect, it did not do me any favors today; the word choices it opted for made me come across as borderline deranged. Oh, well. At least it was comprehensible enough for them to figure out where to find me.

They hurry to the back of the bar where I've sequestered myself, but it's only when they're nearly to my table that I catch sight of the white-blond hair behind them and notice Andie's boyfriend trailing her steps like a lovesick puppy. Wonderful. We have an audience. Eli meets my gaze, and whatever expression I'm wearing is countered with a look of utter bemusement topped with a cherry of unease, like he's not sure he should be here for this.

You really, really shouldn't, I silently project, but he doesn't seem to pick up what I'm throwing down. If there are any doubts festering behind those piercing blue eyes, he keeps them to himself as he slides into the circular booth after my friends.

"What happened?" Ronnie asks, eyeing the highball glass clenched between my trembling fingers as she scooches along the bench to sit beside me. "Are you okay? Or is there a reason you're drinking in the dark alone on a Tuesday like a depressed businessman?"

My gaze shifts from her face to Andie's, then I very quickly look over at Eli, not quite sure how much I should say with him here. In the confusion and surprise of the moment, Damian forgot to have me sign the non-disclosure agreement he mentioned in our email exchange yesterday, but that doesn't mean he won't bring it up later or press charges if word of our arrangement were to get out in the meantime. I can see the headlines now: **Nobody Scholarship Student Besmirches Good Name of Billionaire Heir**. If it wasn't such a dire possibility, I'd laugh at the thought. Good name, my ass.

Still, I'd be lying if I didn't acknowledge that, between the two of us,

Damian has a whole lot more at risk than I do in the reputation department, and as much as I would rather stick hot needles in my eyes than spend a single second more with the cocky bastard, I really, *really* need the money. If he was anyone else, it wouldn't matter; I wouldn't give a damn about pretending to be some rando's girlfriend—I'd fake that shit until I make it—but explaining *this* will take far more creativity than I have. If Ronnie and Andie hadn't been active participants in helping me find the job listing, then I'd take the indignity of this secret to my grave, and just let them think I'd lost however many brain cells would be deemed acceptable to excuse a relationship with the university's biggest playboy. It would still be humiliating, obviously, but for some reason I can't explain, *faking* a relationship with Damian after everything he's done to me feels a lot more shameful than actually being in one. But alas, that isn't an option, and besides, they both know me far too well to know I'd never date Damian Navarro for free.

"I…" I hesitate, stalling for time, and swallow so loudly the sound seems to echo around us.

Think, Lexi, I chide myself, glancing once more at Eli, who watches me, his bright eyes narrowing slightly beneath the quizzical crease of his brow. Yeah, because my continuing silence and the perspiration beading on my forehead don't look suspicious *at all*. No wonder the poor boy looks so confused.

"I…had that blind date I told you about," I say carefully when nothing else comes to me, pinning the full intensity of my gaze on Ronnie. Maybe if I stare at her hard enough, she'll be able to read my mind, unlike Eli.

"O-oh," she stammers, thankfully catching on. "And…how did that go?"

Fan-freaking-tastic. It was like living my worst nightmare, actually. I sigh, and Ronnie quirks one perfectly sculpted eyebrow as if she really can read my thoughts. "So…good," I manage, attempting to force a grin and instead sneering at the rancid taste of my lie. "We're…going to date now."

The cousins exchange a knowing look, but before they can comment, Eli, none the wiser to the reality of the situation (and clearly oblivious to my appalling attempt at improvisation), perks up and says, "Wait, you have a boyfriend now? That's great! Hey, we can double date." He nudges Andie, cracking a smile, and for a moment, I think that's the end of it—that I can just delay this conversation, and tell my girls the truth later when we're in a more secure, secluded location without any unexpected spectators—when Eli asks the dreaded question. "Who is he? Anyone we know?"

I swallow again, prepared to say no, but I can't; the words refuse to come. At my silence, Ronnie's expression contorts into a questioning glare, and though I meet her gaze, I still don't say anything since I have no clue what the fuck *to* say. I don't know what Damian's expected timeline is with this farce, and considering I haven't had a boyfriend in all the time my Conwick friends have known me, it'll look kind of sketchy if I make one up now only to turn around a week or however long later and suddenly say I'm dating someone else. Especially when that someone else is Damian since it's unavoidable that we'll be seen together. Hell, that's the whole point of all this.

No, the only way to really make this believable (and to keep the lie straight in case Eli runs his mouth) is to be honest from the get-go. Well, honest adjacent.

My mouth, on the other hand, has other ideas, and when I open it, I inadvertently expel a very shrill, very unhinged sound that somewhat resembles a laugh. The anxiety which had me running from Damian is now tangible walls closing in on me, threatening to squish me into jelly, with each one representing a different shit thing I'm currently having to deal with. They don't crush me in the end, stopping just short of my death, like I'm Indiana Jones narrowly escaping a cursed tomb. But the claustrophobia that lingers is a hand around my throat, and it chokes me until that laugh is little more than a creepy, monotone chuckle, earning me some very concerned looks from my friends.

I quickly down the rest of my drink to shut myself up since rational thought and behavior seem so determined to elude me.

"You okay there, Lex?" Andie asks.

"Yes, I am…" I force out, fidgeting with my glasses, "and yes, you do."

Andie tracks the movement of my fingers with knowing eyes as Ronnie squeaks, "Wait, what? We *know* him?"

"I hope you didn't have this reaction when we started dating," Eli mumbles with a skeptical side-eye at Andie.

I lift my glass, signaling to the bartender for another drink. Thank god for table service.

"Lexi," Ronnie prods, but her voice gets tangled up in the buzz of chatter that enters my ears as Andie and Eli spout conjecture as to who my new "boyfriend" may be. So many questions are being hurled in my direction, and all this noise is making my brain hurt.

Suddenly, my phone vibrates on the wooden table, and the screen lights up, blindingly bright in the dim lighting of our booth. Thankful for the distraction, I pull it toward me only to glimpse a text alert with Ronnie's name and the following words:

Ronnie

What the fuck? Spill bitch

"Hey, no side conversations," Andie whines, smacking her cousin in the arm.

"We're not," Ronnie retorts, leaning in closer to me when Andie attempts to pluck her phone from her fingers. "I'm merely trying to get to the bottom of this little mystery since Lexi is being so incredibly forthcoming about it."

I roll my eyes as Ronnie thrusts her arms under the table, out of reach of her cousin. While I can't see her hands, I *can* hear the manic tapping of her thumbs, and a moment later—

My phone buzzes again.

Ronnie

Who is it????

I sigh, begrudgingly amazed at Ronnie's ability to type coherently without even glancing at her screen.

"No secrets!" Andie admonishes me, though I'm not entirely sure why *I'm* the one being yelled at seeing as I've said and done absolutely nothing for the last twenty seconds. "If you tell her, you have to tell me!"

"Why is it a secret?" Eli asks, looking almost as dumbfounded as he did when he first walked into the bar.

In tandem, the three all look at me, wearing identical, questioning, probing expressions, and…I can't do it. I can't hold it in any longer. They're all staring at me with beady eyes, and sweat is dripping down my back, and I've only just remembered that I am a *terrible* liar. This whole thing is a horrible, *horrible* idea. As horrible as the ugly truth, which expels from my lips now like vomit.

"It's Damian," I confess.

Silence engulfs the table. Actually, I'm fairly sure it swallows the entire bar, as if everyone in the general vicinity was hanging onto my every breath, waiting for the reveal, like I'm living the world's most cliché soap opera.

Ronnie looks dazed. Andie looks like her two favorite fandoms have just gone to war. Eli's brows are knitting together, like he's attempting some complex mental math.

"As in…Damian Navarro?" he asks when that quiet stretches a moment too long. "Wait, didn't you—" He goes silent when I glower at him, my eyes sharpening like knife points, offering a wordless warning not to finish the rest of that sentence. I may have even bared my teeth. "Never mind," he says quickly.

I exhale, not bothering to hide my relief. The last thing I need right now is to play twenty questions when I don't even have a convincing lie in place to explain why on earth I would willingly date a guy who only fucked me for the sake of a bet.

Stupid Andie and her stupid committed boyfriend who can't leave her alone for five minutes. When I texted our group chat, I envisioned the girls meeting me here and commiserating with me about my terrible luck. Sure, I knew they'd be shocked—I might have even expected a little rage from Ronnie—but more than anything, I expected sympathy, a shared drink, and maybe a hug. I wasn't thinking I'd already have to play the part Damian has cast me in, and I certainly didn't think I would need a cover story prepared so soon. I've barely had time to process how the fuck this all even happened, let alone had a chance to figure out what I would actually tell people.

And thanks to this little interaction, I'm excruciatingly aware I am already doing an abysmal job of selling it.

I'm suddenly regretting running away from Touro Park like I did. If I had stuck around just a few minutes longer, the fuckboy and I could have worked out these details.

Ronnie recovers, jolting in her seat, like someone just hit her reset button. With a toss of her hair, she glances at Eli, but not before her eyes dart to mine. Not for long—just for a split second—but it's long enough for me to notice the devious glint in their depths.

Oh no.

"No, go on," she urges, her voice a gentle coo. "What were you going to say?" She waves a hand, gesturing for Eli to continue.

"What are you doing?" I hiss under my breath, but she just flashes me a saccharine smile.

There it is. I see it clearly now underneath that angelic exterior: the anger and sheer disbelief that I could ever be so fucking stupid.

She's not wrong, but also…what other choice did I have?

I scowl at the side of her face, silently cursing the day she was born. I then immediately take it back—because, as savage as she can be, I love her to death—and choose instead to envy her good luck and the circumstances that have meant she's never had to resort to such awful decisions.

Eli's eyes dance between Ronnie and me, studying us like someone observes a dangerous bear in the woods, unsure whether to flee or stay still. He's probably wishing he had gotten out when he still had the chance. Beside him, Andie is wide-eyed, watching the drama unfold. Despite her sweet looks, she is ravenous for it. All she needs now is some popcorn.

"You were saying, Eli?" Ronnie prompts again.

Although I asked, the truth is, I know what she's doing. She's hoping to prove a point. And that point is more than proven when Eli clears his throat and says, "I'm not trying to rehash shit or anything, it's just…I thought there was a not-so-great history there. You know, with that video last spring."

Another sigh slips past my lips. It would be fantastic if just one person around here didn't know about Damian's stupid bet.

Ronnie shifts in her seat to face me. "He makes a fair point. Your rebuttal, Miss Dornan?"

Hey, brain, you know my genius IQ? It would be awesome if you could use it to give me a logical excuse as to why any sane individual would date Damian Navarro, so I can shut this shit down *now*.

I glare at her. "What do you want me to say?"

The left side of her mouth quirks at the corner. "Nothing. Your silence says it all." She clicks her tongue and then swings her gaze back to Eli. "To answer your question, Elijah, Damian is a very giving lover, and his dick is apparently magical." The disgust in her voice is as clear and sharp as glass. "I mean, it *must* be for Lexi to forget how he publicly embarrassed her."

"I haven't forgotten," I fire back.

She taps a fingertip to her bottom lip. "Is that disdain I sense in your tone?

An odd emotion to feel for one's *lover*."

"Ew. First off, don't ever say lover around me again. And second, he's…sorry," I finish lamely.

Ronnie lifts one pert brow. "Convincing."

"This feels like something you need to work out amongst yourselves, so I'm gonna go," Eli interjects, sliding out of the booth. "Ronnie, always a pleasure. Lexi…congrats?"

"Thanks," I mumble, wondering where the hell my next drink is.

"As for you…" Eli leans down and pecks Andie on the cheek. "I'll see you tonight?"

Her face burns cherry red, and she grins. "Yup. I'll call you when we're done."

With one more uncertain glance between me and Ronnie, Eli backs away slowly, then turns and practically runs from the bar like a criminal fleeing a crime scene. To be fair, it may soon turn into one.

"What's tonight?" I ask, desperate to escape Ronnie's wrath for just a few moments longer now that we're alone, and the mask of deception can finally come off. Not that I wore it very well to begin with.

A manicured finger wags wildly in my face. "Don't change the subject!" she scolds.

I slap her hand away. "I'm sorry you had to grow up with this," I say over her shoulder to Andie.

Ronnie gives a delicate sniff and slumps back in her seat. "That cuts deep, Alexandria. Truly."

I snort. "I'm sorry, but you're acting crazy."

"*Crazy*?" she shrieks. "The only crazy one here is *you* since you have clearly lost your mind!" She snaps her mouth shut, closes her eyes, and exhales a calming breath, searching for her zen or whatever. When she meets my gaze again, she says in a much lower voice, "Seriously, what the *fuck*, Lex. Damian? Ignoring the *several* questions I have, I can't really be the only one who sees what a terrible idea this is?" She turns to Andie, who shakes her head.

"It is pretty fucked up," she agrees.

"Also, how the hell is it even possible that Damian is Craigslist Guy?" Ronnie continues. "Are you certain this wasn't all some stalkery master plan of his and he isn't messing with you? *Again*?" Her eyes bug out, and she lets out a near-deafening gasp. "What if this is another one of his bet—"

"It's not like that," I assure her. "Trust me, if it was, I would kill him myself."

I don't bother to mention that *I* was the one accused of being a stalker.

"How can you be so sure?" Andie asks. "He's not the most trustworthy guy."

I wave a dismissive hand. "You're both giving Damian way too much credit. Aside from you two and Gina, no one else knows what's going on with my mom, so he would have no justification or reason to think a job like that—or the money—would entice me. *And*," I press on when Ronnie looks like she's about to interrupt me, "even if he had posted the ad just in case I might see it to mess with me, that still leaves a one in twenty-five thousand chance that I would be the one to respond to it, and that's assuming every single person in Newport actually looks at Craigslist, including babies. The math just ain't mathin', guys."

Ronnie sighs, retracting her claws, then reaches across the table, gently grabbing my hand. "Regardless, it's a weird coincidence, babe. I just don't want to see you get hurt again."

I offer her a small smile and squeeze her fingers. "I know. And I love you for being so aggressively worried about me, but you don't have to be. It's not like I'm going to *really* date him."

"But you're going to have to pretend," Andie points out. "Is that so different? Fake feelings may lead to certain real feelings resurfacing."

I scoff. "I never had feelings for Damian. I just had a momentary lapse in judgment. Okay, two lapses," I correct when they both shoot me the same doubtful look. "But that's beside the point. This is a business arrangement. That's all."

"A 'business arrangement,'" Ronnie echoes, hooking her fingers into air quotes. "Right."

"It is!" I insist. "Look, it's shocking, I know. Damian is the *last* person on the planet I would've expected to be Craigslist Guy, and I'm still coming to grips with it myself, but…I'm fine. It's fine. In some ways, this is good. It's familiar territory. I know what I'm dealing with."

Andie frowns. "Familiarity might not be a good thing in this case."

Ronnie bobs her head in agreement.

I huff out an exasperated breath. "Hey, let's not forget why I answered that ad in the first place," I remind them. "My hands are tied. I need that money, so if getting it means pretending to be that asswad's girlfriend for nine months, then so be it. Plus, I got him to agree to fifteen instead of ten, so by the time January hits, I'll have enough saved up to pay the deductible in full *and* cover Mom's meds." When the cousins exchange a skeptical glance, I mutter, "Unless either of you know of anyone else offering to pay fifteen grand a month?"

Ronnie holds up her hand. "I offered. And that offer still stands. Honestly, at this point, I'm kind of offended you won't take it."

The bartender chooses this very awkward moment to arrive with my drink, and I mumble my appreciation as he places my third Gin Eyre of the night in front of me on a dainty little napkin embellished with the bar's name and logo: a bunch of grapes sitting on an open book. When he tries to ask Ronnie and Andie if they want anything, they both answer before he can finish his sentence, saying, "We're good, thanks," at the same time, giving major twin energy for two people who aren't even genetically related.

As soon as we're alone again, Ronnie pushes the subject. "Seriously, why won't you let us help you?"

My chest tightens. "You know I can't. It's asking way too much of your family. And while I know you'd give it freely, the reality is…it would massively skew the balance of our friendship."

And right now, my friendship with these two is one of the only good things I have going for me.

Ronnie reels back slightly and crinkles her nose. "What, do you think I'd lord it over you or something? Jesus, Lex, what kind of friend do you think I am?"

Groaning, I run a hand over my face. "Of course not. But…" I hesitate, searching for the right words to explain. If only I could say this with numbers. Numbers don't lie, and math is the one language I know how to speak fluently.

But numbers can't fight this battle for me, and Ronnie deserves to know why I can't accept her generosity, as much as I wish I could.

"It would always be there—this weight of knowing I owe you and can never repay you—and it would change the dynamic between us. Blame it on my pride, but our friendship is too important to me to risk anything changing it. So, I love you and thank you, but it's just not a debt I'm comfortable being in."

"But you're okay being in debt to *Damian*?" Andie counters.

I shake my head. "That's the thing. I wouldn't be. I won't go into the details just in case he tries to sue me later, but it sounded like I would be doing *him* a favor. Besides, the Navarros can stand to be one hundred and thirty-five thousand dollars poorer, don't you think?"

The cousins exchange another dubious glance, and that's when it dawns on me what they're really nervous about. This isn't about the money or the possibility of reliving my embarrassment from freshman year. This isn't even about Damian; he's just a secondary factor, connected to but not the crux of the issue.

No, this is about me.

A long-suffering sigh parts my lips. "Look, despite my little…mishap last week, I am not interested in him, if that's what you're both so worried about. And trust me, he is *not* interested in me. This is Damian we're talking about. He wants a girlfriend as much as I want…I don't know, genital warts."

"Sleep with him again and you may just get some," Ronnie mutters.

I glare at her. "I'm not going to sleep with him again." Frankly, I am mortified that my friends think so little of my self-control. I might be impulsive, but I'm certainly not incapable of keeping my vagina to myself.

Ronnie's mouth presses into a line. "Mm-hmm."

"I'm not! Hey, what's that look?" I snap at Andie, whose lips are peeled back in her best impersonation of a set of wind-up teeth.

She holds up her hands. "We love you, Lex, but you're two for two."

"Meaning?"

"*Meaning*, you've hung out alone with Damian twice, and both times, you've jumped straight on that dick, girl. This arrangement you have…it's tempting fate."

I grimace. "Oh, not you, too. I get enough of this destiny mumbo jumbo from that one." I thrust my thumb toward Ronnie, who leans forward and flicks me on the head with her finger.

"Don't sass the universe, dummy. It's *listening*."

"Jesus Christ, you two are making me need a drink more than this whole thing with Damian. Who, speaking of, I have been alone with *three* times now, not two as you incorrectly stated. Those bullshit tutoring sessions at the start of the year don't count as there were witnesses present, which leaves us with once in the library when we…you know…once last week, and then today at the park. And guess what? I managed to escape said park without his dick entering any of my orifices. So, no, contrary to what you believe, I am *not* going to fuck him again." Throwing my head back, I down my Gin Eyre in one go, and then slam the glass down on the table, wiping my lips with the back of my hand. "Like I said, this is all purely transactional."

"I'm sure Julia Roberts thought the same thing," Andie retorts.

Ronnie blinks large, owlish eyes at her cousin whereas I opt for a much more intelligible, "Huh?"

Andie glances between us, aghast. "*Pretty Woman*? God, you guys need an education in movies."

I suck in a breath, wincing at the sudden throbbing pain in my temples. These two are beginning to give me a migraine.

"Andie," I begin, pinching the bridge of my nose, "I say this as a fellow nerd, but I absolutely *cannot* with your random eighties references at the moment."

Ronnie makes a little *hmph* sound that has me turning on her next.

"Is there something you'd like to add?"

She crosses her arms. "Only that Andie's right. You become chemically imbalanced around that twatweasel, and it's *because* you hate him that we know you'll fuck him again."

"That doesn't even make sense."

She scoffs. "Sure, it does. They call it hate sex for a reason. All that anger and loathing you feel toward him has to go somewhere."

I don't bother dignifying that with a response. Mainly because I don't want to give her the satisfaction or opportunity to tell me I "doth protest too much," but also because I can't be one hundred percent certain that she isn't right.

I fucking detest Damian Navarro…but goddamn, if that boy isn't fire in bed.

God, I really, *really* hate my vagina's taste in men.

"Also," Andie chimes in again, "if you're serious about this, and you guys plan to sell the illusion of you as a couple, that will mean abstaining from sex with other people because there is no way to keep that shit quiet in a college that gossips as much as ours. And if you aren't having sex with each other…" She does that annoying elaborate shrug people do when they think they've made their point. "I'm just saying, nine months is a long time. One of you is going to crack."

"The question is: which one of you will it be?" Ronnie asks.

Frowning, I sink down into the booth cushions, sulking. "I really don't like when you two gang up on me."

Ronnie grabs me by the shoulder and gives me a commiserate shake. "Sorry, fam. Just speaking the truth."

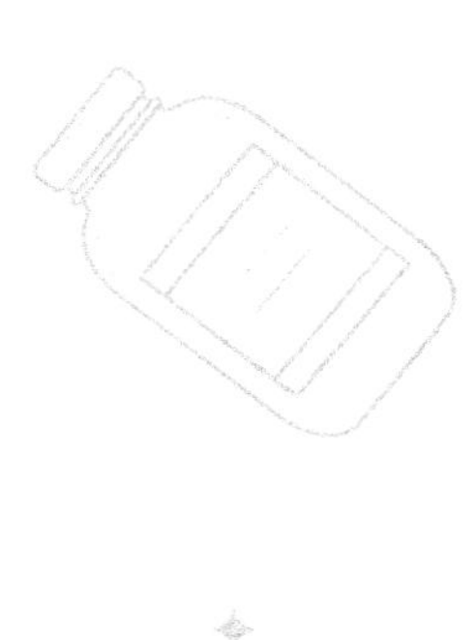

CHAPTER
TWELVE
✦ *Damian* ✦

Camarón que se duerme, se lo lleva la corriente - The shrimp that falls asleep is swept away by the current

Translation: If you snooze, you lose...and I will do whatever it takes to win.

"*You have reached your destination,*" my car's GPS informs me as I hook a right onto a quiet residential road a few blocks from Conwick's campus. Noting the passing numbers of the neighbors, I pull up to the curb outside the house I'm looking for, and throw the gear stick into park, then peer out the window at the bright azure blue Victorian with its even brighter red door. I don't know what I was expecting, but it certainly wasn't this. The house is…cute, with fish-scale shingles and a cozy white porch that extends along the front width of the residence—not at all the kind of property I envisioned Blondie living in. It's not that I had anything specific in mind, but I definitely pictured something more ominous, like a shed full of knives she spends her time sharpening with the intent of chopping off my balls.

Then again, it does look like there might be a backyard, so I guess I can't completely rule out the shed.

Leaning back, I lift my hips and tug my phone from my pocket, then pull up my contacts and tap the text icon for the most recently saved number. As I type out the message, a momentary flicker of doubt stills my thumbs.

This is a bad idea. I already know Blondie has a short fuse, and she could very well blow up in my face for turning up out of the blue like this. If she backs out of our deal, all hope I have of working for the family biz—the one light in the dark tunnel that my life has become—will be completely kaput, and then what? Crawl on my hands and knees back to my parents, and beg Daddy Dearest for forgiveness and mercy? As if.

No, this *has* to work. I need to make it work.

"Be brave. Be bold. Be fearless," I say to myself, regurgitating the inspirational message on my mother's decorative sofa cushions. I wouldn't usually quote cliché home decor, but it seemed more appropriate than "live, laugh, love," and something tells me I'll need all the bravery I can get to face Blondie today. She's the one uncertain factor in this equation, and I can't be sure she won't fuck this up on purpose to get back at me for what happened between us at the start of the year.

If only I knew what was going on with her that made her agree to this arrangement, then I'd at least have some leverage. But I don't, and I have a feeling she won't ever tell me, so I guess all I can hope is that she's as desperate for money as I suspect. Desperation keeps even the most fickle people in line.

"You got this," I murmur. Then I finish typing the partially written text and hit send.

> **Me**
>
> **Knock knock Blondie. Let's go somewhere**

A long moment passes before my phone vibrates with a response.

> **Blondie**
>
> **Who is this?**

A mischievous smile curls the edges of my lips. Under any other circumstance, I might be tempted to use this brief anonymity to mess with her, but the sensible part of me knows I can't afford to get on Blondie's bad side any more than I already have. Besides, time's a wastin' and I'm eager to get this show on the road.

So, instead—and using tremendous effort to keep Naughty Damian in check—I text back:

Me

Come outside and find out

Movement in the corner of my eye lures my gaze away from the phone screen and back to the house, where I glimpse a familiar face staring down at me from one of the second-floor windows, through a gap in the curtains. From what I can make out of Blondie's expression, on a scale of indifferent to "fuck this guy," she looks somewhere between confused and annoyed, but she disappears before I can read any more into it, like a ghost in a haunted house that makes you question whether you ever saw them at all.

I hesitate for a few seconds, then push open the door and slide out of the car, unsure what else to do. Is she going to come outside, or is she expecting me to go up to her door and knock? Maybe she's just biding her time, hoping I'll go away if she ignores me long enough. Considering how she left Touro Park the other day, the latter seems the most likely.

I'm about to hop back in my car and abandon my plan altogether when the front door swings open and Blondie appears at the threshold. She meets my gaze, but hesitates for a few seconds before tugging the door shut behind her and hurriedly descending the porch steps, her cheeks slightly pink and hair unruly. Agitation glimmers in her stormy green eyes.

"What are you doing here?" she hisses, speed-walking toward me. "And on that note," she adds, her brows drawing together as she glances between her house and my car, "how the *hell* do you know where I live?"

My lips twitch at the corners. "I have my methods."

She crosses her arms, her mouth puckering into an adorable—but no less terrifying—scowl.

I roll my eyes and let out a put-upon sigh. "*Fine*, I bribed one of the admin ladies in the office at Conwick to give me your details. She was quite the flirtatious one for a woman of her age. I'm not usually into cougars, but I might make an exception."

The scathing look Blondie gives me could melt steel.

"If you're talking about Meredith, she's, like, sixty-eight years old and about to retire, so…ew," she says, sounding utterly scandalized. "Second, that's a major breach of privacy, *and* I'm fairly certain it's illegal."

I blow out a dismissive breath. "Well, you didn't really leave me much of a choice. I didn't exactly have a chance to ask for your number the other day before you ran off. You're fast, by the way."

"Only when I'm running from assholes," she mutters. Then, combing a hand over her curls, she asks, "If you wanted to talk to me that badly, why didn't you just email me? You know, that method of contact we were literally just using on Monday? Or just text me like you did *just now* since you apparently also stole my number?"

I make a show of considering this, scratching my chin with one hand and propping the other on my hip. "Oh, yeah. I suppose I could have. Truth be told, it didn't even occur to me."

That's a lie. It totally occurred to me. I drafted (and then deleted) at least eight emails to Blondie since our meeting in the park on Tuesday, after which I compiled just as many texts upon retrieving her number this morning from that old fox, Meredith. But in the end, I couldn't bring myself to send any of them. I think because it felt too distant, like keeping our communication to the digital space would make it easy for her to pretend none of this ever happened, and ultimately use it as a way to get out of our agreement. All she would have to do there is block me.

Ambushing her at her house on the other hand…well, good luck blocking me here.

Blondie blinks large, bewildered eyes at me. "Okay, so email didn't occur to you, but bribery and stealing my personal information did…?"

With a coy smile, I step back and lean against the side of my car. "Listen, Dornan, unless you're planning to come over here and spank me for being a very bad boy, then I think you need to get over it. We have unfinished business to discuss."

Fire sprouts across her cheeks. "You are insufferable," she growls.

"And you're being pedantic," I shoot back. "Any other insults you want to hurl my way, or are you done?"

To my surprise, the anger in her eyes dissolves, replaced by a faint glint of amusement.

"Pedantic," she echoes, each consonant as sharp as a blade on her tongue. "Big word. I'm surprised you know what that means."

I shrug. "My word-of-the-day calendar clearly knew I'd need it."

When she huffs out a laugh, I know I have her.

I open my mouth to say something more—to firmly hook the fish on the line—when the front door to her house opens again and a full-figured, middle-aged woman steps out onto the porch. Her hair is even curlier than Blondie's (more coiled spring than loose corkscrew), but a mousy brown, and her face is covered in freckles, which surround bright, curious green eyes.

"Lexi? What's going on out here?" Her gaze jerks from Blondie to me, and her brow instantly lifts. "Oh, hello." She proceeds down the stairs, beaming at me. "And this is…?"

I return her smile and push away from the car, holding out my hand. "Damian. Nice to meet you." When she accepts my proffered handshake, I wink at her. "I'm assuming you're Lexi's older sister?"

She barks out a booming laugh. "I'm her aunt, Romeo, and twice your age, but nice try."

Before I can come back with a witty retort, Blondie steps between us, using her body as a battering ram to break our hands apart. "And on *that* note, we're leaving." She glares at me, silently daring me to say another word, then turns to face her aunt. "We have a…project we need to go work on." I hide my snort. Very convincing. "G, could you let Mom know I'll be home in a few hours?"

With a blink-and-you-miss-it smirk in my direction, the older woman shoves her hands into the pockets of her acid wash jeans and retreats to the porch. "Don't rush back on our account. It's Friday! You two go enjoy yourselves."

Blondie exhales as she turns toward the car, a sneer curling her upper lip. "*Ugh*. Gross."

With a cheery wave at her aunt, I lean over and pull open the door—have to show her I'm a gentleman, after all, if I'm going to be fake dating her niece—and as Blondie steps past me to slide into the passenger seat, I bring my lips close to her ear.

"I bet that wasn't what you said when I was making you come," I purr.

Blondie sputters, choking on either air or saliva—I honestly couldn't say which—then tumbles into the car, her body a tangle of long, slender limbs, the motion knocking her large glasses lopsided. Chuckling to myself, I make my way around to the driver's side, ignoring the death glare she throws at me as I buckle my seat belt and press the button to start the ignition.

"The fact that you aren't even sure says it all." She crosses her arms, giving a delicate sniff. "Nice car, by the way. How many suckers like me did you have to fuck to win it?"

I falter for just a second, then shift the car into drive and push my foot down on the accelerator. I didn't even think about how it might look to her if I turned up at her house driving this car, but there's no undoing my thoughtlessness now. "I think, for the sake of keeping my balls attached to my body, I won't answer that."

Silence swells between us as I continue to the end of her road and turn right, then take the next street over, coming back on myself and heading northbound. I can feel Blondie shooting me a questioning look as I loop onto the 138 and continue onto Newport Bridge, but it's only when we've passed through Jamestown and crossed the last stretch of the bridge, carrying on into North Kingstown, that she finally asks, "So, where are we going?"

"Like I said. Out," I reply without meeting her gaze.

"As in…out to the countryside where you plan on hiding my body?"

I snort. "I was thinking something a little more public."

"Public," she echoes, blanching at the word.

I chuckle. "That's usually how this dating thing works."

Although I try my best to keep my eyes on the road, I can't stop myself from glancing at her. Our eyes meet for the briefest of moments, and she must see the question in mine because she says, "I…didn't realize we were starting already."

A thoughtful hum passes my lips. She seems nervous. And of course— because why would I have had the foresight to consider this sooner—I only now wonder if she suffers from performance anxiety or if, maybe, she is physically incapable of public displays of affection. Her icy personality certainly supports that theory.

I shift my gaze ahead again, set on saying whatever it takes to persuade her that she can do this. That we can *both* do this.

My future literally depends on it.

"Relax, Dornan," I croon, my tone easy and—to my satisfaction—

convincingly reassuring. "Today, we're just going to lay down those ground rules you're so fond of."

She huffs, and I turn my head toward her again just in time to catch her rolling those lovely green eyes.

It seems the small trace of humor I felt between us earlier has evaporated, like a drop of water on scorching hot pavement. I can practically hear the sizzle as it dries up.

"Out of curiosity," I begin with a casual wave of my hand, "are you always a ragey ball of sunshine, or did you just wake up today wearing your cranky pants?"

"Well, I've woken up in a nightmare," Blondie states matter-of-factly. "You can't blame me for not being happy about it."

I take a moment to mull over her words, but though I try to see this from her perspective, it doesn't change what needs to happen. While I can't begrudge her the hard feelings she's holding on to when it comes to me, the fact remains that this arrangement will never succeed if she can't find a way to put our past behind her.

"You know, you'll have to work on transforming all that disdain you feel for me into affection, otherwise no one will ever believe we're an item."

She slaps on a broad smile and bats her eyes, her lashes so long and dark they fan across her cheeks when she blinks. "Better?"

I peek at her for a second, then look back at the road. "Hardly. Also, I should warn you, my parents are *not* fans of sarcasm. They have zero sense of humor whatsoever—trust me, I would know. They'll see through…whatever *that* is."

"My…face?" she asks, confused.

I shake my head. "Your smile. It's fake as shit, and they'll know it."

Sinking low in her seat, she taps her thumbnail to her bottom lip in contemplation. "Okay, so then how am I supposed to convince a couple of human lie detectors we're dating?"

"Well, like all boring old people, they'll see what they want to see, and what they *want* is to see me settled and serious about my future," I explain. "*You* just need to relax and not think too much about it. Act natural, you know? Think of how you acted with the last boyfriend you had." A beat passes as something occurs to me. "You *have* had a boyfriend before, right?"

I can feel her stony glare on the side of my face. "Yes, I've had a boyfriend. Have you?"

"You know, that is the second time someone has asked me that this week," I muse, recalling my conversation with my abuela on Sunday. "Anyway"—better move on before Blondie gets the wrong idea about why I don't want a girlfriend—"just think of the money, Dornan, and I'm sure you'll be channeling Meryl Streep in no time."

Blondie pushes out a strained breath, then taps the button on her door, rolling the window down a few inches. The air outside funnels through the car, whipping her curls into a violent frenzy. "Well, if I'm going to sell it, don't you think I need to know where we're going?" she presses, her voice raised over the wind. She lifts her chin, and that movement, though slight, distracts my attention from the road. I only glance at her for a moment, but it's long enough for me to realize that, as smokin' hot as she looked when I woke up to find her in my bed last week, I think I prefer her like this: with her natural curls on display, no makeup, those obnoxiously large glasses sliding down her nose, and not a single fuck to give.

I gotta admit, it's kind of working for me. If anything, she's even sexier now.

That thought settles in my stomach like curdled milk, and I grimace, yanking my eyes away. I don't know where that came from (or the sudden boner I'm really hoping she won't notice), but I blame the perfume, or the female pheromones, or whatever that smell is the wind is blasting in my face. It's subtle, so much so I didn't detect it before, but now that I do, I can't ignore that Blondie smells great, like citrus and vanilla. I'm finding it hard to think clearly with that dizzying scent suddenly wafting around me. Or at least, Damian Jr. is. And we both need clear heads for this.

Shifting a little to ease the pinch of my jeans against my straining cock, I jam my finger down on the master control on my door until her window is all the way up. Then, for good measure, I crank the air conditioning to flood the car with the faintly metallic—and far less sexy—aroma of the cooling coils.

Blondie's blistering gaze finds my face yet again.

"Fine," I say quickly to distract her from the bulge in my pants, locking the window so she can't roll it down again. Or fling herself out of it. "But just know, you're in a moving vehicle, so there's no backing out now."

"Oh, god," she mutters, apprehensive.

"We're going shopping!" I exclaim, like a show host who just told the contestant they've won a washing machine or a lifetime supply of socks.

"Shopping," she repeats, as if it's the first time she's ever heard the word. I'm starting to think Blondie might actually be a robot.

"That's what I said, isn't it?"

"Yes, but shopping for what?" she asks, then holds up a hand. "On second thought, don't tell me. Just let me out at the next intersection."

"A new wardrobe," I answer before cautiously adding, "For you, obviously. I dress impeccably."

The atmosphere instantly darkens, and I pray that Blondie cares about her own life too much to strangle me and risk me crashing the car with us in it. When I will myself to cast another glance in her direction, I'm unsurprised to find that her expression is mutinous.

"And what, exactly, is wrong with my clothes?" she demands through clenched teeth.

"Nothing!" I assure her, and I mean it when I say, "You rock those Old Navy jeans. Like, *really* rock them." When her face doesn't soften, I add, "I'm trying to say you have a nice as—"

"Moving on!" Blondie interrupts.

Huh. Who would've thought complimenting her posterior could somehow make her hate me even more than she already does. You really do learn something new every day.

I clear my throat. "I'm not trying to give you a makeover or anything. You can still wear your normal clothes. This would just be for when we might be seen and photographed together…so, you know, the days you're at Conwick, and when we go out on fake dates."

"I'm still failing to see the necessity of that," she retorts, her tone haughty.

I suppress a groan, hoping the truth won't get me killed. "It's just…your current wardrobe doesn't really fit the image I need to convey."

Blondie repositions herself in her seat, turning her upper body to face me. "Which is…?"

I shoot her an incredulous look. "Come on, Dornan. I'm the heir to a billion-dollar fortune. I can't be seen with some chick who looks like she shops in the bargain basement. I want my parents to take me seriously, not think I'm going through a phase."

"And what kind of phase would that be?" she snaps. "God, could you be any more offensive?"

A droll sigh parts my lips. "This isn't a personal attack on *you*, feisty. If anything, it's a commentary on them." I flap a hand at some invisible presence in the distance. "The tabloids, my parents, the anonymous Karen hiding behind her computer screen, who spends her time complaining about everything to give herself a sense of entitlement and importance. They're all judgy assholes, and believe it or not, I'm trying to spare you from the toxic bullshit I've been dealing with my entire life."

She barks out a scornful laugh. "Right. Just like you spared me public humiliation last spring."

Her words are a slap in the face. A well-deserved slap. And if we weren't attempting to trick the whole world into thinking we're dating, I would take the verbal beatdown she's so obviously desperate to unleash on me like a man. But we don't have time for this, and if she can't find her inner Elsa and let it go—or at least push her feelings aside for the time being—then this will only end in disaster, and we're just fooling ourselves even trying.

"Don't you get it?" My voice comes out harsher than I intend, but I don't backtrack or apologize for it. Blondie needs a reality check about what she's in for. "If I go out with you as you are…" I trail off, gesturing to her T-shirt, which has the word "I" followed by a heart, and then a picture of a pie with the symbol for the mathematical pi (which I know now; I Googled it after Blondie gave me grief for misconstruing her email address) forming the top of the crust. "Well, let's just say, social media will have a field day. Best case scenario, everyone will think you're a gold digger. Worst case, they'll tear you down in ways you have never experienced simply based on your looks, and trust me, that shit is hard to ignore. Don't get me wrong, Dornan, you're attractive. I'd even say you're a ten out of ten—and cute as a button in your nerdy shirt, I might add—but my parents will think this is some kind of joke and that I'm not taking their threats seriously. *But* if we dress you up, give you a nice little backstory…"

Silence throbs between us like a heartbeat, pulsating and loud. I bite back the temptation to fill it, from digging an even deeper hole for myself, if her lack of response is any indication of how she's perceived my words. I turn my full attention to the road to stop my gaze from shifting to Blondie again— from trying to read her mind on her face.

"So, you not only want me to lie about us dating, you want me to lie about who I am." It isn't a question. Just a simple statement of fact. A confirmation.

I let out a bitter laugh. "It's not as hard as you think. I do it all the time."

She snorts. "Oh, yeah? Like when?"

I shoot her a caustic look. "How about when we met? You believed me when I said I was struggling in class and really needed a tutor."

"That's hardly the same as lying about your entire identity."

"Is it?" I challenge. "A lie is a lie. The only difference between any of it is how well you sell it. And you believed me, didn't you? So, I obviously sold it well."

She instantly bristles. "Yeah, and the joke was on me because *I* was the one who got hurt, not you. So, forgive me for not jumping at the chance to lie like that to somebody else."

Ouch. That's her second zinger today. Point two for Blondie. Damian: zero.

"Listen, the whole bucket list thing…it was a dick move," I admit. "And I get why you're mad, I do. But for what it's worth, I'm sorry. Really."

"You're only saying that so I won't quit," she grumbles, and I can practically hear the pout in her voice.

I heave an exasperated breath. "Can't it be a little of both?" Turning on my right indicator, I switch lanes and steer onto the hard shoulder, then cut the engine when the car rolls to a stop. Blondie begins to ask why we've pulled over, but I cut in. "Come on, Blondie. Let bygones be bygones." I shift in my seat to face her and give her my best puppy dog eyes. "Besides," I continue, hoping a little boost to the ol' self-esteem will go a long way, "you got me back pretty good."

A subtle grin tugs at her cheeks, forming tiny dimples I didn't notice before. "That's true," she concedes, looking pleased with herself. She arches a brow at me. "How's your dick by the way?"

She peers down, and I'm beyond grateful my semi has had a chance to deflate, and even more relieved that it doesn't immediately spring back to life when she curiously examines my crotch. "His ego is bruised, but he'll survive," I say with a withering sigh. "Though, he might cheer up if you give him a little kis—" Blondie punches me in the arm. "Joking! Joking!"

I cower away from her, feigning terror, and hold my hands up in surrender. To my immense relief, she laughs.

Grinning, I lower my hands to the wheel again. "In all seriousness, I really am trying to do right by you with this." I gesture vaguely between us. "I don't want either of us to come out of this arrangement worse off than we were going into it…financially or otherwise."

Blondie looks…decided, but on what, I don't know. On new clothes? On our agreement? On telling me to go fuck myself?

I'm about to ask when she says, "Just so we're clear, I'll wear your fancy clothes, but I won't lie about who I am." A strange look crosses her face, and it occurs to me that I recognize it from somewhere. It takes me a moment to recall where from, and my stomach sours all over again as I remember when she confronted me about the list back in March.

Yeah. She had a similar look on her face then—the same anger wrapped in a shroud of hurt.

"If you're…embarrassed to be seen with a 'Poor Girl'…" She trails off, rolling her teeth over her bottom lip. Then that look of determination returns, and she jerks her chin up, as defiant as always. "Well, then that sounds like a *you* problem, and you're more than welcome to go find someone else to play this little fucked-up game of pretend with. I'm perfectly content with who I am."

There it is. Another verbal slap. Blondie: three. Damian: nil.

I balk, ready to protest, but the words get jumbled in my mouth. "What? I'm not—" *Trying to change you,* I almost say, but my tongue seems to tie itself into knots, preventing me from finishing that sentence. Frustrated, I grind out, "I was only thinking—"

That I don't want to know you.

And if she pretends to be someone else, I won't have to.

But I can't exactly tell her that, and when I glimpse the hurt in her expression again, all the air rushes out of my lungs, like I've just taken a punch to the diaphragm.

"You know what?" I say once I've caught my breath. "Never mind. It's fine.

No lying necessary. You just be your charming self, Dornan. Should be easy for you."

Whether it will be easy for me, though, remains to be seen.

"So, we're good?" she hedges.

I force a smile and make the Scouts honor three-fingered salute, then press the button to turn the ignition back on. "More than good. Now, let's go! We don't have all day!"

I flick on my indicator to merge back into traffic, and as I drive onto the freeway, I hear her mutter under her breath, "This is going to be a long nine months."

For once, we're in total agreement.

A short journey later, I pull into the small, mostly empty parking lot of The Couture Room, a luxury fashion boutique located on the outskirts of Warwick. It's what my mother would call a hidden gem because it's just outside Providence instead of inside the city (meaning no crowds), and shopping here is by appointment only, so customers can browse and try on all the high-end brands in peace…and without the hassle of uptight divas like my mother having to integrate with the common rabble. There are also personal shoppers on hand to help, making it the perfect place for this particular outing since I have a feeling Blondie's going to hate playing dress up and the last thing we need is for our first public appearance together to devolve into an argument. Plus, the staff here have strict conduct rules regarding discussing their clientele, so I feel safe in the knowledge that whatever happens at The Couture Room will stay at The Couture Room, and not get blasted on social media, meaning we have some control over how—and when—our relationship is introduced to the world.

Parking, I turn off the ignition and climb out of the car, and Blondie follows suit, though I note only one set of footsteps on the sun-soaked pavement as I amble toward the door. Looking over my shoulder, I notice Blondie lingering beside the car, the passenger-side door still open, staring up at the boutique shop sign like we've just entered her own personal hell.

"You're not trying to…Richard Gere me, are you?" Her tone is accusatory as she pins the full force of those lovely eyes on my face. "Like, you do know we aren't re-enacting *Pretty Woman*, right?" She then mutters something I can't quite make out, but sounds a lot like, "Fucking Andie."

I release a long breath. "Nothing in there will kill you, I promise. And if it makes you feel better, you can veto anything you try on today. I want you to be comfortable in what you're wearing."

Blondie hesitates. "I don't care about any of that. It's just…before we go in there, about the rules—"

"Rules again?" I groan. "Wow, you're just heaps of fun, aren't you?"

"I'm serious." She throws another uneasy glance at the boutique, this time at the mannequins donning designer labels and handbags displayed in the window. "Wearing nice clothes and plastering on a fake smile is one thing, but…is that"—pulling a face, she brandishes a hand in the direction of the shop—"really all you're expecting of me?"

I stiffen. "What do you mean?"

She sucks in her cheeks and gives me a skeptical look. "I *mean*," she begins after a discomforting pause, "you're paying me fifteen grand a month. There has to be more you want."

My mouth pops open at the implication behind her words, framing a silent gasp. I'm not sure whether I should be more offended that she thinks I would need to pay for sex or that I would go to such tedious lengths to specifically fuck *her*, especially when I've already had a taste of that particular pie. I might have done some crazy shit for the sake of my conquests before, but even I can admit this would be excessive.

I narrow my eyes at Blondie, who takes advantage of my shock to double down. "I need some assurances you won't try any…funny business."

"Funny business," I deadpan. "What are you, a 1930s gangster? Just say what you're really thinking, Dornan."

Her brows knit together. "There won't be a repeat of what happened between us last week, got it? As far as you're concerned, I have a bubble that says 'Do not touch' around me at all times."

"Well, we'll have to touch *sometimes*," I point out. "To trick the parentals, of course," I tack on when the scowl on her face deepens. "And the internet.

But if it will put your mind at ease, I wasn't planning on trying to fuck you again. Ever."

I already learned the hard way what comes from fucking Lexi Dornan, and I don't plan on making the same mistake twice.

Three times, my memory corrects me, and I silently curse Past Damian's drunken decisions.

"I don't really want to relive getting kneed in the junk. *Again,*" I add to appease her, because if she can trust anything, it's Damian Jr.'s need for self-preservation. "Now, come on. We've been standing out here a while, and we're starting to look a little sus."

Blondie glares at me as she closes the passenger door, her scowl locked firmly in place as she crosses the tarmac to where I wait. "So, the king of manwhores is totally okay with going nine months without sex? Why do I find that so hard to believe?" she asks as we approach the boutique entrance.

An attractive sales associate in the back of the shop catches my eye as we walk through the door, and I grin, flashing her a flirty look that says I'm definitely interested. "Who said anything about giving up sex?" I ask when the girl smiles back. "Besides, it wouldn't be cheating. This is a *fake* relationship, remember?"

Blondie follows my gaze and scoffs. "Yeah, a fake one you want your parents to believe. Last I checked, rumors spread around Conwick like herpes. I guarantee that if one of your so-called friends were to see you bringing home someone who wasn't your girlfriend, all of Newport, including your parents, would eventually catch wind of it. Are you really going to risk that after going through so much trouble to trick them?"

I don't bother telling her I don't have any friends—not real ones, anyway—or that she's right about Conwick. But the university campus is hardly the only place I look when I want to get laid, and there is such a thing as a hotel. But then…there are the paparazzi and literally anyone with social media to consider, and as soon as word gets out about my new girlfriend, the vultures will start to circle. It might be harder to get away with than I considered before, and getting caught cheating on my fake girlfriend would not be a good look for either of us.

"I have my ways," I retort, trying to ignore how lame that comeback sounds or that I'm probably too recognizable for any of those ways to actually work. Especially once the world takes an interest in the fact that Damian Navarro, heir to the Navarro fortune, will be off the market.

"Yeah, well, those *ways* of yours will cost me this money, and I just…" Her hesitation takes me by surprise, but no matter how hard I try to read her face, I can't discern her expression. When she realizes I'm watching her, she gives an assertive shake of her head. "I can't let that happen. So, keep it in your pants or I'll cockblock you so fast you won't even be able to finish saying Viagra."

I press a hand to my chest in mock horror. "Hey, I do *not* use the pill and you know it."

"Do I?" she counters, cocking an incredulous brow.

I spend the next hour perched on a sofa outside the changing room, sipping a cucumber and lavender spritz, while Blondie begrudgingly tries on all manner of clothing, to her increasing annoyance and to my unending amusement. Although I would never say so, she looks great in everything. She might seem uncomfortable in designer brands (she's clearly fixating on how much they cost) and—when it comes to styles—figure-hugging dresses…but dios mío, they agree with her.

The only hiccup is that Damian Jr. approves a little *too* vehemently of many of her outfits, and his judgment tends to impact my own. Hence, why I am now standing far away from the changing room after Blondie threw a hanger at my head when I tried (unsuccessfully) to convince her to model some lingerie for me. Oh, well, you miss one hundred percent of the shots you don't take, and the bump on my head was worth the chance of catching even a partial glimpse of those perfect tits again.

"Hi," a voice says behind me, and I turn to find the sales assistant from earlier beaming up at me. "Sorry, excuse me. This is really awkward, but are you Damian Navarro?"

I resist the urge to point out that I booked this appointment under my name, so she could've easily found that answer without having to ask me.

Still, I'm nothing but a gentleman when it comes to a prospective fuck.

"I'd have to check my driver's license, but I'm fairly certain I am," I say with a suggestive grin, spinning my inner charm dial to max.

Her smile broadens, revealing a set of nice teeth. Teeth which now bite at her plump bottom lip, fully redirecting Damian Jr.'s attention. "I thought so." Stepping closer, she touches her fingertips lightly to my forearm. "I'm Rosie. If you're free later, I'd love to give you my numb—"

"Hello, lover," a sultry voice interrupts, and I glance past the consultant to find Blondie standing behind her, wearing a red ruched mini dress I picked out. The fabric fits the contours of her body like a glove, with full-length sleeves that accentuate her slender limbs, and a high neck that works just as well as I knew it would against the delicate bone structure of her face. Not to mention, the short hem makes her legs look about eight miles long.

Shit, Blondie could be a model, I note, all thought of the other woman before me forgotten. I suddenly doubt Stella McCartney has ever looked so good on anyone.

Strutting past the sales assistant, Blondie slinks to my side, and drapes an arm across my shoulders. "Are you going to introduce me?" she asks with an innocent flutter of her lashes.

Instead of answering, I wonder if she's somehow gotten drunk off the spritz or if she's been bodysnatched by an invading alien species. First, the lover comment and now this? The Blondie I know doesn't have game, which can only mean she's been possessed.

The lust in the other woman's eyes dims, her cheeks flushing pink as she casts an uneasy glance between my face and Blondie's. "Oh, uh, are you his girlfriend or something?"

Blondie lets out a beleaguered sigh. "*Ugh,* I *wish.* He's just the best."

She presses a hand to my chest, giving me a loving but very staged smile—the same one she wore in the car earlier that I called her out on for being fake as shit. I can only smile back, completely clueless but curious to know where she's going with this, and why she's acting all coy and seductive…and when the hell she got so good at it. Even Damian Jr. is convinced.

Looking back at the consultant, she shrugs. "But hey, when they're gay, they're gay, you know? The good ones usually are." She sighs again. "Oh, well. All I can do is be the friend he deserves and love him for who he is."

I stare at her, gobsmacked, unable to form words or even a coherent thought. There's a victorious curve to Blondie's mouth as the sales assistant apologizes and excuses herself.

"Seriously?" I whine.

I watch, forlorn, as the other woman hurries away, and disappears into a room at the other end of the shop without a single backward glance, silently consoling Damian Jr., who mourns the loss of a potential new friend. Sorry, buddy. Looks like it's just you, my hand, and some Kleenex for the foreseeable future.

Once she's gone, Blondie drops the act, rounding on me. "Cockblocked." She jams a fingertip into my chest. "Don't think I won't do this everywhere you go, dickface. I will be the goddamn Ghost of Christmas Past to your Scrooge."

Frowning, I rub at the spot where she poked me. "First off, are we talking about the Muppets version? Because I love that movie. Second, okay, woman, damn. Point taken. Calm down."

Blondie crosses her arms, and I instinctively hold up my hands, like I'm that dude in the Jurassic World movies, who actually thinks he can tame bloodthirsty raptors.

Easy, girl.

"Okay, okay, you win," I tell her. "I won't jeopardize the arrangement. Not that I was ever really going to anyway." I last all of five seconds under the heat of Blondie's doubtful glare. "Fine, I *might* have, because I'm a guy, and I obviously tend to think with the wrong head, but you're right. This is too important to risk, so I'll behave. I promise."

Appeased (for the moment), Blondie turns on her heel, and trots back to the changing room while I follow behind like the dutiful fake boyfriend I am.

"That dress is a definite yes, by the way," I call just as she's about to close the thick velvet curtain. Our eyes meet, and a blush warms her cheeks, but she averts her gaze, which catches instead on the price tag hanging from the hem. A strangled sound escapes her when she flips it over.

"As long as you're paying," she breathes out, eyes round with shock.

We're back in the car twenty minutes later with several bags in tow, much to Blondie's protestations. She nearly keeled over when she saw what the total for her new wardrobe came to, but promptly shut up when I reminded her of my family's net worth and that what I spent today was just a drop in the Navarro fortune. Her lips had pursed at that—maybe she didn't like the reminder of just how vast the class difference is between us—but when I asked if she would consider it a gesture of good will that I'll hold up my side of our bargain, the tension in her shoulders had eased, and she didn't fight me anymore on the matter.

It was at that moment that I knew our truce had officially begun.

We don't speak much as we speed down the I-95 back toward Newport, aside from a brief conversation about our plans for the weekend, and confirming that we'll have our first official outing on Monday. Blondie and I both agree we should start small with a coffee date at Izzy's to test the waters and get those in our immediate vicinity accustomed to seeing us together. Considering my reputation for keeping my life girlfriend-free, a steady build up to a relationship will seem more legit than going big on the first date. Plus, this way, we can see just how well the rumor mill on campus really churns.

It's nearly four o'clock by the time I turn onto Blondie's road. Pulling up to the curb in front of her house again, I put the car in park, and push the button to cut the engine.

"You know," I begin as she reaches for the passenger door handle. When she turns to look at me, I notice her gaze lacks the aggression it held this morning. Well, shit. I'd call that progress. "Your performance back there with that sales consultant was pretty impressive. I'm guessing that means I don't have to worry about you convincingly selling your part of our little arrangement."

She shrugs one shoulder. "As long as I get paid, I'll sell whatever you want."

"Okay, in that case, there's just one thing left to discuss." She gives me a cautious look, and I suck in a sharp lungful of air, hoping this won't result in the testicle-chopping I envisioned when I first pulled up to her house. I blow out a breath. "I need you to kiss me."

The hostility from earlier abruptly returns, circling Blondie like storm clouds. "I'm sorry, did you not hear what I said before about ground rules?"

"Yeah, yeah. No fucking, I got it. But"—her eyes narrow slightly—"do you really think anyone will believe we're together if no one ever sees us kiss? Or hug? Or hold hands?"

Her face pales a little at that. Clearly, she didn't consider that a fake relationship would still entail some level of PDA. To be fair, I did try to warn her. We agreed to no sex, but as I already stated, we'll have to touch *sometimes* if we're going to stand any chance of making this whole thing believable.

"I get that you hate my guts, but come on," I say. "There's a logical person inside you somewhere that must know I'm right. And before you accuse me of just using this as an excuse to fuck you again, I promise that's not what I'm doing. I really have no interest in you that way."

That last part isn't entirely true—Damian Jr. is *definitely* interested in her physically. But she doesn't need to know that.

"We'll keep it to a minimum," I continue when she doesn't respond, "and if it'll make you more comfortable, we can even come up with some kind of signal, or a code word, or something prior to any physical contact to make sure we're both on the same page about it."

Her eyes scan my face, narrowing further. "But we aren't in public right now, so why do you need me to kiss you?"

I huff out a laugh. "I'm not asking you to shove your tongue down my throat, Dornan…though I won't protest if you do. Just a peck, so I can be certain our chemistry is solid before we go public. You wouldn't buy a car without taking it out for a spin, would you?"

She sneers. "Please don't compare me to a piece of machinery."

"Considering how much I love cars, you should really take it as a compliment."

Blondie rolls those beautiful eyes again, but says nothing—no witty jab, no retort of any kind. An uncharacteristic muteness consumes her as she nibbles on her bottom lip.

"Okay," she whispers after a loaded pause.

My eyes widen. "Okay?"

I wait, searching her face for a definitive go-ahead, and it's only when she nods at me that I lean over the center console and sweep my hand across the back of her neck, gently pulling her face closer. A sharp breath punches from her lungs at my touch, but she doesn't jerk away or say anything to deter me. She just watches me with those stunning eyes as I close the remaining distance between us.

When our lips meet, it's familiar, but not because we did this only last week; the haze of alcohol has wiped that night from my memory. Instead, the graze of her mouth against mine brings me back to junior year, to when we hooked up in the library in January. Back then, I was so focused on winning the bet with Mason that I didn't take the time to fully appreciate my time with Blondie. I had spent days with her there, flirting and enjoying her pretty smile, pretending to need help with math, and when I finally got her to fuck me, despite how hot and reckless that hook-up had been, all that had mattered was getting off and ticking a box. Whereas now…well, now, this feels weirdly weighted, and not just because of how much is depending on us selling this image of us as a couple, but because this is the first time I'm kissing a girl without the intention of trying to get her into bed. I've never kissed a woman just to kiss them—it's always been a precursor to sex. The necessary foreplay. But with Blondie, sex is off the table, so this…this kiss that will lead absolutely nowhere…is just that. A kiss.

And it's nice, soothing almost, sparking something warm deep in my belly. There's arousal there, sure, but this is different. Comforting. If I was someone else, someone who didn't feel the need to always push people away, I might be swayed to want this on a more permanent basis—this closeness with another person. Not necessarily with Blondie, but just the closeness of intimacy in general. And I don't mean the intimacy of sex, but the intimacy that comes from affection just for the sake of affection.

But the reality is, I'm not someone else, and because I can't trust that life won't fuck me sideways, I don't want this. I can't. Not ever. That's why I make it a point—my prime directive, like I'm a goddamn robot—to always keep everyone around me at arm's length. So no one—not friends, not family, and especially not a dangerous temptation like Blondie—has the power to bring my world crumbling down again.

But if that's how I feel—and it is—then why can't I prevent myself from deepening the kiss or running my fingers over Blondie's soft hair? And why the fuck doesn't she push me away?

The tip of her tongue brushes mine, and when she moans into my mouth, I am instantly hard. Too far. This is going to only end one way if I don't put a stop to it now, and while part of me is eager to be inside her again—to remind myself what it feels like—I can't. Too much is on the line, and I need to be the sane one, for both of us.

Breaking the kiss, I lean away, and reposition myself in my seat, my heart thudding against my rib cage. Blondie does the same, her soft, panting breaths filling the space between us. I don't think either of us intended for *that* to happen, but I am relieved to see I'm not the only one affected.

"Well?" She swallows loudly, adjusting her glasses. She's nervous again. Her cheeks are flushed, her lips slightly swollen, her gaze hazy. It takes everything in me to stop myself from leaning over and resuming our kiss.

This is a business agreement only, Damian. Keep it professional.

"It was...adequate," I manage, hoping she doesn't notice that my voice is hoarse.

Her left eye twitches. "Adequate?"

"I mean, I'd rate it up there with being kissed by my abuela—"

"You are such an asshole."

She pushes open the passenger door, and then slams it behind her, glowering at me through the window before walking to the trunk. Suppressing a laugh, I climb out of the car as well to help her with her bags.

"Hey, for what it's worth, I adore my abuela."

Blondie's cheeks flare dangerously hot, and her brow dips into a deep, angry vee.

"God, I'm joking, Dornan," I say, nudging her shoulder. "You really do need to relax."

Ignoring me, she glares down at the bags, her temper on the verge of boiling over. "Am I to assume these clothes were my payment for this month?"

I open my mouth to say something, but think better of it since she may actually kill me, then fish my phone out of my pocket and tap open my cash app. After typing in her name, number, and the amount I want to transfer, I hit send and wait. Her own phone beeps a few seconds later, and when she sees the notification, her face goes slack.

"I—This is—"

I grin at the startled look on her face. One perk of being a billionaire is having access to higher sending limits than the normal people of Earth. "You said you wanted to be paid upfront, yeah? Well, there's your fifteen grand for September, plus a little bonus for a job well done today. As for the clothes… well, a lot of jobs have uniforms, right? Consider those yours."

Scooping up the bulk of the bags, I brush past her, and stride up the stairs of her porch, then deposit them on the wooden boards just beside the front door. Blondie follows behind me holding the rest, her steps languid, that stricken expression still ruling her features. Though the thought occurs to me, I don't ask her how she'll explain all the new clothes to her parents, or her aunt, or whoever it is she lives with because, honestly, I don't really care so long as whatever lie she spins doesn't jeopardize our agreement. Anything done on Blondie's personal time is her problem.

"Remember, Monday," I remind her, patting her on the shoulder like one might pat the head of a snarling dog before retracing my steps down the stairs. Blondie just nods, her eyes unfocused.

Once back at my car, I shut the trunk, and I'm about to climb into the driver's seat when I find my gaze straying back toward the house. Blondie remains on her porch, looking…well, kind of shell-shocked, actually, her eyes glued to the phone clutched in her hand. It dawns on me that the twenty thousand dollars I just sent her is probably the most money she's ever seen at one time. That puts things into an uncomfortable perspective, so I steer away from that thought, redirecting my mind to another.

"Hey, Dornan," I call, and her head jerks up at the sound of my voice, her glasses slipping an inch or so down her nose. "About that kiss…"

I draw out the suspense for a moment, relishing the conflicted expression on her face. She looks like she's not sure if she should be worried I'm about to insult her again, or if she's secretly hoping I'll ask her to pick up where we left off. To her possible dismay (and mine), I do neither.

"It was good," I say instead.

And with that, I climb back into my car, turn on the ignition, and drive.

CHAPTER
THIRTEEN

Today's lesson: add an unpredictable fuckboy to the equation, and the result will likely be chaos.

"*It was good.*"

I frown as Damian's voice enters my thoughts again, tormenting me for at least the hundredth time since Friday afternoon. I don't know if he said it to mess with me—to get under my skin—or if he genuinely meant it, like some sort of reluctant confession, but those three words have been rattling around in my skull without pause for the past 2.73 days (even invading my dreams), distracting me from far more important matters. Like my Applied Discrete Mathematics lecture, which I really need to focus on. I already missed class last week; with my scholarship dependent on my academic performance, I can't afford to fall behind this early in the school year, genius-level IQ or not.

Pushing up my glasses, I rub my eyes, and flip my pencil between my fingers, straining my ears to make out Professor Bensen's masculine baritone past the unwanted memory of Damian's.

"—by finding the shortest path from your starting source to all other vertices in a graph with non-negative edge weights. Of course, it works for both directed and undirected graphs, but only if the weights are non-negative…"

His words quiet to a hum in the back of my head as my attention threatens to once again drift. Except, this time, it isn't just Damian's voice rising from my hippocampus like a tidal wave to drown me, but the recollection of the kiss itself.

Seriously, what the actual *fuck* was I thinking? While I could see the logic of where he was coming from with the whole touching thing, I did *not* need to let what was meant to be a simple peck on the lips escalate the way it did.

But god, if it wasn't nice. No…nice isn't even a strong enough word. It was freaking transcendent, like Damian's mouth was pure magic. Or the last slice of homemade triple chocolate cake.

Or crack.

It's not like I've never kissed a guy before, though my experience is mostly limited to my ex-boyfriend, Parker. But even then, kissing him was nothing like kissing Damian. Kissing Parker was fine, if not a bit boring and perfunctory, whereas kissing Damian…well…it's addictive. The instant his lips brush mine, I am consumed and lose all sense of self, his every touch the fuel that turns the quiet embers burning inside me into a raging inferno. Before meeting him, I never felt that kind of intense passion, that *lust*, and annoyingly, it's set such a high bar that I have my doubts about finding it with anyone else. Which, of course, only makes me despise him more because of the simple fact that it is utterly wasted.

Why can't I feel those kinds of feelings for someone who doesn't majorly suck?

Jesus, I'm starting to think Ronnie was right. Maybe Damian does make me chemically imbalanced. That's the only explanation for why I keep making decisions with my vagina instead of my head, like I'm a teenage boy in the throes of puberty and all I can think about are boobs.

Focus, Lexi, I scold myself. *That fuckboy Damian is not worth the brain cells you are wasting on him.*

Dropping my pencil on top of my notebook, I lean my elbows on my desk and dig my fingertips into my temples, rubbing vigorously, as if doing so will somehow make me concentrate, like a self-inflicted Vulcan mind meld. Not that I've ever watched *Star Trek* to even know what that is, which makes me think that I lend far too much of my cognitive resources listening to the wonder twins talk about their interests and hobbies, and enduring their personalities in general. That certainly seems to be the case given how I unwittingly channeled them when Damian and I went out on Friday.

First, with the *Pretty Woman* comment, and then when I lost my mind and called Damian "lover" in front of that mortified retail assistant. I didn't know who Richard Gere is until last week when I Googled the movie after Andie made the comparison between me and Julia Roberts, so I could actually understand what she was talking about. As for the whole "lover" thing…I have no defense other than it was the first word that popped into my head when I saw Damian being *Damian* with that attractive sales girl, who was definitely into the "let's fuck" vibes he was giving off like an animal in heat. And I couldn't have that—not because I was jealous (gross), but because he was so flippantly ready to risk blowing up what I was sacrificing *literally* all of my dignity for at the first sign of a willing vagina. And well…I just couldn't let that fly.

Someone coughs, the sound jolting me out of my thoughts, and I glance reflexively at the front of the room where Professor Bensen is pointing at something on the board. Crap, what is he talking about again? We're learning Graph Theory, and he was explaining algorithms before, so…

Dijkstra's Algorithm! The answer hits me like a lightning bolt to my prefrontal cortex, and I snap my fingers in victory, attracting some bewildered glances from my classmates.

Heat warms my cheeks as I sink down in my seat. I really have to get a grip on myself. All this just because Damian said I'm decent at kissing? It's official. I have gone off the deep end.

As if I even care what that asshat thinks.

"Get your shit together, Lexi," I mutter.

"Can anyone tell me what the time complexity of Dijkstra's Algorithm is?" Professor Bensen asks, and I instantly perk up, straightening in my chair.

Perfect. Just the distraction I need.

I thrust my hand in the air, like an overeager kindergartner on her first day of school.

Professor Bensen points to me as he returns to the lectern. "Yes, Lexi."

I clear my throat. "Well, it depends on the data structure used to implement the priority queue, but using a binary heap, the time complexity is Big O of V plus E, times the logarithm of V. If you're using a Fibonacci heap, you can reduce the complexity to Big O of E plus V times the logarithm of V, with the logarithm applying only to the V." The numbers and connections dance before me as the words leave my lips, the colored shapes only I can see locking into place, the edges of each one sharp and precise, like Tetris blocks falling into their intended positions.

Professor Bensen gives me an approving nod. "Excellent answer. Now, some real world applications would be…"

"A Fibo-what now?" a voice says right next to my ear, and I practically jump out of my seat. I careen forward, my fight or flight instinct kicking in, then whip around when I've regained my senses only to find the very source of my distraction and unending annoyance sitting directly behind me.

"Damian?" I gasp stupidly, then blink several times to ensure I'm not hallucinating.

Did I somehow materialize him in the middle of Professor Bensen's lecture because I can't stop obsessing over what he said? Because I can't stop *agonizing* over our kiss on Friday?

No, don't be stupid, I tell myself. He's here because…well, not because he takes this class, that's for sure. I'm not even certain he knows how to do math. We certainly didn't do any during our tutoring sessions last school year. Those were composed solely of verbal foreplay prior to our big finale in the mathematics section. I think humping each other against those textbooks was the closest we ever got to math.

"What are you doing—" I start to ask at the same time he says, "What the hell are you learning?" It's only now that I notice his dark gaze is fixed over my shoulder on my open notebook instead of on my face, his brow creased in confusion.

"Graph Theory," I answer, my tone neutral.

Reaching past me, he flips the pages of my notebook, his expression growing increasingly perplexed. "What is this, some kind of ninja math?"

I sigh, shoving Damian's hand away from my desk, then turn my back to him to at least give the appearance that I'm paying attention, even if all hope of that has been decimated for good with the fuckboy's unwanted presence. Professor Bensen doesn't seem to have noticed the interruption, but the other students around me certainly have.

"What do you want?" I hiss as a few of my nearby classmates watch us intently.

Damian leans forward, resting his elbows on the back of my chair. "You've been dodging my texts. I wanted to make sure we're still on for our date today."

I shiver at the touch of his breath on my neck, and tilt my head just enough to glare back at him over my shoulder. "I'm not dodging your texts. My phone is off because I'm in class. *Learning.* Like you should probably be doing now, too."

His nose wrinkles. "You turn your phone off for class? How…studious of you."

I scoff. "Yes, well, *some* of us had to earn our spot here, and I would very much like to keep mine. So, if you'll just—"

"All right, all right, I'm going," he says defensively, scooting back on his seat, his hands held up in surrender. "But we are still on for Izzy's after this, yeah?"

He stares at me, waiting for my reply, as my own gaze drifts to the students around us, taking silent count of how many are watching our whispered exchange. A few mutter to each other, the rumor mill already fast at work. They don't even try to hide their obvious gossiping or the skepticism slapped across their faces like overdone foundation. No doubt they're wondering what Damian Navarro is doing talking to someone like me: a poor little nobody scholarship student with nothing to offer except her big brain. So much for all those new clothes making me look the part.

But then, that's assuming the other students in this lecture even know who I am…which I'm almost positive they don't considering that, unlike me— who is here because of my academic prowess and lack of financial means— they're all future investment bankers or aspiring company owners planning to use the Bank of Mom and Dad to fund their eventual tech start-up. Or in the case of the rare few like Damian, heirs to major corporations, and taking this Applied Discrete Mathematics class is just one step on their path to a degree that will show they are remotely qualified to inherit Daddy's billions.

All that to say, people like that do not tend to befriend people like me— Ronnie and her cousin excluded, but then, they are the wonderful exception to the Conwick rule. Come to think of it, aside from the cousins—and by extension, Eli—the only people I interact with at school are other scholarship students, and even then, only when conversing is absolutely necessary at our required work study. Outside of that, I rarely even see the other scholarship math majors; there are only a few of us, and none of our classes overlap due to varying academic trajectories and us being in varying years in the program.

Not that having them in this class would in any way make this more tolerable. In truth, they'd probably be judging me just as much as the rich kids are, albeit for entirely different, wealthy douchebag-shaped reasons.

A fresh wave of heat burns my cheeks as my mind whirls in about eight hundred directions. I'm not normally the kind of person who would care what anyone thinks of me, but after the fiasco with the bet in the spring, my skin isn't quite as thick as it used to be, and I can't stop myself from wondering what the students muttering around us might be saying. If seeing me with Damian has reminded them of my humiliation freshman year…

And if this whole thing is just setting me up for more of it.

"Dornan." Damian's voice snaps me out of those thoughts, and my eyes dart to his. "Izzy's?" he prompts.

I swallow past the sudden lump lodged in my throat. "Yes, okay, fine," I say in a rush, my heart like a snare drum, beating aggressively under my skin. "I'll text you when class is over. Now, go. *Please.*"

I don't want to see Damian's reaction to my plea, so I turn my back to him again, and focus on Professor Bensen where he scribbles across the white board at the front of the room.

Or at least, I try to. In reality, I'm far too aware of the heat of Damian's body behind me, and of his footsteps when he stands and walks away. The surprise of his appearance here has left me feeling somewhat claustrophobic, and I only seem able to breathe again when I hear the faint thud of the classroom door closing.

"Now"—Professor Bensen taps the board with the tip of his marker—"who can walk us through the process of applying Dijkstra's Algorithm to find the shortest route from A to each of these other four locations?"

Come on, concentrate, damn you, I scold my brain. Then, inhaling a deep, calming breath to slow my pulse, I once more raise my hand.

The next forty minutes go by without any fanfare or any more interruptions on Damian's part, though I can feel the curious eyes of my classmates, their questioning stares following my every move, even as they begin to funnel out of the room the moment class is over. Trying my best to ignore them, I pack up my bag, and turn on my phone to find several messages from Damian along with a single text from Ronnie. Sometimes, I really do wonder if she's actually psychic.

Fuckboy

Are we still on for today?

Is that a no?

You haven't changed your mind have you?

Why aren't you answering me?

Dooooooornaaaaaaaaaan

????

If you don't answer me I'm going to go put my in the nearest just to spite you

Rolling my eyes, I exit out of the texts from Damian, and bring up my chat with Ronnie.

Ronnie

Fancy meeting at Izzy's? I'm not in the mood for psych class today so totally happy to skip! x

I frown at the message, chewing on the inside of my cheek. I went out of my way to avoid Ronnie and Andie this weekend so I wouldn't have to tell them about my impromptu shopping day with Damian on Friday… and to avoid the very real judgment I would be on the receiving end of if they were to find out we kissed. And they *would* find out because Ronnie would torture it out of me, like verbal bamboo shoots under my nails. I also might have failed to tell them about a certain planned coffee date happening this morning. I didn't see the point as neither of them approve of this fake dating agreement, and I honestly didn't want to endure another minute of the cousins attempting to psychoanalyze me. I swear, Ronnie takes one psychology class, and now everything is a damn therapy session.

Me

Sorry can't today. I have a meeting with my advisor

Then for good measure (and to avoid her showing up uninvited), I add:

Me

And you shouldn't skip. What if they teach something that's on your midterm and you fail and then you need to make up the credits and we end up not graduating together? I wouldn't forgive you for that

It's surprisingly easier to lie to her than I thought it would be, which I guess is a good thing considering how much I'm going to need to lie over the next nine months. Though, I don't feel great about the graduation comment. Ignoring the fact that it's still nearly three years away, the odds of skipping one class affecting her grade enough that she fails altogether is highly unlikely. Still, I can't risk her going to Izzy's and seeing Damian and me together. In *public*. She'd only end up butting her head in where it doesn't belong, and the last thing we need is some wild rumor that she's one of Damian's jilted ex-fucks. Which she isn't, but her reaction would definitely give that impression because it would almost certainly be aggressive. And possibly violent.

She's going to find out about it regardless, my conscience rudely reminds me. Ronnie can smell gossip eight miles away, and as soon as word of our first outing hits social media—and whatever trashy magazines Ronnie subscribes to—she'll know I lied to her.

But as far as I'm concerned, that's Future Lexi's problem. For now, I just need to focus on my first "date" with Damian not turning into a catastrophic disaster. Which means ensuring Ronnie stays as far away from us as humanly possible. Her showing up unexpectedly would be the very definition of cataclysmic.

My phone buzzes in my hand as I make my way up the auditorium steps.

Ronnie

Curse your big brain and the good point it just made   le sigh   I guess I'll see you this afternoon after ALL my classes then 😔

Exhaling a breath of relief, I stow the device in my pocket, and pull open the heavy wooden lecture hall door.

"There you are! Finally!"

I nearly jump out of my skin again at the jubilant voice booming in my right ear, and I stumble a little as I turn to find Damian standing to the side of the doorway.

"Fucking *hell*, you scared the shit out of me! Are you trying to give me a heart attack?" I snap. Although I stare very sharp, very stabby daggers at him, he just laughs me off.

"You'll be fine," he assures me with a placating grin. "Ready to go?"

When he steps toward me, I glower at him, only now grasping just how tall he is. I'm hardly short, and he nearly has a whole head on me.

And I really, *really* detest how my body reacts to that knowledge. Clearly, I have an as-of-five-seconds-ago undiscovered kink for guys who tower over me, and I almost swoon at the realization. It takes the reminder that this is the guy who fucked me to tick a box on a bucket list to keep me on my feet.

My mouth is a desert, but I force out the words, "Have you…" only to trail off when the auditorium door opens again, and a few more students exit the lecture hall behind me. They glance at us as they pass, speculation sparkling in their eyes like gemstones. Once they're out of earshot, I redirect my attention to Damian, drop my voice, and try again. "Have you been waiting out here this whole time? I did say I would text you."

Damian shrugs. "I mean, not to put too fine a point on it, but I didn't trust you not to flee the state at the first opportunity. I figured, if I stuck around, I would at least make sure we got our date today since I did pay in advance. Gotta get my money's worth and all that." Panic ratchets up my heart rate as I glance down the length of the hallway to see if anyone heard him, but we're the only two in the immediate vicinity. "Besides…" He leans in close, a teasing smirk on his lips. "It can't hurt for everyone to see just how into you I am."

I snort. "Right, because waiting for someone to finish class is a huge sign of devotion."

"Hey, it is if you have a reputation for being a playboy."

"I believe the term you were looking for is manwhore," I correct him.

Damian waves a dismissive hand. "Po-tay-toe, po-tah-toe. The point is,

Damian Navarro doesn't waste his time loitering in hallways for just anyone." He then reaches out and boops me on the nose.

I flinch, batting his finger away, and step back to put some space between us. His smug expression falters, and a slippery feeling slides down my back, like an icy fingertip along my spine. He's peering at me strangely now, almost…deviously. Which cannot be good.

"What?" I hedge. "Why are you looking at me like that?"

He blinks as if my question has snapped him out of a daze. "No, nothing," he says. "I just realized you're wearing some of the clothes I got you."

My brow twitches as I peer down at myself. I don't hate what he got me, which is surprising seeing as my wardrobe typically consists of pun-related graphic tees, hoodies, and the odd knitted sweater. The few skirts, revealing tanks, and high heels I own, I reserve for the rare occasion I attend a party or function that requires upselling myself on an aesthetic level to the opposite sex, which isn't often considering I find most social situations exhausting. The party where I encountered Damian at the start of the semester was an anomaly—a deviation from my quiet hermit life where my idea of a good time is drinking at home in my pajamas while watching Netflix, or the odd night out at Grape Expectations in whatever I wore to class that day. I am the definition of casual when it comes to my wardrobe, which typically means sneakers and jeans.

Today, however, I'm wearing an incredibly soft beige fitted turtleneck, with flattering high-waisted tailored shorts and matching over-the-knee black suede boots, which, ironically, *do* resemble something Julia Roberts would wear in *Pretty Woman*, based on the stills I saw on Google Images. All three items are from a luxury designer I've never heard of before (though that says very little), and while it's not something I would've picked out for myself, I find I like how I look in it, even if I am terrified of food or drink coming within a ten-foot radius, given how much it all cost. It's not that I'm self-conscious when it comes to my looks—even next to Ronnie and Andie, who are both genetically blessed, I know I'm considered conventionally attractive—I just…don't care. I have way more important things to worry about, like Mom, and my scholarship, and ensuring my life in general doesn't implode. But today…dressed like this…well, for the first time, I can kind of understand why Ronnie always makes such a fuss about fashion. There's a certain power in feeling good in what you're wearing. If you feel good in the clothes, you'll feel good in your skin, and I suppose that's worth more than any amount of money.

Not that I'd ever tell Damian that, or give him the satisfaction of thinking I'm happy about this. As far as I'm concerned, he can go to hell for treating me like his own personal Barbie.

"Uhh…wasn't that the whole point of buying this stuff?" I remind him. "So I would look *acceptable* when we're together?" I don't bother masking the disdain in my voice. I don't think I could have even if I'd tried. "If I recall correctly, you even called it my uniform."

Damian gives me an incredulous look. "Man, you really can't take a compliment, can you?"

"Was there a compliment somewhere in there that I missed?" I ask dryly.

He rolls his eyes. "You look fit, as the Brits would say. Take the compliment, Dornan."

A deep heat blossoms in the bottom of my abdomen, then spreads until my entire body is lit up like a match. Oh no. If I can feel the flush on my cheeks then there's no doubt he can see it.

No. *Nope.* I refuse to accept that Damian Navarro of all people is making me blush. Maybe I'm having an allergic reaction? Yeah, that must be it. An allergic reaction to bullshit.

"Let's just…go to Izzy's," I grumble, dipping my head as I brush past him so he won't see my face. "But please refrain from referring to yourself in the third person moving forward."

I glimpse Damian's tall form out of the corner of my eye as he falls into step beside me. "Okay, but only if you promise to smile at least once during our date. A *real* one this time. I can't have this looking like a hostage situation."

I consider telling him to take that smile and shove it up his billion-dollar ass, but ultimately decide this whole thing will be far less painful (and way less tragic) if I just swallow my pride and agree.

But because I'm me, and Damian is the human embodiment of a bag of shit, I, of course, can't do that without first making my displeasure known.

So, I huff out a disgruntled breath, and only then do I begrudgingly say, "Deal."

It's another beautiful, warm sunny day, so we sit outside at Izzy's. The fact that doing so means we're out in the open and more visible for the masses to see is just a bonus.

We settle at a table as far from listening ears as possible, though stay in sight of prying eyes—this will work best if we're seen and not heard, at least until we get our story straight. Or a bit straighter than the crooked mess it is at the moment. Damian, for all his fuckboy ways, plays the part of a gentleman well. He pulls out my seat, pays for my coffee, gives me his coat when a breeze blows through and I shiver. He even buys me a slice of lemon cake completely unprompted, which is absolutely to die for.

We only have an hour until my next class and Damian's first lecture of the day (so he says, though I have a sneaking suspicion that's not entirely true, and he skipped his morning seminar just so he could come harass me), so we decide to spend that time pretending to get to know one another… by actually getting to know one another, but only a little and only on the surface. We agreed as soon as we sat down: nothing personal. Nothing too deep. Only the superficial shit that people should probably know about their significant others. Like blood type. And where one stands on the topic of pineapple on pizza.

We discuss favorite colors (green for me, dark blue for the fuckboy) and favorite foods (mine are tacos, without a doubt, and Damian's is his abuela's "it should really be famous" tres leches cake) before moving on to favorite movies. Mine will forever be *Good Will Hunting*—what can I say, I relate to the whole awkward math genius thing—and, questionably, Damian's is apparently *Twilight*, though I sincerely hope he was joking. I've only seen the *Twilight* movies once—Gina, who is a self-proclaimed Twihard, made me watch them with her when I was in high school—and let's just say, the character I related to the most was Charlie. I wanted to see him use that shotgun.

Now, we've shifted to the topic of friends, and I really wish we were talking about Bella and Edward's vampire baby instead.

"Ronnie Hayes…" Damian takes a sip of his coffee, his face a mask of contemplation. "The name rings a bell, though I can't place her. Have I smashed her before?"

I grimace. "No, you have not 'smashed' my best friend."

Damian's eyebrows reach for his hairline. "Statistically, that seems unlikely given how much pussy I get at this school, but I guess it's not impossible."

"Charming." I sneer at his word choice, but he just shrugs as if to say, *What? It's the truth.* I shake my head. "Statistical impossibility or not, you haven't, and you never will," I assure him.

That piques his curiosity. "What makes you say that? Is she into girls or something?"

I scoff. "Not that her sexuality has anything to do with why she wouldn't touch you without a hazmat suit…but if you must know, she's pan. And you are definitely *not* her type."

"Devilishly handsome, you mean? Rich? Fantastic in bed? Baby, I'm everyone's type."

That smile I promised him almost tugs at my lips. I don't want to give him the satisfaction, but damn if the thought of insulting him doesn't bring me joy. In the world of Marie Kondo, the opportunity to knock Damian down a peg is one thing I would not dispose of. At the last second, I manage to keep my expression in check. "Sorry, she's not really into fuckboys."

Rather than take offense to my words, Damian counters, "Well, she's not had a taste of this particular fuckboy. Maybe I'll hit her up when this whole fake relationship is behind us."

A smile once again threatens at the mental image of Damian hitting on Ronnie, and I almost cackle with delight. "You know what? I take it back. I would *love* to see you shoot your shot with her. She would absolutely destroy you."

"Is that a promise?" Damian purrs, a sly curve to his lips. "Wait, you do mean sexually, right?"

I shrug. "Emotionally. Mentally. I've seen her make a grown man cry—"

He shudders. "Okay, okay, I get the picture. Do you have any other friends who aren't psychos, Dornan, or is it just the one?"

I take a sip of my coffee, then set my cup back down on the table. "Well, there's Andie. She's less intense than Ronnie, though they *are* related, albeit not genetically. They're cousins. But she's taken," I warn him. "She has a boyfriend. Not that that's stopped you before, I'm sure." I mutter that last part under my breath. "He's in my year, but you might know him. Eli Winslow? He's rich like you, but the dickhead gene seems to have skipped over him."

"As in the hotel chain Winslows?" Damian asks. "Yeah, I know of them. I've stayed at their hotels a few times. Nice places."

"I wouldn't know," I admit, wrapping my hands around the cardboard cup, and relishing the heat seeping into my fingers. "If I could afford thousand-dollar hotel rooms, I wouldn't have to fake date you, now would I?"

He lets out an amused breath and nods. "That's true. And then where would I be?"

My lips quirk. "Still waiting for someone to answer your ad, I imagine."

"And you?" he says, cocking an eyebrow. "In another reality, where we didn't agree to this arrangement and you weren't here on this *amazing* first date, what would you be doing instead?"

"Sleeping in Winslow hotels, obviously," I deadpan. "In this alternate reality, I'm filthy rich."

He laughs again, more heartily this time, and I'm taken aback by the sincerity of his smile, which, if I didn't know him better, I would almost think is real. I have to remind myself this is all fake. That Damian is *acting*. And that, if I'm going to survive this ordeal unscathed, I have to start acting, too.

"Are you ever going to tell me?" he asks out of the blue.

Confusion furrows my brow. "Tell you what?"

That smile vanishes as he takes another sip of his coffee, and it's only when he sets the cup back down on the table that he answers, "Why you need the money."

My entire body goes icy cold. I've been hoping we'd avoid this subject, and I ignorantly assumed that because he hasn't asked maybe he never would.

I sidestep the question. "Don't worry, it isn't for drugs or anything illegal that could be traced back to you."

He narrows his eyes. "Wow, that wasn't a totally sketchy response. Now, I *definitely* think you're up to something weird."

"I'm not—" I begin to protest, but he cuts me off.

"It's porn, isn't it?" He nods to himself, and before I've had a chance to process the stupidity of his words, he adds, "You have a porn addiction in need of funding. I had a feeling you were kinky, Dornan, but this—"

"It isn't porn!" I shriek, earning a few bewildered glances and giggles from the other customers sitting nearby.

Damian stifles a laugh with his fist. "Rare Pokémon card collector?" he guesses.

Christ, he's not going to drop this, and I think I'm literally getting dumber every time he opens his mouth. I could just tell him the truth, I suppose, but then that means exposing a part of my life to him that I don't want him to know about. He's already caught on that I'm desperate, but the why is just too personal, and I need to do everything in my power to keep some boundaries between us since my traitorous body is clearly not on the same page as my brain or my heart.

"Oh, *I* know," Damian muses, rubbing a hand along his jawline, "it's totally for—"

"Cosplay," I blurt out without thinking.

I stiffen, silently cursing myself. Why the *hell* did I say cosplay? I've never cosplayed a day in my life! Or played video games aside from *Mario* when I was a kid, and the only anime I've ever seen was a Studio Ghibli film Andie once made me watch—which, admittedly, I did greatly enjoy. And don't even get me started on comics, or *Star Wars*, or Marvel, or any of the major fandoms. I like some of it well enough, but that stuff is Andie's bag, not mine. I'm all about true crime, psychological thrillers, and numbers. Give me a murder mystery or a quirky genius story any day.

"Cosplay," Damian echoes, and I can tell from the look on his face that he doesn't believe me.

"Uh…yup." I swallow a sigh. No going back now. "It's a…new hobby, and I lack the skills to make the costumes myself, and um…" Crap, where does Andie get her costume accessories from when she doesn't have time to make them herself? *Take a wild guess, idiot! Just say something!* "Etsy is expensive?" I finish, trying not to wince at the obvious question in my voice.

Damian holds my gaze for a moment, and I can't help feeling like a suspect sitting opposite a detective in one of those dimly lit interrogation rooms in a crime drama. I've seen this scene play out hundreds of times on TV, and it is already a well-known fact what a terrible liar I am, so this can only go one way. Oh, my god, what if he starts asking me questions about cosplay? I know absolutely nothing about it other than the general notion of what it is.

Shit. I'm so busted.

But the cross-examination I expect doesn't come. Instead, Damian just looks me up and down, his lips stretching into a lecherous grin. "Please tell me you're doing the Princess Leia gold bikini sometime because that would be *noice*."

I snort, trying to ignore the itch in my hand that wants to slap that ogling smile right off his face. "You're such a perv. And also kind of a nerd," I note with a touch of surprise.

He points a scolding finger at me. "There is *nothing* nerdy about appreciating a fine woman in swimwear. That scene blew twelve-year-old Damian's mind… and his load."

"Gross!" I admonish, though I laugh despite myself.

Damian's attention shifts ever so slightly, and I follow his gaze to a table at the other end of Izzy's outdoor seating area, where two girls are watching us. I'm not sure if they're trying to be subtle, but if they are, they're doing a terrible job of it. One of them is even holding up her phone—probably to film us. The other girl shoves her arm down when she realizes we've noticed them.

A flutter of anxiety fills my chest as I anticipate the shitstorm that will hail down from Ronnie when she eventually sees whatever picture or video that girl just took. Hopefully, by the time she comes across the unavoidable social media post, it will have gone viral enough (at least within the bounds of Conwick) that she'll forget all about being mad at me for lying, and instead kick straight into defensive mode, making it her new life's mission to protect me from ridicule. And with news of Damian and me out in the world, she'll have to finally accept that she and Andie won't talk me out of this agreement. I am *all* in—nothing will change my mind—so she'll have to support me or risk losing me, and I know she would never choose the latter.

Our friendship might seem unexpected or strange to some people given how little we have in common, but Ronnie is my ride or die. The moment we met at my freshman orientation, she imprinted on me like a newborn bird—or like that werewolf kid in the *Twilight* movies, who imprinted on Bella's vampire baby. We had barely even introduced ourselves, and yet, we both knew without saying a word that this connection between us would be for life. It was the closest thing to love at first sight I've experienced or ever seen for myself, and I was just lucky enough to get Andie as a bonus. Two for the price of one.

And though I suck at verbalizing it, they mean everything to me. They've given me the unconditional love I've only ever known or received from my mom and Gina, but more than that, they've been there for me without fail through the hardest time of my life. Hell, they *met* me when I was in the throes of my mom's cancer diagnosis, and instead of running away from the messiness of the situation, they chose to put their hands on my shoulders and try to help me through it. Frankly, I don't know what I did in a past life to deserve them, but I'll forever be grateful for it.

"Well, would you look at that? This plan of ours is already working," Damian coos delightedly, grinning at me over his coffee.

"That reminds me. When you said you need this to work to 'get my parents off my back,'" I paraphrase in a crude imitation of his voice, "were you—"

"Whoa, party foul!" Damian interrupts before I can finish my question. "You *never* bring up my parents without advance warning. Geez, and just when I was starting to enjoy myself. You're such a buzz kill, Dornan."

I blow an exasperated breath through my nose. "And you're so dramatic," I mutter. "Seriously, though…are they really threatening to disown you?"

I don't know why I ask or why I even care. It doesn't matter why he needs this to work so long as he fulfills his end of the bargain. And it's not like I feel bad for him.

And yet, my stomach twists when Damian bristles. "Oh, believe me, the threat is real," he says, averting his gaze to some far-off point in the distance.

"Is it because of the bet? Because of what happened last spring?"

I'm impressed I manage to ask that without flying into a blind rage. Damian seems surprised, too, because a weed of panic takes root in his eyes as they snap back to mine.

"What?"

"It was quite the scandal, right?" Wow, I've even managed to maintain my composure enough to press the issue. Huh. Maybe this is that whole personal growth thing people are always talking about. "I can't imagine they took it well."

He chokes on a bitter laugh. "That's the understatement of the century."

"So, that's it. That's why?" I need to know—not because I care about his well-being, but because there's a side of me that still clings to the hurt he caused me last school year. Call me petty, but I want to be able to sit here in the contentment that he fucked around and is about to find out, and that I'm going to benefit while he does all this for nothing, only to crash and burn. Welcome to the consequences of your actions. He would certainly deserve whatever comes to him.

He shakes his head, stops, then nods a little only to stop again. "It's…part of it, but not the only reason. Let's just say, I've been doing things to piss them off for a very long time now."

I raise a brow, intrigued. "On purpose?"

"Well, it wouldn't be any fun if I did it by accident," he says, his mouth curling at the corners.

I scoff. "What a fuckboy answer. Color me shocked."

His responding grin is shameless. "What can I say? I am nothing if not true to form."

Damian raises his cup to his lips, and my eyes inadvertently lock on his throat…and on his Adam's apple, which bobs when he swallows. The sight shouldn't do anything for me. Woo, a dude swallowed some coffee, alert the press! And yet…for some reason I can't explain (and despite hating his guts), it's remarkably sexy. *He's* incredibly sexy. His gorgeous bronze skin, the strain of his chiseled jaw when he draws the liquid into his mouth… Honestly, the scene before me seems to straddle the edge between PG-13 and downright pornographic.

Seeming to sense my thoughts, he sets his cup down and licks his lips as if to taunt me. Heat pools in my belly, in that place that demands physical gratification, and—

I have to look away. I have to think about something—*anything*—else, but all I can seem to focus on is the memory of his tongue on my breasts, which, of course, only makes my mind wander to other places. To how it would feel to have his tongue—

No. Nope. I do *not* think so.

I grab my own coffee and throw my head back, downing it like it's a glass of water. Then, when I'm sure my vagina has ceded control, and I won't accidentally ask him to fuck me senseless, I say, "What will you do if they follow through on the threat?"

Damian blinks at me, confused. "Well, that's why *you're* here. To help ensure that doesn't happen."

I nod and decide to let go of the subject for now. He clearly doesn't want to get into it, and considering my own evasive answers to his questions, I can't really blame him. It's best we don't know the full extent of each other's motivations. Surface level only, like we agreed.

Because god forbid he say something that might actually make me feel something for him other than loathing. Like *sympathy*. I shudder at the thought. My vagina is already sympathetic enough. Or dumb enough to not care about the caliber of person we fuck.

"So, we've covered favorite color, food, and movie," Damian counts on his fingers. "What other relevant information might someone be likely to question us on?"

"Major?" I suggest, thankful for the change in topic. "I feel like what you're studying would be a girlfriend thing to know."

"Speaking of, what the hell kind of class did I walk in on earlier? What are you majoring in, time travel or something?"

I bark out a laugh. "Math. We're learning about Graph Theory."

Damian gives me a blank stare. "Yeah, I have no clue what that is."

"Well, don't try figuring it out now," I warn him. "You might hurt yourself."

"Wait, so that's it? You're majoring in just…math?"

"Just math," I parrot, rolling my eyes at him. "My 'just math' major would probably have your brain melting out of your ears in less than a week."

"Most likely," he agrees, unashamed of that fact. "But in all seriousness, you plan to do what with that? Like, specifically. It's just kind of vague is all."

"You mean, like, for work?" I clarify.

"That is usually the next step after college, yes."

I open my mouth to answer, then pause. Because the truth is…I don't have a clue. For as long as I can remember, the one thing I've been exceptionally good at is math. Numbers agree with my brain in a way nothing else in this world ever has. I'm not creative like Andie or performative like Ronnie. My social skills are utterly lacking, and I have a tendency to shove my emotions so far down people often question if I actually have them. Which I do, I just don't like to wear my feelings on my sleeve, and I'm fairly good at compartmentalizing. Most of the time, at least. Clearly, that is not the case around Damian, who seems to bring out the worst in me, like I'm Dr. Jekyll and he triggers my internal Mr. Hyde, but that's not my norm. It's the exception.

Math, on the other hand, isn't my exception. It's my rule. My secret power. My safe space. Since I was very young, it's been the one thing I was always better at than everyone around me, the one thing I could always rely on when I could rely on nothing else. Math is consistent. Math is *constant*. And so many factors in life just…aren't.

But while I excelled at it, I never really had the opportunity to consider how I would use math in the real world, not even once I hit high school. It was just expected I would fall into a job that centered around it because… well, why wouldn't I? I love math, and math *definitely* loves me, so why squander that talent, especially when it was going to guarantee me a full ride to college?

My advisor at the time agreed, though I think she only cared about doing the bare minimum of her job description by ensuring I was applying for colleges by the deadline; there was very little actual advising being done on the matter. As for Mom…well, by the end of senior year, she had other things on her mind. She didn't have time to worry about what I would do beyond college, and neither did I, not when it was four years away and we weren't even sure she would survive the one. Compared to that, deciding on a future job that seemed a lifetime away was insignificant. It wasn't my priority, and I guess I also never really thought about it because I didn't feel I had to. It was math, after all, and don't all jobs use math in some respect? I mean, look at my mom. She's a bookkeeper, so math is a necessary part of her work. And Gina, who is a nurse, utilizes math to dispense medication at the hospital and calculate IV flow rates. Math is all around us. Just like love, in that old Christmas movie with Hugh Grant my mom loves.

But I'm not going to say any of that to Damian. Instead, I redirect his question. "What about you?" I ask. "What are *you* majoring in?"

"Business administration," he answers, yawning as if the words themselves bore him, "with a minor in biotechnology."

My brows spring up. "Wow, that's…"

"Impressive?" he says when I trail off. "I know. I am an impressive guy, after all."

"I was going to say surprising," I counter. "The business major I can understand, but the minor…well, it sounds like a lot of work, and your whole aesthetic hardly screams 'dedicated student.'"

"Maybe not," he agrees, "but I am definitely dedicated to inheriting my family's billions."

I let out a dry laugh. "Wow. Well, at least you're honest about it." *Which is a first.*

"I'd say Honesty is my middle name, but I think that would be a touch hypocritical considering everything." When he gestures back and forth between us, I nod.

"You would be correct in thinking that."

Damian clears his throat, and to my amazement, he looks almost contrite. He may be acting still, wearing fake remorse for show, but even if he is, I can't help it. He's like an injured puppy on the side of the road; I can't *not* feel sorry for him. Or maybe not sorry, exactly. But I do suddenly find I don't want to kill him quite as much as usual.

Internalizing a sigh, I shake that thought away and focus back on our conversation.

"So, biotechnology. That's really interesting."

Damian's eyes, which had drifted down to the table, pop up again at my comment, and he meets my gaze with a slight upward tug to his lips that gives him the appearance of a mischievous child. "And indispensable if you want to get into the drug-pushing business."

I expel a sound that's halfway between strangled choke and flabbergasted laugh. Is there anything he won't try to make a joke out of? "You are unbelievable."

He flashes that infuriating, shit-eating grin of his. "Unbelievably *awesome*, you mean," he corrects me, and I don't know if it's his unfathomable cockiness that does it, or if he's actually driven me to insanity, but I find myself giving him the one thing he asked for before we came to Izzy's.

A genuine fucking smile.

"There it is," he whispers with a victorious fist pump. Then, with a strange look I can't decipher, he reaches across the table and takes hold of my hand. I startle, gaping first at our intertwined fingers, then up at his face. Was that look he gave me supposed to be the signal he mentioned on Friday? We never did come up with a code word for these moments of physical contact.

I open my mouth to say something, but Damian just gives an imperceptible shake of his head before subtly jerking his chin, signaling for me to look over my shoulder. When I shift in my seat, following his gaze to yet another student either filming us or taking our picture, he leans in just enough so I can hear his whispered voice.

"Now, show that beautiful smile to the camera."

CHAPTER
FOURTEEN

Damian

**Donde hay humo, hay fuego - Where
there is smoke, there is fire**

**Translation: Where there are rumors, there is truth...
unless you're the one in control of the narrative.**

OCTOBER

Just as I hoped it would, news of my date with Blondie spreads like wildfire. The hashtag **#DateGate** trends on both Instagram and X, and the pictures snapped of us at Izzy's wind up on at least three separate gossip sites—well, the ones I think to check. Blondie was skeptical when I said people would be shocked to see me in public with a woman, and though I had pointed out that being seen at a party chatting up a hot chick is very different to a daytime date, it took seeing the viral posts about us for her to believe it. There were people who were so confused by our outing that some even commented on one Instagram post questioning if it was one of those Make-A-Wish things and I was granting Blondie her dying request. Let's just say, she did not find that nearly as amusing as I did.

In the nearly three weeks and multiple additional outings since our initial date, the conspiracy theories have run rampant, and I've been stopped several times by other students on campus with every single one pestering me about Blondie. Mason was the first to corner me for answers, and had acted utterly scandalized when I caved to his probing and revealed that the mystery woman in the pictures circulating the internet was actually Poor Girl. At the time, it hadn't occurred to me that telling him she was the same one-night stand from the start of the semester would be a bad thing—after all, it wasn't like he remembered her name or knew anything about her other than what box she had ticked on the bucket list, about which he has since been sworn to silence again. But then the real interrogation began, and his main question hadn't been how we ended up on the covers of multiple tabloids together, but *why* I would willingly date someone who seemed to make a habit of trying to obliterate my dick with her knee.

"What can I say?" I told him in response. "I guess the shock of that last hit to the balls must've gone straight to my heart."

But my answer did not appease his horror, nor did it settle the building unease in my gut that Mason could very well turn around and start spreading rumors about us, the gossipy little bitch that he is. My dude knows not to mention the list or the bet, but what if someone were to make the connection themselves based on whatever else he says? My parents used their rich people powers of we-will-ruin-your-life persuasion to threaten lawsuits against every person and publication that screenshotted and shared the list in the weeks following Mason's video. They even paid off Conwick, and the school was more than ready to bend over backward for them as my family is one of the university's largest donors, announcing it would expel any students who posted, shared, reposted, retweeted, or contributed to any rumors related to the bet. But this college has an abundance of assholes, and who's to say someone won't remember the names Mason posted, make the connection to Blondie, and try to ruin our lives just because they can? Some people love drama and live to stir shit, and the internet provides the platform not only for them to do just that, but to do it anonymously.

That hadn't occurred to me, and it really fucking should have considering there was at least one tabloid still printing stories about the bet as of last month. They didn't publish the list—the article was more about that board member at Hallazgo my parents mentioned going on the record about my "questionable behavior"—but that doesn't negate the possibility that the list could end up published again. If there's one thing the internet loves more than a TikTok trend, it's celebrity drama, and because of my family, I'm recognizable enough on a global scale to fall into that category.

It's quite possible I underestimated the universe's devotion to fucking with my life. If someone *does* link Blondie to the list, then her trigger-happy knee will be the least of my worries.

Or would it? At this point, I don't even know if that knowledge being out in the open would help us or hurt us, and I'm mad at myself for not considering the fuckery that might ensue. I was so focused on the clock ticking over my head with this whole graduation deadline and seizing the only option I saw before me, that, like always, I didn't stop to consider the consequences. And I *should* have thought about it since it *is* inevitable that Blondie's identity will come out sooner or later. Shit, the only reason it hasn't yet is because she is bafflingly anti-social, and because, as established, I am clearly an idiot. Jesus, what the fuck did I think would happen? Well, I didn't—that's the issue. I didn't think this through at all, and now, I have to figure out whether this is a problem before said problem kicks me in the ass.

But then…maybe I'm not entirely hopeless since none of this has occurred to Blondie either as far as I can tell—or maybe it has and she just doesn't care, though that seems very unlikely given what I know of her personality. Or maybe the money matters more to her than reliving the humiliation I exposed her to last spring, even if her reaction to said humiliation would certainly beg to differ. In any case, I've been too afraid of spooking her to ask. She's like a deer in headlights—the slightest wrong move from me and she'll bolt, and her running out on me now would be worse than us weathering any possible storm together.

So, to keep things calm, and to buy me some time to figure out a solution to this maybe-problem, I made the split-second decision to threaten Mason. I kept my warning vague; I don't really have anything blackmail-worthy to hold over him, but that doesn't mean I'm above finding something and getting receipts to silence the fuckwad if that's what it takes. Then, for good measure, I told him Blondie would crush his balls like grape jelly if he so much as breathes a word about her or about our relationship. *That,* thankfully, seemed to get his attention.

As for everyone else who's asked, I've remained…well, not silent but silent adjacent on all things pertaining to Blondie, brushing off any questions with ambiguous answers about how we're just friends getting to know one another. I make sure to never say her name, and I discover it's surprisingly easy to keep her identity locked down. Despite being mentioned in the comments of Mason's video regarding our bet, it seems very few people on campus—or anywhere, for that matter—actually know who Blondie is, and as of yet, no one appears to have made the connection between her and the list. It helps that no pictures were ever posted along with the names Mason outed, and Blondie isn't on any social media that I could find, like some kind of ancient relic from the pre-internet days. It also doesn't seem like she has many friends, and without a digital footprint for people to stalk, there's really no possible way for anyone to work out who she is.

In a strange, eerily convenient way, it's almost as if Blondie doesn't exist. Shit, if I hadn't made a note of her name in my phone after we met in Touro Park last month, I'm not confident the admin ladies in the office would've had any clue who I was talking about, and that's saying a *lot* considering Conwick isn't exactly known for handing out scholarships, let alone academic full rides. And that includes that silver fox Meredith, who Blondie might know on a first-name basis, but the old bat sure as shit doesn't know her back. Though, to be fair, Meredith is nearly as old as the Crypt Keeper, so that might have something to do with it.

Still, even despite getting entangled with me, Blondie's found a way to stay incognito as if she really is Conwick's very own Clark Kent. It's strange how invisible she is, but then…was I ever aware of her before recently either? We might have hooked up last school year, but only because I was specifically looking for someone of her social caliber. Anyone of her socioeconomic background or worse off would've fit the bill, which the more I think about it in hindsight, the more I realize just how truly fucked up of me that was. Because really, it's no different to how I feel whenever people try to befriend me because of my family's money, and I hate that I didn't have the common sense to see the comparison sooner. No wonder Blondie despises me. It also makes me think…if I hadn't made that bet with Mason, would I have ever noticed her at all? Or would I be as oblivious to Blondie as everyone else on campus seems to be? Even now, dressed in the designer clothes I bought her, people only notice her when we're together, and even then, it's like she's being viewed as little more than a pretty accessory on my arm; the talking point is always me. Part of me blames the media, but I also can't shake the suspicion that it's intentional—like Blondie is *trying* not to be noticed.

Well, regardless, whatever she's doing is working, and as the rumors spread, I find her perceived anonymity turning out better for us than I could've ever imagined. A dozen or so brief appearances together in just under three weeks, and the media (and all of Conwick) is hungry to know who she is, so much so there's absolutely no way my parents haven't caught wind of our romance. Though the thought makes me giddy, I keep my excitement in check. Things in my life have a funny habit of going wrong, and even if this all goes according to plan, it's far too early in the game to start feeling smug. Blondie and I have a lot more work to put in for my parents—or anyone else, for that matter—to take us seriously.

Which is why we're starting small, with simple walks on the quad between class and coffee dates at Izzy's—nothing too big to avoid arousing suspicion while still being public enough for Conwick students (and paparazzi with long-lens cameras) to snap as many pictures as they like. After my well-known dating drought, small is more believable, and we need everyone watching to buy into the idea that we're together.

As for Blondie, she's playing her part far better than I could've expected given how bad she is at lying. She laughs at the right moments, holds my hand without complaining, and only grimaces slightly whenever I go in to kiss her on the cheek.

On the first Friday of October (the three-week anniversary of our shopping day and official commencement of our agreement), I even wake up mid-morning to an unexpected text from her.

Blondie

Let's go somewhere tomorrow

Blinking the sleep from my eyes, I roll onto my back.

Me

Wow and here I thought I'd be the one organizing all our dates

I yawn as I stare up at the phone screen where it hovers above my face, watching the little dancing ellipsis until she texts back.

Blondie

**Shocking I know but you are paying me so I
figure I should put in some of the work**

I snort.

Me

You are a terrible liar even in text

A long moment passes before she responds.

Blondie

**You got me 🌚 the truth is I don't trust that you
have any ideas that aren't coffee related and
believe it or not I need this to work out just as
much as you do**

"Wow, she must *really* be into her cosplay," I muse just as my phone buzzes again.

Blondie

**People will start to get bored of us soon if we
don't shake things up 🎭 and if it makes any
difference I could use the distraction**

Sitting up, I press my back to the headboard. She's not wrong about us needing to up the ante a little, though I've been wary of doing that with the worry of what might happen once her name gets out. I might even finally muster the nerve to talk to her about it, except…that last part of her message sinks its claws into me and refuses to let go.

She needs a distraction? From what?

I'm about to ask her when I remind myself that Blondie's personal life isn't any of my business. I wouldn't have cared three weeks ago, and I definitely do not care now so long as it doesn't interfere with or impact our agreement.

Shaking away my fleeting concern, I text back:

Me

**Okay but nothing weird like a couples painting
class or some shit**

Her next message arrives quicker than the previous ones.

Blondie

Oh you mean weird like taking a total stranger on a shopping trip and buying them tens of thousands of dollars worth of clothes they don't actually want?

Me

Can you technically be considered strangers if you'd had your dick inside the other person? Asking for a friend.

Another text comes through a split second after mine.

Blondie

Or what about showing up in said stranger's lecture like some kind of stalker? That kind of weird?

Me

If I recall correctly you were the one stalking me pill lover

My phone vibrates with her response, and as I read it, I stifle a laugh at the mental picture of Blondie's face. She's like a Jigglypuff, adorable even when angry.

Blondie

Call me that again and I'll shove a up your

Me

Don't threaten me with a good time

It occurs to me that she might not be above poisoning my coffee one of these days, so I hastily add:

Me

All joking aside what did you have in mind?

My phone is quiet for so long I start to worry she's ignoring me. When it finally vibrates again, my heart does a leap, kicking me hard in the rib cage. My brow wrinkles as I peer at the dropped pin she sent, but I don't get a chance to work out what I'm looking at before another message pops up beneath it.

Blondie

Meet me here tomorrow @ 11am. Bring 🎧 and don't be late or I reserve the right to draw a dick on your face with permanent marker ✍

This time, I can't hold it in. I bark out a riotous laugh that evolves into another until I'm completely in stitches.

It's almost as if Blondie is reading my mind, and it takes nearly a full minute for me to compose myself enough to type back a coherent response. When I do, a broad smile pulls at my lips as the Pokémon theme song plays in my head.

Me

Whatever you say Jigglypuff 🐱✍

"A mansion tour? *Seriously?*" I groan, peering over my shoulder at the admittedly luxurious property with disdain. "If I wanted a history lesson on the Vanderbilts, I'd just ask my mom. She's, like, second or third cousins with them or something like that. I'm not entirely sure what that makes me—the whole second and third cousin once removed thing has always confounded me—but I *do* know we're related. I think. I could be confusing them with someone else."

Blondie rolls her eyes as she pushes me through the door to the Breakers Welcome Center, where we join the end of the line to check in for our tour of the largest and supposedly grandest of the historic mansions in Newport. I can't remember the last time I willingly waited for something, let alone something *I don't want to do.* Usually, I would name-drop that I'm a Navarro, and cut to the front of this bullshit line, but alas, I doubt Blondie will allow me to use my billionaire status for evil.

"This is the Vanderbilts we're talking about," she scoffs. "Who could you *possibly* be confusing them with?"

I lift a hand to my chin and release a long, contemplative hum. "The Vanderpumps, maybe? It would explain why my mom hate-watches their show every week."

A tiny furrow forms between Blondie's brows. "How do you know she hate-watches it and doesn't just…watch it? You know, because she likes it?"

"Oh, my sweet summer child," I coo, affectionately patting her on the top of the head. She smacks my hand away, and I grin. "First, my mother despises the majority of our distant relations. Second, something you should probably know is that my mom is the definition of a Karen. Hate-watching is the *only* way she watches TV because it empowers her to complain about everything. The only exception is *The Great British Bake Off*, but that's only because she has a massive lady boner for Paul Hollywood."

Blondie blinks those lovely eyes at me. "I find it disturbing you would use the phrase 'lady boner' while referring to your mother. Also, I have no idea who Paul Hollywood is, so I literally have zero reference for your comment."

Shock grips me at this revelation, and I immediately pull out my phone, Google Paul Hollywood, and turn the screen around to face her. "Nothing?" I ask when Blondie doesn't react.

"Baking shows aren't really my thing," she says, shrugging.

I snort. "Okay, *Bake Off* is everyone's thing."

Blondie just shakes her head. "Not mine."

It only now occurs to me that, while we previously discussed movies, our personal taste in television programs has yet to come up during any of our dates. But then, we do spend the majority of our limited time together throwing verbal hands, and there are only so many hours in the day, so I suppose it was unavoidable we'd eventually miss out on something important.

I cross my arms, assessing her unflinching expression with narrowed eyes. "If you aren't streaming *Bake Off* like the rest of the civilized world, what *do* you watch?"

The line moves forward before she can answer, and we're suddenly greeted by an older man wearing a blazer embellished with the Newport Mansions logo.

"Good morning, sir. Miss," he adds with a genial smile at Blondie. "Have you pre-booked your tickets for today?"

Blondie holds up her phone and shows what I'm assuming is a booking confirmation email to the man, who then directs us to a nearby counter, where we collect our printed map of the mansion and are advised on how to proceed with the tour. As we exit the Breakers Welcome Center and head for the property's eastern entrance as instructed, Blondie pulls an off-brand earbud case from the pocket of the Balmain denim skirt I bought her.

"Wait, we aren't *actually* doing the tour, are we?" I ask, genuinely aghast at the idea. Walking around this old house is one thing, but listening to some boring old troll talk about boring old history stuff while we do it? I shudder at the thought.

"What, afraid you'll learn something?" Blondie challenges, raising one eyebrow. At my disgusted expression, she laughs. "Don't worry, it's just for appearances."

"Oh, well, in that case…" Following her lead, I pull my own (not off-brand) earbuds out of my jeans pocket and pop them in my ears.

We trail a small group in front of us into a large entry foyer that Blondie informs me in a hushed breath is called the Great Hall. Four massive chandeliers and an ornate gilded ceiling hang overhead with intricate motifs patterning the walls on all sides of us. It's beautiful—a work of art, some might say—but to me, the surrounding marble and stone is too cold. It's an uncomfortable reminder of my own home. Or rather, my parents' home. To me, that house has become little more than a prison, which is why I've made it a point to return there as little as possible since I started attending Conwick. While the aesthetic isn't remotely similar, it has the same discomforting coldness—the same vast emptiness. Kind of like a show home, everything in its designated place. Almost like no one actually lives there.

To be fair, it certainly doesn't feel like they do anymore.

"Why do you look so constipated right now?" Blondie asks.

I glare at her, defensively crossing my arms. "Of all the things we could've done this weekend, you picked this…*why?*"

"I mean, it was this or the scenic trolley tour—"

"Why were those the only two options?" I sputter. "I know Newport caters to an older demographic, but surely, it has something a little more modern to offer."

Blondie gives me an exasperated look. "So, am I correct in assuming you've never come here before, and that this isn't something you would normally do on, say, a Saturday morning?"

I respond with a delicate sniff. "Yes, and obviously not," I say, sulking.

"Then would I also be correct when I say that seeing you someplace like *this* with a girl you are rumored to be dating might possibly be newsworthy?"

I frown at her logic. "I mean, yeah, maybe. But come on, Dornan"—I gesture around us—"this place is hardly hoppin' with youths. Does anyone here even *own* a smartphone?"

"You say that, but check this out," she whispers, her tone conspiratorial. She tugs on my coat sleeve, and pulls me behind her, leading me across the hall past a large fireplace mantle carved with lions and a horde of what looks like drunk naked babies, only stopping once we reach the doorway to the adjacent room. The furnishings and decor in this space are not at all to my taste, more chintzy than elegant, the colors clashing. It immediately gives me a headache.

"What are you—" I start to ask, but Blondie presses a cool finger to my lips.

Look, she mouths, and I follow her gaze to two girls, who are on their phones beside a small piano positioned in the round window nook. They look to be no older than us—they might even be younger—and seem to be alternating between making TikToks and taking selfies with the furnishings.

"I saw them go in there just as we came in," Blondie explains.

"Uhh…okay?" I mutter back, confused.

Blondie puts her hands on my shoulders and pushes me back out into the Great Hall.

"What I'm trying to say is that, while yes, you're right that mostly older people come here, so do tourists, which includes romance-loving girls obsessed with Jane Austen, and *Downton Abbey*, and *Bridgerton*. They are *dying* to live their best Regency lives, and for many, these mansions are the closest they're going to get. Not that this place is Regency era," she adds as an aside, almost to herself, her eyes wandering in that way I've started to notice they do when she's made an observation that she finds particularly vexing. Then she shrugs, brushing the thought away, and meets my gaze again. "Every single time I've been here, especially in the last few years, I've seen girls just like *that* in this same exact room and everywhere else on this property taking pictures, and making TikToks, and posting every second of their visit here on social media. And considering who you are and…what you look like"—she flaps a hand at me, begrudgingly waving it up and down the full length of my body—"these same girls probably spend their nights drooling over thirst traps or whatever it is you post on your Instagram."

"Thirst traps?" I would honestly laugh if I wasn't so fucking confused about what she's talking about.

She brushes me off with another wave of her hand. "Whatever. My point is, there are definitely people here who own smartphones, and you are famous enough that they will one hundred percent take our picture should they see us because our generation is literally incapable of *not* posting everything online."

"People who love Jane Austen?" I clarify, trying to follow.

She nods. "Exactly. And trust me when I tell you that bitches *love* Jane Austen."

"Okay. I think I get what you're saying, but what I'm *really* wondering is how you know this."

Blondie sighs. "I've been here a lot. You remember my friend Ronnie I told you about?" I nod. "Well, she is one of the aforementioned bitches."

"Ah." I nod again, more vigorously this time, her point finally sinking in. "And are *you* one of these bitches as well?"

Blondie purses her lips. "Serial killers are more my speed, actually."

I blanch, choking out a strained laugh. "Excuse me?"

She arches a sardonic brow. "Crime documentaries? Psychological thrillers? You asked me earlier what kind of shows I like watching. Well, I like anything with murder."

Huh. I would say Blondie is full of surprises, but with two murder attempts on Damian Jr. under her belt, that honestly tracks.

"Anyway…" She extends her hand for me to take the same way I've offered her mine on all our dates since that first one at Izzy's—albeit not without a put-upon sigh and an even more put-upon roll of her eyes. "We look a bit shady standing here, so we should probably go walk around or something."

I hesitate for only a second—just long enough to get over my shock that she's initiated the physical contact between us for once—then accept her gesture, threading my fingers through hers. Her hand is cool against mine, her skin still chilled from the fall air outside, and as we amble toward the red-carpeted staircase on the other side of the hall, I'm struck with the bewildering urge to press my lips to the back of her hand and keep them there until she's warm.

I immediately shoo the compulsion away, blaming my self-enforced celibacy for such uncharacteristic, intimate thoughts. I'm just pent-up, that's all. No sex for a month will do that. Shit, I could be holding hands with Shrek, and I'm sure I'd be considering giving him a kiss, too.

As Blondie leads me by the metaphorical dick through the house, spouting off random facts I only partially listen to, I find she's right. There are more young people here—specifically women—than I would've anticipated, and just as she predicted, they all zero in on us whenever we enter a room.

We encounter at least half a dozen instances of other tour-goers taking our picture, with many more pointing and whispering as we pass, but we both pretend to be too caught up in each other to notice. The whole time, Blondie's hand never once strays from mine, though her fingers occasionally twitch and then tense as if she's overly aware of my touch. Not that I can blame her—I'm weirdly aware of it, too. As I peek down at our intertwined grasp for the fifth time in as many minutes, I wonder why that is.

After an hour spent wandering the house, we stash our headphones and head outside for a change of scenery, and to stroll the sprawling grounds and enjoy the sweeping panoramic of the Atlantic.

"I never get sick of this view," Blondie says as we cross the manicured lawn, still hand in hand.

I nod. "I have to admit, it's pretty nice." I glance back at the northern face of the mansion where it stands in all its dominating glory behind us. "And props where props are due…today didn't totally suck."

"Ha!" Blondie releases my hand and steps in front of me, poking a finger gently into my left pectoral. "I knew it. You're a Jane Austen stan, aren't you?"

I raise my arms in defeat. "You got me. I, Damian Navarro, am secretly a Regency bitch. Though, in truth, I actually prefer *Bridgerton* over Jane Austen."

Blondie lets out an honest-to-god giggle, which does something weird to my chest. "Why am I not surprised you watch *Bridgerton?*"

I huff out a derisive breath. "Who can blame me? That Duke is a *total* smokeshow. Being straight doesn't mean I'm blind."

She laughs again, those adorable dimples on full display, as we carry on down the lawn toward the sloping crest of the bluff. "There's a cliff-side walk if you're up for it," she suggests, and I shoot her an incredulous look.

"Why, are you hoping to shove me off the edge?"

Her lips twitch at the corners. "Maybe. But if it softens the blow at all, I would pretend to be very sad about it after."

Her words echo in my head— *"if it softens the blow"*—and for an unguarded moment, we just look at each other, Blondie awaiting my answer, and me, coming to the most ingenious solution to the maybe-problem she's not even aware we have. Probably.

"That's it." At the silent query in Blondie's gaze, I pull my phone from my back pocket. "Do you trust me?"

She snorts. "Absolutely not. What kind of question is that?"

I hold up a hand. "Let me rephrase. If I initiate an intimate gesture between us that isn't holding hands or a quick peck on the cheek, will you shove me off this cliff?"

Blondie considers me for a moment. "No. I've decided I'm saving that for month nine after I've been paid my due. Besides, my arm strength would have to be phenomenal to yeet you into the Atlantic from here. The edge is still a long way off."

"Do people still say yeet?" I counter, earning me a light smack on my bicep.

"You're such a smart-a—" she starts to say, but her words cut off when I wrap a hand around her waist and pull her toward me. She huffs out a soft *oof* when her chest bumps into mine, her eyes wide with confusion. They grow wider yet when I raise the hand gripping my phone and open the camera app to capture the moment.

"You're taking a picture?" she asks, slightly breathless, her cheeks flushing pink. "I mean, obviously, you are, but why?"

Because what better way to soften the blow of a potential scandal than by getting ahead of it? If people think Blondie and I are truly in love, then when— not *if*—her name gets out, one of two things will happen. One: people will question why the hell Blondie would date me after what I put her through last spring, and we'll both become the targets of public ridicule. Or two (and I'm banking on this): our current romantic involvement will lead people to wonder if the bet was possibly overblown by the media, leading to them downplaying the overall shittiness of the bucket list for the same reason as number one, but from the other side of the coin—why would Blondie willingly date me if what I did was really so bad? And if I use that narrative to shift the focus away from the bet and turn it to our budding romance? Well, then our relationship could even be seen as a happy ending to the entire ordeal.

But I don't say any of that because it's too long-winded, and I don't want Blondie to worry about something that might not even be on her mental radar. So, instead, I say, "Because you were right." I'm not sure what shocks her more—that admission or the playful wink I flash at her. "We do need to shake things up. And nothing says romance quite like a picture to make it Instagram official."

Our breaths collide as I lean into the already narrow space between us, and when she doesn't protest, I press my mouth to hers without another word. Though I'm tempted to, I don't deepen the kiss—not like I did last time, in my car outside her house. It's important that this moment looks sweet. Romantic. And I manage it like a pro, but *god*, does it take effort. Blondie's lips are so soft and warm, and the smell of her perfume, or natural aroma, or whatever the hell that scent is permeates my headspace again just like it did when we were driving to Warwick, making me dizzy and my brain go all foggy. Suddenly, I am a feral dog—I want nothing more than to drag her inside, bend her over the nearest antique table, and remind us both of just how good it feels to fuck her.

Not for the first time, I lament not remembering the details of our hook-up last month. All I have is the memory of our library quickie in January, but I was having so much sex at the time, and I was so drunk on the challenge of my bet with Mason that I didn't really think of her outside the context of getting off. She was just a body. Another number. Another tick on my list. And I fucking regret that. I remember how it went down clearly enough, but I should've savored our time together. I should have documented every single second of how it felt to be inside her so I could recall those moments now instead of filling the blanks with my very wild, very *vivid* imagination.

When I feel myself growing hard, I snap the picture, then pull away, breaking the kiss before I lose my mind completely and do something that will get us both thrown in jail for indecent exposure. Like an old computer, Blondie experiences a few seconds delay, blinking her eyes open so languidly it's like she's moving in slow motion. When she finally meets my gaze again, her pupils enlarge, and her cheeks instantly heat, going from a pretty flower petal pink to burnished red.

And…shit. She is *beautiful*. I mean, I already knew she was, but it staggers me now more than ever that I never noticed it until recently. Seriously, how wasn't I stopped in my tracks the very first time I saw her? Because it isn't the clothes I picked out for her that do it, even though she wears them *really* well. No, what makes her beautiful is the flush of her cheeks that tempts me to run my hand over her skin and feel that warmth against my fingers. It's the way she parts her lips, goading me to kiss them until we're both breathless and sated. Above all, it's the way those piercing eyes fix on mine, making me feel like she can actually see me—or is at least trying to—when I don't think anyone has seen the real me in a very long time.

I immediately shake that thought away. *Stop it, Damian. This isn't real. It's just an act. She's only doing exactly what you're paying her for. Nothing more. This is business. Keep it professional, and stop reading into shit that isn't there.*

Clearing my throat, I shift my gaze to my phone and open Instagram—not only to distract myself from her bottom lip, which is begging me to suck on it, but because I have a narrative to control. A role to play. We both do.

The rehearsal is over. It's time to lift the curtain and step onto the stage.

Blondie says nothing. She just watches me in silence as I select the picture I took of us kissing and tap through to the next screen on the app. I don't tag her (not that I could) or include any explanation or context for the photograph in the caption. Instead, I put only a single emoji.

A heart.

And when I hit 'share,' I try my best to ignore that my actual heart is racing.

Instagram

I wake up Monday morning to what seems like eight hundred texts in my group chat with Ronnie and Andie, but I only get through the first few before I decide it might be best to switch off my phone for a while. It's not that I'm not ignoring them—I just don't have the mental energy for anything other than my nine a.m. class at the moment, and I have exactly one hour to prepare myself and get to campus for that. I meant it when I told Damian I wanted to go out on Saturday because I needed a distraction. Between Mom's illness, coming up with excuses to explain my new clothes and where I got the money to pay the deductible and cover her meds, classes, and keeping up this whole act with Damian, my days have been pretty full up the last month. To be honest, I'm exhausted. And things are only going to get more chaotic moving forward.

Since Damian publicly made our fake relationship official this past weekend (or as official as a heart emoji can be), his Instagram has blown up with comments, and news that the Hallazgo heir is off the market has spread like a venereal disease. So far, my name has stayed out of the media, which I guess isn't all that surprising given my self-imposed cave troll status, but I also have enough brain cells to know it's only a matter of time before it does get out, especially if there are tabloids willing to pay for that information. Then again, most people at Conwick don't need the money, and since it wasn't that long ago that Damian last made headlines, I suppose everyone still remembers his family's and the school's threats regarding what would happen to anyone who was found to be contributing to the media circus, and they're likely hesitant to risk the possible retribution. The more I think about it, that fear is the only reason I can fathom for why no one at Conwick has tried to out me yet, since there are a few who know me by name, mainly within the scholarship program. I guess we're just fortunate that the ones who do know me are the last ones who would risk the school's wrath. As for everyone else, they might fear expulsion and potential legal repercussions, but that fear certainly hasn't stopped them from taking pictures and posting theories about us on Instagram and X; it's just prevented them from digging deeper. For now.

Although she hasn't come right out and said it, I know that's what worries Ronnie the most about my agreement with Damian—that his bet and the bucket list (along with my name) will be unearthed, and the scrutiny I escaped last spring purely by chance will finally bite me in the ass like Death in a *Final Destination* movie. I got lucky the first time around; that douche Mason might have name-dropped and shamed every woman on the bucket list, but he used my full name, so nobody thought to look at me since no one at our school—not even the other scholarship kids—knows me as Alexandria. Plus, there were far juicier names on the list than some Poor Girl who no one even thought to associate with Conwick, let alone with Damian. For all anyone knew, Alexandria Dornan was just some random schmuck he had sex with on a night out at a club. No one had any reason to connect her to me, not even when I confronted Damian and gave him a well-deserved piece of my mind. The only witness to that was Mason, and the shitstorm that was brewing was far bigger than some nobody who was just one in a growing line of furious women with a bone to pick.

Not that any of that makes what he did okay. It was still humiliating, and for weeks after, I had major anxiety about showing my face in public, certain someone would finally make the connection. *That's* what Ronnie is stressed about now—about the effect that kind of public scrutiny might have on me—and I know she's right. Things are different now that everyone thinks I'm with Damian. People have cause to try to dig up dirt on me.

But the thing is, what I wish Ronnie understood, is that even if they *do* link me to the list and it gets out again, I honestly don't give a damn. While the public humiliation was less than ideal, it wasn't what hurt so much about what Damian did. It was the lie—the way he tricked me into thinking he could have actually liked me. *That* was the part I resented him for. That I *still* resent him for. And not because I can't handle rejection, but because it came at a time when I was in a vulnerable emotional state and it felt like the entire world was already against me. Getting ghosted after having what was easily the best sex of my life was one thing. Getting ghosted and then, two months later, finding out said amazing sex only happened at all so he could win a bet? Let's just say it made me feel used in a way I can't even put into words. Then again, I've always sucked at verbalizing my feelings, which is probably why my reaction to the whole ordeal was just to kick Damian in the dick. At least then I was getting my point across.

As for public opinion itself, both surrounding the bet and otherwise— well, recent events have put a lot into perspective for me, and since I couldn't care less what any of these assholes think of me, at Conwick or anywhere else, it really doesn't matter. All I care about is obtaining the money I need to help Mom; if my name has to get dragged through the mud to accomplish that, then so be it.

Besides, it's not like I have to worry about Mom or Gina ever hearing about any of this. Neither of them are on social media or interested in celebrity gossip, and we don't have any extended family, or anyone close to us who might reach out about a questionable tabloid headline. And I know I don't have to worry about their co-workers. Gina is constantly on the move at the hospital, and spares zero minutes a day for mindless chit-chat except for passing chatter with patients to put them at ease, and her days off (when she's not doing favors for people) are always spent with Mom or chilling out at home unless she's urgently needed elsewhere. As for Mom, well, she works with a bunch of middle-aged dudes in construction. I highly doubt any of them are prowling the pages of *Us Weekly* or spending their evenings checking TMZ.

But no matter how many times I say all this to Ronnie, it's like she doesn't believe it—or maybe it's just hard for her to imagine not caring about public opinion when she comes from a family that has made its fortune being in the Hollywood spotlight. Regardless, it's not a conversation I'm prepared to have again at eight a.m. on a Monday, so I text Damian confirmation that I'll see him after class and then shut off my phone.

And see him after class, I do. By now, my Applied Discrete Mathematics classmates have grown accustomed to seeing him waiting outside the lecture hall to meet me each week (the shock has finally worn off, I guess), and I must have grown used to it, too, because I slide under the warm weight of his arm as if it's my favorite place in the world, all the while doing my absolute best to convince myself it isn't, that I hate this, that it's all for show…even if I'm finding it far too easy to outwardly pretend otherwise.

We do this every time he meets me after class the few times a week our schedules align, and as has become routine as of late, he gives me a quick tap on my shoulder (our agreed-upon signal that he'll be coming in for a peck on the cheek) before bending down to kiss me softly, only an inch or so from my mouth. Sometimes, I imagine turning my head and leaning into that kiss just to feel his lips on mine again, and that urge is stronger than ever since our little display on Saturday. That kiss was tamer than our "test" one in his car, but there was something new there, an electric current that still tingles across my skin even now, two days later. I tell myself it's just attraction and perhaps some pent-up sexual frustration—that Ronnie and Andie don't have to be worried, and there are absolutely no warm, fuzzy feelings to be had on my part. Feelings and attraction aren't mutually exclusive, after all. I can detest Damian and still really, *really* want to fuck him.

But then there are moments like this—us walking to Izzy's, him flashing me a wink as he goes to order us drinks—that feel so real that I begin to wonder if I'm wrong. And more than that, I contemplate if I would actually be stupid enough to let myself feel something for him—to have another momentary lapse in judgment, as I phrased it to Ronnie and Andie. Especially now when I know all too well it's a lie.

"Okay, bitch, what the *hell?*" a familiar voice says on my right, and it's a good thing I don't have my coffee yet because of how violently I jump in my seat. My eyes snap away from where Damian stands in line at the outdoor counter of Izzy's, and shift up to Ronnie, who hovers over me like a disapproving parent scolding their child.

"Ronnie, I didn't expect to see yo—" I cut off mid-sentence, falling silent at the sight of her scowl as she pulls out the other chair.

As she plops down across from me, she says, "I have been a *very* gracious friend, Lexi. I forgave you last month when you lied about meeting with your advisor so you could get coffee with Fuckboy over there because I know how you feel about confrontation, and I can admit, I was not being the most supportive bestie at the time. But"—she slams her hands down on the table—"to leave me on *read*? How dare you."

I muster up an apologetic look. "I'm sorry I didn't respond to your texts earlier, but there were so many between you and Andie that I would've been late for class if I had taken the time to actually read them all. What did you expect first thing Monday morning? I wasn't even caffeinated yet."

"That's fair," she concedes. "Although, I am feeling quite sour that I had to find out about *this*"—she shoves her phone in my face, showing me the picture Damian took of us kissing outside the Breakers on Saturday—"from some no-name gossip account on my Insta feed and not directly from my best friend."

I stare at the photo for only a second, then swallow and avert my gaze to get the image of Damian's lips out of my head.

"I'm not really sure what you want me to say. You already knew we were dating. Given who he is, you must have known this would come with the territory." I flail a hand in the direction of her phone.

Ronnie pulls her bottom lip between her front teeth and looks at me hard for a moment. "Yeah, about that. I would just like to reiterate again that *this*"—she holds up her phone and waggles it a few times—"is going to cause you more problems than it will solve."

My heart leaps into my throat at her words, and I glance around to make sure no one is paying attention to our conversation before leaning in close enough to hiss, "Haven't we been over this?"

Ronnie lets out a petulant sigh. "I'm just worried you haven't really thought this through, and all the lies are going to catch up with you. Like, for example, telling your mom and Gina that *I* gave you all those new clothes."

I lean back in my seat and cross my arms. "According to Andie, you clear out your closet at least three times a year. Of the lies I've told, that one's the most believable."

Ronnie's mouth pops open into an affronted O. "Okay, smarty-pants. But if they haven't already, they're eventually going to notice that you're, like, *several* inches taller than me. Then what?"

I shrug. "Bold of you to assume that my fashion-challenged mother and aunt have spared any thought at all for the clothes I'm wearing and whether or not they actually fit me." Given some of the outfits my mom's seen me come home in since I became friends with Ronnie, I think she just assumes it's best not to question it at this point. Like the definitely-not-work-appropriate outfit I had on when I last fucked Damian.

Ronnie plants her forearms on the table like she's about to ask me to arm wrestle. "And the money? Is Carol still swallowing the charity lie?"

I sigh. That lie is my biggest yet—bigger even than making the world think I'm romantically interested in Damian Navarro…or that I like him as a person.

I had always planned on telling my mom the cash was given to us by a cancer charity—that I had applied on her behalf, and we'd gotten approved for monthly stipends to ease the burden of prescription and treatment costs, even if the amounts we're receiving are far beyond the norm for that kind of thing. I just had to hope she didn't know that or wouldn't care enough about where the money came from to ask.

But when Damian sent me that first payment after our shopping trip last month, it dawned on me that my mom would definitely notice the transfers were coming from me. Not from a charity. From *me*.

And she did notice. She questioned me the moment she saw the twenty thousand in her account, demanding to know where I'd gotten the money.

It took a bit of convincing, but panic and desperation must make me a better actor than I predicted because she believed me when I told her I put the wrong account information on the application paperwork by mistake, and that was why the money was coming from me instead of the charity directly—I was just playing the part of the middle man, getting the cash from point A to B. She had seemed skeptical initially, but when I offered to show her my bank statements to prove it, she thankfully didn't call my bluff.

And the subject hasn't come up again. Probably because she can't think of any reason why I'd lie.

"All is fine on that front," I assure Ronnie. "Mom is none the wiser."

She scoffs. "Well, it seems you've thought of everything, then."

On the outside looking in, anyone might think Ronnie is searching for negatives—that she *wants* this whole thing to blow up in my face—but I know her better than that, just like I know that her love language is concern, but that it often masquerades as passive-aggression. Besides, you don't stand by someone the way she's stood by me and help them through something as awful as that first year of my mom's cancer diagnosis unless you truly care. Unless you genuinely only want good things for them…and want to protect them from the bad.

And that's Ronnie to a T. My teeny tiny firecracker of a protector.

"Oh!" She snaps her fingers. "What about the tax implications? Have you considered how receiving that kind of money could affect your taxes? Or your mom's?"

I stiffen. Shit. I *hadn't* thought of that. It's not like my agreement with Damian is a legitimate job…is it? Would pretending to be someone's fake girlfriend and getting paid for it make me self-employed? I suppose we could always say any money I get from him is a gift, but I have no idea if we'd have to pay taxes on it in that case. I *should* know this considering I handle my mom's tax return every year, but we've never received any monetary gift for me to need to know it.

I roll my eyes. "Okay, you thought of the one thing I haven't." Ronnie's face falls at my tone, and I flinch, feeling like I've been sucker-punched in the gut. I reach across the table and take hold of her hands. "Look, I know you're worried about me, but it's fine. I have it under control, and anything I haven't figured out yet, I will." *Because I have to.* "You can stop worrying about me."

"But I won't. You know that, right?" She squeezes my fingers like she's holding on for dear life. When I nod, she leans in close and whispers, "At least promise me that you aren't letting this whole thing with Damian get in the way of your studies. I know how much you need this scholarship."

"Don't worry," I whisper back with a smile. "I'm going to make those midterms my bitch."

Ronnie exhales a quiet laugh that dies as a shadow falls over the table.

"Well, well, this must be the famous Ronnie," Damian says, placing my coffee down a few inches from where Ronnie and I still hold hands. "If I had known you'd be joining us, I would've gotten you a drink."

We pull apart as Ronnie sits back in her seat. "I'm not staying. I was just checking in with Lexi. You know, making sure everything between you two is going *smoothly*." There's a quiet menace behind that word that only an idiot would miss. Fortunately for him, it seems Damian is *not* an idiot because his brow hitches at the obvious threat in her voice. "I saw your Instagram post, by the way. Congrats on bagging yourself one hell of a woman. Not that you deserve her," she mutters under her breath before tacking on a sweet smile.

"Well, gee. Thanks, Red," Damian quips with an equally affable grin.

"That reminds me, we should all get together sometime," Ronnie suggests. She pushes out her bottom lip in an innocent pout, though I can plainly see the devil behind it. "It's important to me as Lexi's best friend that I get to know whoever she's dating."

"Of course," Damian agrees, still playing nice, but I think he's figured out her game. "How about this weekend? Invite your friends, and we can all go out on my yacht this Saturday if the weather is good."

"Sounds great!" Ronnie bounces up from the chair with a broad smile stretched across her face that sets my nerves on edge. It wouldn't surprise me if she's plotting to throw Damian overboard. Her eyes lock on mine. "Text me the details, Lex." Then, with an exuberant wave, she walks off with a peppy, "Cheerio!" like she's Mary freaking Poppins.

Once she's gone, Damian blows out a breath and slides into the seat she vacated. "I know you said she was intense, but I feel like that was an understatement."

My brain is telling me to agree, but my mouth chooses to respond with, "You have a yacht?"

Damian looks at me like I've hit my head. "I come from a family of billionaires, Dornan. Owning a yacht is like a right of passage for us."

I press my lips together and nod, not quite sure what I should say to that. He almost makes it sound like billionaires have membership cards.

"Why?"

"No reason," I murmur, looking down at my coffee.

"Do you have some boat-specific grudge against yachts I need to know about?" he jokes. When I don't dignify that with a response, he says, "Wait. Seriously?"

I open my mouth to speak, pause to consider what I'm about to say, then try again, still not meeting his gaze. "Not a grudge, no. I've just…never been on a boat before." My insides turn cold as the words leave my lips. So much for surface-level information only.

A beat of hesitation.

"Didn't you grow up in Newport?" There's a hint of surprise in his voice.

Yes, but not all of us can afford to just go out on a boat whenever we like, I almost snap back.

Instead, I nod again, more timidly this time, curling my fingers around the hot cup so I don't fidget with my glasses. When Damian doesn't say anything, I force myself to look up again.

Understanding dawns on his face when our eyes meet.

"Are you scared of them?"

"It's not that," I insist with a vehement shake of my head. "I just…don't tend to try new things unless I'm heavily coerced," I confess.

"Such as?" Damian prompts.

I immediately regret the turn this conversation has taken, and I consider changing the subject, but Damian is looking at me so intently that I suspect he won't drop this until I give him an answer.

I swallow. "Well, one time when I was in middle school, my aunt said she would cut my hair when the hairdresser who normally did it went out of business. I didn't want her to—for good reason. That woman might be a nurse, but she should *not* be trusted with scissors around anyone. Anyway, we didn't have a lot of money at the time as it stood, and I didn't want to go to someone else, so my mom guilted me into letting her do it, assuring me it would come out fine. Long story short, she ended up giving me a hideous bob that made me look like a blonde version of orphan Annie. I refused to come out of my room for three days after that."

Damian snorts. "That's understandable. I wouldn't want an amateur cutting my hair either."

That should be the end of that, but for some reason, my mouth is moving again, and words are coming out of me so fast I don't have time to stop them. "And when I was in high school, I left my first party after only five minutes because the music was too loud. I went home and watched *Zodiac* instead."

Why are you telling him this? a furious voice shouts from the back of my head. I don't respond because I don't have a good answer.

"I've…not seen it," Damian says, his tone stilted, but I continue as if I didn't hear him.

"And if we're talking transport"—I choke out a laugh—"well, I only went on a plane for the first time last semester for spring break, and only because Ronnie made me."

Dear god, the word vomit won't stop. It takes biting hard on the inside of my cheek to get me to shut the hell up, after which I can feel my skin flushing a blistering shade of red.

"Oh." Damian gives me another strange look. "Well…good thing she'll be there on Saturday then."

My hand launches upward and latches onto my glasses, jiggling them a little. "Yeah. Good thing," I agree with a tight-lipped smile, feeling more exhausted than ever.

When Saturday arrives, the sky is clear, and the sun is beaming, promising a beautiful day and perfect boating weather. Meaning there is absolutely zero way to get out of this.

Ronnie tugs me along beside her, our arms intertwining as we amble away from our now departing Uber through the gated entrance to Newport Shipyard, Andie and Eli close at our heels, giggling behind us like lovestruck pre-teens. After checking in at the welcome office, we're directed to Pier #1—where Damian's yacht is moored—and told the slip number to look for, which, given my limited boating knowledge, I'm assuming is maritime lingo for "parking space."

As we walk down the length of the pier, I'm astounded by the size of the boats around me, some of which I'm fairly confident are even bigger than my house. What kind of money does a person need to buy something like this?

The kind that could easily pay out of pocket for chemo, my conscience mocks.

Anxiety prickles my skin as a discomforting feeling takes hold in my chest, the financial berth between me and Damian more apparent than ever. Surely, any moment now, someone is going to realize I don't belong here—that although I'm wearing nice clothes and may look the part, I'm an impostor. Not like Ronnie, who is in her element like she was born for this life, channeling her inner sugar baby in her designer jeans, tailored blazer, floppy hat, and sunglasses.

She lowers said sunglasses as we approach the end of the dock, her eyes trailing up to take in the massive yacht stationed precisely where the shipyard staff said it would be. I follow her gaze, noting the name *Lucia* painted on the stern in elegant, swooping letters.

"Wowza," she says, letting out a long whistle. Her steps slow to an awestruck standstill, and she shoots me a curious look. "I know you said he's, like, *amazing* in bed or whatever, but I mean"—she gestures toward the yacht with a flabbergasted expression—"he's gotta be compensating for *something*…right?"

I can't prevent the flash of amusement that crosses my face when Damian pops into view, waving down at us from the top of the boat. "Afraid not." He might be a smug asshole at times, but if there's one thing Damian has every right to be cocky about, it's that.

Ronnie sighs. "Unbelievable. A billionaire *and* he has a huge dong? Whose side is the universe even on?"

We're welcomed on board by an older gentleman who tells us he's the captain, then guided to the upper deck by what I'm beginning to suspect might be waitstaff. Jeez, I guess it's true what they say about how the one percent live.

Damian greets us at the top of the stairs, wearing cream-colored chinos and a white linen shirt, which is unbuttoned to reveal his tan, chiseled torso as if we're in the height of summer and it's not actually mid-October.

"Welcome aboard!" he announces, brandishing his hands to the sides with all the showmanship of a circus ringmaster. He then approaches me, leans down to give me a peck on the cheek, and murmurs, "Dornan," by way of greeting before slinging his arm over my shoulders as has become our signature couple's stance. I silently curse my cheeks when they heat from the contact.

"Ronnie, a pleasure to see you again," Damian says with a polite nod at my best friend when she clears her throat to get our attention. Out of the corner of my eye, I catch the snarky ghost of a smile twitching at the edges of his lips.

She gives him a thorough, assessing once-over, though I can't help wondering if she's actually trying to see through his clothes like a human x-ray machine to determine for herself if I was telling the truth about the generous size of his dick. "Damian. Nice vessel you have here."

"Thank y—" he starts to say, but Ronnie interrupts him, shoving a hand in his face.

"Is that *champagne?*" she squeals, bouncing up and down on her heels as she grabs and shakes his shoulder with one hand, pointing with the other to a table laden with flute glasses in what appears to be a lavish dining area nestled within a built-in section of the yacht.

"It is. Feel free to help yourself," Damian answers, but I doubt Ronnie hears him. She's already halfway to the table by the time he even opens his mouth.

With the spitfire gone, our attention simultaneously shifts to Andie, who approaches us with a wary smile now that Ronnie's out of the way, her hand tightly clasped in Eli's. Though she's definitely the more easy-going of the two cousins, she's no less protective of me, and I can see her sizing Damian up before he's even met her gaze.

"You must be Andie," he says, holding out a hand, which she happily takes. After a quick shake, he repeats the gesture with Eli. "And I take it you're the boyfriend?"

"Eli. Good to meet you, man."

With the greetings all out of the way, and nothing to fill the uncomfortable silence that rises, I jump at the opening to ask the one question that's been burning in my head since I first saw this boat. "Who's Lucia?"

A warm smile instantly lights up Damian's features. "My abuela. This yacht used to belong to my grandfather, and he named it after her."

"How sweet," Andie says with a fond look at Eli before letting out a loud gasp that would give her dramatic cousin a run for her money. "Oh, my god, is that…a jacuzzi?" She points to what looks like a small inset pool at the opposite end of the deck.

Damian follows her gaze with a bewildered frown tugging at his brow, as if a jacuzzi on a two-hundred-foot mega yacht is to be expected. Hell, for all I know, it is. "You're welcome to use it if you like."

Andie's eyes lock on mine, and she stares at me like a child wordlessly pleading for their mother's permission, excitement bleeding across her face. Honestly, between this and Ronnie's elation over the prospect of free champagne, you wouldn't know the pair come from a family with money. Eli appears to be just as excited—though, I think that's likely more to do with the thought of being in a hot tub with his beautiful girlfriend than the hot tub itself.

I shake my head. "I didn't bring a swimsuit. But you guys go."

Andie exchanges a glance with her boyfriend, and then they're off, leaving a trail of clothes in their wake until they're down to nothing but their swimwear. In the Uber over here, Eli had complained about how uncomfortable it was wearing swim trunks under his pants, but Andie had insisted they wear their suits "just in case." I had thought it an odd choice given the time of year, but joke's on me, I guess.

Damian chuckles, and his breath tickles my ear when he leans in close and murmurs, "You could always just go in wearing your underwear, Dornan. It wouldn't be anything I haven't seen before."

I shrug off his arm, which still hangs across my shoulders, and take a step away. "No thanks," I grumble, rolling my eyes. "By the way, who else are we waiting for?"

He gives me a perplexed look. "No one that I'm aware of. Why?"

I turn my head, taking in the expansive deck around us. This level alone could comfortably hold fifty people, and yet, it's only the five of us here.

"It's just us?"

"Yes?" he answers, like he's not entirely sure what I'm asking.

I stare at him hard for a moment, unsure which of the two of us is more confused. "I thought you said we could bring friends."

"Yeah…?" Damian draws out the word, slow and deliberate, like he's trying to communicate with someone speaking a different language. Sometimes, it really feels like we are. "I said, 'invite your friends,' and you did."

"But *you* didn't invite anyone?" I clarify since he clearly has no idea what

I'm getting at.

"Was I supposed to?" he asks. He cocks his head to study my face, like he's a golden retriever and I'm a doberman, and he's not sure if I'm friendly or not.

I let out a frustrated sigh. "I just mean…what about *your* friends?"

"Ah. Right. I understand the confusion now." He nods vigorously for a moment as if in silent contemplation, then shrugs. "The truth is, I don't really *do* friends."

"Like you don't *do* girlfriends," I retort, hooking my fingers into mocking air quotes.

Damian gives me a surprisingly withering look. "Pretty much."

I consider this information, trying to make it fit into the puzzle that is Damian. Before we started this whole fake-dating agreement, I thought he was fairly predictable and easy to figure out. After all, he only seemed to care about two things: status and sex. But the more time we spend together, the more I'm beginning to realize that might not be entirely true, and the overall picture isn't as apparent as I once thought it would be. Trouble is, I'm missing too many of the pieces to work out what I'm meant to be seeing.

"That doesn't make any sense," I mutter, speaking more to myself than to him. I glance around the deck again, taking in all the empty space, before swiveling my head to look up at his still perplexed face. He reels back slightly at the accusation in my gaze. "Aren't you, like, in a frat or something?"

Damian barks out a mortified laugh. "What? No. What made you think that?"

"Well, you're always partying with them," I point out, my tone biting. I don't bother adding that we hooked up last month because we literally bumped into each other at a frat party.

"I've also partied with the Kardashians," he counters. "Doesn't mean I'm looking to become one."

"I—" My skin flushes as I try and fail to think of a comeback. "I'm not following."

Damian averts his eyes, running a hand through his thick hair, and it takes all my inner strength to stop myself from reaching my own hand out and doing the same. Brief flashes of the two times we had sex fill my mind, my fingers twitching with the flesh memory of what his hair feels like and how good I know in my gut it must have felt to touch it. To grip it. To clench it in my fists.

Jesus, my vagina really does have way too strong of a hold over me if I'm getting this worked up over *hair*.

"There's not much to follow," he finally says, an edge to his voice that snaps me out of my horny reverie. "It's quite simple, actually. The reality is, when you come from a rich family like mine, you never know who's genuine and who's just trying to get close to you because of your money." He scoffs, waving a hand toward the jacuzzi where Andie and Eli look one heated glance away from fucking right there in the water. "I'm sure your friend's boyfriend gets that."

"Are you implying that Andie is with Eli for his money?" The hair on the back of my neck rises like the hackles on a hissing cat. "Because she is *not* like that—"

Damian's eyes blow wide at the ferocity in my voice. "I'm not," he insists, holding up his hands to placate me. "I…didn't mean it like that. I just meant that *I* find it difficult to make friends because of my family and who we are. That's all."

I scoff, unconvinced. "How do you know *you* aren't the problem? You say you struggle to make friends, but the common denominator in that equation is you."

His apologetic expression hardens into something that feels all too close to the anger gripping me. "You know what else is the common denominator?" he seethes, then flings his arms out to the side, gesturing all around us. "My family's wealth. And every single time without fail, my 'friends' would take advantage of me for it. 'Oh, Damian can get us into this nightclub because he's on the VIP list,'" he says in a crude imitation of one of these so-called friend's voices. "'Damian, take us on your private jet.'" He snorts maliciously. "People are superficial and phony, and *that* is why I don't have friends."

"What about Mason Harris?" The question comes out more like an accusation. But then, I suppose it is.

Damian bristles. "What about him?"

I hold his unwavering gaze. "He's your friend, isn't he?"

An excruciating lull passes before he answers, as if he's searching for the right words to excuse any acquaintance between them…or to try to justify it.

"I've had the displeasure of going to the same high school and now college as Mason," he explains. "A coincidence of proximity does *not* make us friends."

"Then why did you make the bet?"

His responding laugh is strangled. "Because I was bored, and I like a good challenge." And yet, there's something behind his expression that seems to refute that claim. Something that almost looks like pain. Or sadness.

"Is that really why?" I press, because I need to know there's more to it than that—that the chaos that decision caused didn't come down to something as fickle as boredom. When he doesn't say anything more, when he doesn't contradict himself, I sneer. "Wow. Well, that's a shitty answer."

"Welp." He flings his arms out again, but this time, he lets them fall dramatically to his sides, his palms slapping against his thighs. "I'm sorry to disappoint you—"

"What are you guys talking about?" a voice interrupts, and my heart jumps into my throat when I wheel around to find Ronnie double-fisting a glass of champagne and a very fancy-looking shrimp cocktail.

"Jesus, Ronnie, you startled me," I wheeze, pressing a hand to my chest.

How much of our conversation did she hear? I wonder.

Hopefully, none of it, my conscience answers, and I internally nod in agreement. As if Ronnie needs another reason to disapprove of this arrangement.

Her dark eyes swing between my face and Damian's as she takes a careful sip of her drink. Under the watchful reproach of her gaze, it occurs to me that she asked us a question.

What were we talking about? Nothing I can tell her about, that's for sure.

"Uh…" I huff out an awkward laugh. "Damian was just telling me why his favorite movie is *Twilight*," I say, partly because Bella's vampire baby is the first thing that pops into my head (for reasons I can't possibly fathom) and because I feel like getting back at Damian for being such an insufferable chode.

"Wait, seriously?" Ronnie gasps, glancing between us. "No way! I *love* those movies. What team are you?"

"Yeah, Damian, what team are you?" I ask, smirking.

He makes it a point to ignore me, looking only at Ronnie when he says, "Team Jacob, obviously."

Her eyes narrow, and her lips push out in an exaggerated pout, like she's not quite sure she believes him. Crossing her arms, she gives him a dubious look. "Favorite film in the series?"

"*New Moon*," he answers without hesitation.

Her eyes glint with determination. "Favorite scene," she demands.

Damian laughs as if the answer is obvious. "Any time Taylor Lautner takes off his shirt. Oh, and that whole montage of Bella trippin' adrenaline-fueled balls and seeing those weird hallucinations of Eddie. That was wild."

Ronnie blinks up at him, her face a mask of surprise and amazement that I'm certain must mirror my own. At first, I genuinely thought he was joking when he said his favorite movie was *Twilight*, but his answers to Ronnie's questions have me second-guessing myself. I remember what part he's referring to from the time Gina made me binge-watch all five movies with her, and I'm not convinced that answer is something he could've magically pulled out of his ass unless he had, in fact, seen them.

Ronnie opens her mouth to speak—either to gush that there's something she and Damian have in common or to grill him with more *Twilight* trivia— but before she can get a word out, I say, "You were serious? *Twilight* is *actually* your favorite movie?"

Damian meets my gaze, his expression grave. "I am as serious as a one-hundred-year-old virgin vampire, Dornan. I don't joke about *Twilight*."

"So, you enjoy those movies, like…unironically?" Ronnie asks, quickly tossing out, "No shame if you do. I obviously love them. It's just kinda rare that a straight dude would, too. And before you come at me, just know that I say this from a place of experience. My gay dads are the ones who got me into *Twilight* because of their mutual crush on Peter Facinelli. Not like I can blame them. Carlisle is totally bae."

"They're cringe, don't get me wrong," Damian quips, "but that's what makes them fun, isn't it? And besides"—he slings his arm around my shoulders again—"who doesn't like a good love story?"

Says the guy with an aversion to real relationships, I think to myself.

We spend most of the day out on the water, sprawled across sun loungers on the upper deck, soaking in the unseasonably warm autumn rays, and gorging on expensive canapés, champagne, and cocktails, like we're at some fancy charity event or an awards show after-party. We don't go out to sea, staying close to the harbor to "make it easier to moor again," Damian explains. Though I try not to think about it, the question of how much this day out has cost the Navarros is never far from my mind.

How many monthly supplies of my mom's chemo meds could I buy with the amount Damian spent today hiring the waitstaff alone? Anger seizes me at the thought, and I have to force myself to focus on something else before I lose my shit at the injustice of the medical system and the ever-increasing divide between the majority and the one percent. I'm not one to begrudge anyone the fruits of their hard work, but when those fruits are staring at you while you struggle for scraps, it's a tough pill to swallow.

Thankfully, the conversation proves adequately distracting, especially when Damian reveals exactly how he got into *Twilight*. We all listen with rapt attention as he spins a tale from his freshman year when he caught his not-friend Mason watching the second movie in the series alone one afternoon when he walked past his dorm room. Though Mason had scrambled to shut it off, Damian had seen enough to know the truth. But instead of judging Mason (who claimed he was only watching the films because he thought Kristen Stewart was hot), Damian sat down and watched the whole series with him to see what the fuss was about.

His explanation of these events confounds me, especially considering that, for someone who claims to not have any friends, the actions he took in his story sound very much like something a friend would do. But then…he never said anything about not *wanting* friends, just that he doesn't actually have them. And even I can acknowledge there's a difference.

As this notion settles in my brain, a sour feeling spreads through my gut at the memory of what I said earlier today about how, maybe, Damian is the problem. That *he* is the common denominator as to why he doesn't have any friends. Now, I'm starting to wonder if I was wrong to judge him so quickly, and that there might actually be some merit to what he said about his family's wealth. After all, if it's so easy for me to make assumptions based on how he spends his money, then I can imagine it's just as easy for others to want to take advantage of him for it.

That thought lingers like an itch I can't scratch, and I'm not sure what to do with it. Mostly because it makes me think that, maybe, *just* maybe, he's not quite as much of a shit as I've been telling myself he is since freshman year, when he ghosted me after the first time we had sex. I don't look at that particular line of thought too closely, though. My body is already a traitor when it comes to my disdain for Damian; the last thing I need is my mind entertaining any ideas about potential positive feelings.

For the rest of the day, I distract myself with shallow conversation and by snacking on as many expensive canapés as I can physically fit in my stomach. By the time the yacht makes anchor in the shipyard again, the sun is starting to set, and I feel roughly five hundred shrimps and a gallon of champagne heavier than when I first stepped on board.

We collect our things—I'm fairly certain I even see Ronnie shove some shrimp cocktails into her bag—and I walk with Damian as he sees us all off to the gangway, still playing the part of the dutiful host.

"Well," Ronnie says with a demure sniff. "Today was…enlightening. Thank you for your hospitality, Damian. We must do this again." Which, from Ronnie, is as much of a seal of approval as he's ever going to get.

Lifting her chin, she trots down the ramp to the pier as Andie and Eli step forward to say their farewells.

"Thanks, man." Eli nods as they pass, and Andie waves, chirping out a jovial, "Bye!"

I linger behind as they congregate with Ronnie, then wave for them to go on ahead as I turn to say my own goodbyes to Damian.

"Your friends are interesting," he comments before I can spare a thought for what to say. "Do they know, by the way? About us?"

"Ronnie and Andie do, yeah. They keep trying to talk me out of it." I ignore the question in Damian's eyes. No way am I expanding on the why of that. What was discussed at Grape Expectations among the safety of friends will stay at Grape Expectations. "Eli doesn't, though. I think he's just confused by the whole thing, honestly."

"I doubt he's the only one," Damian muses. "Oh, by the way, how are you feeling?" At my perplexed expression, he elaborates, "Earlier this week, you said new things can be tricky for you, but you seem like you managed okay?"

There's a hopeful, questioning note to his tone that catches me off guard. There it is again—the thought that maybe he's not so terrible after all.

I quickly shake it away.

"I'm fine," I assure him. "You were right. Having Ronnie here helped. Plus, that whole conversation you guys had going about *Twilight* was a brilliant distraction. Especially the part when you said Mason initially tried to convince you he was watching furry porn and not a teen movie about glittery vampires."

Damian chuckles. "Yeah, I'm not really sure why he thought his apparent furry kink was the less embarrassing option, but then, he *is* an idiot."

He gestures to the gangway, and I match his smile as we walk down the ramp side by side.

"Well, I guess I'll see you—" he starts to say, but he's interrupted by Ronnie shouting my name as she runs down the pier toward us. Panic floods my chest at the stricken look on her face.

"What is it?" I ask, stepping forward to meet her. "What's wrong?"

She shakes her head. "I was checking my phone since I didn't have signal all day, and it finally came back just now, and…" She trails off, as if she can't bring herself to voice whatever it is that has her so rattled. Her face is uncharacteristically pale, and when she holds up her phone to show me something on the screen, I notice her hand is shaking.

I glance down, and as my eyes trail across the top trending post on her X feed, my heart falls into the pit of my stomach.

BET YOU DIDN'T SEE THIS COMING!
PHARMHEIR MYSTERY GIRLFRIEND UNMASKED AS MATH PRODIGY NAMED IN SEX BET SCANDAL

CHAPTER
SIXTEEN

Damian

El que por su gusto muere, hasta la muerte le sabe - He who
dies by his own choice, even death tastes sweet

Translation: If you choose your path, you must accept
the consequences...even if they suck.

It's been a week since the unveiling of Blondie's identity broke the internet. One week since the world discovered that the mystery girl I've been seeing is, in fact, one of the ladies named on the infamous "Fucket List" (as it became known following the media shitstorm all those months ago). And while the tabloids, and literally all of my socials, are in an absolute uproar about the revelation, I'm elated to find that most of the commentary on the matter is positive.

Just as I hoped, the revelation that I'm now "dating" one of the women mentioned in my bet with Mason has much of the online community questioning if the whole situation with the bucket list was really as bad as it was made out to be, or if the media purposely blew it out of proportion to sell trashy tabloids and get clicks. It's not a stretch—everyone knows the quickest way to make a few bucks is with a celebrity scandal. It's a well-known fact that nothing gets the attention of the people quite like the downfall of a public figure.

But this isn't a downfall at all—it's a goddamn resurgence. A one-eighty in societal perception from the outrage I was bombarded with in the spring following Mason's video. Many on the internet are even shipping my relationship with Blondie and romanticizing the circumstances that brought us together, with headlines like, **A Bet Gone Right: The Heartwarming Story Behind Damian Navarro's Sex-Bet Controversy** and **Alexandria Dornan: The Girl Who Turned a Dare into a Love Affair** gracing the front pages of several prominent news sites. Of course, most of the information in the articles I skimmed in the spare time I had between midterms this week was absolute bullshit with so-called "sources" who claim to know us both spewing so many lies I could literally wallpaper my entire dorm room with them.

But with others, it's harder to separate the truth from the lies, the facts from the fabrications. For example, the article that lit the fuse on the current media interest referred to Blondie as some sort of "math prodigy," which could be an exaggeration, of course, but considering she's at Conwick on a notably rare full-ride scholarship, and she was indeed learning some kind of ninja math in that one class I dropped in on, the title certainly fits. There were other truths peppered in the article, too, like how Blondie was born and raised here in Newport and that she's currently a sophomore in college, though it didn't go much more in-depth than that. But then, like the other articles I've read, it turned to rumors of our apparently "impending engagement," and how—according to yet another "close source"—I got Blondie's face tattooed on my left ass cheek, and suddenly, I couldn't be sure what was true and what was just another lie in this facade we've built up around us.

Still, riddled with inaccuracies or not, the majority of what I've seen online has put a positive spin on our fauxmance, and with every day that's passed since that first article dropped, more and more people have commented and posted in support of our blossoming "love." Blondie and I have even been bestowed with our own merged couple names, like we're the next Brangelina or Bennifer. Now, that's when you really know you've made it.

But like with all things, there are the supporters, and there are the haters—Team **#Dexi** (our adoring fans) and Team **#Lamian** (as those who think the whole thing is sketchy have come to refer to us). Whenever I see comments from the latter, I'm beyond relieved that Blondie isn't on social media, and I only hope her friends have the sense to keep her in the dark about what these assholes are saying. I know I sure as shit don't plan on telling her about anything I've read this week—about how countless idiots are questioning her intelligence, her judgment, especially on any articles that specifically highlight how smart she is, as if their ill-informed perception of her is fact and everything else is a lie. As if these anonymous keyboard warriors are themselves the very arbiters of truth.

The worst ones have even suggested I'm blackmailing Blondie into a relationship to make myself look better following the bucket list scandal. That angle on things doesn't sit well with me, probably because it's too uncomfortably close to reality. I can only imagine how the headlines would spin it if they knew what was really going on—how they'd try to make this whole thing between me and Blondie into some sordid tale of extortion. Christ, I can't even begin to guess how she would take that. Blondie might have a tough exterior, like some kind of pissed-off turtle, but I have a sneaking suspicion that what's on the inside is softer…*vulnerable*…even if she tries hard to hide it.

I think that's the real reason I've been avoiding her since that day out on the *Lucia*. This past week, I had an excuse. We had midterms, and we both agreed to put our outings on pause until all our respective exams were over. But moving forward? I have absolutely no idea what to expect the next time I see her. If she knows what people are saying about her. If she regrets making this agreement with me. If she's going to freak out and call the whole thing off. Since we started fake dating, she's been surprisingly blasé about being seen together, about being in the public eye, but that was before her identity was blasted to the masses, and before she admitted that she apparently has a hard time with change. And let's face it, becoming one of the most Googled people in the country is a big fucking change.

Sure, I could sit here and say she knew what she signed up for, but I don't think that would be fair since no one can really understand the full scope of something like this unless they've previously had to endure that level of scrutiny. I can't exactly rewind to last spring and check (and it's not like I was paying that close of attention to the blowback on specific people other than myself at the time), but from the lack of familiarity surrounding Blondie—both physically at Conwick and in regard to her name in recent media coverage—I think she might have gotten off easy when the list was first exposed, even flown under the radar completely…which means this might be her first real rodeo with this kind of attention.

As for me, I've experienced enough negative press about me in the last four years alone that I've learned how not to give a shit.

Except…with my father's warning hanging around my neck like a noose, I realize that's not entirely true. I *do* have one fuck left in my arsenal. One worry that keeps me up at night and fills me with an unrelenting dread whenever I let myself think too hard about it.

And that is my parents' very notable silence.

I know it's only been a month and a half since their ultimatum at Fernando's, but it's odd they haven't said a word to me. No praise for attending my classes without incident (I'm sure they're still actively checking). No "well done" for avoiding the party scene and keeping myself out of trouble. And above all, not a single comment about Blondie, not since I posted that picture of us at the Breakers on Instagram, and especially not since news broke of her connection to the bucket list last week.

And here I was thinking that Blondie's name and our messy past going public was somehow doing me a favor. Maybe I've miscalculated this whole thing, and rather than look at the positive shift in commentary and opinion surrounding the matter, my parents are simply pissed that my stupid bet is in the headlines again.

Or maybe they know me better than I gave them credit for, and they've figured out what I'm really up to—that my relationship with Blondie is just a ruse intended to trick them into retracting their threats to disown me.

Or maybe they've taken the side of Team Lamian, and despise us because it's easier to be a hater than to believe people are capable of making mistakes and actually growing from them.

Or…maybe the real problem—the real reason for their silence—is because they're waiting for me to make a move first. Maybe the real issue is that I haven't been vocal enough—that I've been playing it safe, playing it vague, because I thought that was the easiest and quickest route to my goal. My parents want me to get serious about my life, but I'm starting to think that what they really want is to see me take initiative…and responsibility. To stop making excuses and just fucking *do* something.

And actually have the balls to stand firmly behind it.

An idea pops into my head as I prop myself upright in bed, where I've spent the last hour doomscrolling my socials instead of actually trying to sleep, and tapping open my notes app, I begin to type.

The time for half-assed apologies and ambiguous gestures is over.

Damian Navarro is officially stepping into his proclamation era.

By the following Friday, the public's opinion of me and Blondie, and the general perception around how we got together, has improved even further, whereas my mood has taken a nosedive.

I still haven't heard a single word from my parents, not even an "Oh, hello son, just checking in to make sure you're still alive and well." Nope. Nothing of the sort.

Just that same unbearable, judgmental silence.

Which means it's time for drastic measures, hence why I'm now sitting at my parents' usual table in my least favorite place in the world: Fernando's. Blondie sits across from me, a vision in a black Givenchy plunging neckline dress (one of a handful of dresses I bought her when we went shopping last month), and it's a triumphant return to her Superman alter ego, which I haven't seen since the night we fucked, when I was so blind—and drunk—I couldn't even tell who she was. Though I'm a diehard fan of her first-evolution Pokémon, Clark Kent, au naturel form, I can't ignore how great she looks tonight; she clearly put in some effort when she was getting ready. Her curls are pinned in a stylish updo, her glasses are nowhere in sight, and she's even wearing makeup—to her chagrin. On the way over here, she had grumbled about how I'd sprung this date on her at the last minute, about how she'd had to enlist Ronnie's help to make her look presentable for such an upscale restaurant, and then went on in detail about just how torturous the whole experience had been. She might have also muttered something about being treated like everyone's personal mannequin lately, but I couldn't quite make out the words with the way she was gnashing her teeth as she spoke.

I had hoped she'd leave her anger in the car once we got here, but she seems just as sullen this evening as I am. Or maybe she's just picking up on the negative energy radiating from this side of the table, and has opted for the ease of silence rather than trying to force uncomfortable conversation.

I risk a glance at her, wondering if she's being quiet because she's mad about how long it's been since we last saw each other.

But why would she be? I ask myself. It's not like she's my *real* girlfriend, and besides, I sent her the cash I owed her for the whole month in advance just as she requested. If anything, she should view these past two weeks as generous paid time off from her employer.

The man in the corner who was strumming the arpa jarocha the last time I was here is replaced by an older woman singing Mexican ballads, accompanied by a rather dashing gentleman playing a flamenco guitar. Although the music they're creating together is beautiful, it provides a weird contrast to the tension pervading the air, the silence an almost tangible cord that's pulled so taut it could snap at any moment.

"You're unusually quiet tonight," Blondie notes, giving that cord a firm yank. I can practically see it start to fray. "Something on your mind?"

I watch the easy movements of her knife and fork as they dance across her plate.

"Nah. I just don't particularly like this place."

Her hands still, and those gorgeous green eyes lift to mine. "Really?" Her attention dips to my own untouched dinner. "Do you not like the food or something?"

I heave a sigh, taking a generous sip of my wine. "More like…the general vibe," I answer with a vague wave of my hand at the restaurant around us.

Blondie follows the gesture, then meets my gaze again, staring at me hard for a moment. She relaxes her grip on her utensils, setting them down beside her plate. "Okay…" she says slowly, her tone tinged with confusion. "Then *why* are we here?"

When I don't answer, a familiar scowl settles across her face, pinching her brows.

"Seriously, Damian, what's going on? I haven't seen or heard from you in two weeks, and then you call me out of the blue for some fancy date at a place you apparently hate?" The *What the fuck?* I glimpse in her eyes goes unsaid.

Well, I guess that answers *that* question about whether or not she's mad that I've been kind of ghosting her lately. Clearly, I haven't learned my lesson from the last time I did it.

I slump back in my seat, the frustration of the past couple weeks scratching at me, like fingernails that keep obsessively picking at a scab, never giving the wound a chance to heal. Blondie's piercing eyes demand an explanation, but I can't bring myself to meet them, not when guilt tugs at me alongside that annoyance. Guilt that I might have turned her whole world upside down for absolutely nothing.

"I just… I thought this might get their attention," I finally say, staring down at the pristine white tablecloth with the focus of a scientist examining microbials through a microscope. "This is their favorite place, and I figured… maybe it would make them notice."

Blondie is silent for so long I start to think she isn't listening, but then, after what feels like ten minutes but was probably closer to one, she whispers, "Who?"

My jaw tightens. "My parents." That frustration now clutches me with a suffocating strength. "I thought they would've shown more interest in our relationship by now. I don't get it." I shake my head, my temper flaring. It takes all my self-control to keep my voice from rising. "I've been the good, obedient son they want. I've turned things around. I'm showing the commitment they asked for, and yet, nothing. Nada. Zilch." I fling a hand in Blondie's direction, nearly knocking over my glass in the process. "I thought if I brought you here, sat at their *favorite* table, it might finally get their attention since nothing else fucking seems to."

Silence again, aside from that haunting melody filtering into my ears, stirring something deep inside me. "Y aunque la vida me cueste," the woman sings behind me. *And even if it costs my life.* Those words feel eerily prophetic at this moment.

My eyes snap up at the sound of the strangled breath Blondie blows out through her nose. "Wow."

I blink at her, taken aback by her abrasive reaction. "That's it? Wow?" I just opened up to her about a particularly sensitive aspect of my life, and that's all she can think to say?

She clicks her tongue, her brows rising in disbelief. "No, I just find it kind of baffling that you've actually convinced yourself you've turned things around when all you're doing is pulling the same stupid stunts they're already mad at you for. I mean, Jesus Christ, Damian, do you *hear* the words coming out of your mouth?"

Her scathing retort isn't just a slap in the face, it's a full-blown assault, reaching down my throat, and ripping the very air from my lungs. "What?" is all I can manage to say past the crippling breathlessness gripping my chest.

Those fierce green eyes narrow into disparaging slits. "Tell me, what exactly have you committed to?" she asks. "Nothing real, *that's* for sure. What have you done that shows any actual growth? That would make your parents—or anyone, for that matter—think you've changed, and that you aren't still the immature fuckboy you've always been?"

Fury rises inside me with every condemning word spilling out of her mouth. "What the fuck is your problem tonight, Dornan?" I snap, finally finding my voice. "Someone piss in your Wheaties or something?"

Her nostrils flare, her teeth gritting. "My *problem* is that you're a spoiled brat, who's so blind you can't even see your own privilege staring you in the face. I mean, what kind of asshole would rather lie to their parents and go to such elaborate lengths"—she gestures to the grand dining room around us—"than actually try just being a better person? Being a decent human isn't *hard*, Damian."

Decent? Since we made this agreement, all I've done is try to be decent!

I hold up my hands. "Okay, now, I'm just confused. If I'm such a fucking awful person, and my actions are *so* detestable to you, then why the hell did you agree to help me?" I breathe in, then softening my voice, I ask, more calmly now, "Where is this coming from?"

Looking away from me, she pulls out her phone. Her finger flicks against the screen, and clearing her throat, she starts to read, "'I've made many mistakes in my life, but none were as thoughtless and harmful as the now infamous 'Fucket List.'"

A chill creeps up my spine, my veins filling with ice as I hear my own words spat back at me in Blondie's voice.

"'When I look back at it now,'" she continues, avoiding my gaze, "'I can't believe how immature and careless I was, not just with regard to my choices, but how those choices affected the people around me.'" A pause. "'But sometimes, life surprises you with second chances you didn't earn. Though I didn't deserve her forgiveness, Lexi saw something in me, and for reasons I'll never fully understand, she gave me the opportunity to prove I could be better. This isn't just about her giving me a shot at redemption. It's about understanding that if someone I care about is worthy of respect and love, then so is everyone.'"

When she pauses this time, she lets out a callous laugh.

"'To anyone who has been hurt by my past actions, I am truly, deeply sorry. You all deserved better. I can't erase what I did, and I don't expect your forgiveness, but I promise to spend the rest of my life proving I've learned from my mistakes. To Lexi, you didn't have to take a chance on me, but you did, and it's the greatest gift I've ever been given. I'll never have the words to thank you, but maybe these will do instead. I love you.'" Her eyes seem to flash black in the dim light of the restaurant as she sets the phone on the table and lifts her gaze to mine. "'I love you'? *Really*? And before you ask, no. I still don't have Instagram. Ronnie screenshotted your entire attention-seeking post and sent it to me."

"I don't…" I start to say, then trail off as my brain rewinds back through what she just said, and another thought takes center stage. *Attention-seeking?* "Wait, are you *mad* about that?" I sputter, jerking my chin toward her phone.

Blondie leans back in her seat, crossing her arms, drawing my gaze to her lovely collarbones and generous cleavage. Her sharp tone has my eyes darting back up where they belong. "Up until a few moments ago, I honestly wasn't really sure what I was. But now?" She shakes her head, her tongue pushing out her bottom lip. "Yeah, I'm fucking *mad*," she decides, her eyes hard as she glares at me. "When I first read this"—her finger taps against her phone screen—"I actually thought, for one ridiculous second, that you weren't being entirely selfish for once. That maybe…you were trying to protect me from what some people are saying online."

A heavy weight sinks into the pit of my stomach. So, then she *is* aware of the commentary. Or at least some of it. Does this mean she's changed her mind about our agreement?

Would it even matter if she has?

I want to ask if she's seen any of the positive stuff, or if she's only been exposed to the negative, but before I can even open my mouth, she says, "I told myself you probably thought this post would somehow manage any blowback and paint this whole fucked-up situation in a more positive light." She laughs again, and the sound cuts through me like glass. "But it's obvious now that *this*"—her upper lip curls as she stares down at her phone with disgust—"was never about me, but entirely about *you* and whatever it is *Damian* needs. And I…well, I just feel like an idiot for ever trying to rationalize your behavior."

I gape at her, open-mouthed. Seriously? I was doing her—doing both of us—a fucking favor, and this is how she reacts? "*This*," I counter, echoing the disdain in her tone as I reach for her phone, and lift it into the space between us for emphasis, giving it a shake, "was me helping you. You're welcome, by the way."

"*Helping* me?" she practically screeches before catching herself, taking a calming breath, and dropping her voice. "Aside from the fact that the wording in this escalates the perception of our relationship *way* beyond what we agreed to, can you not see how I might feel used? You have literally set me up as a tool to sell your bullshit redemption arc. For fuck sake, do you even *mean* any of what you wrote? Are you even remotely sorry about *any* of it?" Deflating, she rips the phone from my grasp and tosses it on the table. When she next speaks, it's as if all the fight has left her, the voice that held such fury only a moment before now barely a whisper. "Did you only write that post to stop your parents from disowning you? Because you're afraid they'll take away your *allowance*?" Though her tone is soft, she spits that final word with contempt.

The guilt that gnawed at me earlier fully surfaces now, sinking its teeth into my neck as if determined to rip out my throat. What the hell do I even say to that? Sorry for dragging you into my mess without a proper plan?

Maybe she's right to be pissed at me. The Instagram post, this stupid dinner… I don't even know if any of it is helping or if it's only making things worse. Part of me is convinced that my parents are just hanging me out to dry, waiting to see if I'll screw this up even further before cutting me loose for good.

I didn't want to admit it—not to myself, not to her—but that's the real reason I've been avoiding Blondie the last two weeks. Not because of midterms, not because I thought she might need space to adjust to the media frenzy, but because of this growing fear writhing inside me that all of this might have been for nothing. And the longer I let that silence stretch, the more intense that fear grew until, in a moment of desperation, I convinced myself that enduring this dinner would be better than another day of waiting for absolutely nothing.

So, what the fuck can I say that will in any way make this right between us? That will convince her I'm not the asshole she's making me out to be?

Definitely not what I find myself saying, that's for fucking sure.

"That's an awful lot of judgment coming from a paid accomplice." I sneer, returning her glower with a scowl of my own. "Don't act like you're suddenly above all this."

Blondie scoffs. "*Accomplice*? Accomplices work together, but every decision that impacts how people view us—how they view *me*—you've made without my input. So, no, I'm not your accomplice, Damian. I'm just another pawn for you to use and then cast away at your leisure once I've finished serving my purpose."

Plucking the napkin from her lap, she pushes back her seat and tosses the white cloth on the table before rising and grabbing her phone. As she shoves the device in the five-hundred-dollar clutch purse I bought her, she begins to walk past me, but then pauses mid-step beside my chair.

"These problems you're so worried about?" she murmurs, her tone quiet despite its serrated edge. "They're nothing compared to what other people face every day, so don't expect me to feel sorry for you because Mommy and Daddy aren't paying attention to you…or to play along with this. I refuse to be the crutch you lean on to justify your shitty behavior."

Then she walks away, leaving me to stew over her damning words alone.

The restaurant seems to go completely silent, or maybe it's Blondie's deafening judgment of me—my *own* judgment of me—that blocks everything else out.

Is that really what I did—place the entire weight of my public transformation on her shoulders by unknowingly turning her into some kind of unwilling symbol of my redemption?

I suppose I *did* know what I was doing. I actively chose to cast her in the role of my forgiver because I needed a way to repaint this picture of us in pretty colors, so people will only see the revision instead of the original image underneath. And using Blondie was the easiest way to do that.

It wasn't my intention to demean her. When I made that post, I merely wanted to show my parents that I *am* capable of owning up to my mistakes. Of taking responsibility like they want me to.

And besides, I do regret the list and the bet, so it's not like I didn't mean any of it. I *am* sorry, and I *was* thinking of Blondie's well-being when I wrote those words. Shit, I presented her as a benevolent goddess of forgiveness, but then…I never actually *asked* her for her forgiveness in the first place, and I realize now, that's the problem. I took that choice—that decision of whether I even deserve absolution—away from her, and pushed her into a role beyond what she bargained for just to prove a point to two people who might not even be listening.

Fuck. Blondie was right. This really was just another bullshit stunt, and I was too blinded by my own selfish needs that I couldn't even see it.

Mussing a hand through my hair, I down the rest of my wine in one gulp and push back my chair. When I stand, that's when I see it: the dozens of eyes watching me…and the phone across the room that is definitely filming me. Filming *us*.

And I have absolutely zero doubt that it just caught every second of Blondie storming out.

Limits help you understand where things end, but I can't figure out if I've reached mine or if I'm still heading toward the edge.

I push out a breath through my nose, and tap my pencil against page 356 of the calculus book sandwiched between my own open notebook and the freshman's beside me. It's Wednesday, which means it's tutoring night at the library for my required work study, and today, I'm working with a freckled guy named Warner, who is taking calculus as part of his computer science major…and not understanding any of it.

"Okay," I try again, "think of it this way. You're not trying to find where the function actually lands, but the value of where it's heading as it approaches that point. Does that make sense?"

Warner blinks down at the textbook, and I see the exact moment his eyes glaze over. When he looks up at me a few seconds later, I glimpse the answer to my question reflected in those glassy depths.

With another tired sigh, I lean back in my seat and brush a loose curl away from my face, pinning it behind my ear. We've been stuck on the same topic for an hour already, and I'm one explanation away from suggesting to Warner that he would be better off changing his major.

His pleading gaze meets mine again, and I let out a pensive hum. Maybe it's not that he's incapable of understanding the concept, he just needs to see the picture from a different viewpoint to actually grasp it.

Like Damian needed to see my viewpoint of his stupid fake profession of love, I sullenly muse.

I grimace at the unwanted image of his face in my mind and at the mental whisper of his name. It's been five days since we last spoke, since our not-so-private fight at Fernando's and my dramatic exit (and subsequent escape in an Uber), and I honestly don't know what's worse—that he doesn't seem to understand why I'm so fucking mad or that I'm mad at all.

This agreement was a stupid idea. Ronnie said it. Andie said it. *I* knew it. And yet, I had foolishly convinced myself I could do this, that I could stomach our past and what being his girlfriend would mean for the sake of my mom. And I could. I *was* doing it. And even though I would never admit it aloud except, perhaps, under threat of death, I was enjoying it. For the most part. Even if I actively made it seem like I wasn't.

And that, I now realize, is the problem. That over all these weeks of forced proximity and fake flirting, I allowed myself to forget that he is the sort of guy who would hurt me. Who *has* hurt me. I began to think (albeit not consciously—not until now), that he wasn't the same selfish asshole who pursued me and tricked me into thinking he was interested in me just to win a bet. Who spent *days* with me, smiling, flirting, pretending to need tutoring, just so I'd turn around and fuck him. Which I did. In public. Because I apparently have no fucking self-control.

But despite all that, what really pisses me off is that I let myself believe he meant it when he said he wanted to spare me from the toxic bullshit of the internet, and that maybe…just maybe…he was a decent person deep down, and not the same narcissistic fuckwad I had sex with in this very library. I was swayed by his pretty words, and easy charm, and by my own raging hormones…which I'm starting to think I should probably get checked out.

But then I saw that post and realized I was wrong. Because if Damian actually cared about me—about anyone other than himself, even a tiny bit—he wouldn't have been so self-serving and insincere.

And what's worse is, even though I know I was right to be mad—to call him out on his bullshit apology—the truth is, I'm just as bad as he is. Because more than anything, at this very moment, I'm only thinking about myself. Not about the other women on the list, who might see his post and be gullible enough to actually think he meant it. Not about his parents, who might be getting their hopes up that their son is actively trying to change. But about *me*—about what *I'll* do if Damian decides to call off this arrangement and I lose out on his money.

Because as angry as I am, as much as I'm hungry for vindication, I can't call this off, even though I'm tempted to. Mom's health—and making sure she gets her medication—is far more important to me than my own injured pride.

Beside me, Warner clears his throat, and I shake the thoughts away, willing my brain to focus. A new viewpoint, yes. That's exactly what Warner needs. Hell, I think I could do with one, too.

"Imagine you're driving toward a stop sign," I say, picking up my pencil and moving it along my open notebook like a car. Warner's eyes follow the movement, simultaneously hopeful and apprehensive, though mostly the latter. "I'm trying to guess where you'll stop based on how you're slowing down. I don't care if you hit the sign"—I draw a line at one end of the page—"or slam on the brakes too soon." I draw another line several inches away, then place the pencil down in-between them. "I just want to figure out where you're *supposed* to stop."

I'm about to ask Warner if that analogy in any way helps when a towering presence appears before our table, and my blood runs cold. I don't even need to look up to know who it is; I can sense him like my body has some kind of built-in fuckboy detector.

My eyes dart up, locking on Damian's obnoxious, smug face.

"Hi," he says in a chipper and unnervingly polite voice, as if we've never met before. "I'm looking for a tutor, and I hear you can help me."

My face hardens into a mask of stone. "Look elsewhere," I grumble. "Can't you see I'm already helping someone?"

I gesture vaguely to Warner, but Damian doesn't even spare him a glance.

"It really can't wait," he insists. "Big test tomorrow, and all that." When I don't respond, he places his hands on the table, and leans in until our faces are practically touching. "Please?" That single word escapes him in a quiet, pleading breath. "It's important."

Though my lips curve into a pleasant enough smile, my eyes narrow in disdain. "You know what else is important? Limits." I nod toward the calculus book, but my comment is double-edged. It isn't just math limits I'm talking about, but my own. Limits that he shamelessly crossed. "Now," I say, shifting my focus back to Warner, who looks exceedingly nervous to be trapped in the potential crossfire between Damian and me, "if you'll excuse us—"

"Uh…I think I get it now," the freshman stammers, stumbling as he jumps out of his chair and gathers up his belongings, clearly eager to be as far from our impending fight as possible. Or maybe he's just allergic to drama. I know I certainly am, though I seem to be at the center of a lot of it lately. "Thanks," he adds, actively avoiding both my gaze and Damian's as he shuffles away.

Damian raps his knuckles on the table. "Looks like you're free now."

I scowl. I needed Warner's signature on my timesheet for this session for it to count toward my work study hours, and now, thanks to Damian, the last sixty minutes were nothing but a big waste of time. "Well, that's just great. I hope you're willing to pay my tuition when they strip me of my scholarship for not completing my required work study."

"I mean, you know I'm good for it," he murmurs, then immediately backtracks when my expression turns mutinous. "Okay, that was clearly the wrong thing to say."

"Everything you say is the wrong thing," I mutter as I stand and begin to pack up my books.

Rounding the table, Damian spins the now vacant seat around and straddles it. "Aren't you even going to hear me out?" he asks. Folding his arms along the back of the chair, he plants his chin on top of his hands and peers up at me, pushing his lower lip out in a pout. "I came here to say I'm sorry."

I freeze with my hand halfway in my bag and bark out a loud, churlish laugh. "Oh, this should be good. Go on, then. If it's anything like your Instagram post, it's sure to ooze sincerity."

Damian frowns when I snatch up the last two books on the table and turn on my heel with a sneer.

As I storm off into the quiet stacks, I note the thud of hurried footsteps behind me. "Look, I know I messed up." He throws himself in front of me to block my path, and when our eyes lock, he holds up his hands in a gesture of peace. "The post was impulsive. I can admit that. Shit, it was an act of desperation. But," he quickly adds when I try to sidestep him, "mommy and daddy issues aside, I really did think it would help our situation. I honestly wasn't trying to make you feel used."

I snort. "Yes, because nothing says, 'I respect your autonomy,' quite like shoving words in my mouth."

He flinches. "Come on, that's not what I was trying to do. I was trying to"—he waves a flustered hand as if reaching for the right explanation—"control the narrative, not…force you into an uncomfortable position, though I can see now how you would take it that way."

I clutch the books tight to my chest. "That was almost an apology. Congratulations. Anything else?"

Running a hand through his hair, Damian pushes out an exasperated breath that hits me square in the face. I despise how my body reacts to it, how an unrelenting heat blooms deep in my core at this unwanted proximity of him. I hate it. I hate *him*. And yet…I can't deny how badly every atom of my very being desires him.

"I'm really trying here, Dornan," he whispers, and when those warm, honeyed eyes lift to mine, I nearly cave.

Because I want to believe it—that he can be different despite him proving, time and again, that he's the same old Damian who tricked me my freshman year. I want to believe it because, otherwise, I have to accept that the person I hate more than anyone in the entire world is also the very person my body seems to crave the most…and I'm struggling to reconcile the two.

I shake my head. "That's the problem," I say, forcing a needed wall up between us. "You think 'trying' means everything gets excused with an easy smile or wit because you have your name and your family's money to back it up. But it doesn't."

The light in his eyes instantly dims, taking any hint of an apology with it. "Because my problems are insignificant, right? Nothing at all compared to *real* problems." His tone is lethal and razor sharp, like a knife angled at my heart.

I step an inch closer, unafraid of getting cut. "Am I wrong?"

A tight, sarcastic smirk pulls at the corners of his lips. "Nope, that's me: privileged asshole who never has to face the consequences of my actions. Oh, wait…" His eyes blacken with derision. "Well, you got it half right, at least."

"Yeah," I retort, "the asshole part. Are we done here?"

He smiles again, though this time, the curve to his mouth is serpentine. Like pieces on a chess board, he mimics my movement, stepping closer, his long legs eating the distance between us. "I don't know. You tell me. *Are* we done?"

Part of me wants to be. It's been nearly two months of this, and I am beyond exhausted; I have no clue how I'll last until the deadline, or if there's even any point in keeping this charade going any longer. Maybe I should just swallow my pride and ask Ronnie for the money I need for my mom. It would certainly be easier than dealing with this.

"We could be," I answer. "Our impending 'break-up' is already plastered all over the internet according to Ronnie and Andie."

Thankfully, the video that aired of our fight at Fernando's didn't manage to pick up what we were saying, so it just looks like any other lover's spat, leaving the internet with nothing better to do than to theorize what we argued about. We could use that to our advantage, avoid any further scandal and take the easy out it offers us, ending things here and now. Or we can keep up this sham of an arrangement that I had fooled myself into thinking was actually working when in reality…who the hell knows what it was.

Damian shakes his head. "It's nothing that can't be walked back."

"With another lie?" I ask.

He exhales a strained laugh. "This whole thing between us is a lie, Dornan. It always has been. I don't know why you're suddenly so bent out of shape over that."

He's right. This entire situation *is* a lie, and I have willingly participated in this facade fully knowing that. But things changed when he made that post because that lie now extends into unwelcome territory. Into viewpoints I don't want to lie about…and into words I don't want to hear someone say to me, *about* me, unless they wholeheartedly mean them.

And the fact that Damian can't seem to see that is exactly why this won't work out.

He must see the unspoken decision on my face because he grabs me by the wrist when I try to walk away again. "Wait. Stop. I take it back. I do know why you're mad."

Bullshit. I tug at his grip on my arm, attempting to wrench my hand free.

"Stop," he breathes. "Please?"

I stiffen at that whispered request—at the raw desperation I sense behind that one word. There's no way he's faking that, not unless he's a way better actor than I gave him credit for.

Drawing in a breath, I turn to meet his gaze once more. "Okay, enlighten me. Why am I mad?"

He swallows, and the sound is audible in the hushed emptiness of the stacks. "Because I forced a narrative you didn't agree to. A narrative I had no right to force. It's not my place to say whether or not you forgive me. Or if you should."

His words and tone are alarmingly earnest, so much so I have difficulty discerning if he actually means it or if this is just another calculated lie. The lines between the two are becoming too blurry for me to see clearly.

That exhaustion I've felt far too frequently throughout the last month creeps in again, and I press my back to the bookcase behind me, rubbing a hand over my face. "I just don't know, Damian. This is all starting to feel… messy. I mean, is there even any point in continuing this?" I move a hand back and forth in the narrow space between our chests. "Is there a chance, however small, that your parents *actually* care whether you have a girlfriend or not? Is it even making a difference?"

His gaze bores into mine. "Maybe. More than likely not. But if we quit now, I won't ever know."

I see it then: the fear in his eyes. An achingly familiar terror I know all too well, having felt it every single day for the last year and a half myself. For the first time, I wonder if there's more to his situation than he's previously said. If his problems aren't quite as small as I berated him for.

"Besides," he continues before I can wrap my head around that thought, "it's helping you, isn't it? That's worth something at least."

My chest seizes at the sincerity in his tone and at the unabashed plea in his gaze. He might not have meant the apology he posted online, but he means this. *No one* is that good at lying.

A nervous feeling flutters in the bottom-most depths of my stomach. Would it be wrong of me to accept? Do I even want to?

Think of Mom. Do it for Mom, I remind myself, and that thought is all it takes to sway me.

"If I say yes," I begin, my tone tentative as I push away from the bookcase, "there will be no more spontaneous declarations of 'love' of any kind, got it?" I hold up a finger in Damian's face. "And you won't ever speak for me again regarding my opinion about *anything*, especially the bucket list. And don't for one second think I forgive you for it either, despite what the world might believe."

Damian gives me a curt nod. "Understood." A smile tempts the corners of his lips as his solemn expression slips a little. "Does this mean you're still in this thing with me?"

I release a weary breath through my nose. "What the hell. What's another seven months?"

An eternity, my conscience whines.

His face splits into a grin, and he chuckles. "Say what you want about me, Dornan, but either you have a serious cosplay addiction that requires immediate psychiatric attention…or you like being around me." He holds up one hand, bringing his thumb and pointer finger within an inch of each other, peering at me through the gap with one eye shut. "At least a little bit."

I choke out a laugh as I roughly push past him to return the books still bundled in my arms to their rightful homes on the shelves. "Don't flatter yourself."

Damian trails my every step, his mouth uncomfortably close to my ear as he says, "Oh, I am *very* flattered, Dornan. And for what it's worth, you aren't such bad company either, even when you are being prickly."

"I seriously hate you," I mutter, dipping my head to hide the heat that flares across my cheeks in response to how infuriatingly close he is to me.

"Sure, you do," Damian taunts, his presence nipping at my heels, even when I make a pointed display of quickening my pace to escape him. "Though, for someone who 'hates' me, you put a lot of energy into fighting with me when you could just walk away."

Am I literally not attempting to do that? I nearly shout at him. Instead, I fire back, "Maybe because you make it so easy," and stick my tongue out at him over my shoulder.

What is his problem? Is this just his personality, or does he get some sick pleasure out of riling me up?

"Or maybe," he croons, stepping in front of the exact shelf I'm looking for when we reach the mathematics section, his lips peeling back in a wicked grin, "because you don't actually hate me nearly as much as you pretend to."

I flash him a shit-eating grin of my own as I raise my arm to return one of the books, moving to slide it into a spot over his shoulder. "My homicidal urges around you would suggest otherwise."

He grabs my wrist, holding it and the book clutched in my hand out of reach of the shelf, his eyes piercing. When he speaks, his tone is equal parts flirty and teasing. "Are you *sure* that's what those urges are?"

There's that heat in my face again, except now, it's spreading throughout my whole body, starting at the exact place where his fingers are touching me. They burn into my skin, setting my entire nervous system ablaze. If someone were to come in here with an infrared scanner, I would light up like a damn Christmas tree.

What is happening right now? Damian is still holding my arm, and I'm not trying to pull away, and there's virtually *no* space separating us now. I can feel his heat on my face, and it's only matched by the heat building between my legs, and…oh, shit. That heat is going to make me do something really, *really* stupid.

"Care to find out?" I challenge in a voice I don't recognize because it definitely doesn't belong to me. It one hundred percent belongs to my evil, soul-possessing vagina.

That feral grin turns predatory. "You are positively adorable when you're angry. Has anyone ever told you that?"

Sense slams back into my body, and I glower at him, my words coming out in a gravelly rasp as I snipe back, "And you are insufferable when you're breathing, which is *all* the time. Has anyone ever told *you* that?"

Damian lets go of my arm and leans into my space, forcing me to take a step back. "Insufferable, huh? Hm. Well, it didn't stop you from fucking me. Twice."

His voice is sultry, like a kiss of silk against my skin.

This is dangerous, that line between reality and the lie more blurred than ever.

"Biggest regrets of my life," I retort, digging my heels in and holding my ground.

That irritatingly kissable mouth curls into a lopsided smile. "Don't lie, Dornan," Damian chides, his face so close all I would have to do is rise up on my toes if I wanted to kiss him. Which I don't. Not at all. Nope. *Definitely* not. He chuckles again as if he can read my thoughts on my face. His breath ghosts over my lips, near enough to steal the air between us, but not quite touching mine. It's like he's testing me. *Teasing* me. "We both know I rocked your world."

I scoff as several different comebacks battle for prominence in my head.

Bold claim for someone who doesn't even remember us fucking.

My world? Please, you didn't even rattle the headboard.

I've had more memorable paper cuts.

Do you ever get tired of the sound of your own voice? Asking for a friend.

Wow, you're even more impressed with yourself than I thought possible.

And yet, as he stares down at me with that coquettish glint in his eyes, all that comes out is, "You're a pig."

Then I'm dropping the two books in my hands to the floor and shoving him back into the bookcase, any remaining sanity leaving me completely until I am nothing but a vessel for that wild heat tearing through me. It guides my actions, controlling my every movement as I push up onto my toes to crash my lips into his, knocking my glasses askew.

Damian lets out a soft *hmph* of surprise, but loops his arms around my waist, pulling me closer with an eagerness that mirrors the explosion of need overtaking my senses, his mouth opening to swallow the moan that escapes me.

If this was a test, I failed. *Badly.* But unfortunately for me, I don't even have the mental capacity to wonder what the hell I'm doing. My sole focus is on the smooth slide of his tongue against mine, on the squeeze of his fingers as they inch down to grab my ass, teasing far too close for comfort to the backs of my thighs and that fire at the center of my legs that's quickly turning into a maddening ache.

There is nothing soft or gentle about this kiss. It's rough and sloppy, all tongues and teeth—the culmination of this unspoken tension and the weeks of verbal sparring between us finally coming to a long-overdue head.

Is this what hate sex would feel like? If so, I'm starting to see the appeal because I want nothing more than to push him to the floor and ride him like he's a goddamn pony, fucking him senseless right here in this aisle. If I hadn't already had sex with him once in this library, I might boil it down to an exhibitionist kink I wasn't aware I had. But it's not the location doing it for me—it's him. At this moment in time, I want Damian more than I ever wanted him freshman year, as if this loathing boiling under my skin is somehow feeding the attraction between us.

And there *is* attraction. It's insane, and it's clearly affecting my cognitive ability to make logical decisions, but it's there. If the bulge grazing my thigh is any indication, I think it's safe to assume that Damian is having the same indecent thoughts as me, equally aware of this…chemistry, or madness, or whatever you want to call this thing we have. He nips at my bottom lip, and I push against him, retaking control, knotting my fingers in his hair as I once again plunge my tongue into his mouth.

I could allow this to escalate. I could move my hand a few inches to the left, grab hold of his length, and let nature take its intended course. Maybe we just need to get it out of our systems. One final fuck, and be done with it.

But it wouldn't be enough, I know that. If it was, I wouldn't be standing here, wet and writhing beneath his touch when I've already had a taste. Twice, as he was so inclined to remind me.

That's when it hits me. Not his body, though that's certainly there, hard and unyielding under my wandering fingers, but the cold, unforgiving clarity of what I'm about to do.

Of what *we're* doing now.

Oh, my god. I'm *making out* with Damian Navarro. No, I'm not just making out with him, I'm freaking rutting against him in the middle of a public library like an unneutered dog with absolutely zero sense of shame or control. The same Damian whose face I've spent countless hours fantasizing about punching, not *kissing*. And here I was, about to drop my panties and let him fuck me again.

Some genius I am.

Mortification surges through me like a bucket's worth of ice water, dousing that fire inside me in an instant. I break the kiss, tearing my mouth away from his, and shove at his chest with so much force I stumble back a step.

For a moment, we just stare at each other, eyes locked, chests heaving.

Damian's lips are pink and swollen from the attention I gave them in my brief relapse into madness, his hair so deliciously disheveled I have to avert my gaze or risk tumbling back over that edge.

My eyes only swing up again when he laughs.

"I'm…going to take that to mean I was right," he says with a devilish grin, swiping a finger along his bottom lip.

A new heat rushes through me now, hotter and faster than the last, an inferno of rage and humiliation rolled up into one. Is this all just some game to him? Did he goad me, pushing my buttons on purpose, because he knew I'd kiss him?

If he did, then I really, sincerely hate him.

"This never happened," I growl. Glancing around to make sure the stacks are still empty, I straighten my clothes, adjust my glasses, and clear my throat, locking eyes with him one final time to reiterate my warning. "You hear me? *Never.*"

Damian says nothing, and I decide not to wait for whatever witty retort he's bound to cook up, instead storming off with the fury and indignation of a woman scorned. Part of me expects him to follow me, while another part is grateful he doesn't. The third part—the part I'm actively trying to ignore—is haunted by what just happened between us and by the lingering image of his face in my mind. Of the fleeting expression that crossed it as I spit out those final parting words.

An expression…that looked a hell of a lot like disappointment.

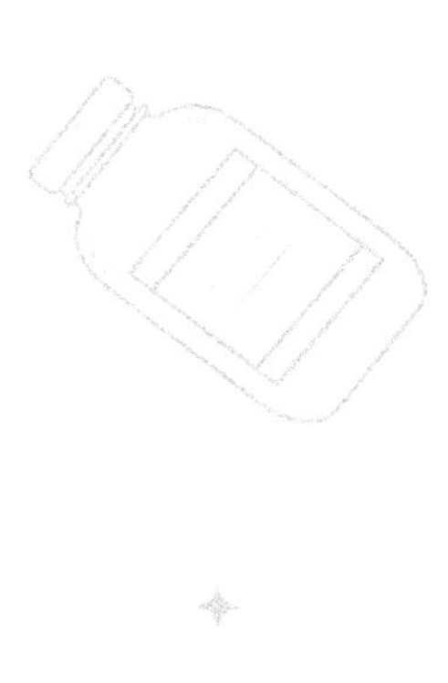

*No hay peor ciego que el que no quiere ver - There is no worse
blind person than the one who doesn't want to see*

*Translation: People ignore the truth when they don't want
to accept it. Which seems legit since I have no idea
what you're talking about.*

I wake up the next morning with a pounding headache and what might possibly be the biggest hard-on of my life. The fading images in my head tell me I must have been dreaming about Blondie—about our kiss in the library yesterday evening. A kiss I haven't been able to stop thinking about despite her warnings to forget the whole thing.

I still don't really know how last night escalated the way it did. One minute, I was pleading with Blondie to forgive me. The next, I was goading her just like I've made a habit of these past eight weeks, doing my best to get a rise out of her because I can't resist how damn cute she is when she's mad.

I don't know if it was our proximity in the library stacks, or some weird sort of mutual unrealized need to relive our previous quickie there, but something about the banter yesterday went beyond our usual teasing. There was a charge in the air between us—something magnetic, insistent, like the tension had been purposely pulling us closer for months, just waiting for the right moment to snap.

My cock aches at the memory of Blondie's tongue tangling eagerly with mine, of those perfect breasts pressed against my chest, of the desperate moans I seemed to so easily pull from her lips, like I was a puppeteer and I knew exactly which strings to tug.

I reach down and wrap my fingers around my aching length, rock hard beneath my touch, giving it a few slow strokes. Jesus Christ, just the thought of her mouth already has me on the verge of coming—

I jolt at the sudden, near deafening buzz of my phone vibrating across my bedside table. Snapping my eyes open, I stare up at the ceiling as I reluctantly release my cock.

What the fuck am I doing? Celibacy clearly does not agree with me if I'm this worked up over a kiss. A fucking *amazing* kiss, yeah, but still…it was only a kiss. I should not be this close to blowing my load like I'm some fifteen-year-old virgin getting his first handy.

My phone vibrates again, more insistent this time, and with a snarl of annoyance, I roll over and grab the device off the table. My erection instantly deflates when I see the name on the screen.

Swallowing, I swipe to answer.

"Greetings, Father," I say, my voice husky.

He scoffs. "About time. Do you always sleep in this late, hijo?"

I pull the phone away from my ear and glance at the screen again. What the fuck? It's not even eight o'clock. I don't know what kind of stimulants he puts in his morning horchata, but I'd hardly consider this sleeping in. Besides, my first class isn't until ten, which I quickly open my mouth to point out, except…that isn't what I end up saying. "Sorry, I was in the shower," I lie because, honestly, it's easier than enduring another second of his judgment.

He grunts (as much of an acknowledgment as I'm likely to get), then finally reveals why he bothered to call. "You do remember what this weekend is, don't you?"

It isn't a question. It's a test. And if my distant father calling me before I'm even out of bed hadn't already killed my erection, that comment and the doubt in his tone would certainly have done the trick.

An uncomfortable tightness grips my throat, and my voice goes hoarse for an entirely different reason when I rasp, "Of course, I do."

"Good." He sounds insultingly surprised. As if I'd ever forget. "I'll expect to see you tomorrow, then. As for Saturday, we fly out first thing, so don't be late. I'll text you the details."

"Okay." That's all I can find the strength to say. In our culture, this is supposed to be a time of celebration—of *joy*—but the truth is, I dread this holiday every year. And every year, I consider asking to skip it. I never do. Not because I don't have the balls to say it, but because I hate myself for even thinking of asking in the first place.

You're a coward, my conscience spits. I don't disagree.

"One last thing," my father adds.

I'm acutely aware of the silence on the other end of the line. It hums in my ears, stretching between us like static, prickling under my skin, buzzing, buzzing, buzzing—

"Your mother and I want you to bring that girl you're seeing with us to Guadalajara."

I go very still, convinced I didn't hear him correctly. Surely, I couldn't have. He and my mother haven't spoken a word to me in nearly two months, and haven't deigned themselves to even acknowledge my relationship with Blondie. And now…they want me to bring her with us to Mexico for Día de los Muertos? Excuse the fuck out of me?

"W-what?" I stammer, trying to wrap my head around what he's asking of me.

"Is there a problem?" he seems to growl, and I hear it again—the doubt in his tone. The disappointment.

He's onto you. Fucking say something.

"No," I answer quickly, squeezing my free hand into a fist to keep from slapping myself silly.

What are you going to do now, genius?

I scramble for words, for a suitable lie…and pray my dickhead father doesn't notice it in my voice. "I just…need to check with her to make sure her passport is up to date."

And try to convince her that this is a totally normal, sane request.

"Good," is all my father says in response. "Your abuela will want to meet her. As do I."

Without another word, the line goes dead.

Grimacing, I pull the phone from my ear.

Welp, this is it. This is the day I die. Because the second I tell Blondie about this, I have zero doubt that she's going to kill me.

The late October air is biting as I exit my building and cross the quad at a brisk pace, my phone call with my dad this morning still playing through my head like a bad song stuck on repeat. If today wasn't Halloween, I might be tempted to skip my planned outing with Blondie, not only to escape her wrath once I actually figure out how to ask her about Guadalajara, but also because—aside from a brief text exchange confirming we're still on for tonight—I haven't seen or talked to her since yesterday, and I don't want things to be awkward between us.

It'll only be awkward if you make it awkward, my conscience unhelpfully reminds me.

I roll my eyes. *Please, like I don't know how to make out with a girl and pretend it never happened.*

But then…kissing Blondie was different. I can't stop thinking about her plush lips on mine, about the feel of her slender curves under my hands, and I'm not sure if I can blame that on the simple fact that I keep allowing these physical things to happen between us despite my No Repeats rule. Shit, that rule is exactly why I should cancel right now and walk away—give us both some much-needed breathing space until our hormones, or whatever it is that's making us crazy horny for each other, have settled and we're thinking clearly again.

But canceling on her would mean missing out on Phi Sigma's legendary annual *Boos and Booze* party—the first shindig of the partying variation I've allowed myself to attend since our fauxmance began—and I refuse to let my costume, which I've been planning in meticulous detail for the past several weeks, go to waste. Sure, I could go on my own, but what kind of message would that send? It certainly wouldn't help to make it look any less like we've broken up. And regardless of what happened last night, I'm not ready to walk away from this agreement. Not when we've come this far already, and there's still a chance it can work.

No, what we need right now is a united front. And if there's one occasion when my parents can forgive me for attending a party, it's Halloween. So long as I behave myself, and don't get drunk or make a scene, it'll all be fine. And hopefully, in the meantime, Blondie and I can put these pesky break-up rumors to rest.

I tug my phone from my pocket and tap the screen, pulling up my chat thread with Blondie as I skip up the steps to Garfield Hall. Our last two messages glare at me, and though they're no tonally different from our other texts, I can't help second-guessing if that kiss yesterday ruined the dynamic between us.

Me

Are we still on for tonight? ◌ Where should I meet you? I can swing by at 9

Blondie

Garfield Hall. Room 237

Blondie has always been rather direct with me, but there was something so…blunt about her answer. Well, more blunt than usual. I'm probably imagining it. And if I'm not—if she *is* pissed at me for…I don't know, kissing her back?—well, then things are about to get a whole lot more awkward.

I yank open the door to the building and make my way up the necessary two flights of stairs to reach Room 237, as instructed. Returning my phone to my pocket, I straighten my back and, bracing myself, rap my knuckles sharply on the door. Beyond it, I hear the muffled cadence of voices, followed by a chorus of laughter, which bodes well for whatever mood I'm likely to find Blondie in. My heart thumps hard against my rib cage when the door opens a moment later, but it isn't my fake girlfriend who answers.

"Damian," Ronnie says, scowling at me from the other side of the threshold.

Right. I forgot. Blondie doesn't live on campus, so that must mean this is Ronnie's room.

"Well, hi there, Red." I grip the rim of my oversized hat and tip it forward in greeting. As I push it back into place, my eyes dip, noting the shiny fire-engine red platform boots and the minuscule Union Jack mini-dress that's barely long enough to protect her from an indecent exposure charge. "Nice costume. What are you supposed to be, some kind of British wet dream?"

"I'm Ginger Spice, dickhead. From the Spice Girls?" When I just stare at her blankly, she clicks her tongue. "*Ugh*, you uncultured swine. Anyway, what are *you* supposed to be?" she counters, looking me up and down. "A giant yellow douche?"

I snort. *Now, who's the uncultured swine?* "As much as I love the inside of a woman's vagina, if you must know, I'm—" Movement behind Ronnie catches my eye, and I let out a disturbed yelp of shock. "Dear god, what are you *wearing*?"

Blondie pauses halfway across the room and looks over at me, confusion furrowing her brow. She peers down at herself—as if, in the span of the last however many minutes, she somehow forgot what she put on her body— then glances back up at me, pushing her glasses up her cute little nose. "I'm a calculator," she answers, shrugging.

I brush past Ronnie and step into the room, gaping in horror at the ungodly sight before me. Up close, the costume is even worse than it had looked from the hallway. Blondie is basically dressed in an ankle-length black trash bag with sleeves that's been decorated with the same buttons and symbols you'd find on a graphing calculator. It's detailed…and beyond hideous.

"Listen, Dornan, I know math is your thing or whatever, but this is too far. That costume is a monstrosity." *And is taking your little cosplay fetish to a whole new uncomfortable level.*

"Hey, I made that!" I hear someone whine, and my gaze shifts to where Andie sits at one of the two desks in the dorm room, dressed in a green cloak, a platinum blonde wig that is striking against her tan complexion, and prosthetic elf ears, her hand frozen halfway to her face with a makeup brush clamped between her fingers. When she frowns at me, I clap my palms together and tilt my head in a plea for forgiveness.

"My sincerest apologies. Truly," I say before turning my attention back to Blondie. Did she run out of her cosplay fun money already or accept this as an act of charity? "Irregardless, you can't wear that."

"Irregardless isn't a word," Blondie retorts. "And why not? It's Halloween, and last I checked, this *is* a costume."

"Yeah," Ronnie barks. "She can wear whatever she wants, fuckwad."

I groan. "But if she wears that then *my* costume won't make sense." I pull the backpack I brought with me off my shoulder and plop it down on the floor between us. Unzipping it, I yank out the treasure inside. "It's our first Halloween together, baby," I say with all the gusto of a man proposing marriage. "We gotta coordinate."

Blondie reels back, her upper lip curling. "What the *hell* is that?"

I hold up the outfit I had specifically designed for her to accompany mine, unsure what part of it could possibly be confusing.

"It's a monkey costume," I answer, waving one hand at the outfit as if that will magically make them all appreciate the genius of my idea. "Monkey," I say again, slowly this time, pointing to the costume, and then gesturing to my own adventurer's ensemble, complete with collared shirt, pants, brown boots, spotted tie, and best of all, a ginormous cone-shaped hat. "The Man with the Yellow Hat," I proclaim proudly. When nobody in the room reacts, I ask, "Haven't any of you ever seen *Curious George*? Adorable animated rascal of a monkey and his BFF slash owner human? No?" A devastated gasp escapes me. "What kind of childhood did you even have?"

"One I clearly grew out of, unlike you, the grown man dressed as a cartoon character," Blondie mutters.

I pout. "Come on, Blondie. I can't be the Man with the Yellow Hat without a George. Please?"

"You don't actually expect me to wear a slutty monkey costume?" she says, aghast. Beside her, Ronnie nods in silent solidarity, which is rich considering the feisty redhead is one gentle breeze away from exposing her vagina to campus.

I press a hand to my chest, insulted. "The audacity," I scoff. "It's not slutty, it's *adorable*! Look at its little tail!" I poke said tail to make it wag, but this doesn't seem to sway her. So, I do the adult thing and resort to sulking. "And, like, not to be rude or whatever, but I refuse to be seen with you wearing *that*," I grumble, pointing at the black bag swallowing her body that's currently masquerading as a costume.

Blondie peers down at herself once again, but this time, instead of confusion, I glimpse a split second of indecision crossing her face. I jump at the opening.

"Come on, spider monkey," I plead, "what do you say?"

Her head snaps up, and she glowers at me. "If that is another *Twilight* reference, I might actually stab you." When I shrug, she lets out an irritated—but defeated—sigh. "*Fine,* but you have another thing coming if you think I'm going to climb you like a tree."

Ronnie and Andie snort at the same time, but otherwise say nothing. The knowing silence that follows is comment enough.

A few minutes later, Blondie is changed and the girls are ready to go, the door to Room 237 swinging open to greet me. It had gone without saying that I would wait out in the hallway to give Blondie privacy to change, and now that I see her in her costume…I can kind of see why she thought it was slutty.

The outfit is a hooded, long-sleeved dress made of soft, chocolate brown fleece, with a full-length zipper down the front, a curved tail that reaches for the floor, and cream-colored ears and a monkey face decorating the hood. While the costume itself isn't inherently slutty, on Blondie, it's borderline indecent, her generous cleavage and lengthy bare legs on display for all to see. Because this is her first time trying it on, I hadn't realized that the zip only goes so far up her chest, leaving a sizable amount of her delicious breasts exposed. And as for the hem of the dress, well…let's just say Ronnie isn't the only one at risk of getting arrested for flashing this evening.

"You look great," I assure her when she steps out into the hallway, and she responds with a glare, clearly less than enthused.

"Let's just go," she grunts.

The Phi Sigma house is on the other side of campus, a ten-or-so minute walk from Garfield Hall. Ronnie and Andie saunter a short distance ahead, occasionally glancing back at us over their shoulders and muttering in hushed whispers to each other, while Blondie and I amble along in what is quite possibly the most uncomfortable silence I've ever endured. I'm tempted to bring up the kiss, but think better of it. If she meant what she said—that the kiss never happened—then the last thing she'll want is for me to mention it now. Best to sweep it under the rug.

"Hey, so, I know it's really last minute," I hedge, "but I have to fly to Guadalajara to visit my abuela on Saturday…and my parents want you to come."

Blondie skids to a sudden halt. "*What?*"

My steps falter, though I hesitate for a beat before finally turning to meet her gaze. Her cheeks are pink (either from the cold or from her rising fury, possibly both) and she's shivering a little, goosebumps pimpling the tempting exposed skin of her—

Focus, Damian.

"I know," I say in a rush, averting my eyes lest Damian Jr. make an unwelcome appearance. It would be pretty hard to conceal him in this outfit, like trying to hide a boner in gym shorts. "My dad just sprung it on me this morning."

It wasn't the only thing that was sprung this morning, but I quickly swat that thought away.

Blondie sputters a few incomprehensible syllables before remembering how to speak. "You don't honestly expect me to leave the country for this, do you? I can't—"

I hold up a hand to interrupt her. "I'm not trying to force you into anything, Dornan, I promise. I learned my lesson." A flicker of doubt passes behind those green eyes, causing my stomach to clench. "Look, I have no issue making up some bullshit excuse about why you can't come. Just say the word, and I'll tell them your dog ate your passport."

"I don't have a dog," she points out.

"*Ugh*, fine. Your cat." I grimace.

She arches a brow. "I don't have a cat either. I'm allergic to them."

Oh. So, she's *not* a cat person. Very interesting.

"Are you allergic to dogs?" I ask, sounding far more invested in the answer than I intend.

She shakes her head. "No. And thank god for that because I adore them."

My heart skips at that, my lips pulling into a grin. Remembering myself, I force a frown in its place. "Whatever, pets are irrelevant. We'll just say you lost it. Or a stray ate it if you want to stick with the dog angle. Assuming you actually *have* a passport, that is."

She gives me a wary look, and my stomach twists again. Is that…guilt I feel? I can't fathom why. I'm giving her an out. But then…Blondie isn't stupid. The option to say no might be there, but she knows damn well I don't want her to take it. After all, isn't this outcome precisely what we've been working toward the past several weeks? Don't I *want* my parents to meet her?

Not like this, a voice whispers in the back of my head.

I don't get a chance to investigate what on earth it could possibly mean before Blondie says, "You *want* me to come, though, don't you?"

Like with my father this morning, the words don't form a question so much as they seek confirmation. I sigh. Which one of us is the terrible liar now?

"Of course, I want you to come. This is the first opening they've given me, Dornan, and I…well, I could really use the win with them. Besides, my dad was pretty insistent about meeting you."

"Yeah, but in a different country?" She winces as if she can't comprehend the idea.

"I mean, you'd technically be meeting them on the way there," I correct her, "*but*…if it makes any difference, it's only for one night, and it's all expenses paid. I'll even pay you overtime for the trouble. Also, we'd be flying on my family's private jet, so no long, boring waits at the airport."

"Um, excuse me," Ronnie says, popping up out of nowhere behind me like a human whack-a-mole. "Did I just hear the words 'private jet' and 'free vacation'?"

I frown at her over my shoulder. "I mean, it's not *really* a vacation, but—"

Ronnie slaps her palm over my mouth. "Say no more. If Lexi doesn't go, I will."

"Ohh, go where?" Andie asks, appearing on my other side.

I sigh behind the dainty hand still clamped around the bottom half of my face and shoot a pleading look at Blondie, who glances between the two possibly over-caffeinated, meddling gremlins she calls her friends. Someone clearly fed them after midnight.

Blondie exhales an equally exasperated breath. "Guess I better dig out my passport," she grumbles. Then, rolling her eyes, she carries on walking.

The Phi Sigma party is already raging by the time we make it to the house, the bass from the music thumping so loudly I can feel the reverberations in the pavement under my feet.

In my peripheral vision, I swear I see Blondie flinch, but before I can ask if something's wrong, she's barreling ahead through the open front door, arms linked with Ronnie and Andie.

The three-story Colonial Revival property is just one in a long line of houses on Greek Row here on campus, but from the crowd inside, I think it's safe to assume that the majority of Conwick is at this party tonight. I squeeze through the throng, making it a point to stick close to Blondie, who stays with her friends, though I don't begrudge her that. If anything, I think their presence is helping to ease the tension between us.

For the next few hours, we play beer pong, dance, and take countless photos for Ronnie's Instagram (and mine), providing all the evidence I need to nip those nasty break-up rumors in the bud. Throughout the night, several people approach us, eager to meet my "girlfriend," and I notice that, despite her increasingly intoxicated state and possible lingering annoyance with me, Blondie plays her role as well as ever, offering me well-timed smiles and pecks on the check when she thinks people might be looking. As the night wears on, I'm surprised I haven't seen Mason come out of whatever dark hole he belongs in, but then it dawns on me that he probably took one look at Blondie and made a beeline for the door. Clearly, he remembers my threat that I would let her crush his balls, and is lurking elsewhere in the house, out of sight.

By the time midnight rolls around, I am all danced out. Considering I haven't really been drinking, I lack the carefree buzz I now realize made these parties so fun, which means there's nothing to mask the exhaustion steadily creeping in. Fanning my face with my giant yellow hat, I retreat to the outskirts of the room, where I can catch my breath, take in the general ambiance, and just people-watch for a few.

And yet…the only person I find myself watching is Blondie. About an hour ago, Andie peeled away from the trio to go spend some time with her boyfriend, leaving me alone with Blondie and Ronnie, who has gone to get refills on their drinks. Or at least, I thought she had. Based on the two Solo cups Blondie's currently double-fisting, I think it's safe to say she's probably set on beverages for a while.

I watch her, transfixed, as she sways in the center of the frat's spacious living room, that adorable monkey hood up over her mane of golden curls, eyes at half mast behind her glasses as she moves to the beat of the music, her cheeks rosy from whatever liquid is in those red cups.

It dawns on me that I've never seen her like this—so at ease—and I can't help feeling that it's a damn shame that it took consuming copious amounts of alcohol to get her to relax. I wish I could see this side of her more, ideally in a sober setting. Though, I'd be lying if I said Damian Jr. wasn't enjoying the show.

Her costume rides up an inch as she swivels her hips, bending her knees and gyrating in a motion that reminds me very closely of fucking. My throat goes dry when she turns and I glimpse the glistening sweat beading between her breasts.

Jesus, she doesn't just look relaxed. She looks totally fuckable…which poses a problem. How the hell can I possibly forget about our kiss with her dancing like *that*?

Was this what she looked like the last time I saw her at a party? If so, I think Past Damian can be forgiven for his previous transgression of breaking our one cardinal rule.

"No," a voice barks beside me.

I startle, nearly dropping my gigantic hat as I jerk one step to the left, my eyes following the sound to Ronnie, who now stands less than a foot to my right, glaring at me. Where the shit did she come from? I swear, this girl really needs to stop popping up out of nowhere.

"Excuse me?" I croak.

"*No*," she says again, her tone firm. "Actually, allow me to rephrase: *fuck* no."

I stare at her blankly, totally lost. "Sorry, Red. You're going to have to elaborate."

Hostility darkens her features. "That look on your face just now when you were watching Lexi. Don't even *think* about it."

My attention shifts back to Blondie, who still dances alone in the middle of the room, completely oblivious to our conversation.

"I have no idea what you're talking abou—" I start to say, but Ronnie interrupts me.

"Cut the shit. The cutesy couple's costume. The trip to Mexico. She told me about the kiss in the library, dickweed, and I'm onto you. I know *exactly* what you were thinking just now, and it's not going to happen. Not on my watch."

So, Blondie *did* tell her friends about last night. Interesting behavior for someone who claims to want to forget it happened. But that's beside the point.

"You have it all wrong," I protest, though the words sound unconvincing. Probably because they're a lie. After all, wasn't I just imagining motor-boating Blondie's perfect breasts? I shake the image from my head before Damian Jr. gets any ideas. "*But* even if you didn't, I really don't see how it's any of your busine—"

She cuts me off again, poking me hard in the chest. "Lexi is my best friend, which *makes* it my business. And as her best friend, I am warning you now that if you don't behave like a fucking gentleman and stick to the agreement as planned, I will quite literally tear your balls from your body. I. Will. Tear. Them. Off." She enunciates each word with painful staccato jabs to my pectoral muscle. "Right off. I'm not above going to prison, bitch, so bear that in mind before you mess this up for her."

I bat her hand away and take a step back. "Chill your grill, Red. I'm not going to mess up anything. Our arrangement is mutually beneficial. I need it to work, too, remember?"

"Which is why you are going to keep your hands to yourself so it stays that way," she warns. Her russet brown eyes slide to the side, watching Blondie for a moment. Then, in a solemn voice I can only just hear over the music, she adds, "I don't think you understand how much she needs this money."

Okay, now, I'm definitely confused.

"Listen, I know she loves cosplay, but that's a bit extreme, isn't it?" I ask, trying not to sound like a judgmental asshole and failing completely. "It's not like she'll die if she doesn't get the cash to buy helmets, or weird wigs, or whatever off eBay."

Ronnie blinks up at me. "Cosplay? EBay? What the fuck are you talking about?"

I match her bewildered stare. "Lexi said she needs the money to finance her cosplay addiction." When Ronnie's frown deepens, I hold up my hands in a *don't shoot the messenger* gesture. "I'm just repeating what she told me."

Angry Spice blows out a loud breath through her nose. "Wow, okay, there's a lot to unpack there. Um, first, that's a load of horseshit. Andie is the one who cosplays, not Lexi. Second—and I have *no* idea why she would keep it a secret—but Lexi needs that money to pay for her mom's cancer meds."

As her words penetrate my brain, the entire world seems to drop away from under my feet, leaving me standing on nothing but air. It's a horrible, weightless sensation, like time has frozen around me, keeping me suspended in a moment I'd give anything to escape.

Or like I'm falling.

It's a feeling I know all too well…and one I never wanted to live through again. And yet, here I am as if the last four years have come full circle.

"What?" I gasp, fighting against the sudden tightening of my airway.

"Yeah," Ronnie says, eyeing me strangely, no doubt picking up on the panic ripping my insides to shreds. "Did she really not tell you? Her mom has leukemia, and their insurance recently stopped covering her prescription. A very *expensive* prescription that they wouldn't be able to afford without this money. So, yeah, you're right. Lexi won't die, but her mom could if this all goes south."

So, *that's* why she responded to the job listing. Oh, my god, I'm *such* an idiot.

It takes all my inner strength to stop the hysterical laugh that threatens to escape. Of all the people who could have answered the ad, what are the odds?

This has got to be the universe's bad idea of a joke.

"No, that can't be right. If what you're saying is true and she needs the money that badly, why didn't you offer to pay it? Aren't you loaded?" I ask.

"You think I didn't?" she fires back, her voice a menacing growl. "I *tried*. Twice. She refused me both times. Said she couldn't deal with the imbalance accepting that kind of money would bring to our friendship. Which is insane because I would *never* hold it against her, and my dads are awesome and would've paid all the costs, no questions asked."

I can easily see the pain behind Ronnie's eyes—the hurt she feels, visible only to those who know what to look for. Because her friend won't accept her help. Because there's nothing she can do to improve the situation that doesn't involve her money.

That's another feeling I'm intimately familiar with. That powerlessness.

It haunts me every fucking day.

"I…" The lump in my throat is so thick it's hard to swallow. "I had no idea…"

Ronnie crosses her arms in a huff. "Yeah, well, it seems like you aren't aware of a lot considering she's supposed to be your 'girlfriend.' Seriously, how well do you even know her?"

That's a great fucking question, Red. Clearly, not well at all.

I look back out at the living-room-space-turned-dance-floor where Blondie takes a swig from one of her two drinks and laughs at a silent joke no one else can hear.

I flail a limp hand in her direction. "I know she's on scholarship and that she's apparently a math prodigy, so she's smart or whatever. And I know first-hand that she can be mean. Like, *really* mean. Though, maybe not as mean as you. Oh, and she likes nerdy T-shirts and…pie? Wait, no. Pi," I correct, then frown, realizing that in no way clarified the difference.

Before I can amend my response, Ronnie snorts out a humorless laugh. "She's not just smart, dumbass. She's a genius. *Literally.* Like, smarter-than-Einstein smart."

"Okay. She's *really* smart. I get it."

"No, you *really* don't," Ronnie counters. "Do you think being intellectually gifted makes her life easier? Because newsflash: it doesn't. In a lot of ways, it's made her life harder."

Harder? I want to scream. *Harder than having a family member with cancer?*

But I don't say that. I can't.

"What is that supposed to mean?" I press.

Ronnie's face scrunches into a grimace as if she's searching for the right words to explain. "It means…Lexi sees the world in ways that you and I can't even begin to imagine. To her, numbers aren't just numbers—they're shapes, colors, patterns. Things she can physically *see* just like I see you standing in front of me now. And I'm not talking figuratively, like imagining something. I mean *literally.* On top of the many other ways her brilliant mind operates, Lexi has number-form synesthesia, so even if she hated math, she would never be able to escape it. It's as much a part of her as breathing. So, while, yes, she's *really* smart," she continues, mimicking the voice I made before when I said these very same words, "there's far more to it than that. The synesthesia is just one aspect of how her brain works—of how she experiences the world and everything in it in a way that isn't considered 'typical' by society's standards. Equations that normal people would need a calculator to solve, she can work out in her head like *that*"—she raises one hand and snaps her fingers—"but she couldn't tell you why someone's mad at her or what they're feeling unless they spell it out for her. Sometimes, she's blunt, or she'll fixate on stuff most of us wouldn't notice. You think she's mean?" She snorts again, the sound condescending. "She's not. She just doesn't sugarcoat things, which, frankly, is what I love most about her. *But* she doesn't always realize how her words or actions can come across. Because of that, Lexi had to learn how to adapt, to weigh every action and word. Of course, that doesn't mean she always gets it right…or that she always bothers. It depends on the situation and who's involved. When she feels the need to, though, she's good at masking—mirroring what people expect of her and becoming that person to help her fit in."

Ronnie must see the question in my eyes because she says, "Didn't you wonder how, for someone who is *so* bad at lying, she's weirdly convincing as your fake girlfriend? That's her masking. It's what makes her seem like she's got her shit together when, in reality, she doesn't. Far from it. Behind that mask, she's always on edge, like she's walking a tightrope, always one misstep from slipping. Always questioning everything because she doesn't comprehend situations or interactions the same way we do. It's why she's not so great with change. She can adjust if she has to, and she's open to some stuff so long as the push to get there is gentle, but she gets overstimulated and anxious easily, so it takes her time.

"Because of that, her childhood was kind of hard. The way she is, it made her…a lot at times. Especially for her dad. Lexi was this brilliant, quirky kid who saw math everywhere she looked, who understood things those around her didn't, but who sometimes needed a little extra patience as she tried to process the world, and he just…bailed. He left her mom to handle everything on her own."

Why are you telling me all this? I'm tempted to say, but I can't find the words. Or maybe I'm just so desperate to hear more about Blondie that I can't bring myself to make Ronnie stop.

"Wait, he left because she was *smart*?" I ask, overwhelmed and completely taken aback by this unexpected onslaught of information. This is definitely way more than Blondie and I ever agreed to share with each other regarding our personal lives, and I'm not sure if she'd be pissed her friend is telling me this, or simply grateful that she didn't have to do it herself.

"*No*," Ronnie counters, her tone defensive, "he left because he was an asshole who couldn't handle raising a kid who was 'different.' And Lexi picked up on that. It's why she is the way she is. Why she alternates between pulling away one minute and overcompensating the next, like she's got to prove she's worth sticking around for. And why she takes it so hard when she's let down. Since her dad walked out, she learned to deal with most things on her own because she grew up with this constant, nagging feeling that she was 'too much' for the people who were supposed to love her."

I shake my head in disbelief. "I haven't met her mom, but I met her aunt, and I didn't get the impression she's the kind of person who would ever treat Lexi that way."

Ronnie scoffs. "Of course not. Gina and Carol are saints. Gina stepped up when Lexi's dad walked out, and together, they raised Lexi and did everything they could to make her feel normal…even when she wasn't. Not in a bad way, but you know what I'm saying. Neither of them ever once made Lexi feel like she had to change who she was. But that doesn't mean other people treat her the same way. She's spent years trying to balance being herself with being what everyone else thinks she should be. Can you imagine how exhausting that is? It's why she doesn't have a lot of friends. Because she's been burned so many times that finding people who would understand and put up with her eccentricities stopped being worth the hassle."

"And yet, she found you," I point out. "And Andie."

"Yes, well"—Ronnie waves a dismissive hand—"I have a sixth sense about people. I took one look at Lexi and knew she was my soulmate. And Andie's a weirdo in her own right. The two of them are like two nerdy peas in a pod."

I consider everything Ronnie's just told me, trying to formulate my thoughts into words.

"Is that…the stuff with her mom, I mean…why she's at Conwick instead of some Ivy League college? If she's as smart as you say—if she really is some kind of math prodigy—then surely, she could've gone to any school she wanted."

Ronnie nods, her face crumpling a little. "Lexi got full-ride offers to every Ivy League and elite research university you can name. MIT practically begged her to go there. Before her mom got sick, her future was set. She was going to attend her dream school, and her high school boyfriend got into Harvard, so they were going to move to Boston together."

Boyfriend? That thought sends an unexpected rush of jealousy racing through me. I should probably examine why more closely, but my attention is diverted when Ronnie continues.

"But then senior year hit, and halfway through the spring semester, her mom got diagnosed. The admission deadlines had already passed, but Conwick made an exception for Lexi, and without hesitation, she gave up her dream college to stay in Newport and be here for Carol through her chemo. If it was just losing out on MIT, I think it would've been less of a blow, but her prick boyfriend dumped her the second she told him she wasn't going to Boston."

That flash of jealousy returns, but it's angry this time. Vengeful. I quickly tamp it down, hooked onto Ronnie's every word with bated breath.

"The last year and a half has royally sucked for her. And all the while, she keeps up this act like she's fine. But she's not. Not really. She's still giving everything she has, trying to save her mom and hold it all together, and meanwhile, you're over here thinking this is about cosplay."

I recoil at the venom in her voice. Well, that certainly took a turn.

"I didn't know! If I had…" I trail off. If I had…what?

What the fuck would I have done?

I can only assume Ronnie is wondering the same thing because her next words are biting. "Lexi's been let down too many times, and ironically, one of those times was by *you*. She can try to downplay it all she wants, but she was really hurt by that whole thing with the bet. It might not seem like a big deal to you, a name on a list—who cares? But for someone who rarely opens up to people…it seriously fucked with her. Not to mention, it *literally* ruined spring break for her, which I am so angry about since you have *no* idea how hard it was to get her to agree to go on a plane in the first place."

Is all of that true? The spring break part lines up—Mason chose then of all times to drop his stupid video, right before a bunch of us were due to go to Cabo, a trip my parents promptly put an end to when the video went viral. But what about the rest? I know Blondie harbors some unresolved aggression toward me for the whole bucket list fiasco, but I assumed that was just because I embarrassed her on a public scale, not because I *actually* hurt her feelings. It never seemed that serious to me.

And that, my conscience sneers, *is precisely why you don't deserve her forgiveness.*

"Do you get it now? Why I don't trust you?" Ronnie hisses, dropping her voice. "Why I *never* wanted her to do this? Things with you two have already crossed a dangerous line, and if you screw this up, it's not just her mom's literal *life* at stake, it's Lexi's faith in people. And any faith she may ever consider placing in someone again. So, if you're planning on just fucking her around, getting your dick wet, and then disappearing again, I'd think twice. Find some other willing pussy and leave her out of it."

"That's not what I'm doing," I nearly shout, surprised at my own vehemence.

Ronnie drops her gaze and shrugs, picking at her polished red nails. "For her sake, I hope that's the truth. And if it's not…" Her eyes snap back to mine. "Well, I suppose it's a good thing I look great in orange."

Without another word, she trots off, leaving me reeling.

I don't know how long I stand there, completely stupefied by my conversation with Ronnie, but when I next look up, Blondie is directly in front of me, staring at me through narrowed eyes. The two cups she was previously holding have mysteriously vanished.

Leaning into my space, she murmurs, "Your head looks like a traffic cone." Then she giggles, dangling off my shoulder with one hand and batting at my hat with the other, like a kitten that's had one too many sniffs of catnip.

Well, someone's had a bit too much to drink.

I fight the urge to laugh, giving her a placating smile. "You look like you're enjoying yourself."

She nods, her eyes glassy. "The jungle juice is really good."

"You know," I say, curling my arm around her waist when she stumbles back a step, "I think this little monkey has had enough of the jungle for one night. Why don't I take you home?"

She considers me for a moment, scratching her chin. "Sleep *does* sound nice," she concedes, her words slurring.

"I agree. Let me just…" I trail off, searching the surrounding faces as I steer Blondie through the crowd of fellow partygoers in the general direction of the front door. As we take a detour through the kitchen, I glimpse a familiar blonde wig by the patio doors leading out back. "Andie, hey," I call to her, crossing the space as quickly as escorting an inebriated drunk allows.

When she turns, I forget what I was going to say, my focus homing in on her costume…and the outfit her boyfriend is wearing beside her.

"Wait, what are you two supposed to be?" The words come out somewhat accusatory, prompting Andie to give me a curious look.

"Legolas and Gimli," she answers as Eli nods at me from behind a large braided fake beard, holding up a prop ax for me to see. "From *The Lord of the Rings.*"

Excitement ripples through me, and I turn to Blondie, about to joyously shout, "Couples' costumes! See? It's a thing!" only to realize she's practically half unconscious at this point and likely wouldn't remember it.

"Cool, cool, cool. You guys look great," I say instead, a rising disappointment extinguishing my glee. "Anyway, could you do me a huge solid and inform your cousin, Satan, the lord and ruler of Hell, that I took Lexi home? To clarify, I mean to her house. Where I will make sure she's settled and safe and then proceed to go back to my own dorm. *Alone.* I feel the distinction is important here." I glimpse a flash of red hair out of the corner of my eye, but when I turn to look, it's gone, leaving only a shiver of dread in its wake. "I'd tell her myself," I stage-whisper, "but I think she might be hiding a shank in that scrap of a dress, and I don't really feel like getting stabbed on this particular evening."

Andie presses the side of her fist to her mouth, suppressing a laugh. "I'll tell her," she promises just as Eli says, "I wouldn't put it past her."

I give him a knowing glance, bro to bro. This guy totally gets it.

"May the force be with you," Eli adds with an encouraging nod at Blondie, who giggles again and boops me on the nose.

"Wrong universe, dude!" Andie frowns, lightly elbowing her boyfriend in the ribs. "Good lord, it's not even the same genre!"

Shaking my head, I carry on, making it roughly halfway to the front door before I feel a light tap on the back of my arm. I turn, shuffling Blondie, who stumbles a little, only to find Andie standing behind us.

"Ronnie means well," she says, her expression apologetic. "Try not to take it too personally, okay? She—*we're*—just worried about Lexi."

We both look down at Blondie, who's discovered a newfound fascination with the tail sewn onto the back of her costume.

"I know," I mutter softly, but what I really want to say is, *So am I.* "Though, I think, for tonight at least, the only thing we have to worry about is the wicked hangover she's going to have tomorrow."

Andie flashes a kind smile at me, then nods and retreats back into the party.

With a sigh, I guide Blondie the rest of the way to the front door, and lead her outside into the biting night air. As the chill rips through me, I find myself peering down at her bare chest and legs, and wishing I had a jacket to offer her. But if Blondie *is* cold, she doesn't complain. If anything, all that alcohol in her system is doing a damn good job keeping her warm.

I keep an eye on her fumbling steps as we pass a couple fucking on the grass by the side of the house and at least four separate people passed out in and around the bushes out front. Jeez, less than two months away from the party scene and I forgot how sloppy Conwick students can get.

Yup. I am definitely ready to call it a night.

Blondie's house isn't far from campus, but it's far enough that it will take forever to get there if we continue at the glacial pace she's setting. Stopping her with a gentle hand on her upper arm, I step in her path and turn in place, bending my knees until I'm squatting on the sidewalk in front of her.

"Come on, spider monkey. Hop on."

When she doesn't immediately move, I pat my lower back for clarification.

A shiver rolls up my spine when she lightly trails a fingertip over my shoulder. "I recall telling you I wouldn't climb you like a tree, Mr. Giant Banana."

I snort, peering back at her. "I think that was *before* you drank a gallon of Everclear. Come on, I'm just helping you home."

That's all the convincing it takes. And I instantly regret it.

Blondie climbs onto my back, hooking those mile-long legs around my waist, and I swallow at the warm press of her breasts to my back and the heat of her breath on the side of my neck. I've never been more aware of her body, which is just so fucking typical when I'm trying to do the gentlemanly thing and take her home. She's drunk out of her mind, for fuck sake. The last thought on mine should be how it would feel to be inside her again.

For the next five minutes, I distract myself with the worst kind of boner-killing thoughts, but even the most grotesque visuals of my abuela wearing lingerie are not enough to stop me from thinking about Blondie. I'm so consumed by the idea of her that it takes me far too long to realize I didn't imagine the gentle rasp of her voice in my ear.

"What?" I choke out, repositioning my grip on her legs, and trying—and failing—to ignore the heat of her bare skin against my fingers.

"Did you know?" she says, her words sloshy, like they're on a spin cycle in a washing machine.

I clear my throat. "Know what?"

"That I was going to kiss you," she breathes.

Her tone isn't reproachful, but curious. Still, I bristle at the question—not at the mention of the kiss itself, but at the notion that I had somehow pre-empted it. Not just that I knew it was coming, but that I had *expected* it.

Did you? my conscience asks me.

"No," I answer, and it's the truth. *But I think part of me hoped you would.*

"I saw it, you know," she mumbles into the side of my neck, coaxing a shudder over my skin. "When I said to forget about it, you were disappointed."

I release a breathy laugh. "What can I say? It was a good kiss."

Out of the corner of my eye, I glimpse her glasses sliding down her nose, and I reach over my shoulder to push them back up before they can fall off her face. When I do, she makes a cute little grunting sound, like she's annoyed I've done something nice for her.

Neither of us says another word the rest of the walk to Blondie's house. I take her as close to the porch stairs as I can get, shifting my back to face them to minimize the drop to the ground, then carefully ease her down as she slides to her feet.

When I turn around to say goodnight, I half expect to find her already at the front door. Part of me is even preparing to find said door slammed without so much as a thank you. What I do *not* expect is Blondie's face hovering within an inch of mine as she steadies herself with her hands on my shoulders.

"It annoys me to admit this," she whispers, her breath hot on my cheeks, "but I'm attracted to you. Like *really* attracted to you. My body"—she inches forward, and I have to literally plead with Jesus to keep my eyes from dipping down to her cleavage, which is dangerously close to my lips—"is very fond of your body. And I think you're attracted to me, too."

The huge lump in my throat is only outmatched by the hardening bulge in my pants.

"Anyone with eyes and common sense would be attracted to you, Dornan," I say, my voice thick. "I have both."

"Well, then…" She leans deeper into my space, her knee nudging between my legs. "We should do something about that."

This is wrong. She's drunk, my conscience scolds me. *Put a stop to this right now, asshole.*

Laying my hands on Blondie's shoulders, I gently push her back. "If you're trying to tell me you want to be my real girlfriend now, that's not part of the deal—"

I barely get that last word out before Blondie laughs. Scratch that—laugh isn't a strong enough word. This is a full-on, evil, "I have a plot to end the world, and now, you will die, Mr. Bond" cackle.

"That's the last thing I want," she wheezes, giddy with amusement.

What do you know? Hits to the ego are effective boner killers, too.

My lips purse. "Then what *do* you want?"

I don't know why I ask. I don't know why I don't just herd her inside and then leave this night in my rear-view mirror, where it belongs. Talking to Blondie while she's in this state is like trying to have a conversation with an actual monkey. Sure, we understand each other a little, but it's mostly hand gestures (often crude ones) and throwing verbal shit.

"To change the rules," she answers, her tongue darting out to lick across her bottom lip, which she now pulls between her front teeth just to torture me.

I force my attention up, meeting her gaze. "The rules?" I parrot, confused. "What rules?"

She rolls her eyes. "Of our agreement. We're in the unique position of sharing a mutual attraction while also despising each other. Which *means*," she continues, surprisingly eloquent now for someone who just downed an unhealthy amount of jungle juice, "we don't have to worry about anyone 'catching the feels.' There's no chance of me falling for you, and well, you're just completely incapable of feelings at all, so, yeah. No problemo."

No problemo? More like no comprendo.

"Dornan, I don't really know where you're going with this. I think you might have to spell it out for me—"

"I want to put sex on the table," she blurts out.

"I…what?" is all I can manage. I'm sure my expression is equally articulate.

"Sex," she repeats, louder this time, like the problem before was her volume. "I want to have it. With you. Again. For the third time. We already had it twice." She holds up two fingers. "Now, I'd like to have it thrice. Then maybe some more times after that." All her fingers are upright now, and she waggles them at me with a mischievous grin.

A weaker man would give in to temptation. A weaker man wouldn't hesitate to take what she's offering, no questions asked. And not because any guy would be an idiot to turn down no-strings-attached sex, but because Blondie is a fucking catch. She's smart, sexy as hell, funnier than she realizes…

And that is exactly why I can't do this.

"I…don't think that's a good idea," I say carefully, inching back to put some space between us.

Her expression grows stormy. "Tell me you don't want to fuck me."

My cock twitches, but I stand firm. "That's irrelevant."

"No, it's not," she protests, stepping off the stair so we're on even ground again, and her words are suddenly so clear and sharp that, if it wasn't for the alcohol smell on her breath, I would wonder if she was just pretending to be drunk before. She takes another step closer. "Let's be real for a minute—I know what I said about no sex, but in practice, it isn't working. We're both horny as shit, and this is a perfect solution to a mutual problem. A workplace perk, if you will."

My jaw clenches as the arousal I've been fighting abruptly dies at her words. Workplace perk? Is she being serious right now? My dick is not a grab-and-go breakfast bar or a dental plan.

For a guy who's seen more ass than a public toilet, I'm surprisingly scandalized by the idea. Anger bubbles under my skin, and I can feel the flush of heat overtaking me like a bad sunburn until I realize that I'm not just angry, I'm *furious*. It pisses me off that she would suggest this, throwing a wrench into what has been, thus far, an otherwise successful arrangement. It makes me absolutely incensed to think that, if I say no, she might get her jollies somewhere else, with some other guy who isn't me. Above all, I'm positively livid that she would reduce herself to something as unfeeling as being my fuck buddy when she deserves so much more.

It takes me a moment too long to process the thought that just steamrolled through my head. I have no idea where that came from. And what the fuck did I even mean by 'she deserves so much more'? More what? Surely not—

My stomach drops. Oh, no. No, no, no. It can't be.

Fuck.

"I wouldn't want more if that's what you're worried about," Blondie says in what is easily the most ironic, cruel twist of the evening.

Because I like her. I *like* Blondie. I can see that now. And not in a platonic, fake girlfriend kind of way, but in a I-want-to-kiss-every-inch-of-your-body-until-you-come kind of way.

In a if-I-let-myself-get-close-to-you-like-that-again-I-might-actually-fall-for-you kind of way.

How could I have allowed this to happen? For fuck's sake, I have actively pushed away every woman I've ever slept with, especially since starting at Conwick, to avoid this very outcome, and I sure as shit didn't go into this fake relationship looking for a real girlfriend. But then, I've never let myself get close to someone like I have with Blondie. And despite trying our best to keep things professional (or as professional as a fake relationship can be), I've come to know her on a level I've never known anyone before. I *know* her… and now, thanks to Ronnie, I can truly see her.

"Are you listening to me?" Blondie asks, and I jerk out of my thoughts, swallowing hard.

My hands curl into fists, as if that will somehow quell the hurricane of emotions thrashing inside me. "You're drunk," I whisper, finding it difficult to speak. "You won't feel this way in the morning."

Will *I*? Or is what I'm feeling now just a weird blip? A momentary lapse in sanity?

One glance at those stunning green eyes and I know the answer. If this is a blip, a lapse in sanity, then the last two months have made me completely deranged. Because I don't just like Blondie, I *really* like her. How could I not? She's gorgeous, has a fiery temper, and is smarter than I'll ever be, genius or not. Shit, I think I've liked her for a while now, and I just haven't had the balls to admit it…or the sense to accept it. Or the courage. Because liking Blondie means embracing the very real possibility that I might eventually lose her, and that is a reality I'm not ready to face. It's easier to never have her at all than to open myself back up to that kind of pain.

But explaining that to Blondie would require telling her about my past, and I don't think I'm ready for that either. Not yet, anyway.

Maybe not ever.

"You honestly think this will just go away overnight? If that's the case, then why did I kiss you?" she challenges, taking a step into my personal space again. When I don't respond, she lets out an irritated whine. "Seriously, I only drank as much as I did tonight so I could work up the nerve to—"

"Ask me to be friends with benefits?" I spit, the words sour on my tongue.

If she was anyone else, I would've had no trouble saying yes. Getting laid was never my problem. The feelings behind it were always the impossible part.

And those feelings, however problematic, are exactly why I have to say no. It would be wrong to do otherwise, and not just because she's drunk, and I'm literally paying her to be around me, but because I'd be taking advantage of a situation she doesn't even want to be in but *needs* to be in to help her mom. Her *sick* mom.

Sick…just like Jamie was.

Blondie snorts, pulling me out of that unwelcome thought. "I mean, we're hardly friends, Damian."

There it is. The real crux of this little *feelings* dilemma. Blondie might want to fuck me, but she sure as hell doesn't like me, and honestly, I doubt she ever will. Not after what I've done to her. Not after how I treated her…

And I just don't know if I can put myself through that.

"I think," I begin, my voice low but unwavering. Firm. "For the sake of our agreement, we should keep things professional…and stick to the rules as they are."

Blondie must hear the finality in my tone because she doesn't argue, though the daggers she shoots at me from those lovely eyes cut through me just as easily as any words. With a delicate sniff, she takes a step back, widening that berth between us once more, then she lifts her hand to the neckline of her costume…and starts to unzip it.

"What are you doing?" I nearly shout, keeping my eyes locked on her face so I don't ogle her. Despite my efforts, I'm all too aware of her black lace panties and bra and all that skin, which is now exposed to the elements.

"Returning your costume," she answers simply, "and reminding you what you're missing out on."

She steps out of the outfit, picks it up off the ground, and hurls it at me before storming up the porch stairs and slamming the front door behind her.

I glance at the bundle of fleece in my hands, then over at the spot where Blondie last stood, unable to find the strength in my legs to move. Well, I guess I was right about one thing when I woke up this morning.

Blondie is definitely going to kill me.

CHAPTER
NINETEEN

✦ *Lexi* ✦

NOVEMBER

When Damian picks me up Saturday morning, I'm forced to acknowledge that the past thirty-one hours were not some lucid fever dream. Nope, that was really me getting drunk in a monkey costume and riding on Damian's back through the streets of Newport. That was really me digging out my passport (which—for someone who has never left the U.S.—I only have as a second form of identification and because my mom said I should have one "just in case") and packing my bags for this insane trip to Guadalajara. A trip I had to lie through my teeth about to explain why I won't be home again until tomorrow evening.

Luckily, Ronnie—albeit reluctantly—agreed to help cover my lie. As far as Mom and Gina are concerned, Ronnie, Andie, and I will be spending the night in Providence to celebrate the end of midterms. And to avoid my mother or aunt finding out that I'm actually out of the country, I will conveniently forget my phone on my desk, half obscured by a few shirts that I "decided against bringing with me and had haphazardly tossed to the side when packing." You know, should either of them ask.

It's definitely not the smartest move I've ever made, but in terms of deniability, it was safer to leave it behind, what with modern technology and its ability to track people. My mom might trust me, but she does have a habit of checking the tracking app at random to make sure I'm alive (and where I said I would be), and her noticing I'm not in Providence but in freaking Mexico is a risk I'm not willing to take.

Ronnie's only demands in exchange for her complicity were that I put her number in Damian's phone (so that, if something *does* happen, one of us can get in touch with her and let her know what's going on) *and* that I check in with her via said phone once every six hours with the exception of the time I spend sleeping. I had tried to tell her that I'll be out of the country for less than a full day—not even one complete rotation of the Earth—and the odds of anything bad happening were practically zero, but she insisted, and I wasn't in the mood to argue.

I had asked Damian to wait down the road so Mom and Gina wouldn't see him parked outside the house, but I still glance over my shoulder as I speed-walk toward his car to make sure they aren't watching me through the windows, either to wave goodbye or just to make sure I get there safely. Although it's fairly early, and the coast seems to be clear, I don't dawdle; I quickly throw my bag in his trunk and then hurry over to the passenger door.

"Dornan," he says by way of greeting when I climb into the seat beside him. I avoid his gaze, but to my unending annoyance, I can see the smug grin tugging at his lips out of the corner of my eye.

Keeping my own expression drawn, I respond with a curt, "Fuckboy."

He barks out a laugh. "Well, that answers that question. You aren't a morning person."

I can feel his eyes burning into the side of my face, and the silence between us swells with a tense sort of anticipation as if he's waiting for me to speak… or just to look at him. I can't bring myself to do either. Partly because I have no idea what to say, but mostly because I don't want to see it—the memory of how I acted the other night reflected in the depths of his eyes.

While certain parts of that night are spotty at best, I unfortunately wasn't *quite* drunk enough to wipe the full recollection from my brain. And even more unfortunately, the segments I remember the clearest are the most mortifying.

Me, propositioning Damian since my raging libido apparently knows no bounds, and it seems I am incapable of going nine months without getting dicked down.

Me, stripping to my underwear when he refused in the hope that seeing me (almost) naked would overwhelm him with such insatiable lust he'd change his mind.

Spoiler alert: it didn't. And now, I just feel like an idiot. Again.

Damian pulls away from the curb, and we drive in silence for a few minutes, the quiet stretching until it's like an overinflated balloon about to pop.

"You know, you're going to have to look at me sometime this weekend," he says. "And exchange more than one word with me. Ideally." When I don't respond, he adds in a soft voice I barely recognize, "It's not too late to back out. If you want me to take you home, I will."

I have to resist the temptation to look at him—to gauge if he's actually being honest with me or if he's only saying that to get me to crack. It would be so easy to brush off the sentiment, to assume it's just another lie, but… the sincerity in his tone tells me it's not.

A flush creeps up my neck, and I can see my cheeks burning scarlet in the side-view mirror. "It's not that." The words tumble out in a rush.

"Then what is it?" Damian asks.

I slump in my seat, lifting my shoulders and tucking my chin into my chest, like I'm a turtle trying to escape into my shell. "I'm embarrassed."

Damian considers that, and I wonder if he's going to press the matter— if he's going to make me spell out what I'm embarrassed about (despite knowing damn well what I'm referring to) just to torment me for his own entertainment.

I wait for it. For the teasing. For the playful, sarcastic remarks. But they never come.

Instead, I sense his eyes on my face again as he says in that same surprisingly gentle voice, "You don't have to be. It's forgotten."

We're both quiet for the remainder of the brief drive to the airport, and I know from the second we arrive that this is going to be unlike any other flight I've ever been on. Not that I've been on many—just the flight to Santa Cruz and the flight back, but still. The fact that Damian drives right up to the freaking plane is indication enough.

Airport staff are waiting for us outside the car, even going so far as to open our doors and retrieve our bags from the trunk as soon as we're parked. I glance at Damian, but he doesn't notice my questioning gaze as he climbs out and tosses his keys to a young man standing nearby, who now slides into the vacated driver's seat. Once we're clear of the car, the valet speeds off to park the assholemobile somewhere secure until we're back tomorrow.

My jaw drops as my focus drifts from the two staff members escorting our bags to Damian, who strolls toward the lowered stairs leading up into the jet as if this is the most normal thing in the world. I suppose, to someone accustomed to his family's caliber of wealth, it is. I stumble after him, climbing the steps with wobbly legs, my hands fidgeting with my glasses. I wonder if I should ask about security and whether we need boarding passes (though, I suspect the rules are different for rich folks with private jets), but all attempts to organize my thoughts are forgotten the moment we step inside the plane.

If I looked surprised before, I must be the spitting image of a cartoon character now, mouth hanging comically wide, eyes bugging out of my skull.

The jet itself is, obviously, much smaller than a commercial airliner, but the interior is a thousand times more luxurious. Shining wooden panels accent the white walls and ceiling, and five pairs of cream-colored seats that resemble recliners await us on the beige carpet—four positioned toward the front of the plane and one at the back opposite a long sofa, complete with cup holders, throw pillows, and blankets.

It's from one of these seats that a woman exuding the elegance of old Hollywood jumps up to greet us.

"Ah, there he is," she says, reaching over a small wooden table to the man sitting across from her, gently patting his arm to get his attention. His back is to us, but he turns at her words as he folds and places down the newspaper he was reading.

Damian grabs my hand, tugging me forward from where we entered at the rear of the plane, and I promptly snap my mouth shut when the woman's eyes flit to mine, taking me in, her smile kind enough but reserved. Behind her, the man looks like he'd rather be just about anywhere else at this specific point in time, a feeling I can relate to.

"Mom. Dad," Damian says, looking at each of his parents in turn. I can feel the rigidity of his entire body in the way his hand tightens around mine—can hear the careful distance in his voice when he speaks. Most of all, I see it in his face when he peers down at me. "This is Lexi. Lexi, these are my parents, Lenore and Hector."

My heart races, pounding against the cage of my ribs, and I wonder if his parents can sense the anxiety bubbling under my skin. If they can see the sweat beginning to bead along my hairline.

It was one thing posing for pictures and letting Damian spin the lies about our relationship across his social media—I was never actively participating, but rather…omitting the truth through a lack of denial. But now? Now, I'll have to quite literally put his money where my mouth is and lie my ass off like our lives depend on it.

Like Mom's life depends on it.

That thought is all the encouragement I need to slide my game face on.

I plaster on a pleasant smile, and curl the fingers of my free hand into a tight ball at my side so I don't touch my glasses. "It's nice to meet you both."

His mother—Lenore—offers me her hand, and I shake it. "Likewise. Though, to be honest, Damian hasn't actually told us anything about you."

I let out a quaint, tinkling laugh and shrug. "Well, this is still pretty new, so…" I purposely trail off, leaving his parents to fill in the blanks. Damian doesn't meet my gaze, but he squeezes my hand, and that's when I feel it— the ever so slight trembling of his fingers.

"Why don't you take your seat," his father says in a gruff, unfriendly voice. "We'll be departing soon now that you've arrived."

His parents return to the seats closest to the front of the jet, but this time, they sit in two adjacent chairs on either side of the narrow aisle, gesturing for us to take the other pair opposite them so we're all sitting across from each other. A handful of strained minutes pass as the boarding crew prepares for take-off, doing the necessary safety procedures. During this time, a flight attendant takes our drink order, returning with a steaming cup of tea for Damian's mother and three cups of coffee for Damian, his father, and me.

It's uncomfortable—the silence that follows as we quietly sip from our mugs, like we're all waiting for someone to speak, but none of us wants to be the first to do it. The tension persists after take-off, and before we're even in the air, I sense the interrogation coming.

"So, Alexandria, why don't you tell us a little about yourself?" Lenore suggests, that kind smile unnervingly tight around the edges of her lips.

Alarm bells ring in my head at the use of my full name. Damian called me Lexi when he introduced me—*not* Alexandria. I suppose it's possible his mom made a wild guess, or assumed, though something tells me that's not the case here. Maybe Damian mentioned it to them, and his mother was just exaggerating when she said he hasn't told them anything about me. He did say they specifically requested I come today, which means they must know about me to some extent, full name possibly included.

Or more likely, they've seen what's been posted online, a wary voice mutters in the back of my head.

Damian is sitting too far away for me to risk a casual glance at him—to try to read his face—the aisle between us suddenly as expansive and broad as an ocean.

You're on your own. Just stay calm.

Straightening my back, I swallow my rather unladylike gulp of coffee and set down my mug. "Well, I was born and raised in Newport. I live with my mom and my aunt. And I go to Conwick with Damian, though we don't have any classes together. I'm a sophomore."

See? No need to be nervous, I assure myself. *Nothing you just said is a lie.*

"And how did you meet?" she presses.

I return her careful smile with one of my own. "In the library." It's still the truth—no need to panic so long as I leave out the part about her son fucking me against the stacks in the mathematics section to win a bet. Given what's been said in the media lately, she already knows. Generally speaking, that is.

"Miss Dornan, we're going to cut to the chase," Lenore drawls, wrapping long, manicured fingers around her steaming mug. "We know you were one of the young ladies connected to our son's ill-conceived…*endeavors* last spring."

And there it is. The topic I had hoped to avoid.

Even with the gulf between us, I sense Damian stiffen as Lenore clears her throat. "We also know you're on a full scholarship to Conwick, that you're studying mathematics, but what we don't know—and what we're trying to understand—is why you're dating him after what happened with you two last semester."

I mask my stilted breath by taking another hearty sip of my coffee. Okay, so his parents are aware of my connection to his bet, and they've clearly read enough about me to know a bit about my personal life, but what's most important is they're under the impression—or at least open to the idea—that this fake romance between us is real. They're skeptical, sure, but they aren't in complete disbelief. Not yet. Which means there's still a chance, however slim, that we can pull this off.

"It's just…unusual," Lenore continues, her fingers now moving to the string of pearls around her neck. "And after everything, why *now*? It almost feels like—"

"Someone's twisting someone else's arm," Hector finishes.

All eyes swing to Damian's father, who watches me with narrowed eyes, like a hawk tracking an unsuspecting rodent. It takes all my self-restraint to not cower under his withering gaze.

"That's not—" Damian interjects, but his father cuts him off with a warning glare.

"We would like *her* to answer."

Damian visibly recoils, shrinking into his seat, his eyes dipping to the table between him and his mother, and it dawns on me as his hands squeeze into fists on his lap…he's afraid. Not *of* his father—that's not the vibe I'm getting—but of the ramifications that will no doubt arise if I say the wrong thing.

Worry stretches across his features, and in the briefest sliver of a moment our gazes meet, I see him—his real face past the easy-going mask he's always wearing.

Like armor, I realize.

It occurs to me then that Damian's joking demeanor, his sarcasm…it's all a guise—another piece of that bewildering puzzle I'm still failing to see the complete picture of. He uses humor to protect himself, I can see that now. I think I've known it since that day on the Navarros' yacht when he explained to me why he doesn't have any friends.

But why? What is he hiding that makes him so determined to keep everyone at a distance?

The answer doesn't come to me. All I know is the man beside me—the one who's trying so hard to look calm but has a frightened-looking boy in his eyes—is the *real* Damian, and the fuckboy I met at the beginning of the year is the costume he wears to hide that person. But there's something else here I'm not seeing—something beneath the surface that I know will explain this almost tangible hostility between him and his parents. Something that might also give me the answer as to why he got so mad when I called his problems small.

As that thought crosses my mind, another follows. There has to be more to his parents' ultimatum than what he told me, just like there's more to why I need his money than I was willing to tell him—the truth hidden behind that ridiculous cosplay excuse. It seems that secrets abound between us, and I suspect they're each just as consuming and present as our irrefutable attraction.

Unease stirs in the pit of my stomach because, on some distant level, I can relate to what he must be feeling. I might have an unshakable bond with my mother, but I would be lying if I said our relationship hasn't been complicated by her cancer diagnosis, and as for my dad…well, I remember a similar tension with him that makes this situation hit too close to home. Damian's father might not have left him like mine did, but I suppose his threat to cut him off is a kind of abandonment of its own.

Perhaps it's for that reason that, for the first time since we made this agreement, I find myself wanting to *help* Damian—to be more than just a participant in this lie, but an active contriver. And not for my own selfish reasons, not just for the money, but because I know how it feels to be a constant disappointment in the eyes of someone who is supposed to love you unconditionally. And perhaps it's for that same reason, words start flowing out of me without reservation.

"With all due respect, I can appreciate how it must look, but no one's twisting anyone's arm here." I peer across the aisle at Damian and offer him a reassuring smile before turning my stony gaze back on his parents. "I was furious with your son about what he did last spring, but I don't regret that it happened. If it hadn't, then I never would've known the person he is now. The person who is *more* than those bad decisions."

It's not the truth…but it's also not entirely a lie. If the bucket list hadn't existed, I wouldn't have gotten a glimpse past Damian's fuckboy shell, and

I wouldn't be sitting here desperate to see more of the real him he keeps tucked away.

You hate him, a small voice reminds me from a space in the back of my head. *Why should you care?*

But as those words flood my thoughts, I can only respond with, *Maybe I don't hate him. Not anymore.*

Or maybe it would be more accurate to say that what I feel for him now is more nuanced than something as straightforward as loathing. In the weeks we've spent together, I've seen so many little pieces of him, and while the picture they form might still be disjointed and unclear to me, I see enough to grasp that there's more to him than the guy who ghosted me freshman year. There has to be.

"You want to know why I'm dating Damian?" I ask, not meeting his eyes, though I can sense him watching me, just as curious about the answer as his parents. I shrug. "It's simple. He owned his mistake, apologized for it, and I *chose* to forgive him. The person he is with me now is not the same person who made that bet."

Another half truth. His apologies so far have been apathetic at best, and I'm not sure I can ever forgive him, not really…but I also know he isn't the same guy I fucked in the library at the start of the year. Because I wouldn't be capable of anything but hatred for that man, and the Damian sitting beside me? Well, I'm certain now I no longer despise him.

If I did, I wouldn't be this eager to clap back at his parents.

"It's just all very sudden," his mother persists, exchanging a concerned glance with her husband.

"It's not." My tone dances on the knife's edge between polite and argumentative. Though it wavers, I make sure to keep it mostly on the side of politeness. "Damian spent months trying to get in my good graces again," I say, submitting myself to the outright but necessary lie. "The only recent part is us dating. Before that, it was more of a…tentative friendship." When they still don't seem quite convinced, I add, the words clipped, "Just because it hasn't been documented doesn't mean it hasn't happened."

That last statement seems to get their attention. Lenore gapes at me, looking utterly stymied, while Hector appraises me, his eyes considering.

"Don't take this the wrong way, my dear, but why *you*?" he asks after a lengthy pause. "Of all the women he wronged with that immature stunt of his, why only apologize to you? Why apologize at all? What could have possibly triggered this uncharacteristic burst of conscience?"

It's a good question. One I don't have an answer to.

In the weeks since we our fake romance began, Damian and I discussed at length what we would say if anyone asked how we got together, and—worst case scenario—what our explanation would be in regard to how I could have forgiven him to the point we ended up dating in the event my connection to his bet ever became public knowledge. Our agreed-upon response: that we've actually been friends for months, and he's done the work to earn my forgiveness. Easy. Simple. Vague but believable enough. Kind of.

But the question we never prepared for is that someone might ask us why Damian is with *me*. Given how I was the wounded party with the bet, and he was the villain, it wasn't an angle that seemed likely to come up…so it didn't occur to us to consider it.

A mistake that might very well cost us now.

I part my lips, pleading with my brain to come up with something—to process my scrambled thoughts and turn them into suitable words to get us through this conversation. But Damian speaks before I get the chance.

"Because she was the first one to call me out on my shit, long before either of you," he snaps. My eyes dart to his face, and I notice that the frightened boy I saw in his gaze is now gone, hidden behind a hard expression I've never seen before. He looks…determined. No, not determined…

Defensive. Protective, even.

Of me.

"You might not believe it, but I did feel bad about what happened— maybe not about the bet, not at first, but definitely about the video." He's looking at his parents, but part of me can't help wondering if these words are intended for me. His eyes slide to mine for a flash of a second, and in those honey-tinged irises, I glimpse the answer to my unspoken question. *They are.* "I was just so used to doing whatever I wanted, consequences be damned since there never were any"—he scoffs—"that I didn't really feel the need to be sorry. I figured it would all blow over and be forgotten just like everything else, and life would carry on as normal. Except…Lexi didn't *let* me forget it. At every opportunity, she gave me hell."

His parents don't speak, riveted into silence. I don't dare breathe a single word either, caught in the suspense of what he'll say next.

Damian blows out a frustrated breath through his nose. "For a while, I was too proud to apologize, and when I finally did to get her off my back, she didn't want to hear it. She just wanted me to own what I'd done—to acknowledge that I'd hurt her, hurt the other people involved, and actually mean it when I say I'm sorry."

A half truth of his own. Or is it? He certainly has me pegged correctly.

Damian lets out a bitter laugh. "It bothered me…that I couldn't just smile and charm my way into her forgiving me. For a while, I didn't understand why. Why I cared about her opinion. Why I cared if she accepted my apology or not." He shakes his head, shame creeping across his face, but I can't tell if it's just an act, or if I might actually be seeing another small glimpse of the truth. Of the *real* him. "It took me realizing that *I* wouldn't forgive me either to finally get it. To realize I didn't want to be that person. Just another rich asshole making life miserable for everyone else."

His eyes, which had drifted down to the table in front of him, snap up again, locking hard on his father.

"You want to know why Lexi? Why *now*? Because after years of having my behavior excused or covered up thanks to our connections and money, *she* was the only one who didn't let me hide from it. She held me accountable. And not just with threats"—his eyes harden at that, and I know he must be referring to his parents' ultimatum—"but by actively trying to understand *why* I did it." He reaches across the small aisle between us, taking my hand, his thumb brushing along the backs of my fingers. A shiver runs up my spine at his touch, but I'm so transfixed by his words that I'm barely conscious of it. "Because of that, she made me want to be better. Or good enough to deserve her, at least."

He doesn't give his parents a chance to respond, rising from his seat in a righteous fury, and dragging me behind him until we're at the opposite end of the plane and safely deposited on the sofa, out of earshot if we keep our voices low.

"That was…dramatic," I whisper, turning my face into his shoulder. I want to ask him about what he just said—demand to know if any of it was true—but I don't dare risk it out of fear his parents might overhear us.

Damian looks down at me, and when a sly smile curls those luscious lips, the anger fading from his eyes, I grasp that the defensive outburst, the storming off—it was all a calculated move.

Disappointment sours in my gut. Was it all an act, then?

"Yup," he says. "And now, they can stew on it."

Though neither of us speak for a long time after that, he doesn't let go of my hand once the entire flight. His thumb lazily grazes my skin without pause, and that touch, the tenderness in each passing brush…it's enough to settle my unease.

And it makes me wonder if, maybe, what he said wasn't at least somewhat true after all.

Our plane lands in Guadalajara five hours later, and after another forty-five minutes in a private car, we arrive at Damian's abuela's house, a hacienda-style three-story mansion located in an affluent residential area known as Colinas de San Javier. The house itself is gorgeous, with red clay roof tiles, dark wood doors and windows, countless archways, ocher walls, and so much greenery the property almost feels alive.

The stairs leading up into the house are decorated with colorful floral tiles, and the warm yellow and wood accents I spotted outside continue in the mansion's interior as we step through the arched double front doors into an expansive entry hall.

I've barely taken two steps inside when I hear a woman's voice shout from nearby, "¿A poco es mi nieto el que oigo?"

"Sí, abuelita," Damian calls back. "We're in the foyer." When I glance at him, the smile lighting up his face is blinding. Taking my hand again, he says, "Come on," and then guides me forward, around the upcoming corner to our left, and down a short corridor into the most beautiful kitchen I've ever seen.

The ceiling is a masterpiece in wood carving, and the walls—where they aren't covered in shelves and plants—are decorated with that same yellow paint and exquisite patterned tiles that almost seem to tell a story with the imagery printed upon them. The cabinets lining the walls and the island in the center of the kitchen are a soft sage green, topped with more of that warm wood used elsewhere in the property, and wrought iron sculpted into elaborate chandeliers hang from the ceiling.

An older woman who looks to be in her early seventies stands hunched over the counter on the opposite side of the island, but she immediately straightens when we enter the room, dusting her floured palms on her apron.

"Damian," she coos, skirting the island at an impressive speed and crossing the distance between us at a brisk walk. Damian bends down as she takes his face in her hands and kisses him twice, once on each cheek. "My beautiful boy. ¿Como estas?" she says fondly, pulling back a little to look at him, then startling when she notices me standing beside him. "And who is this?" She looks me up and down, and then a mischievous smirk I recognize all too well tugs at the corners of her lips. I realize now where Damian gets it from. "Ella es muy bonita," she stage-whispers to him, raising her eyebrows suggestively.

Damian coughs into his fist to cover his laugh. "Abuelita, this is Lexi. Lexi, this is my abuela, Lucia. And yes…she is very pretty."

My cheeks flush, first at his words, then again when Lucia cocks a brow at him and asks, "Your girlfriend?"

Damian's grin falters only a little—only just enough that I notice. Forcing it back into place, he nods.

If Damian's smile in the hallway before was the sun, then his abuela's smile is the entirety of all the stars combined.

She beams at me, lovingly patting my cheek. "Bienvenida, mi amor." Her eyes snap back to Damian, narrowing. "Espero que este muchacho te esté tratando bien."

Beside me, Damian snorts. "Of course, I'm treating her well, abuela. Geez. What do you take me for?"

I glance between them, mirroring their smiles and trying not to feel completely out of my depth. "It's really nice to meet you," is all I can think to say before hastily tacking on, "Thank you for having me in your home."

Lucia, possibly noticing my lack of understanding where her native language is involved, spares me the discomfort of asking for a translation and says in English, "You are welcome any time. Ah!" She raises her hands at the clack of paws on the earthy terracotta tiled floor as her attention shifts to the hallway behind me. "And there is Xolo, no doubt coming to see what all the fuss is about."

"Xolo?" I ask just as Damian shouts, "¡Ven acá, Xolo!"

Barking ensues, and I glance toward the sound, turning as a medium-sized hairless dark brown dog bounds into the room and into Damian's awaiting arms.

"Buen perrito," he croons in a baby voice I would never expect to hear coming out of that mouth, scratching the whining dog behind the ears.

I watch them for a moment, taken aback by the unexpected display of warmth I've just witnessed, then—because I've never met a dog I didn't immediately want to pet—I squat down to the floor beside them.

"Wow. What a cool-looking dog," I murmur, reaching out and stroking a hand along Xolo's smooth skin. It's a weird sensation, but I am fascinated by it.

Damian casts a sidelong glance at me. "He's a Xoloitzcuintli, also known as a Mexican hairless dog. And he is the goodest boy in the whole world. Yes, you are," he adds in that sickly sweet baby voice again before smacking an obnoxiously loud kiss on Xolo's nose.

A grin slides across my lips. Who would've thought that Damian Navarro, a guy who would rather pay someone to be his fake girlfriend than form any meaningful human attachment, would be such a simp for dogs?

"Damian." Lucia taps her grandson on the shoulder to get his attention, then waves him over to the kitchen island where several plates of pastries and a floured chopping board cover its surface. She gestures to one of the platters. "Take these buñuelos to your abuelito's ofrenda. It will give you a chance to say hello before we leave."

Leave? To go where? I nearly say, but I keep quiet and shoot covert daggers at the back of Damian's head instead. Curse him for not telling me anything about what to expect on this trip. And curse me just as equally for not thinking to ask. I was so focused on meeting his parents—and internally celebrating that I wasn't having a massive panic attack on the plane—that I didn't stop to think about the real reason for this little foray out of the country. I wish I knew more Spanish. *Any* Spanish. Does Damian's abuela think I'm disrespectful for coming here during a family holiday? Not that I had much choice in the matter. I wish I knew more about Día de los Muertos. *Ugh*, why did I leave my phone at home? I could really use Google right now.

With one final pat to Xolo's head, Damian rises and walks over to the counter, scooping up the plate, then promptly returns to my side. "Come with me," he says, taking my hand again. At my questioning look, he jerks his chin to the doorway behind me, and I follow his line of sight to where his parents are seconds away from entering the kitchen. "Lest my parents try to interrogate you again," he explains.

Before I can nod or say a word in agreement, he tugs me toward the opposite end of the room, through an archway leading into another hallway.

My eyes swivel all over the place, jumping between the shining tiled floor to the wooden beams overhead, each one beautifully carved with patterns and painted in those same bold colors seen throughout the rest of the house.

As we walk, I take in every detail of my surroundings, peering into the open doorways we pass in an effort to consume as much of this stunning home as I can in the limited time I have here. It's crazy to think we're going to be in Guadalajara for less than twenty-four hours; I don't think I could even fully appreciate this property in that time frame, and the expense of just flying here for such a brief visit must have been nauseatingly immense. But then, I suppose that kind of money is just a drop in the ocean to people like Damian and his parents—and from the grandeur of this mansion, his abuela.

"So, I'm not sure how much you know about Mexican culture," Damian begins, steering me into a two-story living room, the upper level surrounded by ornately carved mesquite banisters, overlooking the open space below. Like the other rooms I've been in, the walls are that warm, welcoming ocher color, and wood accents and plants cover nearly every available surface. Opulent red sofas frame a wooden coffee table with a large brick fireplace serving as the centerpiece of the room.

"I've seen *Coco*," I quip.

He snorts. "Oh, so you know all about Día de los Muertos, then."

I shrug. "A little. But it's been a while, so maybe don't quiz me on it. You know, to be safe."

Damian gives me a look that clearly says I'm a smart-ass, then smirks, gesturing for me to keep following him.

He stops just as the wall opens up on my left, and that's when I see it: the explosion of color that encompasses the display in the corner of the room. I hadn't been able to see it from where I was standing when we first walked into the space, but now that I do, I realize this is the true centerpiece of the house, at least for today.

A table covered in white linen with three smaller identical tables atop it stands in the middle of an arched nook, which is bordered by marigolds of the richest orange and paper banners in every color of the rainbow, each one cut into intricate patterns of flowers and skulls. The tables are accented with even more of the marigolds along with a magenta runner that unfurls down the center of the display toward the floor like a waterfall of fabric, with framed photographs, ornaments of all shapes and sizes, and lit candles filling almost the entire space. On both sides of the shrine, two additional surfaces are decorated with even more of those vibrant orange marigolds and plates of so many different foods that I don't even know where to look first.

Noticing my gawking stare, Damian says, "Well, the abridged version is that this holiday is a way for us to honor the people we've lost. It's about remembering them and celebrating their lives rather than mourning them… though, that's easier said than done in my family."

He steps forward, placing the platter of fried pastry on one of the side tables, and I notice that it resembles the fried dough I used to have at the Fourth of July celebrations in Newport when I was a kid. As Damian inches back, I follow his now forlorn gaze to one of the photographs before us—of him and an older smiling man that I realize, based on his age, must be his grandfather.

I glance at the other pictures around it. There's one of his grandparents' wedding day, and another of Damian's abuelo and abuela with Hector when he was a child. But most of the photos on display feature Damian—some when he was young, others more recent, though none within the last few years it looks like. In many of the pictures, he's alone with his grandfather, and their close bond is evident in the matching smiles they wear. There are also images of Damian with both of his grandparents—a happier, younger version of him that I struggle to see in the Damian I know now.

Then there are the other photographs, and a creeping feeling of dread rouses from somewhere deep in my gut as I examine the one face I don't know among the other Navarros. Except…he isn't entirely unfamiliar. I see glimpses of Lenore and Hector in his features, and Damian's mischievous nature reflected in his toothy smile. If Damian wasn't also present in the pictures, I might assume I was looking at a younger version of him, but he's also there in every image—as the teenager I never knew.

My mouth goes desert dry as I stare at the little boy's grinning face.

The little boy who isn't Damian.

"This is the ofrenda your abuela mentioned, right?" I force myself to ask to fill the silence, though it's another question altogether that beats against the inside of my skull. "And it's like…an altar?"

Damian nods. "Every ofrenda is different, but they typically all have pictures, candles, mementos, food. In the case of my abuelo, we put out things like pan de muerto, tamales, atole. Basically, all his favorite stuff. As you probably remember from *Coco*"—he shoots me an amused smile—"during Día de los Muertos, the veil between the living and the dead is temporarily lifted, which means it's the one time of year when we can reunite with our deceased loved ones. This"—he waves a hand toward the ofrenda—"is meant to guide their spirits back to us."

I once again take in all the plates of food cluttering the two round tables on the sides of the shrine.

"So…the food is an offering." It isn't a question so much as a confirmation, to help me understand his culture and the significance behind this holiday that is clearly a monumental part of their lives. Especially if they would travel so far for such a brief time just to pay their respects.

"Right. Buñuelos"—I follow Damian's gaze to the plate he just set down a few moments ago—"were my abuelo's favorite treat. If he does come back to us, I guarantee it's for these."

My focus shifts to the pictures atop the ofrenda once more—to the smiling face of the Damian in those photos. To the kind face of his grandfather. And to the face of that young boy, notably missing among the still living Navarros.

That feeling of dread intensifies, and I blink up at Damian, my heart aching with the weight of that unspoken question. A question I can't bring myself to ask.

So, instead, I say, "And you do this every year?"

Damian considers his next words carefully, his expression drawn. "Growing up, we celebrated in Newport, but that was before my abuelo died and my abuela moved back to Guadalajara, since this is where they both grew up, met, and got married, and she wanted to spend her remaining days close to where he's buried. Now, we split the celebration between the two places."

I don't ask how his grandfather died or when; judging from the photographs, the most recent of them pegs Damian around the age of sixteen. A hard age to deal with such a profound loss.

Not much younger than I was when my mom got diagnosed, I realize.

That thought rams into me like a truck, and I find myself not quite sure what to do with it—this notion that he's experienced a significant trauma that's possibly shaped him just as my own experiences have shaped me. It was always so easy to discount Damian as just another player, a fuckboy, a rich asshole with nothing to lose because everything and anyone could be bought.

But now, I'm starting to see that's not true.

After all, even wealth can't buy your way out of death.

My chest tightens, and moisture pricks at my eyes as I stare at the ofrenda with a newfound appreciation and respect. I'm lucky—my mom is still here, still alive. But something about seeing this, something about what Damian's told me about this holiday…it brings me some semblance of peace knowing there are people out there who strongly believe that death is not the end. I only hope they're right.

"It's beautiful…the idea that the dead don't really leave us."

Damian exhales a breath that sounds eerily close to a scoff, and when I peer up at him, I'm startled by the devastated expression marring his handsome features. He shakes his head, not meeting my gaze.

"If only it was true." Then he turns away from the ofrenda and walks off without looking back.

We spend the next several hours at the Panteón de Mezquitán, a historic cemetery in Guadalajara about twenty minutes from Lucia's house, visiting the grave of Damian's abuelo. Like with his grandfather's ofrenda, the cemetery is splashed in countless colors, with more of those intricately cut flags hanging between the mausoleums and headstones, as well as sugar skull decorations, and orange marigolds (cempasúchil as Damian calls them, or flor de muerto—flower of the dead) and red cockscombs in such abundance that there must be millions of flowers in this one location alone.

Though I feel out of place, Damian's abuela is kind and guides me through the process of cleaning her husband's grave and decorating it with candles, framed photographs, and personal mementos—much like his ofrenda at her home. Damian and his father both help as well, with Lenore quietly standing to the side and carefully arranging the bouquets we set down in front of the headstone. Once the decorations are finished, and offerings have been placed, I listen in respectful silence as Lucia, Hector, and Damian each pray and pay homage to his abuelo. Then, for a while, we just enjoy the warm afternoon—and later, evening—air, the glow of the flickering candles around us, and the traditional music that can be heard playing nearby, all of it adding to the spiritual atmosphere pervading the cemetery.

None of the Navarros really speak during those hours, not even once we return to Lucia's home and sit down to eat dinner. On several occasions, I'm tempted to break the hush, if only to tell Lucia how *incredible* her cooking is, but I hold my tongue…and the moan that nearly escapes at the bold diversity of flavor bursting across my palate. There are so many foods I've never even heard of, let alone tried before (my knowledge of Mexican cuisine has always been mostly limited to tacos), and I can't get it all on my plate fast enough. Lucia seems pleased by my appetite, grinning at me occasionally across the table. A few times, I notice Damian watching me, too, though I can't quite discern his expression.

It's late by the time we finish dinner, and after, we all work together to tidy the kitchen in that persistent, near-painful silence. Once we're done, Damian's parents inform us that they're going to return to the cemetery for another hour or two, bidding us all goodnight before Damian or Lucia even have a chance to respond. As they leave, I don't miss the curious way Hector looks at me, like he's trying to make up his mind about something, but the glance is so fleeting I can't be entirely sure I didn't imagine it.

Hector and Lenore's departure doesn't seem to surprise Lucia, who simply smiles at me with that same genuine kindness she's been graciously bestowing upon me all day.

"You'll forgive this old lady for turning in early, but these bones aren't what they used to be…and I'd like some time alone. Damian will show you to your room. Thank you for coming today."

A lump rises in my throat as I squeeze her proffered hand. "Thank you for having me."

Shifting her attention to Damian, Lucia grabs his face and pulls him down so she can kiss his cheek. "Buenas noches, mi cielo," she murmurs.

"Goodnight to you, too, abuelita," he whispers, his lips set in a soft, affectionate grin that's so unlike him and so heartwarmingly tender that it makes my own heart skip.

As Lucia saunters off, humming a lovely tune to herself, I peer up at Damian, feeling the fatigue of today setting in. Before I can ask him where I'll be sleeping, Lucia coyly calls over her shoulder, "Oh, by the way. He might try to sleep with you."

"*What?*" Damian and I both seem to choke on the word, and I stumble back a step, putting some distance between us, my face horror-stricken.

Lucia nods toward her dog, who I didn't notice had meandered into the kitchen and is now bumping his naked head into Damian's shin for attention. "Xolo," she says as if the answer was obvious. "He loves when we have company." When Damian and I both gape at her, speechless, she bats innocent eyes at us. "Why? What did you two think I meant?"

But she doesn't wait for either of us to respond, and as she turns to leave the room, I glimpse the devilish smile hooking up the corners of her lips… along with the twinkle in her eye that tells me she knew exactly what she was implying.

The air shifts the moment we're alone, charged and crackling, like static electricity. Though Damian tries to laugh it off—to ignore this weighted attraction between us that even his abuela can see—I know he's well aware of it, too.

And all it will take now is one little spark to set us both alight.

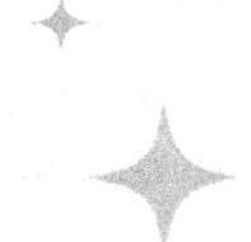

CHAPTER
TWENTY
✦ Damian ✦

Logro resistirlo todo, salvo la tentación - I manage to resist everything, except temptation

Translation: We all eventually give in to our desires... and I am no exception.

The silence is oppressive as I lead Blondie down the long, empty corridor, Xolo striding alongside us, and a rush of heat burning under my skin that sets my entire body aflame. I can't explain how or what, but it feels like something has shifted between us since this morning, since that awkward plane ride with my parents. We were both acting—putting on the necessary show—I know that, but there was also truth behind each of our words, I'm sure of it. There was certainly truth to mine.

Or maybe I'm wrong and nothing has changed at all, and it's just my own deepening feelings I notice, now that I'm actually aware of them. Since Halloween, those feelings—and *her*—are all I seem able to focus on, her presence a constant weight around me, heavier than the thickest humidity, depriving me of oxygen.

Of sense.

This feeling…this was *exactly* why I came up with the No Repeat rule, why I distanced myself from romantic attachment. From any attachment at all. Because this—whatever *this* is—it threatens everything I pretend to be. It threatens to dislodge the mask that serves as a shield to protect the shredded remains of my heart.

I thought I could keep up the ruse. I thought I could keep that needed distance between us, and maybe, with anyone else, I could have.

But Blondie isn't just anyone, and I realize now I was just fooling myself thinking I wouldn't end up liking her. It was stupid of me to think for one second that I would make it out of this arrangement without getting attached.

This is exactly why I didn't want to get to know her. Part of me was smart enough to understand if I did—if I *allowed* myself to get close to her—it would be impossible not to feel something. And I do.

I feel everything.

I can't help wondering…when did this actually stop feeling fake for me and start feeling like something real? Something I would actually want? The Breakers, maybe—when we kissed for my Instagram post? Or was it even sooner—maybe even that kiss in my car? I wrack my brain, but I can't pinpoint the exact moment it happened, and the more I try, the more I think I was down bad for her before I even knew I liked her at all. And when she kissed me the other day in the library…I think that was when it really began to sink in—not consciously, but enough to get the wheels turning until Halloween sent that train full steam ahead.

And now? Well, now, I'm fucked. I thought I could put a boundary in place, keep things non-physical and emotion-free between us, but seeing her here? With my family, my abuela embracing her without question or reservation? It's shaping a future I never dared to imagine because I could never bring myself to picture a future without Jamie in it. I struggle to still, but…for the first time since he died, a bright golden light is starting to break into the unforgiving gloom of my world, and I find that I *want* to envision it—what that future might actually look like.

And in every version of it, I see Blondie.

"Earlier," she begins, breaking the silence that separates us as we walk down the hallway. My fingers curl instinctively at the soothing cadence of her voice, and it takes all my self-restraint to keep from pulling her to me, from running those fingers through her wild curls. It would be a bad idea. I told her as much. But that doesn't mean the temptation isn't there.

The flames broiling in my chest burn hotter as I force myself to look at her.

She analyzes my face, like my guarded expression is a math equation waiting to be solved, and her teeth roll over her bottom lip, her gaze considering. Contemplative. As if she's not sure if she should ask the unspoken question pressing at the seam of her lips.

"Just before we left the house," she continues with a decisive breath, "I noticed a little boy in some of the pictures on your abuelo's ofrenda."

An icy shiver douses that fire in my veins, like a bucket of water has been tipped over my head. My skin pimples, the hairs on my arms and the back of my neck going rigid, standing on end, rising in protest of this topic.

Only forty-eight hours ago, it felt too soon. To tell her about this. For me to be emotionally ready to voice it. But I can't avoid it forever—not anymore. And knowing what I know about her now, about her mom…it wouldn't be fair to.

It's time. Not to get over it—I don't think that will ever be possible—but to accept that what happened…happened. To no longer treat it as something taboo, never to be spoken about or thought of outside of one day a year, like my parents seem so intent on doing. But to talk about it.

To acknowledge my pain with someone who will actually listen.

"I considered that he could maybe be a cousin," Blondie murmurs in a gentle voice before I can find the courage to speak. She casts a wary look at me out of the corner of her eye as we continue our sluggish advance through the hallway. "But…judging from how we're the only ones here, and there weren't any other family members in those photographs, I'm guessing not."

"Jamie," I croak, his name foreign and strange in my mouth, as if my tongue can't comprehend or comfortably form the syllables anymore. When was the last time I actually allowed myself to say it out loud? "My younger brother."

The fire that occupies my chest vacates the premises to move up into my eyes, which burn now without mercy. Four years of pain stored up, ready to unleash in one blistering moment. I dip my gaze so Blondie won't see the tears.

"I didn't know you have a brother." Her tone is careful, even though we both know she's smart enough, perceptive enough, to deduce the truth. She just doesn't want to be the first to say it, perhaps because it's too close to home—too close to what might lie in wait in her own future.

"Had."

Blondie's stride falters at my strangled exhale, and Xolo pauses when I stop walking as well, his large eyes fixed on us, tail wagging, completely oblivious to the tragedy encompassed in that single word. She remains stock-still, not meeting my gaze, and for a weighted beat, we just stand there in the middle of the corridor with Xolo wedged between our legs, unwilling—or maybe unable—to speak.

It's not too late, a voice says in the back of my head. *You could put an end to this conversation before it begins. You don't need to say anything else.*

But then my eyes drift to Blondie's as if pulled there by gravity, and the devastated look on her face makes me realize I do. The wall we've both built up between us has never been thinner or more fragile than it is right now. One word—that's all it would take. One more word and I could knock it down, leave all the lies and omissions in the past, and let her see the me I keep locked away from the world because that is the only way I feel safe.

It's a leap I still don't know if I'm ready to take, but I also know that if I don't, if I yield to cowardice now, I might not get another chance to be real with her…or with myself. And if I back away? If I lie? I would be doing the exact thing Ronnie warned me against. Isn't that what she said? That if I fuck this up, Blondie might not be able to put her faith in anyone ever again? Especially me.

Is that a risk I'm willing to take now that I know how I feel?

She hasn't outright said it, but I can tell Blondie's feelings toward me have changed—maybe not to the extent mine have (or in the same direction), but I've managed to come back from her hating me, which is something. Though it's been brief, now that I've caught a glimpse of what she's like behind that loathing, I realize her hatred was a wasteland. And I don't ever want to go back to that dark place in my life that turned me into the kind of person who got me sentenced there.

No, it's time to be honest. With Blondie…and with myself. About this one thing, at least.

"Jamie, he…" The lump in my throat seems determined to choke me into silence, but I push past the hurdle. "He died four years ago at the ripe old age of eight. He had glioblastoma. Brain cancer," I clarify when her brow wrinkles in question. "It all happened really quickly."

Her mouth opens, but she promptly shuts it again, searching my face, which slips beneath her perusal. "I…" Her voice is thick, and though she clears her throat, she only manages a timid, "That's awful."

"It's the reason things are so strained with my parents," I try to explain, that anger I've been holding onto so tightly for the last four years seeping into every sharp line and curve of the letters forming the words that escape me. "Everyone wants to move on, forget, but I just…can't. And I can't forgive him either."

A flash of doubt passes over her face. "Your brother?"

I shake my head, my nails biting into the skin of my palms. "No, my dad."

I turn and start walking then, needing the movement to calm me, as Blondie's bewildered stare burns into my back like a cattle brand. A few seconds pass, then she falls into step beside me, her breaths uneven. I speak before she can, sensing her question, even though the words are like broken glass inside me, cutting me everywhere that matters.

"When Jamie was diagnosed, the prognosis was grim. Research into pediatric cancers is already severely underfunded, and glioblastoma is extremely aggressive; the doctors said his odds were terrible—that his only real chance was to try an experimental treatment, like stem cell or gene therapy."

Blondie's silence hits differently now, and in the brief pause I take to organize my thoughts, I wonder if she's been told something similar about her mother. I hope for both their sakes she hasn't.

I sense another question hanging in the narrow space between us, where our shoulders are almost brushing. It says, *What does this have to do with your dad?*

Everything, I answer.

"My dad refused." At Blondie's choked gasp, I clarify (not to defend him, never to defend him, but so she can get the complete picture of the situation at the time), "He had taken a very public anti-experimental stance in regard to the family business—not because of any personal beliefs, but because his shareholders had 'ethical' concerns." I scoff. "*Meaning* they were scared shitless about any legal liability that might fall back on them if Hallazgo were to manufacture those drugs and something were to ever go wrong. And what's the one thing my dad cares about more than anything else in the world?"

Blondie looks over her shoulder as if she'll find the answer in the empty space behind us, in the ghost of our footsteps. When she doesn't, she turns her focus back to me, those big green eyes shining with the unmistakable sheen of tears.

"Ensuring he upholds his father's legacy," I say with a humorless laugh. "In his eyes, it wasn't just a financial gamble but a risk to the company name. The *brand*," I mock. "So, you can imagine which of the two was his priority: maintaining that stance or telling them all to go fuck themselves for the only chance he had to save his dying son's life."

The words have barely left my lips when I feel the hot touch of Blondie gripping my hand. Her fingers tremble against my skin.

"I'm so sorry, Damian."

My heart rages—with sorrow, with anger and fury, but above all, with longing for this sometimes unpredictable and surprising but *always* smart and beautiful girl, who is doing more for me by simply holding my hand than my parents have done—or even tried to do—in the four years Jamie has been dead.

I pull away before I do something stupid like lean down and kiss her.

"Needless to say, my high school years sucked," I lament. A sentiment I know she would agree with considering her own final year before college. "First, my abuelo died just after I started tenth grade, after which my abuela moved away. Then Jamie…during my senior year."

In my peripheral vision, I can just make out the way her face shifts against the dim light and shadows—the pursing of her lips, the creasing of her brow—and I wonder if she's coming to the same realization I did when I learned of her past from Ronnie. How our individual experiences have been a strange mirror of each other's, even down to the timeline.

"How come…" She trails off, and the burden of those unsaid words draws my gaze to her face. The hand I was holding before is now gripping the right arm of her glasses, and she shifts them a fraction of an inch, even though they were at no risk of slipping—one of her many little quirks I've come to notice that would endear her to me more if I didn't know what they were masking.

Her cheeks turn ruddy under my lingering stare.

"How come we didn't…honor Jamie?" Her tone is tentative. Unsure. Like she's embarrassed or even afraid she'll offend me for asking.

I offer her a pacifying smile. That she's even trying to understand means more than I could ever say. "Día de los Muertos spans a couple of days. Today, we honor the adults we've lost, like my abuelo. Yesterday was for the children." The one day a year my family actually allows itself to outwardly grieve, and even then, my parents continue to wear their unrelenting shroud of indifference, hiding it behind the guise of celebrating Jamie's life instead, as if acknowledging our pain is something to be ashamed of. As if they don't even have any pain left to acknowledge. Not like me. A sob threatens to escape as I force out my next words. "Jamie's ofrenda and grave are back in Newport, though my abuela has her own ofrenda for him here. We celebrated him yesterday."

Blondie's only response is a slow, contemplative nod.

"Sorry," I add when it seems like she won't break the silence again without prodding. "I didn't mean to dump all that on you." And yet, I can't stop myself now that I've started. Can't stop myself from taking the knife always wedged between my ribs, and using it to spill my guts to her. A bitter sigh scorches the inside of my throat. "Sometimes, I wish I could be like my parents and just let it all go." I wish I could be past this grief. I wish I could be at the point of finding joy in the fact that Jamie lived at all, but the wound is still too fresh. "But I—"

"Maybe they haven't," Blondie cuts in, jostling her glasses again. "Maybe they're just better at bottling it up."

I snort. That's one way to put it. And certainly kinder than I would have.

My parents are experts in avoidance. Shitty decisions aside, I have no doubt they mourned my brother at some point—perhaps, in their own way, they still do—but the problem is I never saw it. And they're so focused on moving on, on pretending his death didn't happen at all, that they never seemed to realize they've only made the situation worse, not only for themselves but for me. They weren't the only ones who lost Jamie, and I *needed* them to acknowledge that. I needed to be allowed to express that loss to them. And when I wasn't…

Well, that was when the rebellious behavior began. Because if I couldn't purge my grief in a healthy way, there was only one option left.

To self-destruct.

"Yeah," I mumble, shoving my hands in my pockets and dipping my eyes to the floor, mindlessly watching our steps. "Maybe."

A hand on my bicep urges me to stop walking again, and I relent, pausing mid-stride, my heart lodged in my throat. Blondie's eyes burn into the side of my face, but I can't bring myself to meet them this time. I'm too exposed, too raw. She'll see the ugly truth of my anger, my pain.

But that doesn't seem to frighten her because she puts her hand on my chin and turns my face so I have no choice but to look at her.

"For what it's worth, I think it's okay to feel what you're feeling."

Her touch lingers for only a moment—just long enough to permanently mark my skin and memory with the sensation of her fingers—then she drops her hand.

"I know this weekend is about celebrating their lives instead of mourning them, and I think that's a wonderful way to look at it, but I also think it's like you said before—it's easier said than done. Sometimes, we get stuck in the past, and we think we're supposed to just let it all go, like none of it ever happened, or only look at the positives, because that's what everyone else seems to do. Because that's how you show that it hasn't affected you, or that you've managed to overcome your grief. And some things we should let go." Her words have a sharp bite to them, and I can't help thinking that she must be referring to her father. To the man who was meant to love her without limit or condition, and yet chose to abandon her just because she was different. Special.

"Some things *aren't* worth clinging to," she declares, and I know then that if there was any part of Blondie that held tight to whatever childhood affection she felt for her sorry excuse for a sperm donor, it's gone with that statement. Snipped, like a fraying piece of thread. "But other things…" She reaches up again, pushing a stray lock of hair from my forehead before flattening her palm to my cheek. "It's okay to hold onto the stuff that matters. It's *okay* to not be healed yet. To still be sad."

If I wasn't already aware of my feelings for Blondie, those words would've been my wake-up call. And not just because of her understanding and empathy, but because…right then, with that sentiment, she sounded so much like my abuelo that I find myself believing that he really is here with us today.

"You sound like my abuelo," I muse. "He would've said the same thing."

A smug smile pulls at Blondie's lips. "I guess I'm just full of unsolicited wisdom."

She moves to retract her hand again, but the irrational part of me grabs it before she can, holding her warm palm to my skin. It's the part of me that wants to say, *To hell with the rules. I'll be whatever you want.*

"Ah, yes." I step closer, my grip unwavering, my heart racing at the wonderful sight of the blush creeping across her cheeks. "Like that time you suggested we become enemies with benefits. Very wise, indeed," I tease, though what I'm really dying to say is, *I don't want to be your enemy. I don't even want to be your friend. I just want you. I want more.*

Her breath hitches, and the raspiness in her voice matches mine when she whispers, "What happened to, 'it's forgotten'?"

I wish I could decipher this new question in her gaze. I wish I could tell if she even remotely feels what I'm feeling right now, or if sexual attraction is the limit of any reciprocity I can ever hope for.

It's crazy. Only last week, this was just a mutually beneficial, purely platonic (if that) arrangement. But now…

How quickly the tables have turned.

I clear my throat. *She's not interested in you,* the scolding voice inside me says. And with that reminder in my head, I drop her hand.

I inch back, and with some needed space between us to think, I realize where we are in the house. Turning, I take a few more steps before stopping in front of an open door on our right. "Here's your room."

Blondie blinks at me, her expression conflicted as if she's once again considering the correct thing to say—or as if the words are already on the tip of her tongue, just waiting to be voiced.

But she doesn't speak. Instead, she drops her gaze and hurries past me into the bedroom. "Goodnight, then."

Xolo whines by my feet when she starts to close the door, and spurred by the sound (or by my own stupidity), I shoot out my hand to stop her. My palm slaps against the wood, and Blondie gapes at me through the crack between the door and the frame.

This is a bad idea, my conscience warns, but I have to know.

"Did you mean it?" I find myself asking against my better judgment, my brain not quite keeping up with the words spilling out of my mouth. "Or was it the alcohol speaking?"

Blondie's brow creases for only a second before comprehension bleeds across her features.

My conscience was right. This *is* a bad idea. A terrible idea. I shouldn't even be considering this—the ache in my chest is proof enough of that. I should walk the hell away.

Because if I'm already this close to falling for Blondie, what the *fuck* do I think sleeping with her will accomplish? She might not hate me anymore (I think), but that doesn't mean she likes me either. Shit, she made it pretty damn clear there were no romantic feelings to be found on her part. Not now. Not ever.

As for me, as for what *I'm* feeling… I've been acting for a while now, with her, with everyone, but I'm not sure I can convincingly play the role of the unattached fuckboy any longer. Especially not if I sleep with her again. Because sex with Blondie won't just tear the mask off. It will burn it, and everything I pretend to be, to ash.

And yet, instead of walking away like I already should have, I hold Blondie's gaze, my every breath ragged with anticipation. It might not be smart, it might blow up this whole agreement, but despite what I said to her on Halloween, I know now that if it's a choice between having her the way she wants and not having her in any way at all, I'll always choose the former. Even if it means my heart will get smooshed into mushy pulp in the process.

The column of her throat shifts when she swallows, the movement agonizingly slow as the seconds crawl by at a snail's pace. She's doing this deliberately to torment me, I know it, and yet, I would take every moment of this torture for the slightest chance she'll say—

"I meant it." The words slip from her like a confession whispered in the sacred hush of a church.

My own lips and mouth have gone completely bone dry. "And now?" A dangerous question—one that will undoubtedly change everything with its answer.

Blondie's startled expression softens a little. "I guess that depends."

My heart hammers against my ribs as if these feelings are trying to truly break me. "On?" I press.

Her eyes don't leave mine as she pushes the door open again. "On whether your abuela will hear us."

I take in the space between the door and the frame and then peer past her into the empty bedroom, aware that once I step inside, there will be no turning back. Not for me.

Don't do it, a voice calls out from that grim, desolate place within me. From that dark place that's made me push away every chance at connection and sabotaged any hope I had of healing over these last four years. That's been so afraid of loss and betrayal I haven't allowed myself to feel anything but that self-inflicted detachment. The place that kept me isolated in my grief.

But I don't want to be alone. Not anymore. And I'm tired of living my life in the darkness.

I take a step into the room. Into Blondie's personal space—into her warm, golden light—relishing the way her eyes roam over my face and the graze of her hands as they reach out to touch my waist. My own rise to curl around the back of her neck, and—

A bark from the hallway has me jerking away from her, and we both glance down at Xolo, who wags his tag and stares up at us with pleading eyes, imploring us to allow him in, too.

I stifle a laugh and break away from Blondie, putting a hand on the door. "Sorry, boy, but I'm about to do some stuff you probably won't want to see."

I've barely clicked the door shut before Blondie is in my arms and I'm pushing her up against the nearest wall, one hand pinning her left wrist above her head and the other thumbing along the soft skin of her jawline. The warmth of her body is intoxicating, her heat, her desire for *this*, radiating through the thin layers of fabric between us. I can feel the rapid thrum of her pulse beneath my fingertips, and her breath is shallow as I pull her closer, chasing her lips. She moans into my mouth as I force them apart with a gentle tug of my thumb on her chin, and I sweep my tongue inside when she opens up for me, capturing the sound.

If our kiss in the library on Wednesday was a hungry inferno, the kiss we share now is a life-ending tsunami. It washes over us, filling our lungs until we're drowning in it. Until I'm completely drowning in *her*.

Blondie's knees turn to jelly when I move my lips lower, fixing my full attention on her throat, pressing open-mouthed kisses to every inch of exposed flesh I can reach. As I kiss her jaw, her neck, her collarbone, her hands knot in my hair, tugging me closer as her body arches, seeking more. *Demanding* more. Another breathy moan punches out of her, and I can't help smirking against her skin. It's the kind of sound I want to hear again, and again, and again.

I resume my eager exploration of her mouth next, high off the little keening sounds she keeps making, and with each smooth slide of her tongue over mine, my brain registers that she tastes like all my favorite things rolled into one, especially…

Blondie reels back and glares at me when I let out an inconveniently-timed laugh. "*What?*"

I trail my thumb across her bottom lip and bring it to my tongue, sucking off the lingering flavor. "You taste like my abuela's tamales," I croon, flashing her a salacious grin.

Pure mortification crosses her face. "Oh, god."

She slaps a hand over her mouth and attempts to retreat, but I grab her before she can get very far. "No, stop." When she doesn't, when she keeps her head averted, fighting my grasp as if worried she'll somehow kill me with her breath, I sigh. "You're being ridiculous, Dornan." To prove my point, I yank her forward, and trap her in the cage of my arms so we're standing so close I only have to bow my head and I could kiss her again if I wanted. I resist the temptation to do so, instead dragging my lips along the shell of her ear. "I like it. It makes me want to find out what you taste like elsewhere."

A shiver rolls through her at my words, and it's all the convincing she seems to need because her mouth is instantly on mine again. As we kiss, I move my hands to her ass and then curl them down her thighs, hoisting her up so her legs can wrap around my waist. She brushes against me, and my cock goes rock hard, aching under the stiff bite of my zipper. I could fuck her like this—shove down my jeans, push up the lovely green dress she's wearing that perfectly matches those stunning eyes, and pound into her until I've found my release. But I want to take my time with her. I want to make this

YOU TASTE LIKE MY ABUELA'S TAMALES.
IT MAKES ME WANT TO FIND OUT WHAT YOU TASTE LIKE ELSEWHERE.

moment last since I have no idea how many more I'll get.

Intent on doing just that, I walk her over to the bed, and lean forward, guiding her back down onto the blanket. I break our kiss, watching her face, watching the way her eyelids flutter with pleasure, as my fingertips skim along her bare thighs.

Flattening my palms, I push her legs open, and yank her hips closer to the edge of the mattress, then sink to my knees before her, like she is an altar to pray at. I might not be a religious man, but when it comes to this—when it comes to ensuring this is the single best sex of her life—I am completely devout.

"Fuck, I've been thinking about this almost non-stop since you kissed me on Wednesday," I admit as I plant teasing kisses along the inside of her leg.

"I didn't," Blondie starts to say, then gasps, biting the back of her hand.

I lift my head and shoot her a dubious look. "Didn't what? Kiss me? Now, now, Blondie," I coo, "no need to be embarrassed. Besides…" Another kiss—this one closer to the apex of her thigh, making her tremble beneath my lips. "I like a woman who can take charge."

I push her dress up until her hips are exposed, and start salivating at the sight of her lacy white panties and the obvious damp spot forming at the center of the thin fabric. I let my fingers trail just over the edge of the lace, teasing her for a fleeting moment, relishing the whine that escapes her. Then, leaning forward, I close my mouth around her—underwear and all. She bucks beneath my lips, letting out a hoarse, "Fuck!" that has me smiling against her heat.

Deciding I've teased her enough, I pull back, then deftly slide her panties down her long legs before chucking them onto the floor somewhere behind me.

"I am going to devour you," I purr, bowing my head again to make good on that promise.

Blondie's back arches at the first hot sweep of my tongue, and I moan as I close my mouth around her again, sucking and licking until she's a trembling mess. Her hands comb through my hair, gripping the strands with ferocious demand, and pulling me to her as she bucks, writhing against my face. I lave at her clit, alternating between broad strokes and taunting circles, absolutely consumed by the knowledge that *I* am the one doing this to her. *I* am making her lose herself.

And I am losing myself, too. Each shift of her hips only stokes the fire burning inside me, and I dip a bit lower, probing her entrance with the tip of my tongue, teasing her just enough to make her whimper. She's so sweet, so fucking responsive, and I'm lost in the taste of her, in the feel of her pulsing against my mouth.

After a few minutes of this, I pull back, needing to see her face—to see what I'm doing to her—and her wrecked expression nearly has me coming untouched. My jeans are so tight now it's agonizing. I trace the shape of her clit with my thumb while my other hand moves to free my cock.

"Why'd you stop?" I hear Blondie ask, her voice a thready gasp, and I flash her a devilish grin before kissing the dip where her leg meets her pelvis.

"I was just wondering if I should tell you what you taste like," I murmur against her skin, and she shudders from the heat of my breath. "Don't worry, it's good," I promise.

I lick her again, and she groans when I slide a finger inside her slick entrance, my hand working in tandem with my tongue. With my other hand, I slowly stroke myself—not enough to come, but just enough to stave off the ache. For now.

Blondie's breaths grow more rapid with each ravenous swipe of my tongue, and I sense her impending release a moment before it happens as her inner walls tighten. She presses something—a pillow, I assume—to her face, muffling the desperate wail that slips from her with one last lick to her clit. I close around her again, unhurried and deliberate, savoring the sweet, heady taste of her climax, the pulse of her orgasm trembling against my tongue.

Sitting back on my heels, I let go of my cock, lest the night come to a premature conclusion, then rising, I climb onto the bed, hovering over Blondie on all fours. The pillow is still propped against her face, though she no longer holds it there, her arms spread out beside her, her body perfectly still aside from her chest, which rises and falls in a steady rhythm. I pull the pillow away, needing to see it—the blissed-out ecstasy I'm certain I'll find on her face. I saw what she looked like in the heat of the moment, and now, I need to see what she looks like when she's been thoroughly taken apart. By me.

Blondie's eyes are hazy, and a loose laugh bubbles out of her throat when she meets my gaze, her dimples popping out to greet me. God, she's beautiful. I want to kiss her, and I lean in to do so before second-guessing myself. Maybe I shouldn't. Some women aren't okay with that—not after what I just did. Not with the taste of her lingering on my lips.

But as I've already come to realize, Blondie isn't like the other women I've pursued. She reaches an arm around my back, pulls me down, and locks our mouths together without hesitation.

This kiss is chaste, soft, and when it's over, I just look at her—at the heat in her cheeks, the swollen plumpness to her lips. At those beautiful green eyes, which shine with an emotion I don't recognize. It's definitely not one I've ever seen in the eyes of the other women I've been with.

Whatever it is, it fades before I can try to make sense of it. Next thing I know, Blondie is dipping her eyes to my erection, which hangs between us, neglected and leaking. With a coy smile, she reaches down and wraps her soft fingers around my length, coaxing a groan to slip free of my lips. Closing my eyes, I drop my head into the crook of her neck.

"Can I fuck you?" I whisper, wincing at the nervous waver in my voice.

Christ, I sound like a pre-teen who just asked the girl he likes to dance.

Blondie stills, and an ice-cold dread washes through me. Was that the wrong thing to say? She might have let me go down on her, but am I being presumptuous thinking she'd want to do more despite what she said on Halloween?

Those fears fall away like autumn leaves when she laughs. "Honestly? I might murder you if you don't."

Relief barrels through me, but it dissipates when a terrible realization hits me. "Shit."

"What?"

I sink back onto my knees and straighten, running a hand through my hair. "I…wasn't exactly expecting this to happen," I admit, furious with Past Damian for being so short-sighted, "so I didn't bring anything."

Blondie immediately catches my meaning. "Oh. Well…" She bites her lip, that contemplative expression returning. Finally, coming to some internal decision, she shrugs and says, "I'm on the pill. And besides, I'm nowhere close to my fertile window, so we should be good."

I bark out a startled laugh. "Fertile window?"

She looks at me as if I'm stupid. "Yeah, you know. Ovulation?"

"Women actually keep track of that?" I ask.

Blondie purses her lips. "What, like it's hard? It's just simple math."

"What about STIs?" I counter. I hate that it sounds like I'm searching for an excuse to put a stop to this, but if I *was* going to look for an out—a reason to walk away—this would be it. I could still say no before I lose myself for good.

She stiffens. "I hope this isn't your way of telling me you really do have the clap."

"Are people *saying* that?" I gasp, clutching metaphorical pearls, like I'm channeling my mother and she was just told her favorite perfume has been discontinued.

Blondie shakes her head. "Just Ronnie."

"How shocking," I deadpan, failing to hide my glower. "But to answer your question, no. I do not and have *never* had the clap or any other sexually transmitted disease. I'm one hundred percent clean. Besides, I've only been with you since that day you nearly kicked my balls off my body. The, er, second time," I amend.

Blondie snorts. "You're the only person I've been with my entire time at Conwick."

My jaw drops. "No way. Really?"

I suppose I'm not surprised she didn't sleep with anyone else after the whole scandal with the bet—if I was in her shoes, that would've put me off penises, too—but before that? We're talking a solid six months from the time she started at Conwick when she could've been going to Pound Town.

But then Ronnie's words at the party the other night fill my head—about Blondie's dickhead ex and how she's so used to being let down that she never lets people in—and suddenly, I'm filled with a deep self-loathing that I became just another one of those people...

And a determination never to be that again.

Impatience wrinkles Blondie's brow, and she averts her gaze, but she can't hide the blush sweeping over her cheeks, leaving the skin a sexy burnished red. "Don't let it go to your head or anything," she mutters. Then, scowling at me, she adds, "Are we doing this or what?"

With a throaty chuckle, I sink back onto my forearms, and when my body brackets hers, those perfect, tantalizing breasts rub against my chest.

So much for self-preservation. God, I am so fucked. "Only if you keep being bossy," I purr, giving her an impish smile. "It's quite the turn-on, you know."

We don't speak anymore after that, and any concerns she had about my abuela hearing us are long forgotten as I push my jeans and briefs down and sink into the welcoming heat of her.

I've wondered what this would feel like since that morning in September when I woke up to find her in my bed. I've wanted to remember how it feels to be inside her since I realized who she was on the list. And fucking her is just as good, if not better, than I imagined—or remembered—it would be. Blondie's body molds to mine like we were made to go together, our every movement perfectly in sync. My only regret is that we push our clothes out of the way instead of fully taking them off, so I miss out on the feeling of her naked skin—of seeing those gorgeous breasts bared to the world. In spite of that, Blondie is a sight to behold, moaning and writhing beneath me, and it's a struggle to hold out for as long as I do. Thankfully, when I do come, she's right there with me, pressing her mouth into my shoulder to muffle her cry.

"Fuck," she breathes when I flop down on my back beside her a moment later. "That was…"

"Yeah," I agree, my chest heaving.

An unfamiliar tingle of nerves ties my already tense stomach in knots. This would normally be the part where my hook-up for the evening would leave. Or I would, depending on where we were. But this? This is unchartered territory, and I don't know how to react. Or what I should assume.

I opt for the safe option. The *smart* option.

Lifting my hips, I yank up my jeans, and move to slide off the mattress.

"Where are you going?" Blondie asks, propping herself up on one elbow.

"I just figured you wouldn't want me to stay," I answer in the most detached tone I can manage.

Her eyes narrow as if she can see through my bullshit. "You can if you want. I'm not that heartless that I'd fuck you and then kick you out of bed."

I snort. "How romantic of you."

Blondie collapses onto the bedspread with an exasperated sigh. "Do you *want* to go?"

Yes, the smart part of me tries to say. But the stupid part, the part that knows this is a very bad idea, takes control of my voice first.

"I mean, it *is* a long walk back to my room." At Blondie's skeptical glance, I shrug. "This is a large house."

She sits up again with a grunt, then grabs my arm and pulls me back down with her until we're lying side by side on the bed. "Then stay, you idiot," she scolds. "Besides"—she snuggles closer to me, rubbing her face against my bicep—"you're warm."

I blink down at her in surprise—at the way she's wrapped herself around me like she's some kind of human koala bear. "Huh," I muse. "I would *not* have taken you for a cuddler."

She scowls at me, those green eyes flashing with warning. "Shut up," she grumbles.

It takes some encouragement, seeing as back-to-back orgasms have Blondie on the verge of a coma, but I convince her to scooch up the bed and get under the covers. The second we're both repositioned and settled, she contorts her body to mine again, firmly gluing herself to my side.

It's strange; she wasn't like this the last two times we had sex. Not that I can recall, anyway. But then, we didn't know each other like we do now. We didn't have this trust between us, albeit tentative on her part. It's enough to almost make me get my hopes up, but then I remember myself. I remember this is temporary. And the mask slides back into place.

Bracing myself for emotional impact, I watch her as she begins to fall asleep, her dark lashes fanning across her still rosy cheeks, her lips parting with every soft breath.

"Goodnight," she mumbles through a yawn as my thoughts drift to how much I want to kiss her again. As I think about rousing her and telling her that I also want to change the rules of our agreement. But not just about sex. About everything.

How I want this to be something real.

It takes so long for me to find my voice that she's already fast asleep when I speak.

"Goodnight," I murmur. Then I bite down on my bottom lip until the tang of copper floods my mouth to keep what I *really* want to say at bay.

Sometimes, the only way to solve a complex equation
is to start over with new variables.

When I wake up the next morning, Damian is already gone; if my panties weren't strewn on the floor, and I couldn't smell his expensive sandalwood and cardamom cologne on the sheets, I might think I dreamed the whole thing.

For a moment, I just lie still in shock, my fingers absently gripping the blanket.

Damian and I had sex again. *Amazing* sex. *Mind-blowing* sex. After what he said to me on Halloween about keeping things professional and sticking to the rules, I didn't expect him to actually change his stance. He had seemed so insistent, so set on not crossing that boundary with me, and yet…

The memory of his mouth on me, of everything we did last night, shows a completely different side to his mindset. As for the thoughts running through *my* head, at the moment, they're singular, and my hand inches toward the ache building between my legs that I desperately wish he was still here to take care of.

But he's not, and something tells me that any orgasm achieved via my own hand won't be worthwhile. So, with no other option but to get the day started, I jump out of bed and into a cold shower before I combust.

Once I'm dressed, I find Damian—along with his parents and abuela—

in the kitchen, all sitting at the table, eating and drinking their coffee in silence, while Xolo paces and sniffs around their feet on the hunt for scraps. Lucia perks up the instant she sees me, and after ushering me to a free seat, immediately makes it her life mission to fix me a plate. I can't bring myself to tell her I'm still full from last night.

Not wanting to be rude, I pick at my food, every bite just as savory and saliva-inducing as the feast I indulged in the previous evening, and proceed to down two cups of what might very well be the world's best coffee. My eyes must light up with that first sip because Damian smiles at me from across the table with amusement and…something else. Something I can't quite put a name to, but that inexplicably has my cheeks burning and my pulse thundering under my skin. I glance away before the others can notice.

We set off for the airport after we eat. Just before we leave, Lucia embraces me tightly, and makes Damian promise he'll bring me back to visit again— soon, and for longer next time. Making that promise, committing to the lie that I *will* come back, physically hurts in a way none of the other lies have. Maybe because I do want to come back. I *do* want to see more of this part of Damian's life, not only because being here is so vibrant and rich, and I want to absorb some of that color into my own existence, which is painted in shades of monochrome lately, but because being here—seeing Damian here—it's like taking a peek behind the curtain. But that peek isn't enough to satisfy me, and I can't help wanting to see more, especially now that those missing pieces that were keeping me from glimpsing the full picture of him are beginning to slot into place.

Both the drive to the airport and the flight back are just as awkward as they were coming here, however, the judgment I sensed from Damian's parents has now turned into a quiet contemplation. Every so often, I feel them watching us. Watching *me*. The one time I dare to meet their eyes, Damian's mother gives me a careful, optimistic smile before glancing away, whereas Damian's father…he holds my gaze—not to challenge me, but as if he shares his wife's tentative hope and is simply more reluctant to show it.

Whatever his parents see on my face must have alleviated their worries, because when we land in Newport, they both express a keen desire to see me again. Agreeing to their request feels less like a lie and more like an inevitability.

A guarantee, especially since the expiration date for our relationship is still months away.

We part ways at the airport once the valets arrive with our cars, Damian's parents going one way, and Damian and I driving off in the other, toward the other side of town. To my dismay, Damian is eerily quiet during the drive. Even that warm smile he offered me this morning has vanished.

Damian didn't talk much at breakfast or throughout the flight, but I had assumed that was due more to the proximity of his parents than anything I might have done. Now, though, as I scan the profile of his face, I can tell something is eating at him. Something he seems wary to voice.

Does he regret what we did last night? Or think I've developed feelings for him despite assuring him I wouldn't? Maybe I shouldn't have let him stay in my room. Maybe cuddling was a step too far.

But the thing is, I needed that human contact. After hearing the story about his brother—hearing about the tragedy that could very soon mirror my own—my anxiety was at an all-time high, clawing at the mask I'd slapped on to play the part of the perfect house guest. In reality, I was on the verge of erupting, every moment testing the limits of my mental restraint, and I couldn't cope with the thought of sleeping in an unfamiliar place by myself. Of being all on my own with the thoughts and fears hissing and snapping at me like violent snakes inside my head. The house, while lovely, was too big, too full of ghosts, and without someone there to hold me together, I knew I'd only fall apart once alone.

But…I didn't. Because Damian was there. Because he *stayed*.

And for the first time in my life, the anxiety bled away like rainwater down a drain.

The drive back passes quickly, and before I know it, we're parked outside my house. It's not that late, but night has already descended, marking the arrival of November and blanketing the quiet road in a thick, heavy blackness. My mom and Gina don't know what time I was due back today since I conveniently "forgot" my phone, but even if they are keeping watch for me, they shouldn't be able to make out who's sitting beside me in the car thanks to the shadows. It's only for that reason I linger.

"Thanks for coming yesterday," Damian says, cutting the engine. "I think my parents liked you. My abuela definitely did, and that goes a long way in my family."

"It was…" I almost say *fun* before having the sense to stop myself.

Damian's mouth hitches into a smile when I fidget with my glasses, as if he's surmised what I was going to say. "Fun?" he guesses. "It's okay, you can say it. Some parts of it were."

My brows quirk up when he winks at me. "So, you don't regret it? Last night?"

He slowly bats long lashes at me. "No? What gave you that impression?"

He sounds genuinely confused—hurt, even. Still, I shoot him a skeptical look. "Last time you were this quiet, something was up. I just don't know what else—"

I clamp my lips together when the scolding voice of my conscience makes an unwelcome appearance.

Seriously? You don't know what else could be bothering him? How about the dead brother he told you about just last night?

I resist the urge to slap myself on the forehead.

I'm about to tell him to forget what I said when he suddenly whispers, "You're right."

My stomach sinks, though I'm not prepared to analyze why. "But not about what you think," he adds when he notices the look on my face and my hand lifts to adjust my glasses.

I shift in my seat to face him, trying—and failing—to ignore my now frantic heartbeat.

Damian doesn't meet my gaze, keeping his focus on the window, staring out into the darkness of night on the other side.

"I meant what I said yesterday. To my parents." His eyes remain on the glass, but even with his head averted, I can see his reflection…along with the miserable expression he's likely keeping his face turned from me to hide. "I know you said what you had to, and I appreciate that, but what *I* said? It wasn't a lie. And I—" His voice breaks, and he clears his throat, trying again. "I'm *so* fucking sorry about the bet. About playing you, and making you think…"

I liked you.

My insides turn slippery and cold at those unspoken words—at the humiliation and anger that are still there, ever present in my memory, but are dulling with time and as I get these tiny, earned glimpses behind his mask, like a knife losing its edge from wear.

"I'm just sorry about all of it," he breathes. His eyes trail to mine, and the ice in my veins starts to melt at their warm, honeyed touch.

"What you said," he continues a moment later, "about not regretting what happened last spring… I know it was just some bullshit you spun on a whim to appease my parents, but for me?" He lets out a quiet laugh, as if he can't quite believe this revelation himself. "That's exactly how I feel about you. The part without a conscience, at least. That part of me is selfish, and it wouldn't change a damn thing that's happened because, if I *had* listened to that voice in my head and stayed away, I wouldn't have gotten this chance to know you. And that would be a real shame,"

A hundred different thoughts whirlwind through my head in response to his confession. But all I can think to ask is, "And the part *with* a conscience?"

Damian considers my question for the length of a few steady heartbeats, and in those silent seconds, that's when I see it: the genuine remorse in his eyes.

"For four years, all that part of me has wanted is for my brother to be alive again. But now… For so long, I've been torn up inside, and hell-bent on trying to punish my parents for what happened to Jamie, that I didn't see how you and so many others were getting caught in the crossfire. It was fucked up—I can see that now. And I—" His slow exhalation is shaky. "More than anything, that part of me only wants to take back all the pain and humiliation I caused you…even if it means I never would've gotten to know you at all."

Those words hang heavy in the air between us, choking all the oxygen out of my lungs until I'm on the verge of gasping for breath. Damian, mistaking the look on my face, quickly says, "I'm not asking for your forgiveness because I know what I did doesn't deserve it. But I hope you at least believe me when I tell you I'm sorry."

He stares at me with imploring eyes, and despite calling us enemies, despite insisting with every bone in my body that I hate him…in this moment, I find it's all too easy to say, "I do."

Neither of us says anything else apart from a brief goodbye after that. Damian doesn't seem like he has it in him for more, like the weekend has fully wiped him clean of words and he just used up the few he had left.

As for me, I'm teeming with them, the letters spelling out the names of all the conflicted feelings rushing through me pushing at my inner walls until I feel like I might explode.

I burst through the front door, managing a quick hello and goodnight to my mom and Gina, who watch me in quiet bemusement as I move through the house like a human tornado. Once in my room, I don't even bother to change before grabbing my phone from my desk and flopping stomach-first onto my bed. The battery in the device is low, so I plug it in before it can die, then quickly thumb open iMessage. My fingers are trembling by the time I text my group chat with Ronnie and Andie.

I tell them everything that happened this weekend. About Damian's parents. About his brother. About his confession just now in the car. And then I tell them about the sex.

Thankfully, they both wait to comment until I'm done purging.

Ronnie

Called it. Pay up bitch

Andie's response follows a few seconds later.

Andie

I scowl at the phone.

Me

Did you two seriously bet on my weekend?
Shameful behavior given my history with bets

Ronnie

Only that you would end up fucking Navarro

Andie

In my defense you threw such a bitch fit about
this the last time we brought it up that I thought
you'd have more restraint

I let out a scandalized gasp.

Me

**Hey! I do have restraint. And in your defense???
How is any of what you just said any better?**

Andie

Ronnie

**Hate to break it to you bae but around Navarro
you have the restraint of a snapped rubber
band**

My skin grows hot as I furiously hunt for a GIF of Mr. Darcy from the 2005 film adaptation of *Pride & Prejudice*—Ronnie's favorite movie and the perfect weapon to voice my outrage. His handsome face fills the screen alongside the quote, "So this is your opinion of me. Thank you for explaining it so fully."

Ronnie's only response is a kissy-face emoji and the words **Sorry not sorry.** I'm still frowning at my phone when it vibrates with another message.

Andie

Do you still hate him?

A whooshing breath parts my lips as somersaulting butterflies fill the now empty void in my stomach. I asked myself that very same question on the flight to Guadalajara, and it has haunted me every moment since. *Do* I still hate Damian?

The answer is immediate when I ask myself this time. Maybe the changes in altitude and time zone have given me some much-needed clarity of mind, or maybe Damian's confession in the car is what's helping me see things so clearly now. Regardless of the reason, I respond truthfully. My *new* truth.

Me

No. I don't think I do

Over the next two and a half weeks, when I'm not in class—or with Ronnie and Andie, bearing the brunt of their unending stream of "I told you so"—I'm with Damian, though our public outings are considerably briefer than usual.

Instead, we spend our time together in a near-constant state of undress, as if having sex again in Mexico unhinged something inside us. We fuck like we're trying to make up for lost time—usually in Damian's room, albeit with a few daring exceptions where that potential exhibitionist kink of mine was really put to the test.

I haven't ever felt this sated, not even when I was with Parker (*especially* not when I was with Parker), and I can't seem to get enough, even as every cell in my body keeps screaming at me that sleeping with Damian is a bad idea. That I'm going to wind up hurt again. That this will only end in heartache.

But then, for it to end in heartbreak would mean one—or both—of us feels something deeper than a simple sexual attraction for the other, and that's absurd…isn't it? Only a few days ago, I would've thought, *yes, that's absolutely ridiculous*, but now, I'm not so sure. Of my own evolving (yet, still conflicted) feelings, despite trying to keep them at a distance.

Or of Damian's.

It doesn't escape my notice that, ever since Guadalajara, he has his own internal conflict that he refuses to talk about. I sense it behind every easy smile and quip, and it's always there between us, in every subsequent touch and kiss. He fucks me like he's working through something. Like he's searching for the answer to a question that relentlessly plagues him, and he'll only find it deep inside me, in a place he can only reach one way. His enthusiasm is appreciated and well-received; I only wish I knew the cause of it.

Neither one of us has brought up what he said to me that day in the car— or those two words I said back—and I can't decide if that's for the best, or if it's simply leaving this, whatever *this* is between us now, unresolved.

Our relationship as it stands is like an ellipsis at the end of a sentence, the thought of it incomplete. In some ways, it's like we're stuck in a bubble in time. Frozen. Never moving forward or back. I'm grateful for the latter; I don't want to go back to what we were before—to being enemies, if you could call us that. But as nice as it is, I don't want to stay like this either, in this weird space between the truth and a lie.

This is my fault. I asked for this. I pushed to be more than enemies, business associates, friends, whatever we are. And now, I'm left drowning in the uncertainty of the unknown.

Perhaps I shouldn't have suggested we put sex on the table. It's complicated everything when so much was already on the line, and I'm no longer convinced we can make it to his graduation deadline without this arrangement blowing up in our faces.

Or at least, blowing up in mine.

Maybe Damian would've been better off making this agreement with someone he didn't have such a murky past with—or a past at all. Someone who is immune to his charms, the way I try so hard to be. Then I could go back to hating him instead of being trapped in this weird limbo where I *want* to forgive him, I *want* to move on, but the lingering hurt in my heart is holding me back. A festering wound that's taking too long to heal.

With a frustrated groan, I lean forward until my forehead is pressed against my open textbook. It's Wednesday, which means it's work study night at the library, but my mind is too preoccupied with thoughts of Damian to be of much use to anyone. A junior statistics major I've been tutoring since last winter asks me if I'm okay, and I make up some lame excuse about having a cold to get her off my back. Thankfully, she's my final tutee of the night, so I don't have to keep up the act for long.

Once she's gone, I pull my phone free from my pocket and stare at Damian's number in my contacts, turning over an idea that's been taking root in me these last two weeks. It's risky—Damian might think I'm insane or find the very suggestion offensive—but I can't think of any other way to finally close that wound and slam the door shut on our past for good.

He needs this as much as you do, I tell myself, and that thought is all the encouragement I need to tap open our chat.

Me

Can you meet me in the library? I want to test a theory

Fuckboy

Color me intrigued 😊 I'll be there in 10

As promised, Damian walks through the door ten minutes later. Since the library is closing in half an hour, most of the students have already left (of the small percentage of Conwick undergraduates who actually utilize the facility), and the librarian is occupied at her desk, so we should be fine as long as we're quick.

Jumping up from my chair, I cross the atrium floor in a direct beeline for him.

"Hey," he says as soon as I'm within earshot. "Are you okay? I—"

"Come with me." With a hurried glance around the almost empty library, I subtly grab his hand and then yank him behind me toward the stacks.

Damian lets me lead him through the path of bookcases without complaint, only breaking the silence once he finally registers where we're going. Although I can't see his face, I can hear the confusion in his voice as he asks, "Why are we—"

But I don't let him finish. The moment we step foot in the mathematics section, I whirl on him, rising onto my toes to kiss him.

I swallow his grunt of surprise as I push his back against the nearest shelving unit, sweeping my tongue inside his mouth with a lack of control—a desperate need—that's entirely foreign to me. Damian kisses me back at first, one hand on my waist, the other creeping up my shirt toward my breasts, but almost as soon as we start, he pulls back.

"Wait, stop," he says, breaking the kiss. He then plants his hands firmly on my shoulders and gently pushes me away a few inches, though whether that's to keep me from kissing him again or to stop himself, I can't be sure. "Just…wait a second," he pleads, "and tell me what's going on." He searches my face with narrowed eyes, but when he doesn't find the answer (and I fail to outright say it), he whispers, "Please?"

His breath is warm on my face, and it either robs me of sense or knocks some into me because I choke out, "I don't know what this is between us anymore. But I look at you, and I don't…" I step back, his fingers sliding off my shoulders, and gesture at him with a flailing hand.

Damian raises a brow. "You don't…?" He trails off, prompting me to continue.

My mouth tightens into a disgruntled pout. "Hate you. I don't hate you."

Considering what he said to me in his car that day we came back from Mexico, I expected Damian to be at least marginally happy to hear this. But his face is unreadable, his expression unnervingly blank.

"I'm sensing a but," is all he says.

I swallow, wincing at the sudden dry grittiness of my throat. "*But* so much of this place, of…*this*"—I wave my hand back and forth between us—"is tainted by what happened last spring. I know you're sorry," I interject when he opens his mouth to cut me off, "and I believe that, I do. And on some level, after everything you've told me, I even understand why you did what you did. But," I repeat, hating the sound of that word, "I think what I"— *What we both,* I silently add—"really need is to wipe the slate clean. Not a fresh start, exactly, so much as a…redo."

The furrow in Damian's brow deepens. "A redo?"

I nod.

But he just shakes his head. "I'm not following, Blondie." There's a note of exasperation to his tone, and I shrink back from it on reflex—at the memory of hearing that same exasperation in my father's voice in the weeks, months, even years before he left.

The comparison makes my insides harden.

There it is. The real reason I've been so afraid to confront my emotions and recognize them for what they truly are. The real reason I told Damian he didn't have to worry about feelings between us when we both know that's a lie.

It was never about the bet or the video; it was about the fact that I had opened myself up to him, and he fucking ghosted me just like my asshole dad did when I was a kid. And part of me is terrified it will happen again, even though we're nothing to each other. Even though I have no reason to expect him to stick around once our agreement ends. It's a moot point regardless. Feelings or no feelings, Damian isn't looking for a girlfriend, and he made it perfectly clear to me on Halloween that hasn't changed.

Even if it had, would it make any difference? It wasn't a lie when I said being his girlfriend was the last thing I want, and while that hasn't exactly changed either, my reasoning for it has. If he put the offer before me now— for a real relationship, not a fake one—I don't think I could accept, but not because I don't feel something for him…but because I can finally admit that I do. Because despite those feelings, I had the nerve to tell him it's okay to hold onto the things that matter when all *I* seem capable of clinging to are all the bad things that don't. What right do I have to expect something real if I can't even find the courage to be real with him? To be honest about what I'm feeling, about my mom, especially when he was willing and brave enough to open up to me? About his parents. About his brother and the grief that's still eating away at him. What right do I have to any part of him when I won't show him all the damaged parts of myself?

Still, together or not—real or not—I don't want things to stay like this, frozen, never acknowledging the truths of our lives, however ugly they seem. And while I might not be ready to face all of them, to unburden my mind and heart of the baggage constantly weighing me down, there *is* one truth I'm ready to confront. One wall I'm finally ready to tear down.

"When we were here together in January, you only had sex with me for the sake of a bet, correct?"

There's no accusation in my tone, but Damian must mistake my blunt question as one because he asks, his voice strained, his eyes glinting with guilt and hurt, "Do I really have to answer that?"

I chew the inside of my lip for a moment. "Let me rephrase. Why are you having sex with me now?"

He snorts. "If we're being technical, right now, I'm being interrogated—"

"You know what I mean," I retort.

Damian takes one look at my face—at the solemn expression shaping my features like fingers molding clay—and sighs heavily through his nose. "I'm sleeping with you, Dornan, because I like it, and because I want to. And because, up until about thirty seconds ago, I was under the impression you did, too."

"I do, shut up," I grumble, my face and the back of my neck burning with a blistering heat. "My point is, there are no ulterior motives this time, correct?"

Damian rolls his eyes. "No. I have no ulterior motive for sleeping with you beside the pleasure of your company…and your vagina. And those perfect breasts."

I glower at him.

"What?" he says defensively. "You have *great* boobs. Own it. Slap it on one of your nerdy T-shirts." When I don't laugh, or even crack a smile at that, Damian exhales, then murmurs in a soft, concerned voice, "Come on, Dornan, what is this really about?"

An uncomfortable tightness clenches my chest as the words tumble out of me in a rush. "I don't want to stay stuck in the past. I *want* to forgive you. Fully. But to do that, I need you to help me overwrite it."

His eyes widen as the meaning of what I've said begins to sink in. With a hesitant breath, he asks, "The past?" At my confirming nod, he adds, "How?"

I step forward, erasing the distance between us. "The last time you fucked me here," I rasp, bringing my lips to his ear, "you only did it to tick a box. But after everything you've said to me, after everything we've been through, I *have* to believe I'm not just some nameless Poor Girl to you anymore."

"You aren't," Damian growls, once again carefully pushing me back, but only enough to look me in the eye. "Dornan, I—"

"Then help me," I plead, interrupting whatever he was going to say, because if I don't say this now, I know I'll lose my nerve. "Let's replace the bad memories we left here with new ones. *Better* ones. So, we can both move on, and leave all that hurt and pain behind us."

"A clean slate," Damian whispers in awe, and the hopeful look in his eyes nearly undoes me.

Lifting my hand, I cup his cheek just like I did in Guadalajara. Then I whisper back, "A clean slate."

Before I can get another breath out, his mouth is on mine.

Our kiss this time is a near identical re-enactment to how it went down when we were last here together—a clash of teeth and tongues, urgent and frantic. But unlike before, when I stopped things from going too far, now, I'm begging for it, leaning into every eager graze of Damian's fingers and spurring him on.

His hands glide over my waist, then slide beneath my shirt to fondle my breasts, his thumbs pushing the fabric of my bra aside to lightly tease the sensitive peaks of my nipples. His touch coaxes a gasp out of me, and he swallows it eagerly, his lips curling into a smile that I can physically feel.

I smile back, losing myself to the sensation of his muscled body against me, of his hard length pressing into my thigh. I reach down, rubbing him through his jeans, and he groans into my mouth, his breath hitching. I never knew a sound could turn me on, but hearing Damian moan like that, and knowing I'm the one who caused him to do it, is a drug I could get high off forever.

He trails one hand down my stomach then and, stopping at my waist, unfastens my jeans with a deftness I would be impressed by if I wasn't so overwhelmed by the hungry heat building in my core. As soon as the button is free, he dips that hand under my panties, reaching down to touch me where I need pressure most. A moan of my own slips out when his finger swirls over my aching bud.

"Fuck, you're already so wet," he purrs in my ear before plunging one finger inside me.

I bite into the fabric of his Henley to keep from crying out. I could come just from this, with his hand in my pants, his palm grinding against my clit, but that's not how things played out last January, and that's not how either of us need them to play out now.

"Fuck me," I manage through my panting breaths, the words husky. "Please?"

I don't have to ask Damian twice. Retracting his hand, he grabs my waist and shifts me, switching our places until I'm pressed to the bookcase where he was standing only a moment before. My back meets his chest when his lips skim the curve of my ear, sending a shiver down my spine.

"You're sure about this?" I note the hesitation in his tone behind his own ragged breaths, and hearing it unknots something inside me—whatever ember of reservation I was still holding onto regarding this.

I nod against the lingering brush of his mouth. "I'm sure. Now, hurry before Mrs. Everly catches us."

Damian snorts. "You know the librarian's name?"

I scowl at him over my shoulder. "I'm here literally every Wednesday. Why is that surprising to you?"

He chuckles into my neck, sending a shudder of pleasure racing through me, and I unwittingly arch my back until my ass is rubbing against his length. Whatever other snarky comment Damian was about to say dies on his tongue as he yanks down my jeans and panties.

The air conditioning nips my skin as he puts one hand on my back, pressing my upper body down a little. With the other, he swipes a finger up my seam from behind, and that single touch nearly turns my legs into limp spaghetti noodles.

I reach back, my fingers brushing across the warmth of his thigh, and my heart skips a beat when I realize his pants are already down, leaving him as bare as I am. The heat of him is unmistakable, and I shift, searching for more. A second later, I feel it: the blunt head of him pressed to my entrance, hot and eager, sending a jolt of anticipation through me.

Damian's hands clamp down on my hips as he pulls me back onto his cock, and as he slides inside me, each inch of him makes my body coil until I'm a spring about to snap. I'm so wet, it only takes one deep push for him to be fully seated, and I nearly cry out from the sudden feeling of fullness.

I throw my head back onto his shoulder as he reaches around me, planting one hand against the bookcase for support. The other inches up my chest to my throat, and as he pumps into me—slowly at first then faster, like he's feeding a need that's consuming us both—I half expect him to cover my mouth to stifle my cries just like he did the last time we were here in this position.

Instead, he curls those long, skilled fingers around my chin and turns my face toward his to kiss me.

We lose all sense of reason after that, and as he slams into me over and over again, hurdling us closer to our impending orgasms, I realize this time together feels less like the lie we keep telling ourselves and more like a foregone conclusion. Though, what that conclusion is, I still don't entirely know.

There's only one thing I *am* sure of as the heat inside me rises to boiling point, and I clench around his cock, his mouth devouring my cry of release. And as he follows suit, groaning against my lips as his pistoning hips slam into me one final time, I sense that he's aware of it, too.

That hate that engulfed us, that tension…it's gone, like a candle snuffed out by the wind. I can feel the weight on my chest lift at once, and I know then we've succeeded. That by coming together again here of all places, the past between us raw and exposed, we've managed to rewrite whatever complex equation we were before, those variables of hate and tension canceling out to leave…this. Something new. Undefined, maybe, but real.

Damian props his chin on my shoulder, but doesn't pull out, as if he doesn't want to lose this physical link tethering us. I know I don't. His cock throbs inside me, and I wish we were anywhere else—his room, a hotel. Fuck, I'd even take the back seat of his car. Anywhere that would keep this moment from ending.

In my peripheral vision, I catch the mischievous grin spreading across his face.

"I'm starting to think libraries are severely underrated," he breathes, wrapping his arms around me from behind and pulling me tight to his chest.

And as he turns my chin to kiss me again, I notice that, for the first time since what happened last spring, this thing between us doesn't feel like something broken.

It almost feels like a beginning.

CHAPTER
TWENTY-TWO
✦ Damian ✦

It's official: I am the world's biggest coward.

I had the perfect opening to tell Blondie I like her—the opportunity presented itself on a freaking silver platter—but I didn't take it despite spending these past few weeks working up to that exact moment. Each time we slept together since that night in Guadalajara, my determination to confess would only grow stronger, and that voice in my head would say, *This is it. This is the day I tell her.* But then, lo and behold, every time without fail, I would shrivel up like an old ball sack.

I kept convincing myself that it just wasn't the right time, that I'd get another chance. But last night in the library? *That* was the moment, I'm sure of it. And I completely fucked it.

Blondie was practically begging me to validate this thing between us, to reassure her she isn't alone in feeling confused about what this fauxmance has become. But I was too scared of what I *thought* she was trying to say— that her wanting to wipe the slate clean meant she would call this whole arrangement off—and subsequently too stunned by what she *actually* meant, that I wasn't prepared for the opening when it arrived, smashing into our conversation like the Kool-Aid man minus the enthusiastic, "Oh, yeah!" Not that Blondie gave me the opportunity to get a word in edgewise, but still, I could have told her if I really wanted to.

Maybe I didn't because last night was about her, about what *she* needed, but I hate myself for not at least trying. For letting her walk away after the single most intense sex of my life without telling her the truth. Without telling her what it meant to me. It kills me to think that she might now be wondering if these past few weeks—and even that redo she asked for—have been nothing more than casual sex in my mind instead of something more, something *else* beyond that wonderful chance for forgiveness I'm still not convinced I deserve. Something I'm terrified to put a name to, even though it's tearing me up inside not to.

I flop back against my pillow with a frustrated groan and stare up at the ceiling, my brain replaying every second of what happened in the library yesterday in excruciating detail until I'm so hard I have to jerk myself off just so I can think clearly again. My orgasm hits me so fast I get whiplash, but it unfortunately does little to uncloud my thoughts. Maybe nothing will until I finally come clean with Blondie. About my feelings. About what I want us to be.

About everything.

Perhaps, more than anything, that's why I couldn't bring myself to tell her I like her. It wasn't timing, it wasn't even my own lack of courage (though that was certainly a factor), but the simple fact that she's in pain, and I don't have the goddamn cajónes to tell her I know about her mom.

Maybe, on some incomprehensible level, I don't want to stir up shit between her and Ronnie, since I don't think Blondie knows her rabid chihuahua of a bestie told me about her current predicament. It doesn't seem like the sort of thing Ronnie would admit to, and if Blondie *does* know, I'm certain she would've mentioned it when I revealed what happened to Jamie. Plus, her not knowing explains why she never invites me inside her house. Why she seems to jump out of her skin any time I broach the subject of stepping beyond the boundaries of her porch. Because she's afraid. She's afraid I'll see her mom and figure out the truth.

Besides, Ginger Spice might be a she-devil, but it's obvious she's a fierce and protective friend, and I don't want to do anything that would ever jeopardize that for Blondie, not just because she's already lost so much, but because coming between two friends like that—especially when Blondie doesn't have very many—would be a major dick move. And even *I'm* not that big of an asshole.

Mostly, I think I don't tell her because I'm terrified of how she'll react. That she'll be embarrassed I know the truth about why she needs the money from our agreement, and that she'll pull away from me—from what this is becoming—to protect herself, even though I would never judge her for it, not for one moment. What wouldn't I give, what depths wouldn't I sink to, if it meant bringing Jamie back? Shit, judging Blondie would be the last thing I'd do.

And I'm sure, after hearing about my brother, she knows that on some level, but still…even after yesterday, I can't help fearing she'd use it as an excuse to take the easy way out and break things off. That she'd insist we go back to the safety and distance of the facade. And though I'd give her whatever she wants, do anything to make her feel safe and comfortable, it would destroy me inside to do that. I don't want to lose this part of her that I only get to see in those moments, when the walls are down and we don't need to lie.

I don't want to lose any of her at all.

My chest heaves with another sigh. This situation is so fucked up. The fact that Blondie had to answer my ad in the first place just to help her sick mom is so fucked up. Has the system always been rigged this way and I've been too blinded by my own privilege to notice? It feels like such a cop-out to say willful ignorance kept me from seeing the obvious power imbalance that exists because of my money and because of her desperate need for it, but that's exactly what I've been: ignorant. Before Ronnie told me about Blondie's mom, this felt like a mutually beneficial arrangement, and I could dismiss that imbalance. But now, I'm awake to the truth, and I just feel dirty, like the sex we have is only because Blondie feels indebted to me, even though the explosive attraction between us is enough to assure me that's not true. Still, that voice of doubt is loud. Sometimes, it's so loud I could scream.

With another agonized groan, I force myself upright and swing my legs over the side of the bed. I hate how helpless I feel. I hate knowing that Blondie is in any way suffering and that I've only contributed to it. Hindsight is a bitch, and while I was unaware of her situation at the time of the bet, it isn't an excuse, nor does it help me figure out what to do about it moving forward. I just wish there was something I could do *now*, some way I could be useful beyond my fucking wallet. Anything to guarantee her mom's story has a different ending to Jamie's.

Suddenly, I hate myself for wasting these last four years dwelling in my grief instead of doing something productive with them. Seriously, what the fuck have I achieved? Punishing my parents and everyone else around me hasn't brought Jamie back. All the mindless sex I've had since starting college hasn't in any way assuaged my suffering, or filled the void in my chest my brother left behind; the only thing that's managed to do either is being with Blondie, and it's killing me that I don't know what to do to help her.

I wish I knew more about her mom's cancer, about their insurance, about fucking *anything*, but I can't exactly ask her about it without telling her Ronnie spilled the beans. And besides, even if I *did* know any of that information, what the fuck could *I* do?

Nothing. The sad truth is I can't do shit.

I lean forward, propping my elbows on my knees, and comb my fingers through my hair before lacing my hands around the back of my neck. The consequences of my actions these last four years have never felt heavier than they do at this moment, when I'm so close to having a real seat at the table and yet farther than I've ever been because I was stupid and immature enough to fuck it all up. If I hadn't been so short-sighted and angry, then in another six months, I would be working for Hallazgo, and I would have the access and means to try to do something, *anything* at all, to help people like Blondie's mom. Like Jamie.

I only wish I knew what that something was.

I rub my hands across my face and blow a loud breath out through my nose. My mind spins in circles, searching for an answer, for even the smallest drop of inspiration, but I got nothing. As usual, I'm fucking useless.

What I wouldn't give to have a brain like Blondie's right about now.

My eyes drift to my bedside table where my phone sits on top of it, silent and still, and it dawns on me that, while I might not be a genius, I *do* have the next best thing.

Swiping my phone, I open my recent contacts and select my abuela, who answers on the first ring as if she sensed I would be calling.

"¡Hola, mi cielo!" she trills, and my worried heart instantly warms at the unabashed affection in her tone. It wraps around me like a soothing embrace.

"Hi, abuelita." I put the phone on speaker and set it back down on the table. "Are you busy?"

She clicks her tongue. "For you, mi amor? Never." I can hear the smile in her voice when, not even two seconds later, she asks, "How is that charming girlfriend of yours?"

My stomach flips, and my mouth reflexively stretches so wide my cheeks begin to ache. Never in a million years did I, Damian Navarro, self-proclaimed asshole, think I would grin like a lovesick idiot at the word "girlfriend," but here I am.

"Lexi is fine," I tell her, and the words sound like fucking sunshine on my lips. "I'll tell her you said hi."

"Please do," my abuela insists. "Now, as much as I love hearing from you, mi cielo, I'm assuming this isn't a social call given the hour?"

My smile slips as I glance at the time on my phone. Shit, it's nearly midnight in Newport, which means it's eleven o'clock in Guadalajara, which on a normal day might as well be three a.m. to my elderly grandmother. Aside from not realizing just how late it is, I forgot all about daylight saving time and assumed I was still two hours ahead.

"Lo siento, abuelita. I didn't even look at the time—"

"Nonsense," she interrupts before I can finish apologizing, say a hasty goodnight, and hang up. "I will always answer your calls, no matter the time of day, mijo. But Xolo is looking at me as if to remind me that it's our bedtime, so perhaps you could tell me what's wrong so we can talk it out and this old lady can go to sleep?"

I nod, even though she can't see it, then dart out my tongue to wet my lips. "I just…well, what I wanted to ask…" I trail off, struggling to put the thought into words.

A beat of silence passes before my abuela asks, "What's bothering you, mi amor? You know you can talk to me about anything."

A shaky breath expels from my lungs. "I don't know where to start," I admit. "I feel like I've completely screwed everything up. Like…I had a chance to make a difference, to do something good with my life like abuelo did, and now, it's just…" *Gone.*

Or close to it. At this point, it's impossible to tell what my parents are thinking, or if they'll allow me to take that seat at the table once these nine months are up.

"Did you get into another fight with your father?" my abuela asks.

"No," I retort, then clear my throat, checking my tone. "No, I haven't. It's just… I've been thinking about Hallazgo and everything abuelo built. About how he wanted to help people, and he just…*made* it happen. Looking at my own future"—I let out an exasperated breath at the thought—"I don't know. It just feels like the whole system was constructed to hurt the people who need it the most, and I don't know how to fight that. How did abuelo manage to do it?"

My abuela's lengthy pause is telling. "Oh, mijo," she coos, and the sadness in her voice has alarm bells screaming in my head and red lights flashing behind my eyes. "Your abuelo was a great man, but what you saw in him, and the stories and ideals he instilled in you when you were young, that was the dream. *His* dream, yes. But it wasn't always the reality."

Goosebumps pimple my skin. "What do you mean? He always talked about wanting to make medicine accessible to the masses, and he did it. It wasn't some unattainable dream. He made it happen."

I was raised on stories about my abuelo—about how he grew up in near poverty, and built Hallazgo from nothing to become the conglomerate and major foothold in the health industry it is today. It was always framed as the classic underdog story, an inspirational tale about a man with a passion for chemistry, who—after developing a breakthrough treatment early on in his career—realized the power he had to use science to change the world.

His goals were altruistic, his kindness and compassion were unparalleled, and though he didn't believe in unearned handouts, he was always the first in line to donate to charity. To offer help to those who needed it most. I know all that about him for certain—I saw it with my own eyes—and yet…my abuela's comment makes me wonder if there was more I *didn't* see because I was too young, too afraid of shattering that image, to look beyond what was right in front of me. If I was only seeing what I *wanted* to see instead of the truth. If I idolized the grandfather I loved and the man he desired to be instead of who he actually was.

Her next words only compound that fear.

"It might not feel like that long ago to you, but you were still so young when he passed. You only ever saw the success. You didn't see what it cost him."

What it cost him? I shake my head, confused. My abuelo was an exuberant man, full of life, and energy, and ideas. And he turned those ideas into a reality using his brilliance and innovation. Our wealth and the dominance of Hallazgo in the global market are proof enough of that.

But if that's true, then why is that voice of doubt that was only just pestering me about Blondie now whispering in my ear again, beckoning me to consider that, maybe, I've always had it all wrong? I grew up with these stories about my abuelo, this incredible self-made man, but even I know wealth and opportunities don't just appear from thin air, and as someone who came from nothing, it was unavoidable the poor chemist from Guadalajara had to make sacrifices, or pay some price, to reach the impressive heights he did. As that understanding sinks into my skin, another unsettling thought takes shape. What devils did he have to bargain with to create this life I've taken for granted?

What monsters did he have to sell his soul to?

A feeling of disquiet curdles in my stomach like spoiled milk, and I'm overwhelmed by the sudden urge to retch.

"I don't…" I shudder at the sticky bead of sweat forming along my hairline and brow. "I don't know what you're talking about," I force myself to choke out. "He only talked about the good, about what was possible if I worked hard enough. He always said we could change the world."

"That's because he wanted you to believe it," my abuela insists, though her tone is gentle. "He wanted you to see the best of what he was trying to achieve while also shielding you from the ugliness of the truth."

"The truth?" My heart is racing beneath my rib cage.

A few seconds tick by, marked by the call time on my phone screen as if taunting me. Finally, my abuela says, "How difficult it was to create anything good in a system designed to put profits ahead of people."

"But he did," I counter, clinging to that image of the man, the grandfather, I revered as a child. "He built Hallazgo on his own, and turned it into something huge. He found a way to beat the system."

Didn't he?

The silence that follows is deafening. I can hear the crinkle of the static between us in the dragging moments it takes my abuela to speak.

"No, mijo." There's a heaviness to her voice now. "He didn't beat it. He *survived* it."

Her words hit me like a blow to the chest. I'd always imagined my abuelo as a man who commanded respect, who bent the whole world to his will. The idea that he'd been forced to bow to it instead…it doesn't sit right with me. It doesn't sit right at all.

"When your abuelo came to this country, he had hopes and dreams, as so many do. And he thought, with perseverance, and with the right people behind him, he would have the reach and means to create medications that everyone—regardless of income bracket—would be able to afford. He thought others would share his ideals. That science and the desire to do some good in this world would be enough to sway them."

"Let me guess," I deadpan. "It wasn't."

"No," she says sadly. "It wasn't. The insurance companies, the industry regulators, the investors—all of them wanted to make money first and help people second. Your abuelo's biggest struggle wasn't in the lab; that part was always easy for him. The real hurdle was convincing everyone else with a hand in the pie to take a chance on his ideas. Every formula, every breakthrough—he had to fight to get them funded, to get them approved, to get them into the hands of the patients who needed that medication. And each step of the way, there were compromises."

That horrible sour feeling in my stomach rises in my esophagus until I taste bile in my mouth. I try to spit out the bitter tang, but what escapes instead are accusatory, venom-laced words. "So, he sold out," I growl as that pedestal I put my abuelo on seems to crumble before me.

"It's not that simple," my abuela protests at the clear vitriol in my voice. "Your abuelo never once abandoned his ideals, but he also knew he couldn't create what he did on his own. He didn't come from wealth—you know this. His funds were not unlimited. So, he had to find a way to work *with* the system, not against it. The success of the company had to come first. He hated it, but if he didn't play by the rules, there would have been no Hallazgo. No way to distribute the medicine he was creating, least of all to the people who needed it. Do you think he *wanted* to see his drugs priced so high that only the wealthy could afford them? Do you think he *wanted* to partner with predatory insurance companies? Of course not. But without them, the people who needed his drugs the most—the ones who couldn't afford to pay out of pocket—would never have been able to access them at all. And without the funding, without the patents and approvals, there wouldn't have been any medication to sell. He didn't have a choice, Damian. All he could hope was that, someday, whether under his leadership or your father's…or even yours," she adds after a meaningful pause, "that maybe, someday, things would be different."

For the first time since losing Jamie, it feels like my entire world has been turned upside down. All these years, I thought our family's wealth was a benefit of my abuelo's selfless ambitions, not in spite of them. At least when I was a child, I had the self-centeredness of adolescence to blame for never thinking to question it, but what excuse do I have now? Clearly, I'm *still* a self-absorbed child, too consumed by my own issues to see beyond the end of my nose. And I should have seen it. I should have realized. After all, I know first-hand what Hallazgo has become—where its investors' values lie. I think I just didn't *want* to see it because seeing it would have forced me to finally lift the rose-tinted glasses. To realize my abuelo wasn't the infallible figure I've built him up as in my mind.

And I suppose because it was easier to blame my father, like I have for so much else. To lay the burden of fault at his feet. After all, it's not like he's trying to make the world a better place, or doing anything to help people like Blondie's mom. His concerns are singular, and none of them are altruistic.

"Everything your abuelo did," my abuela says carefully when it's clear that I won't break the silence first, "was for survival. For stability. And for the chance, however small, that his actions would eventually do some good in the world. Do you know what it's like to come to a new country with nothing? He had his ideals, yes, but he wasn't just building a company,

Damian. He was building a life for his family. For *you*. Your abuelo wanted to help people, and he did as much as he could *when* he could, but it was also extremely important to him that he take care of his family. To guarantee and protect *our* future. Unfortunately, along the way, there were times when a choice had to be made. And the more Hallazgo grew, the more your abuelo stood to lose."

I swallow hard, fighting back the tears threatening to break though. "I just assumed he… I don't know. The way he always talked about it, I thought he found a way to stay above all the bullshit."

She sighs. "There is a reason they refer to it as the ignorance of youth, mijo. You only saw the man he wanted you to see—the dreamer who believed he really could change the world. But he carried a lot more that he didn't show you. He worried constantly about whether he was doing the right thing. Whether he was doing enough. Your abuelito was a good man, Damian. But even good men can't fight the whole world on their own. He never stopped trying to help, but he also knew the system was far bigger than he was. That he was just one cog in a much larger machine."

"A machine Dad was more than happy to keep being a part of," I mutter. My father is a businessman, after all, not a chemist or idealist, like my abuelo was. His priority will always be the bottom line.

My abuela exhales a loud *tsk*. "Your father inherited a company that was already deeply rooted in the system. He didn't create it. He's simply trying to keep it alive, keep it from falling apart. Do you think he hasn't made sacrifices? That he hasn't struggled with the same questions your abuelo did, or that he doesn't have regrets about the decisions he's made?" I can't recall the last time my abuela raised her voice, or the last time I heard that fire in it that burns brighter with every word. Shit, I can count on one hand how many times my abuela has shouted at me. And unfortunately for me, she's not done yet. "*You* think he's selfish, but *I* think he's scared of losing everything your abuelo fought for. Of being the one to ruin this family."

The insolent part of me bites back, "But he's lost sight of why it all started. Abuelo wanted to help people. Dad only cares about profits and keeping the shareholders happy."

It's an unfair thing to say. I know it the moment the words leave my lips.

After all, my family's wealth isn't anything new. It isn't something we've only had since my father took over the company. I was raised with the private jets, the yachts. We had all that and more under my abuelo's leadership. We grew richer while the poor got poorer, and all this time, I've been ignorant and selfish enough to convince myself our fortune wasn't at the expense of someone else.

I wanted to believe it wasn't. I wanted to believe one could live by their morals and make positive change in the world, and still have the success, the wealth, the lifestyle I was raised to inherit. And while I could sit here and say that inheritance isn't behind why I always wanted to work at Hallazgo—that I was more interested in holding onto that last tie I felt to my abuelo, despite it being the truth—I can also see now how easy it is to say something like that when you have a safety net to fall back on…even if said safety net is one wrong move away from being ripped out from under me.

A deep sigh filters into my ear, and when my abuela next speaks, I notice that fire in her voice is gone. Extinguished. Now, she just sounds tired, like she's grappled with this topic for far longer than the brief span of this conversation. "A legacy is a heavy burden, mijo. Maybe more than you can imagine. Do you know how many times your abuelo thought he was going to fail? How many times he sat at our table with his head in his hands, wondering if he'd made the wrong choice? If he'd done the wrong thing? Your father grew up watching that. He learned to fear failure more than anything, learned just how much was always at stake, at least in those early days when we first came to this country." Silence for a beat. "Years have passed since then, but still, that fear remains. Maybe now, you will understand why."

"But I don't," I say as the tears I've been holding in for what feels like a lifetime escape, sliding down my cheeks in hot, scalding lines. "I don't understand any of it. Because if Dad gave a fuck about what abuelo stood for, he never would have let Jamie die."

I can sense my abuela's shock through the phone, and she's quiet for a tenuous moment. Finally, after what seems like an hour, a year, a decade, she murmurs, "That was a terrible decision to make, but it wasn't only your father who made it." Her every word is measured to hide the waver I clearly hear behind them. "The truth, mi cielo, is that Jamie was going to die no matter which way your parents chose."

"But they could have at least tried!" I shout, slamming my hand down hard on the table.

"Yes, they could have," she agrees, and I'm sobbing in full now. I can't seem to wipe the tears away quickly enough. "But it would've taken a miracle to save Jamie's life, whereas the blow to this family's livelihood, and to everyone who helped build the company, would have been certain. And I'm not talking about the shareholders, but the employees—the scientists who worked alongside your abuelo to make Hallazgo a reality. Do not make the mistake of thinking it didn't cost your father dearly to choose the way they did."

Wiping my nose on my sleeve, I fling myself backward onto my bed and cross my arms over my chest. "How lucky then that it didn't cost him his precious legacy," I scoff.

My abuela's responding laugh is completely devoid of humor. "No, but it cost him one child and the love and respect of the other." She pauses then as if considering what to say next, and another few weighted seconds pass in silence before she adds, "Believe me when I tell you that it wasn't money or legacy your father was thinking about in that moment…but ensuring there would still be a future for the child who would actually live to have one."

Those words evoke more pain than one of Blondie's swiftly-timed kicks to the nuts, and I grimace, rolling onto my side until my face is mere inches from my phone.

"Are you just saying that so I'll forgive him?" I mutter.

I hope she is. Because the thought of it being a lie is so much easier to swallow than the possibility that what she's said is true.

My abuela tuts at the question. "No, mi amor. If your father seeks your forgiveness, he will have to ask for it himself. Though, I do pray you will try to remember that you are not the only one who lost your brother. We are all still hurting."

As if on cue, my heart squeezes, reminding me of that pain, and I curl into a ball as my tears continue their now silent descent, the pillow growing cold and wet where they pool beneath my face.

So much for walking away from this conversation feeling fucking inspired. I called my abuela so she could make me feel better, so she could give me hope that I can still find some way to help Blondie since I'm clearly incapable of doing it on my own. I wanted to spark an idea, not discover that everything I grew up believing was bullshit, and that my anger these last four years has maybe been severely misguided.

"Are you still there, mijo?" she asks after a while.

My responding grunt lacks enthusiasm.

"Talk to me, Damian. Tell me what you're thinking."

I sniff, rolling onto my back again, wiping away my remaining tears with the heels of my hands. "I won't lie to you, abuela. I'm thinking this has all been depressingly eye-opening."

She lets out a sardonic laugh. "Why? Because you've finally learned your abuelito was human? Because your father is not the heartless monster you've convinced yourself he is?" My silence says it all, and she snorts. "Good. Maybe now you can let go of this idea that you need to become either of them. Instead, you should become your own man."

I blink at that, the words like a slap in the face that rouse me from my indignation and grief.

Become my own man?

"But I…" A lump rises in my throat. I swallow hard. "Even if Hallazgo didn't become what abuelo envisioned, he was still the one with the ideas and the skills. What the hell do I have to offer? What can I possibly hope to achieve that he couldn't?"

If he couldn't find a way to make a real difference, how can I?

And then there's my dad to contend with. Regardless of his reasons for what happened with Jamie, his priority is ensuring the survival of Hallazgo. And maybe his motivation for protecting it really is the same as why I'm so set on working for the company—that lingering thread connecting us to abuelo. Maybe he knows me better than I care to admit if he knew to snatch that thread away. But that sentimental connection—the one that makes me want to fight for a different Hallazgo, and makes him want to protect it— means it'll only be that much harder to convince my dad to let me change anything. He wants to preserve, but I want to evolve.

I only wish I knew how to do that.

"You listen to me, mijo," my abuela commands, and I soften at the consoling cadence of her voice. "You are a bright young man, and you have your own skills and passion that you will use to make a difference. I'm certain of it. But you don't need to have all the answers right now, and no one expects you to. Give it time. Give *yourself* time."

But I don't have time! I nearly shout into the phone.

Blondie's mom might not have time.

As if reading my thoughts, my abuela says, "Besides, I hear your Lexi has quite the gifted mind. Perhaps, you will one day work together on this and find those answers together."

My abuela's words echo in my head.

Together…

Together?

Holy shit, that's it.

I don't need to *have* a big brain like Blondie's. I just need Blondie herself.

That spark I've been waiting for ignites, and a vague concept of an idea starts to form. Well, fuck. This was a super traumatic way to go about it, but it looks like I found my inspiration after all.

Way to deliver, abuela.

I thank her for her brutal honesty, and after a quick goodbye, a goodnight, and a, "Yes, abuela, I will bring Lexi to visit again soon," I hang up the call and get ready to brainstorm. And as that ember of hope building inside me explodes into a vibrant flame, I start to believe that, maybe, I really can succeed where my abuelo didn't. Maybe his role wasn't to finish what he started, but to lay the foundation. To build something strong enough for me to take further—to push beyond survival, and use Hallazgo as the tool to create something that will actually bring real change to the world the way he always wanted.

Maybe that's *my* legacy.

I understand it now—the reason for all the stories, the convictions I was raised on…

My father might have inherited the company, but I inherited my abuelo's dream.

TWENTY-THREE

**Exponential growth is the rate at which
my problems are multiplying.**

I never knew grudges could feel physically heavy, like a weight literally pressing down on my heart, but now that the weight has been lifted, I can't help marveling at the difference. At how light I am by comparison now that I've finally been relieved of that burden.

It seems strange to say I've never forgiven someone before. But forgiving someone for something small and forgiving them for deeply hurting you are two different things. And the fact is that Damian did deeply hurt me, and though I wasn't sure if I could ever truly forgive him for it, I do. And that forgiveness—knowing I'm even capable of it—fills me with a drugging euphoria. It's crazy how easy it was in that moment, to let what we were doing wash away all the bad between us, but it did. It washed away my anger and resentment as if Damian's dick really is magical, just like Ronnie said.

And I've been walking around high on that weightlessness since. That is, until this morning, when I realized my mom had her biweekly chemo session, and reality brought me crashing back down to earth. Although Mom is in the second year of her treatment, it's still very much ongoing, and it's uncertain when she'll be safely out of the woods. Days like today—when I have to sit there and watch how frail she looks wrapped in a blanket, the infusion steadily dripping through the IV line attached to the port in her arm—only remind me of that. But I put on a brave face because that's what Mom needs from me right now. She needs me to make her think I have hope, even if some days—like today—it's so damn hard to feel it.

Between the two of us, Gina is the far better motivational cheerleader, and though we usually take it in turns to go with Mom to the hospital (and today would have been her day), I wanted to give her this much-needed chance to relax. She's been drowning in overtime ever since the insurance gods decided to smite us—just in case anything happens that requires draining our bank accounts, impacting our ability to pay the mortgage and bills—and I know she's tired and uncomfortably close to burning out. I don't have classes on Friday, anyway, so I volunteered as tribute to take Mom for her infusion.

Four hours later, we're in the car heading home, and thankfully, since today was a monoclonal antibody day, she doesn't seem as unwell or exhausted as she usually does after her standard rounds of chemo. She's even talking about what we should have for dinner, which is amazing considering her treatments have a tendency to make her feel too sick to eat after. We're debating the pros and cons of Italian versus Chinese food when I turn onto our street, my personal feelings on chow mein abandoned mid-thought when I spot the silver Audi parked outside our house.

"Whose car is that?" I ask, glancing at Mom.

She shakes her head. "I'm not sure. Must be someone visiting one of the neighbors. Or maybe Gina has a guest over?"

The latter seems unlikely. Gina's usually so busy that when she does get some time to herself, she chooses to spend it vegging out on the sofa rewatching episodes of *New Girl*—a rare indulgence, but one she relishes when she can. And the only people she allows to intrude on her personal time are me and Mom. So, unless Edward Cullen himself is in there spilling all his vampire secrets, I highly doubt she has anyone over.

I pull up to the curb in front of the car in question and swing open the driver's door, peering down the length of the mostly empty road for a beat before rushing around to the passenger's side to help Mom. She stumbles a little, catching her toe on the tarmac, and I shoot out a hand to catch her, forgetting all about the Audi.

"Are you feeling okay?" I ask, guiding her along the short path to the porch.

She huffs a humorless laugh. "Same as usual. You don't have to baby me, Lex. I'll be fine." Despite what she says, she doesn't resist my offer of support, and I notice her grasp on me tightens a little as we make our way up the peeling wood steps.

Laughter reaches my ears when I push open the door, and I'm about to call out, "We're home!" when I step far enough into the hallway to have the living room in my eyeline. Gina is sitting on the mustard-yellow sofa, exactly where I expected to find her, and on the armchair across from her is—

"Damian?" His name shoots out of me in a panicked shriek.

What the *fuck* is he doing here?

His head snaps in my direction at the sound of my voice, and my mouth goes dry when I glance over my shoulder at Mom, who shuffles forward to see what all the commotion is about. When I look back at Damian, he jumps up from the armchair, a smile edging his lips.

"Hi."

My stomach twists as my fingers twitch with the sudden urge to touch my glasses. If he sees my mom, he'll know. He'll know I lied about why I need the money. He'll know I'm one crack away from breaking.

"I…" I swallow hard. "Wh-what are you doing here?"

An honest-to-god blush creeps onto his cheeks as he rubs a hand along the back of his neck. "Well, I…" He clears his throat, then offers me a timid smile, which is equal parts endearing and totally unlike him. "I wanted to see you, but you weren't home. So, when Gina said I could hang around until you got back, I figured"—he shrugs—"I would."

I blink stupidly, trying to process this information. "And…how long has that been?"

"Oh, uh…" He checks his watch, and his cheeks inflate like two small balloons before he blows out a whooshing breath. "Two hours?"

"*Two hours?*" I echo, nearly shouting the words.

He holds up his hands. "Don't worry. Your aunt has been entertaining me with some truly riveting conversation. In fact"—a devious smirk hitches up the corners of his lips as his eyes narrow on mine a little—"we actually have a lot in common—"

"Don't say it," I warn, even though I know exactly what's coming, and that nothing will stop him now that he's started.

That smile deepens. "Did you know Gina is a self-proclaimed Twihard as well? We *should* be enemies," he explains with a glance at my aunt, who nods and grins at me as if she is abso-fucking-lutely *delighted* by this turn of events. "You know, since she's on Team Edward and all. But we've agreed to a truce for your sake, so you don't have to choose sides."

I don't even bother to hide my groan as I reach up and pinch the bridge of my nose. "Dear god," I mutter under my breath.

Behind me, my mom clears her throat to get my attention. Shit. In the span of sixty seconds, Damian's weird *Twilight* obsession derailed my thoughts, and I somehow completely forgot she was here. And right after chemo no less, looking very much like she just walked out of an oncology ward. If the sunken cheeks and pale skin weren't evidence enough, the cotton wrap to cover her hairless head is a dead giveaway.

"Lex," she begins, her eyes—the mirror of mine—swinging from my face to Damian's then back again, pinning me in place. "Care to introduce me?"

I turn my attention to Damian, assessing his expression for any sign that he's registered my Mom is sick…but I find nothing. Just a patient smile and a casual lift of his brow to remind me they're all waiting for me to speak. Or maybe that's all I'm allowing myself to see.

My lips part, and my mouth hangs open for a moment before I finally locate my voice. "Mom," I say slowly, "this is Damian. Damian, this is…my mom." I wave a put-out hand toward my aunt. "Gina, you know."

Damian crosses to where my mom and I linger at the threshold to the living room, his long legs eating the distance in only two strides. "It's great to meet you, Ms. Dornan," he says, offering his hand to her. The way he addresses her as Ms. and not Mrs. doesn't escape my notice, but then, I've never mentioned my dad, and he knows I live with my mom and aunt, so he probably just went with the safest option. I watch their interaction with laser focus, especially when my mom slides her hand into his and he shakes it. The gentle way he touches her is another thing that fails to evade my attention. "I've heard a lot of great things about you."

You have? I nearly ask. *From who? Because I sure as hell haven't told you shit.* But I swallow my comment and remind myself that Damian is just being polite. He's acting, stepping into a role, though who can say what part he's supposed to be playing right now.

"Is that so?" my mom says, raising a brow at me before tacking on a kind, "And call me Carol, please. I refuse to be the only person in this room not on a first-name basis."

Damian beams at her, clearly pleased, like a child who's just been told he's on Santa's good list this year. God knows what he's so happy about.

Seriously, why are you here? I try to ping that thought directly into his brain but fail. He just keeps smiling at my mom, completely oblivious to the molten heat of my stare on his face and my many obvious attempts to get him to look at me, so I can mouth for him to get out. To leave before he realizes I've been lying to him and ends up hating me for it, especially after he was so candid about his brother.

I could have told him then, in Guadalajara. I could have told him dozens of times. I *should* have told him, and yet…I could never seem to find the words. Maybe because talking about my mom's sickness only makes it that much more real, and I want just one place in my life where I can pretend that it isn't. That this isn't my life. Maybe I just don't want Damian's pity, which is insane since he's possibly the one person I know aside from Gina who would actually understand.

Or maybe I'm just scared because we have this major thing in common connecting us, and I don't want it to freak him out. For it to be too heavy for him after what happened to Jamie. If it is, he'll leave. And I want so badly for him to stay.

I don't want to be left behind again.

At this thought, I look at my mom, acutely aware of how weak she is despite today being a good day. She needs her rest, but if I make a big deal about it, Damian will realize what's going on, won't he?

Just play it cool, Lex, I tell myself. As if playing things cool is something I'm totally capable of.

"Mom, um…why don't you sit down, and I'll go make everyone something to drink?" I suggest.

Three coffees and an herbal tea (for Mom) later, we're sitting in the living room in awkward silence with mugs in hand, my mom resting in the oversized blue armchair that seems to swallow her whole, and me, Damian, and Gina on the sofa with me sandwiched in the middle. Damian's body heat bleeds into mine, even though I make a conscious effort to keep some breathing room between us. Despite my efforts, I can feel Mom's gaze zeroing in on my movements, no matter how slight, every time I shift, as if she knows exactly what I'm doing.

Her eyes flick from the near non-existent space between our hips to Damian's face. "So, Damian, I'm assuming you go to Conwick, too?"

He nods. "Yeah. But Lexi and I aren't in the same year. I'm a senior."

Beside me, Gina nudges my shoulder. "Older man. Nice. Get it, girl."

My cheeks burst into flame as my eyes snap to my mom, who scrutinizes my face, staring me down like a hawk. I expect her to say something, to call me out on…what, I don't really know, but on *something*. Instead, her gaze settles back on Damian as she questions him about his major and then follows up that question with, "How did you and Lexi meet? It doesn't sound like you share any classes."

"We actually met in the library," Damian tells her, and I nearly spit out my coffee. "I had to take a few math lectures to complete the requirements for my major, and she tutored me a handful of times."

Oh. *Okay, that wasn't so bad,* I assure myself when it seems like he won't add anything further to that explanation. It's not exactly a lie; that *was* how he first approached me, even if we spent that time flirting rather than studying, and the needing a tutor part turned out to be bullshit. Regardless, I'm just glad he didn't say—

"I tell ya, though," he continues, as if the asshole is actually reading my mind, a smug grin forming on his lips, "she really rode me *hard* with those math equations."

Oh. My. God. If I could curl into a ball and die right now, I would. There is no fucking way my mom and Gina missed that conveniently placed double entendre. Gina's raised brow and the smile she's trying to fight are proof enough she heard it. Fucking Damian. My cheeks burn so hot I'm certain they'd rival the surface of the sun.

My mom's eyes swing between me and Damian like a pendulum, her lips slightly pursed, as if she's coming to some internal decision about something.

Eventually, she says, "So, I take it you two are—"

I jump up from the couch. "You know what? It's getting late. Why don't I see you out?" I say, grabbing Damian's arm and yanking him to his feet.

"What? But it's not even four yet," he protests.

I snort, tugging him harder. "Yeah, but it's, like, ten in Sweden," I counter, as if that's in any way relevant to this conversation. When no one comments, and everyone stares at me like I've lost my mind, I add, "So…yeah. Anyway, I'll walk you out."

"All right, pushy," Damian grumbles, breaking free of my hold to walk over to my mother, extending his hand again. "Carol, it was really nice to meet you." His head then snaps to the side and he looks at my aunt. "Gina"—he holds out his hand for a fist bump, which, to my growing horror, my aunt eagerly reciprocates—"keep it real."

"For a Team Jacob girlie, you're all right," my aunt says with an approving head nod. Then, with a flirty wave, she croons in a sugary lilt, "Bye Damian!"

Pure mortification rushes through me as I reach out and grab Damian by the wrist again, my fingers a vise grip on his forearm. He doesn't struggle against me this time as I yank him toward the door.

"Oh, before you go," my mom calls out when I'm just one step shy of the hallway and salvation from this conversation. Plastering on a smile, I turn to face her, but the blood freezes in my veins at the calculating look on her face. She might be sick, but this is a woman who mainlines true crime. When she's paying attention, nothing gets past her.

Except, she isn't looking at me.

"I didn't catch your last name, Damian."

"Navarro," has barely left his lips before I'm tugging him toward the door, lest anyone else feels the undying need to play fifty questions with my fake boyfriend.

I don't release my hold on his arm until we're safely outside and the front door is firmly closed behind us.

"Damn, Dornan," Damian grunts, rubbing his wrist. "You ashamed of me or something?"

"What?" I whip my head to look at him, but my brain fails to communicate this movement to my feet, which continue their forward march and nearly send me plummeting to my death down the porch steps. Damian catches my hand at the last second before I can fall.

Pulse throbbing under my skin, I draw in a steadying breath to calm myself down, and it's only once my heart rate has returned to normal that I realize my hand is still clenched in his. My eyes dart to the living room window, but although the curtains are drawn, I yank my hand away.

"No," I answer, and it sounds completely unconvincing, even though it's true. "I just… I wasn't really ready for…*that*."

Damian's gaze follows mine back to the house, and when I glance at him again, I wince at the look of dejection that crosses his face.

I know what he's thinking. By *that*, he thinks I wasn't ready for my mom to meet *him* when, in reality, it's the opposite. What I wasn't ready for was for him to meet my *mom*. For him to see the truth I've been hiding—the last lie I've kept between us because I'm scared of what it will mean if I do fully tear down that wall. And of what it'll do to me if what I'm feeling is one-sided.

"Got it," he murmurs. And then he's quiet for a moment as we walk down the steps. "I'm sorry if I overstepped by coming here," he says once we're halfway to the sidewalk. "I tried texting, but you weren't answering, so I just wanted to check that you were okay."

A foreign tightness squeezes my chest. I didn't see his messages because my phone has been off all day while I've been at the hospital with Mom, and I obviously haven't had a chance to turn it on since I got home. But seeing as I can't exactly tell him that, I latch onto the last part of his statement instead.

"Why wouldn't I be?" I ask, feigning confusion.

He stares at the side of my face as if he's trying to read my expression. Or see past it. I don't meet his gaze, and if he does sense the false note to my voice, the obvious evasion, he doesn't call me out on it.

"You got me. I just wanted to see you in one of your cute nerdy T-shirts again."

He stops walking then, right beside the silver Audi parked outside my house. Fishing the keys from his pocket, he hits the unlock button, and it's only when the vehicle audibly *boop-boops* that I finally comprehend what I'm seeing.

"Wait…" I glance from the Audi to Damian then back to the Audi again.

"This isn't your car."

"Sure, it is," he says, reaching out and affectionately patting the roof with his palm. "You just haven't met the Renesmobile yet."

The…what?

"Renesmobile?" I parrot in lieu of an actual intelligent question.

Damian's responding grin is borderline maniacal. "Yup. And before you ask, it's *exactly* what you're thinking." He holds out one hand. "Renesmee." Then he extends the other. "Mobile. Put them together"—he claps—"and you have…" He makes a theatrical gesture toward the car. "The Renesmobile!"

"Oh, my god. Did you seriously name a car after the *Twilight* baby?"

Damian chuckles. "What can I say? My obsession knows no bounds. And as a Team Jacob fanboy, it was only fitting."

My nose wrinkles. "I can't believe I have consensual sex with you."

He laughs again, but doesn't offer any explanation for the real question hanging unanswered between us.

I sigh. "Fine, I'll bite. What happened to the douchemobile?"

Damian's whole demeanor changes, the humor and light in his eyes extinguished as suddenly as a flame doused with water. When he next speaks, his voice is so soft I barely hear it. "I gave it back."

I blink at him, not entirely convinced I heard him correctly. "You gave it… back," I repeat, trying to make sense of this admission. "Like…to Mason?"

The tempered smile Damian offers me is strained. "Correct. And the Renesmobile got pulled out of retirement." He pats the roof of the car again. "I was growing tired of the Maserati, and Nessie here is far too good for my parents' garage anyway, so it's all for the best, really."

I hold up a hand. "Wait, I'm confused. Why?"

"Why is she too good for my parents' garage?" Damian asks, his brows knitting together until they're hooding his eyes, darkening his gaze in a way that does something strange to my insides.

I clear my throat, trying to stay on track. "*No.* Why did you give it back?"

He knows what I was asking—I can see it in the way his pupils contract, just as I can see the tremor of unease twitching along his lips when he answers.

"It…was a reminder I didn't want anymore." His voice is only a breath above a whisper now, and I can tell it's taking immense effort on his part to hold my gaze. He wants to look away so badly, his shame rising to the surface, but to his credit, he doesn't. "Truthfully, I should've done it a long time ago."

The air catches in my chest at his words, and I open my mouth to say something, even though I don't have the first clue what to say or what to think. Damian cuts me off before I can utter anything more than an incomprehensible squeak.

"I know this doesn't erase what I did, but after what happened the other day…" Now, he *does* look away, his face visibly flustered. He runs a hand through his hair, disheveling the thick strands. "I thought maybe this would make it clear how much I wanted that redo, too."

I gape at him, not quite sure what to make of this confession. Is this his way of saying thank you for forgiving him, or is he under the misguided assumption that there's still a chance I haven't? To be fair, it's not like I've come right out and said it, but I thought it was obvious I have. That I do.

I *do* forgive him.

I'm about to tell him so when his eyes veer over my shoulder, looking past me at something in the distance. "I think you're wanted inside."

"I…what?"

He jerks his chin ever so slightly in the direction of the house behind me. "Your mom and aunt are watching us from the window."

"Jesus Christ," I mutter, turning my head to see if he's telling the truth or if he's messing with me, which honestly wouldn't surprise me. But sure enough, Mom and Gina are spying on our conversation from the front window, the curtains now thrust aside. God, they aren't even making an effort to hide it.

"Wait, I think Gina is mouthing something…" Damian squints. "'Kiss… him'? Oh, well, if she insists, then you should definitely do that." Winking at me, he puckers his lips.

"No, she is not!" I gasp, half out of embarrassment that my mom and aunt are watching this happen and half laughing at the stupid kissing face he's making.

Damian barks out a laugh. "I'm joking, Dornan. Though, judging from your reaction, I'm guessing this means a rain check on that goodbye smooch."

My face burns again, and the gleeful look in his eyes tells me I am probably as red as a tomato. "I…yeah." I don't need to give my mom and Gina any ammunition when I'm sure they already have an entire arsenal of questions.

My stomach dips, and it dawns on me that I'm…disappointed. I *want* to kiss Damian, and not because of this chemical attraction between us, or as a precursor to sex, but because I simply want to be close to him in that way. Because his goofy, stupid face makes my chest feel light, and I don't want that horrible weight from before to come creeping back in.

"You know," he croons, stepping forward to tuck a rogue curl behind my ear. "You're cute when you're embarrassed, Blondie."

I snort. "What? I'm not—"

"Liar." He flashes a coy smile at me, and before I can protest any further, he opens the door to the silver Audi and slides into the driver's seat with a wave.

I stand on the sidewalk for a tragically long time after Damian drives away, the image of his face in the rear-view mirror—shrinking the farther he got from me—burned into my mind like a bad memory. It's another long moment before I remember my mom and aunt watching me from the window, and the hair on the back of my neck rises as I turn and retrace my steps up the path. My eyes drift to the large glass panes, but my nosy relations have vanished from view. Still, though I can't see them to gauge their expressions, I'm aware of what's coming.

Sure enough, the second I step back inside the house, they are both on top of me like Ronnie on a free samples table. They corner me against the closed front door.

"All right, spill," my aunt demands at the same time my mom says, "What was that, Lex?"

"Damian." I give a little nonchalant shrug as if that answer alone explains everything. "He's a…friend."

My mom scoffs. "A friend who just so happens to be a billionaire. Oh, and also your boyfriend, *apparently*?"

I can practically feel the color leach from my cheeks. "What?"

My aunt puts her hands on her hips. "Navarro? As in Hallazgo Pharmaceuticals?" When I stare blankly at her, she rolls her eyes. "Lexi, I work in a hospital," she reminds me. "Don't you think I know where we get our drugs from?"

My mom bobs her head in agreement. "All we had to do was Google his name, and you were one of the first results to come up. Along with some other interesting information I'd *really* like some clarity on." Despite her tone, her expression is calm. *Too* calm. The kind of calm that comes right before a storm I'm absolutely not prepared for.

"You know," my aunt muses, rubbing her chin, "I knew he looked familiar that first day he came here."

I glance at Gina, surprised by this revelation. The only reason I didn't panic when she met Damian that day we went shopping in September was because I was certain there was no way for her to know who he is. He never told her his last name, she doesn't give a single flying fuck about celebrities or public figures, and she's not on social media where she might stumble across him by accident—simply because she doesn't like to waste what precious little free time she has doomscrolling.

My aunt must gather where my thought process is going because she lets out a tight, mirthless laugh. "Girl, I might not give two shits about celebrity gossip, but the waiting rooms at the hospital are quite *literally* littered with magazines. I obviously don't stop to read them, but I have, on occasion, seen the covers."

"They have them in the infusion room, too," my mom points out. "And unlike my sister, I do, on occasion, partake of the gossip."

I balk, gaping at my mother as if I've never seen her before. Since when does she read tabloids?

"But I… I didn't…"

"Think we'd find out? Christ, Lex, we don't live under a rock." Her expression warps then, and her eyes lock on mine with an intensity that seems so at odds with the otherwise frail condition of her body. "Is this how you've been getting the money for my treatment?" She exhales an incredulous breath, like she can't believe she didn't put it together sooner. "I knew something felt off about the whole charity thing, but I couldn't fathom why you would lie about it, so I didn't press the issue. But if you're getting money from this boy, I'd like to know. *Now*. And while you're at it, why don't you tell me about this bet that keeps popping up when I Google your 'friend.'"

The look on my mom's face is all it takes for me to crack—the stern scolding in her eyes mixed with a very clear concern. I've been holding in so many lies these last three months, I feel ready to explode. So, I do. I let the words erupt out of me like an exponential equation on steroids; they spill over so quickly I can't rein them in, with no upper limit to how much I seem able to say. And there isn't one. I tell them everything, even that Damian and I have been sleeping together, though I make it a point to spare them the gruesome details. I tell them about the bet (minus the very public library sex), about the Craigslist ad, about how I exhausted literally every other option before answering it. I tell them about our fake dates and the trip to Guadalajara. "You left the country without telling me?" my mom had shrieked, but it was hard to say if she was more angry or shocked that I did something so obviously out of my comfort zone. Thankfully, the topic of me crossing the border without my immediate family's awareness was put to rest when I followed it up with the story about Damian's brother and the resulting situation with his parents. I don't tell them about what happened in the library on Wednesday, certain that would be a step too far (and something tells me my mom wouldn't exactly see eye to eye with me regarding my logic on that one), but I do tell them about Damian's car. *Mason's* car. And about what it means to me that he chose to return it.

"We need to pay him back," my mom mutters in a daze the moment I've finally stopped talking. We've settled back in the living room. This time, Mom takes a seat next to me on the sofa, while Gina sits ram-rod straight in the armchair, hanging onto our every word. "And you can't accept any more money from him," Mom adds with a warning glare at me.

"I won't agree to that," I say, as calmly as I can manage. "You need it. That's why I made the agreement with him in the first place. With respect, *fuck* your 'alternative to continuing treatment,'" I air-quote when she starts to protest, reminding her what she said when the insurance first pulled their cover for her meds. "That isn't the solution, Mom. But *this* is. Trust me, if I had another option, I would take it, but I don't. And I refuse to feel guilty about that. Besides, this arrangement is mutually beneficial. I help Damian with his parents, he pays me, and *you* get your prescription." At my mom's perturbed expression, I double down. "We need this. *You* need this. I can't end it. I won't."

And Damian still needs this, too. I can't back out on this agreement, not just because of my mom, but because I can't do that to him. As much as I need his help, he also needs mine, and despite the way things started between us, I want to give it to him now.

Mom's face crumples, and for a moment, I think she might cry. "Oh, honey. This shouldn't be your burden to bear."

Gina's face is drawn, and I can tell she wants to agree with my mom, but can't bring herself to because she knows I'm right. Without this agreement, without this money, Mom never would've been able to carry on with her chemo, and if she hadn't continued her treatment, there's only one way this would've ended.

"But it is," I tell her, taking her hands in mine. "And I won't apologize for doing whatever it takes to help you."

Mom's gaze turns watery, and she sniffs. "I don't like feeling like a charity case, Lex."

"But you aren't," I assure her. "Damian doesn't know about your cancer or what I'm using the money for." At my mom and aunt's pointed glances, I explain with an embarrassed grimace, "He thinks I've been using the money for cosplay."

My aunt's coarse laugh is so loud I'm tempted to cover my ears. "Cosplay?" she sputters, now fully snort-laughing. "As what? The world's worst liar?"

"Lex, come on," my mom chides, rolling her eyes at her younger sister. "If he didn't already know the truth, I think it's safe to say he does now."

She gestures to herself, and my heart breaks a little at the realization that she sees what I see. How I wish the mirrors she looks in would lie so she can at least pretend to feel strong.

A lump swells in my throat. "It doesn't matter." Except, it does. It matters to *me*. But I need her to believe it doesn't, to believe everything will be okay. I need her to believe it as much as I need to convince myself.

My mom's weak grasp tightens on my hand. "It does," she insists. "But not because of me, because of *you*. You're playing a dangerous game, mixing money with emotions this way…" She shakes her head. "It's only going to end with one or both of you hurt."

I bristle. "Why would it? Yeah, we're sleeping together, but we aren't actually dating. We're just…friends," I remind her, even though that doesn't feel like remotely the right word to describe us. "There aren't any feelings involved."

Liar, my conscience growls, but I push its voice down deep, to the dark space in the back of my head where I can't hear it. In its place, however, I notice another voice, louder and much closer to home.

"Does he know that?" my aunt challenges.

I glare at her across the wooden coffee table. "What?"

She arches a cynical brow. "Girl, I just sat with that boy for two hours talking about *you*. And *Twilight*, of course. But mostly you." She shakes her head, and I don't miss the worry in her eyes. The shades of silent disbelief. "I know you struggle sometimes with social cues, Lex, but I can't help thinking you're being willfully blind if you can't see what that means."

"What Gina is *trying* to say," my mom cuts in, "is that you claim this thing between you two isn't real, but that's not what it looks like to us. And I don't think it feels that way to him."

Her words hang in the hush that follows, and in that quiet, I hear that distant, chastising voice surfacing from the back of my head. This time, however, instead of scolding me, it asks a simple question.

What does it feel like to you?

CHAPTER
TWENTY-FOUR
✦ Damian ✦

**Más vale solo que mal acompañado - Better
alone than in bad company**

**Translation: Being alone is preferable to surrounding
myself with the wrong people. Time to cut the dead
weight and focus on what really matters.**

While seeing Blondie flustered is always an entertaining experience, witnessing her crushing terror this afternoon was not. I know I blindsided her by showing up like I did at her house, which sucks since I really didn't mean to. I was genuinely worried about her when she didn't answer my texts. And not in a creepy stalker I-require-all-your-undivided-attention kind of way, but in a shit-I-hope-nothing-bad-has-happened way. Seeing the state of her mom, it seems I was right to worry.

I know Blondie was freaking out about me being there and finding out what's going on at home; I just wish I understood why she's so reluctant to tell me about it. At first, before we became…whatever we are now to each other, I could see why she might not view me as the right person to confide in about her mom's illness and their financial troubles. But now? And after I told her about Jamie to try to show her just how much I understand?

Well, I don't fucking get it.

Though I played it as cool as I could, it hurt when she kicked me out, and that rejection has been screwing with me all day, making it nearly impossible to focus on anything else. Since leaving Blondie's house, I spent the bulk of the remaining afternoon and evening in the campus library (shocking, I know), researching as much as possible about existing programs that help people with healthcare costs, as well as gathering demographic data to work out local cost of living and the gap between available income and the burden of medical expenses. But I don't honestly know how much of any of it I retained. I had planned on talking to Blondie today about working on a proposal for Hallazgo together, but with how things went down at her house, it wasn't the right time to bring it up. Judging from Blondie's reaction when I left earlier, maybe it never will be.

I sigh, trudging up the stairs to the second floor of my dorm. It's weird, calling it a night when it's not even ten p.m. on a Friday, especially when I can hear students hollering from somewhere down the hall, probably pre-gaming with beer pong or flip cup before heading off to whatever frat or sports team house is hosting a party tonight. Just three months ago, I would've been right there with them, getting so drunk I couldn't see straight and scouting campus for my latest hook-up.

Now, the desire to fuck around like that is entirely gone. I'd rather spend my evenings out with Blondie on one of our fake dates, jovially arguing about one thing or another, or better yet, with my face buried between her legs.

It's crazy how much has changed in such a short space of time—how much *I've* changed since she came back into my life…and especially since Halloween, when my feelings slapped me in the face. I wish I knew what she was thinking, and if she's struggling to the same extent I am with the blurred lines of our agreement. If she's also failing to see where the lie ends and the truth begins since we began sleeping together.

But then…I'm not lying. Not anymore. Not about any of it. And despite the terms of our agreement, I don't want this to end. I want her—*all* of her—not just the part I get when we're in bed, or the part she offers to fulfill her side of our arrangement. I want all of her parts, even the ugly ones—the parts she thinks I won't understand. And maybe I won't, but I'll sure as hell try. At this point, I don't think there's anything I wouldn't do for her.

I contemplate calling her to talk out what happened earlier when I turn into the corridor to my room and stop short. Mason is standing outside my door, his back to the wall, hands thrust deep in his pockets. There's zero doubt in my mind he's waiting for me.

I'm about to back away—to find someplace to wait him out since I'm really not in the mood to deal with him right now—but he must sense me because his pale eyes dart to mine.

"There you are," he shouts down the hallway. "I've been waiting for ages."

I cover my grimace by wiping my nose. "I've been out. If you needed something, you should've just called."

Mason's eyes narrow on me as I move closer. "I did."

I blink in surprise. What is he talking about? I haven't received any texts or calls in the last two hours—from him or anyone.

Fishing my phone out of my pocket, I press the side button to turn on the screen. "Shit. Phone's dead." Fuck. I really hope Blondie didn't try to call me. Shrugging it off as if it's no big deal, I slide the device back into my jeans and lock eyes with Mason. "What's up? Did you need something?"

Mason assesses me for a moment, looking first at the general vicinity of my pocket where I just stashed my phone, then at the notebook tucked under my opposite arm. His brow hitches upward when he meets my gaze again. "So, did she forgive you?"

I stiffen. "What?"

Mason rolls his eyes. "Poor Girl," he answers, and it's impossible to miss the note of disdain in his voice. "Considering you didn't exactly offer any explanation before chucking the keys to the Mas at my head, I'm going to go out on a limb and assume she's why you gave back the car."

He points to his forehead where, sure enough, there's a red mark half obscured by his greasy hair.

I snort. "Not my fault your hand-eye coordination is shit." I don't think the guy could even jerk himself off without staring at his dick to be certain he's grabbing the correct body part.

Mason observes me for another lengthy moment, waiting for said explanation or an apology, maybe—neither of which he's entitled to or deserves. I did so much shady, hurtful shit these last three years because I stupidly allowed him to goad me on, and I'm finally done. With all of it, but especially with him.

That's why I didn't bother explaining myself when I returned his keys this morning. I simply walked into his room, tossed him the keys, and told him the Maserati was his. Because that car was just an extension of my association with Mason, and I need to cleanse myself of both—of anything that reminds me of my bad decisions and the pain I inflicted. I can't keep being fake friends with Mason and driving his car and mean a single word of the apology I gave Blondie. The two just aren't compatible, and only one of those two things actually matters to me.

He cocks a brow. "That's it? That's all you're going to say?"

I shrug, eyeing my door behind his left shoulder. The door he's inconveniently blocking. "What do you want me to say?"

He frowns. "I don't know, man. The whole thing just seems weird is all. The bet went public months ago, but you didn't ditch the car then, not even during the worst of the backlash. You didn't even flinch when that shit broke the internet and people were calling you a dick."

No thanks to you, I'm tempted to say, but I hold my tongue.

"But now, out of nowhere, you're done with it?" I shrug again, which only infuriates him because he hastily adds, "It makes me wonder why she's dating you if she's still pissed about all that, but hey, what do I know? *Women,* am I right?" The condescending manner in which he manages to debase the entire opposite sex in a single breath ignites an overwhelming urge to punch him in the face.

No, Mason, you're not right. You're just a tool.

I huff out a sigh. "The bet was shitty of us, Mason. Maybe I'm tired of being a shitty person."

And it's true. The bet might have been Mason's idea—and the subsequent fallout entirely down to his reckless stupidity—but *I* still took him up on the challenge. *I* still participated and demeaned all those women, not unlike the way he's demeaning Blondie now. I was so blinded by my own grief and anger toward my dad that I couldn't even see what a fucking terrible person I was becoming. But now, my eyes are opened, and I don't want to be that person anymore. Not just for Blondie, but for me.

I want to be someone my abuelo and Jamie would be proud of.

"You know, you used to be fun."

Mason sneers, and though I try not to take the bait—not to rise to the insult—I can't help myself. The question is out before I can stop it.

"Meaning?"

His upper lip curls as he looks me up and down, as if he's really seeing me now that the douchey mask has been peeled away.

"Look at you," he mocks. "Returning a fucking Maserati, playing the doting boyfriend, not even pretending to care about your rep anymore." He shakes his head as if he can't fathom anything being more important. "A few months ago, you would've laughed in my face if I told you this is where you'd end up."

I shrug. "Well, I guess it's a good thing I never gave a fuck about your opinion."

As long as I've known him, Mason has just been background noise in my life. It was always easy enough to ignore him, only cranking up the volume when I needed entertaining or an accomplice for some stupid prank, but now, it's time to tune him out for good. To turn off the sound on that part of my life and let something better play in its place.

Mason scoffs. "If you say so, man. I wish you the best or whatever." He pushes away from the door then and starts to walk past me, only turning at the last moment to throw out, "I just hope Poor Girl's worth it."

As he retreats down the hallway, I glare at the back of the head.

"Don't fucking worry," I grind out between clenched teeth as I unlock my door. "She is."

I spend the next hour pacing my bedroom, chewing on my thumbnail and casting the occasional glance at my phone where it charges on my bedside table.

Just call her! the voice in my head shouts for the tenth time in as many minutes.

He's right. *I'm* right. I should just call Blondie. What's the worst that can happen?

That thought is immediately followed by every worst case scenario I can imagine. Blondie screaming at me for showing up out of the blue at her house.

Blondie telling me I suck in bed. Blondie ending our arrangement.

God, when did I get so pathetic? When did I get so self-conscious?

Where the shit is Confident Damian when I need him?

I slap myself hard on the cheek. "Come on. You can do this." With an affirmative head nod, I cross the room, grab my phone, swipe open the contacts, tap Blondie's name, and hit call before pressing the device to my ear.

The ring tone repeats so many times I begin to think she won't answer. Just as I'm about to hang up, the ringing ends, and I catch a faint, "…'ello?"

I pull the phone away from my head just enough to glance down at the screen. I definitely called Blondie, but there's a lot of noise on her end, and I can barely hear her.

"Dornan? Where are you?" I ask, trying to ignore the sudden panic flooding my insides, drowning me from within.

I can just about separate the jumbled sound of laughter and music from her muffled voice when she answers. "Grabe Expep…Expeptasins."

Little cartoon men wearing firefighter hats race around in my head, on high alert, screaming, "Fire! Fire!" Is she drunk? I mean, it's not the first time it's happened, but it's weird that her friends would let her get so wasted she can barely speak comprehensible English.

It takes me a moment longer than I would like to decode her slurred words.

"Grape Expectations?" I ask. "The wine bar?"

Blondie chuckles. "That's the one."

"And how much of that wine have you had?" I press, trying and failing to hide the tense edge to my voice.

There's a rustling noise, like Blondie is shaking her head against the mouthpiece, then a grumbled, "No wine. I'm a big fan of Gin Eyres."

I hear a male voice then, and Blondie giggles at something he says, which instantly makes my jaw tighten. "Is someone with you?" The jealousy in my tone is so blatant I cringe. I know it's ridiculous to think Blondie might be out drinking with the intention of getting laid, but then I remember the events that led to us hooking up back in September, and the caveman inside me rears his ugly head. The thought of Blondie with some other guy—with anyone who isn't me—ignites a possessiveness I didn't know I was capable of.

She's mine. She's been mine since that day we kissed in my car. I only wish she knew it.

She huffs out a soft laugh, like she's amused by my reaction, but doesn't have the energy for anything that requires more exertion than that. "That was just the bartender, silly." I release the breath I was holding, but my relief is short-lived, replaced once again by worry when she asks, "Where are you, anyway? Why can't I see you?"

"Because we're talking on the phone," I say carefully, the dread roiling inside me so palpable I can practically taste it. Then another thought occurs to me, and my whole body goes cold. "Is Ronnie there with you? Or Andie?" Silence. No response. "Dornan?" I press. Still, she says nothing. "*Lexi?*" I almost shout out this time, desperation hitching my voice up an octave.

"Nope," she finally drawls with a long-suffering sigh. "Just little ol' me and the weight of my actions."

Shit. She's not just drunk and alone, she's *upset*. With me? Because I turned up at her house uninvited? Because of what's happening with her mom? I don't know the answer, and the not knowing only stokes the flames of my growing trepidation.

There's a demanding fervor behind my next words. "Stay put. I'm coming to get you."

I've never moved so fast to get anywhere in my life. The moment I hung up with Blondie, I bolted out of my dorm, and raced to the Renesmobile like Batman answering the Bat-Signal. While I still abide by the laws of traffic (safety matters and all that), I definitely put my foot down on the pedal a little harder on the quieter roads, determined—no, *needing*—to get to Blondie as quickly as possible.

Less than ten minutes later, I'm pushing open the door to Grape Expectations, praying that I understood Blondie correctly. The breath that escapes me when I spot her in the back corner booth seems to take my entire body weight with it, leaving me practically floating as I rush over to her table.

Just as she said, she's alone, surrounded by no fewer than a dozen empty highball glasses, her hair a wild mess and glasses askew on her face. I throw an angry glare over my shoulder in the direction of the bartender, who should have cut her off probably six or seven drinks ago—or better yet, not served her at all considering she's not twenty-one yet, though I know from experience he wouldn't have bothered to check her ID—but he's too busy flirting with a busty brunette to be paying any attention to Blondie's blood alcohol level. I'll definitely be having words with that asshole before I leave.

Blondie's eyes are glassy when they catch on mine as I slide into the rounded booth opposite her.

"Well, well, well, if it isn't Mr. Big Dick," she drawls.

A smile twitches at the edge of my lips. The size of my manhood was never in doubt, but it's nice to hear she's impressed by it.

Her brows knit together, forming the cutest little crinkle between her eyes. "What are you doing here? Or am I imagining you?" Her face pales a little, and she shakes her head, covering her eyes with her hands. "God, I hope I'm imagining you. I don't want you to see me like this."

"Like what?" I ask gently. "I've seen you drunk before."

She peeks at me through the gaps between her fingers. "No, all sad and weird."

I snort. "I hate to break it to you, Dornan, but you're always weird." My smile wavers, and I hesitate a moment before asking, "Why are you sad?"

She lowers her hands with a beleaguered sigh, and her bottom lip wobbles as she stares down at the table. "Because Mom and Aunt G know the truth. They know we're not really dating…and all the rest."

My stomach twists. "The rest…like the agreement?"

She nods. "Mmhmm. And the bet."

Now, my insides are doing gymnastics, and I feel like I might throw up. Fuck. I suppose it was inevitable her family would find out about the bet sooner or later, especially with me showing up at her house earlier like I did. One Google search is all it would take to damn me. But still, I wasn't prepared for the terror that grips me at the thought of her mom and aunt knowing about all the shit I did. Or of them disapproving of any relationship I might have with Blondie.

"Oh. Are they, like…demanding you end it?" I force myself to ask.

If they are, then where does that leave us?

Nowhere, that voice in the back of my head taunts.

It's right. If Blondie's mom and aunt want her to end things with me, then that will be that. Agreement terminated. And though it would kill me to lose her, I would graciously accept it. I would never make her choose.

I'm steeling myself for that very outcome—for her to end it here and now—when she surprises me by shaking her head again. "Mom thinks it's a terrible idea, but Gina gets it. We need the money, so…" She trails off, and a shiver travels over my skin, leaving goosebumps in its wake.

I hate the self-doubt that infiltrates my thoughts, that makes me wonder if Blondie is only sticking around for the money I'm paying her and not for more. Not for *me*.

I'm tempted to ask her, but it wouldn't be right or fair—not with the inebriated state she's in. So, instead, I ask, "What's the problem, then?"

Blondie rolls her eyes. "The problem is they think you like me. Like…*like* like," she clarifies.

My heart slams into my rib cage as disappointment chafes at every inch of my soul, rubbing me raw. I never knew words could hurt so much, but hearing that me liking her is a *problem* is a new kind of pain I wasn't prepared for.

She stares at me, waiting for my response. I swallow down the hard lump in my throat. "That's a lot of likes," I deadpan.

She sighs again. "Mmhmm."

Blondie rests her chin on top of her folded arms, slumping over the table, and I don't think I've ever seen her look so dejected. Weirdly, it makes me optimistic. It makes me wonder if I'm misreading the situation, and the problem isn't that I like her, but that she's convinced herself I don't. That she believes her mom and aunt are wrong.

That conviction might be totally off, but it makes me brave. Brave enough to say, "Who says I don't? *Like* like you, I mean."

Blondie blinks those lovely eyes at me behind her glasses, which have slipped a bit farther down her nose, and the hope I find in them has my heart leaping over the damn moon. The disappointment that filled me before evaporates as quickly as the dew coating morning grass on a hot day until I'm brimming instead with an elation that has me near to bursting.

Holy shit, I was right. Blondie *likes* me. Not just physically—not just for sex—but *romantically*.

But if that's true…why does she look so unhappy?

Her bottom lip juts out in a deep pout. "*Because*, Hallucination Damian," she retorts, her tone chiding, "*Real* Damian doesn't do girlfriends."

I wonder if I should be alarmed that Blondie thinks I'm just a figment of her imagination, or if I should correct her by making it clear that I'm actually here. Maybe it's fucked up that I don't. But I can count on one hand how many times she's been candid about her feelings toward me (including those early days when her emotions were fairly singular and isolated to rage and loathing), and I don't want to miss out on this chance to understand what she's thinking. To see behind the mask she keeps insisting on wearing around me, even though I've stripped back mine.

So, I step into a new role: the one she needs me to play. A role that will let me be there for her, to listen to whatever she's willing to tell me, even if the only way she'll open up is if she believes this is all in her head.

"He said that, huh?" I ask, committing to the part. "What a bastard."

And it's the truth. I *am* a bastard, so I suppose it's only fitting that my proclamation from what feels like a lifetime ago should come back to haunt me.

"Yup," she mumbles, heaving yet another dispirited sigh, and it takes everything in me not to reach across the table and touch her hand.

"What if he did?" The words are out before they've even fully formed in my head. At the question in her gaze, I clarify, "What if Real Damian wanted a girlfriend?"

What if I want you to be my girlfriend? Not a fake one but a real one.

I don't know what I expect her to say, but it isn't the "I don't know" she whispers.

I bristle at the uncertainty in her voice. "Is it the bet? I wouldn't blame you if you still haven't forgiven him."

She surprises me again by fervently shaking her head. "It's not that. And I do forgive him," she adds with a vehemence that squeezes my chest.

She hasn't said it before—not outright—and I was starting to doubt she ever would. Not just say it, but truly forgive me. But now, actually hearing it…

It's like music to my fucking ears.

"I just haven't been honest with him." When I don't press her on the matter, she arches a brow and says, "Aren't you going to ask me about what?"

I nearly tell her, "I don't have to. I know." But I stop myself before the words can slip free.

This is it. I've been waiting for her to talk to me about this. To open up. But now that we're here, I don't know what to think. On one level, this seems wrong, like I'm tricking her into it, while on another, I can't help thinking this might be the only way she'll ever feel safe enough to say it.

I don't know how to answer her, what the correct option is, so I settle somewhere in the middle, leaving the decision up to her.

"Only if you want to tell me."

She considers that for a moment before sitting up straight, her eyes slightly clearer than they were when I first walked into the bar.

"My mom has cancer. Chronic lymphocytic leukemia. They caught it early, so if we're lucky, she'll go into remission and we'll have more time."

My chest aches when she says the word "time." The one thing I wish I could have had more of with Jamie.

"But…?" I prompt, sensing there's more she wishes to say.

She lifts her shoulders in a weak imitation of a shrug. "But I can't bring myself to tell Damian about it."

"Why? Do you think I—*he*," I quickly correct, "wouldn't understand?"

A melancholy smile tugs at her rosy cheeks. "No, he would. Probably more than anyone else I know." Her lips part on a shaky breath, and my own hitches as if all the oxygen has been sucked out of the room. "It kills me that he told me about his brother and I can't find the courage to tell him about my mom, but I'm just so afraid that…if I do, it will be too much, and he'll…" She trails off again.

"He'll what?" I press, my pulse throbbing under my skin.

"Leave," she gasps, choking on a quiet sob. "He'll leave."

The dim lighting overhead catches on the sheen in her eyes, and it's like a gut punch seeing those tears and knowing they're because of me. Because my shitty past behavior made her think the worst and only compounded what she already believed.

That she isn't worth sticking around for.

But these feelings inside her aren't just down to me; my actions only contributed to a much deeper issue.

"I'm not your dad, Lexi," I say because I need her to hear it. I need her to know there are men who won't flake like her father and ex-boyfriend did—like *I* did. Men who won't abandon her. I need her to know that she is worth all the love in the world and more.

She lets out a husky, bitter laugh. "And that's how I know you're not real. I never told Damian about my dad, and he never calls me Lexi unless he has to." She grins, but the expression lacks humor. "You're so busted, Hallucination Damian."

I smile back at her, even though my heart is breaking. "You got me."

Looking down at the table, she leans forward again until her chin is once more propped on her folded arms, and for a horrible moment that seems to stretch on for hours, neither one of us says a word.

"Hey, it's getting late," I murmur when her lids start to droop. "You must be really tired."

"A bit," she concedes. "Maybe I'll just rest my eyes."

"Not here, Blondie," I warn with a glance over my shoulder at the bartender. Luckily, he's too busy talking to busty Barbie to notice that Blondie's barely clinging to consciousness because he didn't have the fucking sense to cut her off.

If Blondie hears me, she doesn't acknowledge my words, and within seconds, those beautiful eyes slide shut.

Running a hand through my hair, I dig my phone out of my pocket and pull up the one number I never thought I'd use. The one Blondie put in my contacts just before we left for Guadalajara.

Me

> **Hey it's Damian. I'm at Grape Expectations with Lexi and I don't think she's in any shape to go home**

> **Can you come get her and have her stay with you tonight? Might look kinda sus if I try to leave with her and I don't feel like getting arrested**

That, and it's better for her to wake up tomorrow somewhere familiar and safe.

I'm not sure how many minutes pass between Ronnie's response and the cousins storming into the bar, but their appearance seems almost instantaneous. As soon as they walk in, I wave to them from that back corner booth, where I now sit next to Blondie to shield her from the bartender's line of sight. When we lock eyes, Ronnie nearly bursts into flames, revealing her true Satanic form.

"What the *hell* did you do to her?" she hisses once they reach the table, her eyes practically glowing red.

I hold up my hands in a placating gesture to plead my innocence. "She was already like this when I got here, I swear."

Ronnie glances at her cousin, who shrugs. "I mean, that kinda tracks," Andie says, and though I wonder what she means, I don't press her for details. I can only assume this isn't the first time Blondie has tried to drown her woes with gin.

Crossing her arms, Ronnie glowers at me. "Did she at least say *why* she's drinking alone on a Friday night like the protagonist in a sad indie movie?"

I peer over at Blondie, whose head is still down on her arms, her face partially obscured by her hair. "Her mom and aunt found out about our agreement. I don't think she's taking them knowing too well."

"Shit," Ronnie mutters. Then, coming to some internal decision, she sighs. "Okay. We'll take it from here."

I slide out of the booth so the girls can reach Blondie, and as Ronnie takes my vacated seat, I lean in, speaking just loud enough for her to make me out over the surrounding music and chatter. "She doesn't think I was actually here. She convinced herself I'm a hallucination, and I just…" I give a helpless shrug. "I don't want her to feel embarrassed about anything she said, so maybe…stick with that."

Understanding lights up Ronnie's face, and she gasps. "Oh, my god, she finally told you about her mom?"

I cast a wary glance at Blondie, but she hasn't budged an inch or responded at all to Ronnie's words, so I give an affirmative nod. "Among other things," I admit. "And I'm not sure how she'd react if she knew *this* is how she told me."

Ronnie's eyes follow my outstretched hand to her intoxicated best friend, who is quite literally drooling into her hair.

She frowns, then peers over at her cousin, who is sitting on the opposite side of the circular booth. "Hey, And?" When the other girl meets her gaze, Ronnie jerks her chin toward Blondie. "Would you take care of that, please?"

Her cousin doesn't miss a beat. "On it." Reaching across the table, Andie plucks Blondie's cell phone from her relaxed grip while Ronnie gently maneuvers my fake girlfriend's finger onto the button at the bottom of the screen to unlock the device.

I'm about to ask what the hell they're doing when Andie turns the phone to face me. "Was Lexi here already when you made this call?" she asks, pointing to the latest entry in Blondie's recent calls list.

I narrow my eyes and peer hard at the time stamp. "Yeah," I confirm. "I called to see if she was okay and came here as soon as I realized she was drinking alone."

Ronnie's brow dips into a worried vee as she glances down at Blondie. "All right, delete that."

Andie gives her a thumbs up. "You got it. And for extra measure…"

She taps Blondie's phone screen, and a second later, Ronnie's purse—which the redhead had tossed onto the table upon their arrival—starts screeching and shaking. Reaching inside the bag, Ronnie pulls out her phone and hits the green answer button, letting the call continue for about thirty seconds before finally hanging up.

"Alibi secured," she informs us, and I blink between the two of them, confused.

Andie gestures to the phone held aloft in her hand. "Lexi isn't stupid. She'll check her call log as soon as she's sober. This way, she'll think *she* called *us*, and that's why we came to get her."

"And with the evidence of your call to her deleted, she'll never even know you were here," Ronnie adds.

My startled gaze swings between the cousins. They look nothing alike, and I remember Blondie telling me they aren't even biologically related, and yet…

"That was some really creepy twin-level shit," I breathe, my voice awed, as Andie slides around the bench seat to the other side of the booth, and loops one of Blondie's arms over her shoulders while Ronnie takes hold of the other, hoisting her upright.

As they shimmy out of the narrow space between the table and seat, the cousins exchange a smug smile. "We get that a lot," Andie says.

They're about to walk past me with Blondie in tow—her eyes are still heavy-lidded, but she's conscious enough to at least shuffle along at their urging—when I choke out, "Hey, could you, um…keep me posted? Just the odd text to let me know she's okay."

Ronnie's responding stare is assessing, as if she's trying to make up her mind about something. Finally, she inclines her head. "Sure."

I exhale a strained breath, my chest and shoulders visibly deflating with relief. "Thanks."

"Let's go," Andie urges. "I love this bitch, but damn, she's heavy."

I expect them to leave then, but Ronnie stands statue-still, ignoring her cousin's goading, her brown eyes locked intently on my face. I don't think she blinks once in the seconds that pass, and I'm about to ask what she's looking at when she says, "It pains me to admit this, but…you're *maybe* not as much of an asshole as I thought."

My lips curl into a smile, and I snort out a laugh. "That is the second best compliment I've received today."

Andie pokes her head around Blondie's wild mane of curls. "What's the first?"

My smile deepens as I remember the sultry way Blondie called me Mr. Big Dick. But I don't tell them about that. Instead, I tap the side of my nose and wink. "That one's between me and my girlfriend."

"I think you mean *fake* girlfriend," Ronnie corrects me in a hushed breath before leading Blondie toward the door.

Maybe, I muse as I watch them walk off. But now that I know what's actually going in Blondie's head, it hopefully won't stay that way for long. After weeks of wrangling with my feelings and the kind of person I want to be moving forward, I'm ready for the real thing, and I want it with her. I just need to find a way to prove that I'm not going anywhere if she'll have me. That nothing could ever scare me away.

First, though, I remind myself with a heated glare over my shoulder, locking eyes on the laughing man behind the counter.

I've got a bartender to deal with.

My emotional state today is like a fraction.
My numerator is panic, and my denominator is dread.

I wake up Saturday morning feeling A) like trash, B) confused about how I ended up in Ronnie and Andie's room, and C) with a bone-deep dread that I did something stupid last night.

I groan, a headache splitting my skull in half, as I sluggishly force myself into a sitting position on the coral pink futon the cousins keep in their room just for me—for movie nights and the rare occasion they convince me to go out with them, because it's easier to crash here than make the short walk home. After fumbling around for my glasses (which I locate on the small table beside my makeshift bed), I slide them on to find Ronnie and Andie are already awake; Ronnie is primping herself at her desk-turned-vanity, while Andie is curled up on her baby blue bean bag, reading *Dune* for what must be the eight hundredth time.

They both stop what they're doing the moment I'm upright. Andie puts down her book and jumps up to hand me a much-needed bottle of water. As for Ronnie, she grabs her sunglasses off a hook on the side of her vanity mirror, kneels before me, and slides them onto my face in front of my glasses.

"Here, sweetness," she coos. "You'll need these."

After gulping down half the water and inhaling the painkillers Andie benevolently folds into my hand, I glance between the cousins, finally ready to ask them about last night. Their answers are frustratingly vague. They make sense—that I was drinking alone at Grape Expectations (again, oof), that I called them, and they rushed over to get me—but it still feels like I'm missing something important. Some memory of the previous evening that my alcohol-addled brain refuses to conjure.

Ronnie and Andie are both appropriately sympathetic to my Gin Eyre-induced hangover, and they even convince me to go to breakfast with them. I don't bother informing the cousins that the thought of eating anything turns my stomach.

The campus cafeteria reeks of scrambled eggs and bacon—a smell that would normally have me salivating, but which only exacerbates my queasiness today. I'm quiet as we eat, poking at the food on my plate as Ronnie and Andie chat animatedly about topics I only half listen to, my eyes drifting instead between the surrounding tables. Though it's not a fully conscious intention, I know I'm scanning those tables for Damian.

Weirdly, I don't really know if I'm looking for him because I want to see him, or because I want to hide from him. I feel bad about yesterday—about being too much of a coward to own up to the truth—but the lie has been going on for so long now that I don't know how to broach the subject. Part of me thinks it would be easier to just…not. But when I consider where the road I'm on will lead if I continue down it this way, the future I imagine is lonely. In theory, Past Lexi might have been okay with that since, at least that way, I wouldn't get hurt…but that was before Damian.

He's infuriating sometimes, cocky beyond belief, and annoyingly smug, but under all that sarcasm, he's thoughtful and genuine in a way I didn't know he could be—in a way that makes me want to lower my walls. And while I want to strangle him more often than I don't, he's brought an excitement into my life these last few months that was missing before.

And that scares me. Because now, when I look at that distant future, I struggle to separate him from it.

If Ronnie and Andie notice my quiet contemplation, they don't comment on it. Nor do they pry. They do, however, walk me home ("The fresh air will do you good!" Ronnie had insisted), and while I don't say more than maybe five words collectively between breakfast and that brief stroll, I'm grateful for their company and for the distraction. By the time we turn onto my street, I'm even starting to feel better. I might not engage in their conversation beyond a snort at something Ronnie says about a date that went horribly wrong on whatever reality TV show she's currently watching, but it's enough to take my mind off other matters, at least momentarily.

When we reach my house, the only car parked outside is my mom's. Relief slams into me at that, but I'm surprised by the tinge of disappointment that follows. I shake it off and take the porch steps two at a time, trying my best to think of absolutely anything else as I unlock the front door.

When I step inside, the house is quiet, which is my first sign that something is wrong. I don't expect to hear Gina—she told me yesterday she has a shift at the hospital today—but I would have expected to hear *something* since Mom usually spends the days following her treatments on the sofa wrapped in a blanket watching TV. It's possible she's napping, but she doesn't like to sleep in silence, and there is no other word to describe the sheer soundlessness pervading the house.

"Mom?" I call out, a tremor of unease distorting my voice.

No response.

That's my second sign that something isn't right.

My heart is a jackhammer against my ribs, and behind me, Andie barely gets out the words, "What's wrong?" before I tear Ronnie's sunglasses from my face and fling them aside, lunging forward. Ice-cold terror consumes me the moment the front room comes into my eyeline.

"Mom!" I scream at the sight of her prone figure on the ground.

She's unconscious on the floor next to the sofa, and I drop to my knees beside her, pressing a shaking hand to her throat. Thankfully, I feel a pulse, but it's weak.

Too weak.

Behind me, I hear an audible gasp, and I snap my head in the direction of the cousins, who stand at the threshold of the room, terror etched across their faces.

Andie is already yanking her phone from her pocket when the command rips from my airway, fast and forceful, like the nausea surging up my esophagus.

"Call an ambulance!"

I pace the ER waiting room at Newport Hospital, one arm curled around my middle, while the other remains in the same place it has for the better part of the past hour—with my hand to my lips as my teeth gnaw unconsciously at the tip of my thumbnail.

The ambulance arrived seven minutes and three seconds after Andie called 911, and in another ten minutes, my mom was being triaged, and I was diverted outside to wait for an update where I've spent the entire time on the verge of a meltdown.

My anxiety is like a hand—not just around my throat but pushing at me everywhere from within until I feel too big for my skin. My breaths come in short bursts, and I'm sweating from how overheated I am. Is the thermostat cranked up in here or something?

Ronnie and Andie—who stayed with me until the ambulance arrived, then went back to campus to get Ronnie's car so they could follow me here—sit nearby, and though I rarely meet their gazes, I can sense them watching me.

"Lex," Ronnie says carefully, her tone persuasive but not pushy, "maybe sit down for a bit. Wearing a hole in the floor isn't doing you or your mom any good."

Before I can respond, Andie pipes in, "Hey, there's Gina."

My head snaps to the side, in the direction of the ER doors, and sure enough, I spot my aunt clad in her usual ceil blue scrubs. She gives me a hesitant smile when our eyes lock as she crosses the busy waiting room to meet me.

"Hi, honey," she calls out once I'm within earshot.

Her curly hair, which is usually kempt in its work bun, is a tangled mess, and her eyes are bloodshot as if she's been crying.

"Mom?" I croak, unable to form any other comprehensible words with the way my heart is pounding violently in my throat.

Gina must realize how she looks because she quickly shakes her head. "Don't worry, she's fine—"

"She didn't *look* fine," I retort, my fear evident in my quavering voice. That image in my head—the one of my mom on the floor, unmoving—is something

I don't think I'll ever shake for as long as I live. Though I can't bring myself to say the words aloud, there was a moment when I thought she was dead.

That's the opposite of *fine*.

"I know," Gina murmurs, giving my arm a consoling rub. "*But* she is going to be okay."

Guilt claws at my insides. While I was out throwing a hissy fit and getting drunk alone, then waking up hungover in my friends' room, my mom was suffering. She could have *died*. She very well might have if I didn't arrive home when I did.

"What's wrong with her?" Ronnie asks when I don't respond to Gina, and I jolt at her sudden appearance at my side. When I glance at her, she reaches out and takes hold of my hand when she catches me trying to touch my glasses, and proceeds to give it a gentle squeeze. With a tremulous breath, I squeeze hers back.

My aunt, who adores my best friend, gives Ronnie a grateful smile, and I know she's relieved that I didn't have to face not only finding my mom but this last hour alone.

"The simple answer?" Gina says after a pause. "Anemia. The medical explanation: her hemoglobin levels were critically low. It's not uncommon for them to fluctuate after infusions, especially this far into treatment, and especially with a cancer like CLL, which can suppress bone marrow function."

"But she seemed fine yesterday," I protest. "Better than normal, even." While I was busy worrying about Damian, I should have been more focused on *that*. I should have been concerned that she was different instead of elated at the prospect of gorging myself on fucking chow mein. "And this has never happened after an infusion before," I add. While that may be true, it's also an excuse—a way to sidestep the guilt now threatening to tear me in two.

Gina looks at me like she knows exactly what I'm thinking. "I know, but the longer you go through something as grueling as chemo, the more fragile your body becomes. Your mom's bone marrow is less resilient than it was when she first started treatment, so it's possible her hemoglobin levels were already declining and just hadn't reached a critically low point to cause such a severe reaction. Monoclonal antibody treatments can also cause a decrease in white blood cell counts, further worsening that suppression."

I swallow hard, my eyes blurring. My aunt steps forward, pulling me into a crushing embrace that suffocates the breath from my lungs, but also offers the weight I need to keep my brain focused. To keep me from falling apart. Ronnie releases her hold on my hand so I can hug my aunt back, and I hear her retreating footsteps as she returns to where Andie remains in one of the waiting room seats, the two of them giving us space.

"I know you, sweetheart," Gina breathes into my hair once we're alone. "I know you're blaming yourself for not being there, but you can't. Hell, I've been a nurse for over a decade, and even *I* didn't see any cause for concern before I left for work this morning."

I sniff as she pulls away and takes a step back.

"I know it was scary"—her cadence is soothing as she reaches out and brushes away the single traitorous tear that slides down my cheek—"but this can happen sometimes after an infusion, even if it never happened before. And in cases like your mom's, delayed effects of anemia like this aren't that unusual. It's just unfortunate that, when it does hit, it hits hard."

"Okay," I say, drawing out the word as I try to wrap my head around her explanation, "so, what are they doing for her? What's the plan?"

Gina exhales a heavy breath. "For now, we're going to keep her overnight and see how she responds to fluids. If her hemoglobin levels start to improve, and she's feeling stronger tomorrow, the doctor will probably discharge her. But if she's still weak or her numbers don't come up enough, they might keep her an extra night and consider a transfusion."

I can practically *feel* my face go pale as the same fear that overwhelmed me the day we got those fateful letters from the insurance company once again rises to the surface. My mom's health and well-being will always come first, but now that I know she's going to be all right, I can't help panicking about the cost of all this. I had run the figures back in September, when I needed a ballpark estimate of how much money I'd need to keep my mom's treatment going, and the numbers running through my head were scribbled plainly across the "worst case scenario" page of my notebook. Those same figures build up before me again now in those taunting blocks of color that seem as physical and real as the chairs surrounding me. The fee for the ambulance. The emergency room visit. The IV fluids. The overnight stay. The potential need for a blood transfusion. The numbers skyrocket into the five-figure range and keep climbing as my anxiety ratchets to an all-time high.

Sure, I have the money from Damian that we've been saving, and there should be more than enough to cover this in the event our insurance tries to fuck us again, or to pay the difference between what they *will* cover and what they won't, but that money is supposed to pay our deductible and for Mom's prescription when our policy changes in January. At best, the total sum I'll receive for the nine months of our agreement will only cover eight months of her pills. If I start chipping away at it now, who knows how long it'll last.

"How much—" My voice comes out as little more than a rasp. I clear my throat and try again, clamping my hands into tight fists at my sides, resisting the urge to touch my glasses and to hopefully hide how badly they're trembling. My nails bite into my palms to the point I think I might have drawn blood. "How much will this cost?" I breathe.

Gina hesitates. "You don't have to worry about that."

I blink, then stare at her hard for a moment. Her word choice was oddly deliberate. Not "You don't have to worry about that *right now*," but "You don't have to worry about that," period.

"What do you mean?" I counter. "Of course, I have to—"

She interrupts me with a hand on my arm. "Lex." She says my name slowly. Pointedly. "It's already taken care of."

Taken care of?

I narrow my eyes, and I'm about to ask her to clarify—to fucking insist on it—when her gaze drifts over my shoulder to something I can't see behind me. She jerks her chin, gesturing for me to look.

My heart plummets into my feet as I turn in place, following my aunt's line of sight, and that's when I see him: Damian at the opposite side of the room holding a ridiculously large bouquet of flowers.

I blink the sudden onslaught of tears from my eyes, and my knees knock together as the ground threatens to rush up to meet them. Damian begins to cross the room, navigating the maze of chairs, and the only thing I can think beside the incessant, repeated beating of *he's here* in my ears is that, if what Gina just implied is true, then *he* was the one who covered my mom's hospital bill. Which can only mean…

He knows.

I stand rooted to the spot as he closes the remaining distance between us.

"Hey," he murmurs. The corners of his lips twitch into the barest ghost of a smile.

"Hi," I whisper, unsure what else to say. I feel completely gobsmacked, like someone just told me that two plus two really does equal five.

My eyes dip to the obnoxiously-sized (and obviously expensive) flowers held close to his chest.

"For your mom," he says in response to my unasked question, not even bothering to dance around the subject. "How is she?"

I try to answer him—to apologize for lying for so long—but my confusion wins out over logic, and what actually comes out is a very ungrateful sounding, "What are you doing here? *How* did you…" My throat closes around the rest of my words as that panic I felt yesterday when I saw him at my house once again claws at my insides.

Now, instead of hearing that persistent *he's here* in my head, all I hear is an unending string of *he knows.*

"Ronnie," Damian answers point-blank. "She texted me and told me what happened."

An unexpected and absolutely ludicrous jealousy twists my stomach in knots. "I… How did she get your number?"

Damian shrugs. "Guadalajara? From the eight times she made you check in with her, I presume. She must have still had it saved in her phone."

My lips twitch. "As I recall, it was three max."

He snorts. "Per day, maybe."

That fleeting pang of insecurity fades, and I release a shaky breath. Ronnie would never go after Damian—or anyone I was sleeping with or remotely interested in, for that matter—and I have to believe, after everything we've been through, Damian wouldn't go after her. Unless I've read this entire thing between us wrong, and in that case, I—

My brain screeches to a halt mid-thought as my eyes catch on Damian's right hand. His knuckles are mottled with blackish-purple bruises, like he hit it against something hard. Like a wall.

Or someone's jaw.

HEY.

HI.

"What happened to your hand?" I gasp, reaching out and carefully prying his hand away from the bouquet so I can get a better look at it. He relents to my touch without a fight, though I notice him wince in my peripheral vision when I brush a thumb over his swollen skin.

"Oh, this?" he asks with a dismissive *pfft*. "It's nothing, just the result of a *really* intense game of rock-paper-scissors. Spoiler alert: paper won." When I give him a flat look, he responds with that annoyingly charming grin of his.

"Sounds like a totally real thing that happened," I deadpan.

Damian nods. "Absolutely. You should've seen it."

My only response is a scoff, and then we fall into a silence so thick and all-encompassing it seems to engulf the entire waiting room. In it, I hear all the unspoken words between us.

I stare down at Damian's hand to avoid his gaze, my thumbs still mindlessly tracing soothing circles across his bruised skin. I don't even realize he's leaned in toward me until I feel the warm brush of his breath on my face.

"How are you holding up?"

My thumb stills. "I…don't know how to answer that," I admit. "Or what to say to you about…" That swell of familiar panic expands in my chest, and instinctively, I drop his hand. I'm about to take a step back, to put some space between us, when he stops me, reaching out with his injured hand and fervently grasping my fingers, even though the movement must be excruciating for him.

"Hey." His voice is a contradiction—hard but soft. A warning wrapped in the warm embrace of a consolation. "You don't have to say anything if you don't want to."

I risk a glance up at him through my lashes, and the look he gives me makes my chest tighten.

I've never had anyone look at me like that—with such affection and understanding, as if, having felt my pain himself, he would do anything in the world to take it away so I don't have to.

Fresh tears creep in at the edges of my vision as he leans in a little more, just enough to say in a voice only loud enough for me to hear, "But if you *do* need or want to talk, or you just want to cry on someone's shoulder or scream into their shirt, or if you want to do nothing at all but sit here in silence and eat your weight in waiting room M&Ms, I'm here. I'll be whatever you need—that ear, that shoulder, that shirt, or the guy who gets you as many dollar bills as you need to empty that vending machine over there." He jerks his chin toward the vending machine in question, and I choke out a wet laugh before meeting his gaze again. When I do, he says the very words I need to hear. Words that make me feel like my heart might explode. "I'm *here*," he promises. "And I'm not going anywhere."

My bottom lip wobbles.

You can't say things like that to me, I nearly let slip. Because when he does, it makes me want to do something really stupid like fall in love with him.

Assuming I haven't already.

That thought clicks into place like a missing link, and I emit a strangled, mewling sound that has Damian lifting his brow in concern.

Letting out a hysterical laugh, I say (partly because it's true, and partly because I want to distract him from the realization I just came to that is probably written all over my face), "I could actually go for some M&Ms right now."

Damian snorts out a laugh of his own before releasing my hand. "Then it looks like I better hunt down an ATM." With a tentative smile, he lifts his fingers to my face and brushes his bruised knuckles along the curve of my jaw, sending a shiver racing through me. "I'll be back in a jiff."

When he steps out of my direct line of sight, I'm not surprised to find Ronnie a few feet behind where he just stood, looking at me with a sheepish expression. She waits until Damian has left the room before shuffling toward me.

"Are you mad I asked him to come here?" she asks, clamping her hands in front of her waist in a completely out-of-character display of nerves.

I shrug. "That depends. Did you text him just so he could come pay the bill?" There's an acidity to my tone I don't fully intend, mainly because I don't really think she'd do that. I wholly believe Ronnie would sooner cover the debt herself than breach my trust that way.

And yet…she still told him about my mom. I need to know why.

She gives me a steady look, though that nervous energy is still there. "I texted him because, despite my reservations about what's been going on between you two, I can see that Damian cares. And honestly? I thought having him here might help. And not just on the money side of things," she clarifies when my lips purse. At my sharp exhalation, she reaches out and takes hold of my hands. "You're carrying a lot, Lex. I just wanted to make sure you weren't doing it alone."

"But I have you," I retort. "I have Andie. I'm clearly not alone."

"I know," Ronnie says. "But I also know he can offer something we can't, and I think, maybe right now, you need that."

I gape at her. Is this really the same woman who has called Damian every insult under the sun and spent the last three months trying to discourage me from fake dating him?

I shake my head, bemused. "In that case"—I heave a sigh—"no, I'm not mad. Honestly, I should've told him about all this sooner."

"Why didn't you?"

I part my lips to answer, but…can't. It's as if voicing the words—pulling them out of mere thought and turning them into a form that others can hear—will make them real, and that terrifies me.

"You can't even bring yourself to say it, can you?" she challenges.

I bristle. "Say what?"

The look Ronnie gives me lacks the judgmental edge I expect. Instead, it's surprisingly sympathetic. "That you have feelings for him."

I huff an incredulous laugh. "I don't. We're just…friends."

There's that bullshit excuse again, I muse, mentally calling myself out. *That's twice in two days. Well done, me.*

My face scrunches into a frown. How can I admit my feelings to Ronnie if I'm not ready or able to admit them to myself? It's not that I'm blind to them, I just…fear them. *And* the possible rejection that might coincide with them if he doesn't feel the same way. Damian might like having sex with me, but that doesn't mean he likes me romantically. There's a definite distinction. Trouble is, for me, those two things have now become intertwined.

But instead of saying any of that, I do the mature thing and double down. "It's all fake, you know that."

She scoffs. "Yeah, and Timothée Chalamet is my secret fiancé, and we're eloping to Mars next week. It's okay to admit it, Lex. If you're worried how he'll react, you might be surprised." She winks at me, and I once again just stare at her, completely flabbergasted by her abrupt Damian-related one-eighty.

"I don't get it. I thought you hated him."

She shrugs. "I did. But opinions can change, can't they? Yours did." I'm starting to wonder if she grasps the full extent of just how much my opinion of him has changed even more than I have. "Don't get me wrong, I still think he's an ass for the bet, but he's clearly not the same guy he was last spring. And as appalled as my past self would be to hear this, I think he might be good for you. He's pulled you out of your comfort zone, and what's more, you've *let* him. And with way less convincing than you usually need, I might add. How many people can you say that about that aren't related to you or aren't me and Andie? That's huge, Lex. He's changed, but so have you, and I think you know why."

I balk at that. First, my mom and Gina, and now Ronnie? I want to wonder what they're all seeing that I don't…but the thing is, I see it, too. I'm just afraid it's a lie, like so much in my life has been. That what I'm seeing isn't real.

As if reading my thoughts, Ronnie squeezes my hands again and says, "I know you're scared, but I don't think you have to be. Not everyone will leave you, Lex. *I* haven't. Andie hasn't. And I know you're afraid your mom will, but if she does, it certainly won't be by choice, and it won't be today. We all *love* you. It's okay to let someone else in so they can love you, too."

I consider that for a moment, then ask, "If I did…you wouldn't judge me? Considering everything that's happened between me and him?"

She surprises me again by shaking her head. "While I might *sometimes* question your life choices"—she leans into my space and gives me a playful nudge to my shoulder—"I am also grown up enough to admit that if our places were reversed and I had a second chance with Jay…" She falters as if lost in the memory, then gives me a rueful smile. "Well, I'm not sure I'd have the strength to reject it. This is your second chance, Lex. Don't let it slip away just because you're scared."

The words lodge in my throat. It's not that I don't know what to say, but that once I say it aloud, there's no turning back or denying it any longer.

I take a breath. Then another. Ronnie watches me, waiting, her patience stretching out the hush between us until it's unbearable. Until the truth I've been choking on has nowhere left to hide.

"I like Damian," I finally admit. "So much that I think I might actually *love* him. And you're right. That scares the shit out of me."

The second the confession leaves my lips, I feel it—something shifting. Settling. A truth I've been running from at long last catching up to me.

I glance at Ronnie, expecting some kind of "I told you so," but all she does is squeeze my hand again, a quiet acknowledgment that she already knew.

And now…so do I.

CHAPTER
TWENTY-SIX
✦ *Damian* ✦

**Vale más dar que recibir - It's worth more to
give than to receive**

**Translation: Love and compassion hold more value
than wealth...so I intend to make a difference with mine.**

True to my word, I return to the waiting room with enough M&Ms to feed a small army of children. One of the receptionists I passed during my hunt for vending machines took pity on me and gave me a plastic shopping bag to hold my bounty, and—when I told her why I'm here—even volunteered to take the flowers I got for Carol off my hands, promising to deliver them straight to her room or to Gina, depending on which she comes across first. I graciously accepted her offer; that bouquet took up more arm space than I was prepared for and was severely impacting my ability to efficiently stockpile candy.

The waiting room is quieter than when I was last in here, and I immediately clock that Blondie is nowhere in sight. It's like I have an internal radar that was designed to detect her, and its sudden silence is unnerving. I don't see Gina anywhere either, and I can only assume they're with Carol, which bodes well if she's able to have visitors now. For Blondie's sake, I hope that's the case.

Ronnie and Andie are here, at least—still sitting in the same seats as before—so I saunter over to join them, rustling, overpacked bag in hand.

Ronnie glances at me when I slide into the empty chair beside her.

"Hey," I say. "Any news?"

She shakes her head. "Not really. Though, I think I overheard Gina say they're going to transfer Carol out of the ER soon, which is good. Lexi is with her now, so we should know more once she's back."

I nod. If they're moving Blondie's mom to a different ward, that must mean she's stabilized. Definitely a good thing.

Ronnie snorts. "Are you planning for the apocalypse or something?"

I follow her gaze to the bag dangling from the tips of my fingers between my open legs. "Lexi said she wanted M&Ms," I state simply.

Ronnie stares at me blankly for a moment. "So, you robbed a candy factory on the way over here?"

I bark out a laugh, and to my immense surprise, the she-devil grins at me—not like someone plotting my death, but like someone who might actually, one day, be my friend.

"I didn't get a chance to say it before, but thanks for texting me," I say to her, and I mean every word. "Really. Thank you."

Her lips twitch at the corners, that smile faltering, a hint of sadness peeking through. "Thanks for coming. I'm sure Lexi won't ever come out and say it, but she's glad you're here. And I am, too," she adds reluctantly, her voice a disgruntled grumble.

I smirk as I lean back in my chair. "Is that your way of saying you want to be besties?" Ronnie scoffs and rolls her eyes when I hold out my hand. "How about it, Red? Will you be the Alice to my Bella?"

Her lips purse, and with a delicate sniff, she retorts, "Jessica is the best I can do."

I consider that for a moment, then nod. "A fair counter-offer. Frenemies, it is."

Ronnie takes my hand, and we shake, affirming our newfound friendship… although, truce might be a better word to describe it. On her other side, Andie huffs out a soft, mocking laugh.

"And you call *me* a nerd."

Roughly ten minutes later, Blondie returns, and I jump up from my chair the instant I spot her, my chest tightening when I notice her eyes are red-rimmed from crying. Shit. I hope that doesn't mean anything bad. I weave around the chairs blocking my path until I'm standing in front of her.

"Hey." God, she looks so dejected and meek, and so damn small in spite of her height. I want to grab her hand, or hug her, or just do *something*, but I'm not sure she wants to be touched. I know I didn't. But then, maybe I would have if Blondie had been the one who was there with me all those years ago when I was in her shoes.

Swallowing the rising lump in my throat, I ask in a muted breath, "How's your mom?"

Despite the redness ringing her eyes, a look that can only be described as relief crosses her exhausted—and definitely hungover—face. "She'll be okay…which I already knew from Gina, but it helped to see it for myself."

"Of course." I understand that well. Unfortunately, I never got that moment with Jamie.

"Thanks for staying," Blondie whispers, giving me a shy smile before dipping her chin to look down at her shoes. "I—*Jesus*, how many packs of M&Ms did you buy?"

I follow her bewildered gaze, which has shifted to the bulging plastic bag by my side. "All of them, I think? In this hospital, at least—well, excluding the staff rooms." I don't bother clarifying that "all of them" includes the gift shop stock on top of what I found in every last vending machine that crossed my path. It might seem excessive, but if M&Ms were what my Blondie desired, then I would bring her as many of those small chocolatey candies as I could physically get my hands on.

Despite the weariness on her face, Blondie cracks a smile—dimples and all—and chuckles. "You're ridiculous."

My heart does a somersault in my chest at the fucking *delightful* sound of her laugh. "Just doing my part," I declare with a grin, and I wonder if she can sense what I'm desperate to say to her. If she can read it on my face.

The words push at the boundary of my lips, and they're about to slip out when I hear a familiar voice behind me.

"Lex?" Andie interrupts, and I turn to see the cousins anxiously inching toward us. I completely forgot about them the moment Blondie re-entered the room. I'm certain they caught sight of her, too, so I can only assume they hung back to give us a minute alone. But now, I can see on both their faces how eager they are for news of her mom.

Blondie puffs out her cheeks and blows out a loud breath before offering them each a tentative smile. "Mom is okay," she assures them, answering their unspoken question. Glancing between the three of us, she gives us a brief rundown on what's happening with Carol, and what she plans to do in the interim. "Gina said there's no point sticking around since I won't be allowed in with her outside of visiting hours, so I'm thinking of going home and coming back again in the morning. Gina will be here overnight, and she said she'll call me if anything changes."

"I'll get you home," I offer before quickly adding, "if you want." Blondie's face flushes when our eyes lock, causing my heart to do something entirely new, something weird, and fuck…if this feeling writhing inside me isn't love, I don't know what the hell it is.

"Okay," she says, her voice so soft it barely qualifies as a whisper.

Ronnie clears her throat, and Blondie blinks rapidly as if suddenly woken up from a trance. Her long dark lashes flutter against the porcelain of her cheeks.

"Th-thank you both for being here," she stammers, remembering herself as she breaks my gaze and glances between her friends' faces. They each respond with the same patient smile.

"Any time, Lex, you know that," Andie murmurs.

Ronnie steps forward and clasps Blondie's hands in hers. "Call us if you need us. For anything, regardless of the time, okay?"

"I will," Blondie promises as the two girls throw their arms around her.

We part ways with Ronnie and Andie outside the hospital, the cousins crossing the road to the lot where Ronnie parked her car, while Blondie and I wait at the drop-off loop by the main entrance for our Uber.

When I got Ronnie's text, my first instinct was to jump in my car and race over here, but then I considered how much time I might waste looking for a free parking space, assuming there were any at all, and though I was ready to ditch my darling Renesmobile in the middle of the street if I had to, taking an

Uber seemed preferable to causing a potential traffic collision. It took longer than I would have liked—not to mention the pit stop I made to buy flowers—which meant calling the hospital from the car to take care of Carol's bill so the Dornans wouldn't have to worry about it, but in hindsight, I think it was the best choice. I doubt I would've been in the right headspace to drive, and now, it means I can give Blondie my full attention on the way to her house.

When the Uber arrives less than two minutes later, I climb into the back seat with her, the bag of M&Ms sandwiched between my feet on the floor, and my heart gallops when she opts to sit in the middle, gluing herself to my side. My eyes dip to her hands, which she clenches nervously in her lap, then lift to her face—to her eyes, which shine behind her glasses. I don't think as my arm seems to move of its own accord, sliding around her shoulders and pulling her close to me. I'm not sure if it's the right thing to do. I'm not sure if I should give her space. But those doubts are silenced when she lets out a stilted breath and sinks into my chest with a sigh.

Neither of us says a word during the car ride. I just hold her to me, occasionally pressing my lips to her hair, trying (and failing) to ignore her hand on my thigh. There's nothing remotely sexual about what we're doing—this moment is strictly about comfort—but embracing her like this, having her so close that her scent is the only thing my brain is aware of, is only making me all the more attuned to how fucking much I want her. And not just in bed, but in all the ways. I want every part of her.

Because I love her.

I fucking *love* her.

That realization rings through my head in a constant loop right up until we pull in front of Blondie's house. Then, as we walk the short path to her porch, all I hear in my head is *tell her, tell her*, like my heart is pumping those words into my blood so I feel them everywhere.

"So, it looks like I have the house to myself tonight," she says once we reach her door, her tone casual, though the implication behind it is obvious. "Do you…want to come in?"

Yes! every part of me screams as she unlocks the door, but I stop myself from crossing the threshold.

"Only if you want me to." Her brow furrows, and she opens her mouth to say something, but I hold up my free hand to stop her. "And just so it's clear, if you *do* want me to come in, I'm not expecting anything. I'm here for you for whatever you need, bag of M&Ms and all."

I lift the overstuffed bag dangling from my other hand to prove my point.

Blondie stares at my haul as I lower it back to my side. "I need you to stop being so…*this*."

"This?" I echo.

She huffs out an exasperated breath. "Charming. Sweet. *Thoughtful.*" Annoyance punctuates every word. "It makes me confused."

A jolt of something that feels a lot like guilt hits me like a lightning strike to my heart. "Confused about what?"

She shoots me a vexed look before moving her hand back and forth between us. "What this is…exactly."

As her words—and the understanding of them—sinks in, that pang in my chest grows more pronounced. I guess it looks like my hunch at the bar last night was right. Blondie doesn't believe I like her—or at least not enough to break my "no girlfriend" rule.

Fuck, has she been walking around these past weeks since Guadalajara thinking I'm only in this for the sex? That this thing we have is just physical to me, as fleeting as a car passing by on a busy street? If so, how long has she been speculating when this will end—that I'm not fully in this, up to my neck in deep water?

Jesus, my dad was right. I *am* a pendejo. Ronnie told me that Blondie sometimes needs things spelled out to her, and because I'm the biggest idiot in the world, I've only added to her confusion by not being upfront with her from the moment I realized what I was feeling.

This is it. The timing might be completely fucked considering everything going on with her mom, but I have to tell her now or risk never telling her at all.

"Isn't it obvious?" I whisper, committing to what I'm about to do by taking that step over the threshold into her house. Blondie holds her ground as I inch closer to her, my movements slow and measured, my gaze unwavering.

Gentle, I remind myself. That's another thing Ronnie said. That Blondie is open to new things so long as the push to get there is gentle.

And accepting what I feel for her after everything we've been through *is* a push. But she feels it, too; I know she does. If she didn't, she wouldn't be so terrified of me leaving, a fear I plan to quash for good.

"Clearly not," she breathes, her voice tremulous as she jerks her head. "Not to me."

Another step closer. I lean in toward her a little, cocking my head with a smirk. "Are you being deliberately obtuse right now, or do you really not know?"

My question has the intended effect. Banter has always come easy to us. It's familiar territory. Comfortable. And most importantly, it puts her at ease—I can tell by the softening of her shoulders, which were previously tense and raised.

Blondie rolls her eyes and snorts. "Obtuse? Is that another word from your word-of-the-day calendar?"

"You know it," I say with a laugh, taking another step closer. "This month is math words. Are you going to answer my question?"

She hesitates, giving me a skeptical look. "I don't know what you mean."

"Then let me spell it out for you." Lifting my free hand, I pinch the end of one of her curls between my fingers, tugging it gently and then letting it go, watching with a tiny, fond smile as it springs back into place. God, I love her hair. "I like you," I murmur.

Blondie slow-blinks at me once…twice…like a computer processing a command input.

"You *like* me," she repeats. "Like someone likes a really good taco?"

I snort out a laugh. "I *love* your taco, actually. But…I was thinking more like *Twilight*-level feelings."

Her lips purse into the cutest little pout. "So, you have a huge boner for me?" she asks in a surprisingly sultry voice that immediately has Damian Jr. taking notice of this conversation.

I nod. "In my pants *and* in my heart." Her eyes go wide as I raise a hand to my chest and lay it flat over my left pectoral. "Right here. The biggest of boners." She stares at that hand for a moment, saying nothing, and I frown at the lingering uncertainty I find in her gaze. Maybe I'm being *too* gentle with this admission. I want to heed Ronnie's advice, do this right for Blondie's sake—give her time to process by spelling out every word and emotion so she doesn't doubt it—but then, I've never held back with her before. Maybe blunt honesty is what she needs from me now.

"I'm sensing there's still some confusion here, so allow me to be perfectly clear. I have feelings for you, Dornan."

"Like…homicidal feelings?" she hedges, echoing what she said to me before kissing me in the library last month.

I scoff. I swear, she's doing this on purpose now.

"Romantic feelings, you smart-ass." I lean in so close her warm breaths puff against my face. "I *like* you, Blondie. *Like* like."

It's when I say those last two words that I see it: the cautious understanding on her face that tells me she *knew* (or at least suspected) how I feel about her but was too scared to believe it.

"You like me," she breathes, looking up at me through sooty black lashes, "like someone would like their girlfriend?" A grin explodes across my face, and I'm about to respond when her wary voice cuts through the silence like a knife. "But you said you don't want a girlfriend."

It isn't a question. It's a condemnation. And as the smile slips from my face, I have never hated my past decisions more than I do at this moment.

"I know what I said. But that was Past Damian, and I think we can both acknowledge that Past Damian was a bit of a bastard."

Her lips quirk at the corners, but whether she remembers our conversation at the bar last night remains to be seen. It doesn't matter if she does so long as she believes me. "And Present Damian?"

I drop the plastic bag in my hand to the floor and curl my arms around her waist, gently pulling her toward me. "Present Damian would like to retract all previous statements regarding his lack of interest in a girlfriend…because he's crazy about you, Dornan. *I'm* crazy about you."

She sucks in a sharp breath. "Well, then we have that in common. Because you make me crazy."

I arch a wry brow. "Is that your way of saying you have feelings for me?"

"Homicidal ones, definitely," she quips.

"And…non-homicidal ones?" I ask, our mouths only an inch apart now as I dip my head.

"I have a huge boner for you, too, if that's what you mean," she deadpans.

My eyes drift to the nonexistent space between us—to where those perfect breasts are flush to my chest.

"In your pants or in your heart?" I rasp.

"Both," she whispers, and my own heart fucking implodes when she says, "I like you, too, Damian. And I don't want this to be fake anymore."

I raise one hand and press it flat to the side of her neck, and she trembles when my thumb grazes the skin of her jaw. "Then it won't be," I promise.

I don't plan to kiss her, even though it's killing me not to. I meant it when I said I'm not here with any expectations. But when she rises onto her toes, closing the last of the distance between us, and her plump lips mold to mine, any self-control I had slips away.

Thankfully, our heads seem to be in the same place because, before I know it, both our jackets and shirts are discarded in a heap on the ground, leaving us standing topless in the hallway, pawing mindlessly at each other. I roam over every inch of soft skin I can reach—her stomach, the curve of her back, the delicate line of her neck, those perfect breasts—my lips following the path my hands take. I kiss her like she's something I can't get enough of. Something I need to consume. Devour.

Her responses are just as eager, and I swallow her moan when I back her against the nearest wall, my hand skimming the underside of her thigh as I hoist it upward and step between her legs. Her nipples are as hard as my cock as I push closer—so close nothing could get between us, not even air—and I fucking *relish* the debauched whine she exhales when I grind my length against her.

This isn't what she needs right now, I try to remind myself, but it's like shouting into the void. I can barely hear that voice of reason in the back of my head, too drunk on her touch, her lips, her hot center, and the remaining layers of clothing I'm dying to rip off.

It's only when Blondie claws at my back and yanks me closer that I realize I must've said that out loud. "You're wrong. I do need this. I need *you,*" she pants against my cheek.

My heart races as her hands move to my jeans, and I barely have time to process the sound of my zipper before I feel her palm on my cock.

"Fuck, Blondie," I hiss, thrusting into her touch.

Our movements are clumsy as we help each other out of our pants, and then I'm kissing her again, crowding her against the wall, my dick (which is so erect I could hang a damn coat on it) grazing the wet heat of her entrance. My hands find the underside of her thighs again, and understanding my intention, she wraps her legs around my waist when I lift her as if she weighs nothing. It's easy to slide into her at this angle, but while fucking her this way is the single hottest thing I've ever done—a fantasy come to life, hotter even than our library sex—there's also an intimacy to it that I've never known before with sex. Maybe it's the fact that we've been honest with each other after months of dancing around the lies and the tension. Maybe it's that I've finally opened myself up to feeling something again. Something real.

And I feel everything as I pound into her.

Pleasure.

Euphoria.

Complete fucking bafflement that I could ever deserve this happiness.

As she screams my name, her orgasm crashing around me, I wonder if she finds herself overwhelmed by the same feelings, the same satisfying sense of completion, like the world used to be out of focus, and it's sharp and clear now that we're together.

More than anything, I wonder just how deep her like of me goes. As I set her down, and she guides me over to the sofa before kneeling between my open legs, I wonder if there's a chance, however small…

That she might love me, too.

Blondie and I spend the next several hours exploring each other's bodies to the fullest, as if admitting our feelings has unlocked some primal need and erased any and all inhibitions. We fuck on the sofa, against the wall, on the kitchen table. Between the sex, me eating her out, and her sucking me off (which is spectacular, I might add), I honestly don't know how we haven't collapsed from exhaustion. It's like we've made fucking an Olympic sport, and she makes me orgasm so many times, I'm starting to think there isn't a drop of cum left in my body. I'm so spent, I feel borderline malnourished, but I can't bring myself to move from the sofa for sustenance or even for water. Not when doing so means untangling my limbs from hers and the warm blanket wrapped around us.

If this is how I die—with Blondie between my legs, her back to my chest, her fingers mindlessly caressing my arm where it rests across her stomach— then I will accept my death with gratitude, because nothing in this world is better or makes me happier than this moment.

My lips graze her forehead when she shifts her head to look up at me. "Not to be that person who needs to put a label on it," she begins, her voice rough from what I'm thinking is likely sex-induced dehydration, "but…"

I notice the undercurrent to her tone as she trails off—not of uncertainty or even fear, but of expectation. She needs me to say it, not just that I like her, but where that mutual liking will now lead us. She needs to hear it out loud.

And maybe I do, too.

"Yes," I say, answering her unspoken question, "you're my girlfriend, Dornan. And before you ask, no, I don't mean my fake girlfriend. I mean my for-real one. And I couldn't be happier about it." I catch a glimpse of her smile as I pull her tight and kiss the top of her head. "Truthfully, I've wanted this for a while."

"Really?" She shifts again to lock her big, beautiful eyes on me. "Since when?"

"Hard to pinpoint," I admit, "but it really sank in on Halloween, so some time before that."

Blondie stares up at me for a moment, rolling her teeth over her bottom lip. After what she did to me earlier, those delicious lips will undoubtedly feature in all my future dreams. "Can I ask…" She hesitates as if considering her next words carefully, then finally says, "Why was Past Damian so intent on no girlfriends?"

When I don't immediately answer, Blondie sits up and turns so we're now lying stomach to stomach. Resting on my chest, she props her chin on the back of her arm while the fingers of her other hand trace feather-light circles across my shoulder.

I want to blame the shiver that wracks my body on her wandering touch, but I know that's not the cause. It's this final sliver of truth I've been hiding from these last four years. Although it's difficult to voice, I'm ready to face it—I *need* to face it if I'm ever going to truly move on. And I want to move on, I *want* to be free of this pain I allowed to eat me up for so long. To do so, I just have to say it and hope to god that it really will be like that saying: that the truth will set me free.

"When my abuelo, and then Jamie, died, it left a gaping hole in my life," I explain, and I can see the weight of my words reflected back at me in Blondie's softening gaze. "I was desperate to fill it, but too scared to let anyone in, certain it would end badly and I would be forced to go through the pain of losing someone I loved all over again. So, I substituted the emotional connection I *needed* with empty physical ones. To protect myself, I kept everything and everyone at a safe distance. No friends—not real ones I actually like, anyway, which was easy enough since people only ever looked at me and saw my family's money. No girlfriends. Just parties and sex. And absolutely no Repeats. Until you." I flash a small smile at this gorgeous, smart, incredible woman, who blushes scarlet at my profession. "So much of my life, so much of who I was before…was until you. Until I met someone who made the risk worth it, and reminded me how it feels to live."

Blondie's breath catches when I stroke a hand along the length of her naked arm, then, interlacing our fingers, I slowly pull our joined hands to my lips and place a tender kiss on her knuckles.

"What I was doing before wasn't living. Shit, I wasn't even surviving. I was *drowning*, and you pulled me out." I shift my other hand to her face and trail the pad of my thumb across her bottom lip, which quavers at my touch. "You not only saved me, but you made me want to re-examine my life. What I want to do with it. Who I want to be. And I think I finally found that answer."

I spend the next several minutes telling Blondie about my abuelo, about the dream I was raised on, and the hope I have to turn that dream into a reality. Her eyes brighten with quiet pride when I tell her I want to use my name and family's wealth for good, and when I eventually tell her how I plan on taking that first step—about my proposal to convince the board at Hallazgo to implement a program that would aid families struggling to afford life-saving medication and care—that admiration in her gaze becomes silvered with tears.

But as much as I want this, as much as I believe in it, I can't ignore the shadow hanging over it all—the threat that I might not even be allowed to work for Hallazgo. That the means to instill real change might be taken away from me, no longer mine to inherit. I've spent four years purposely destroying my life; my grades had already dipped from dealing with the loss of my abuelo, but after Jamie, I ended up nearly failing my senior year and only graduated high school at all due to "extenuating circumstances" and a sizable donation from my parents. I wouldn't have even gotten into Conwick if my dad hadn't bought my way in, and I proceeded to float by doing the bare minimum since and fucking up everything in my path. I think my parents assumed I would grow out of it, out of this "phase" they refused to acknowledge for what it really was: grief. And when I didn't…well, they made their feelings clear: step out of line again and they'll cut me off, not just financially, not just from the family, but from the company my abuelo built. It doesn't matter that I'm their son. If they don't approve of the man I'm becoming, they won't let me be a part of their empire. And without their backing, I don't know if I'll even get the chance to pitch my proposal, let alone make it happen.

Still, Blondie's approval means more than I can put into words, and for the moment, it's enough to quiet those fears.

"Damian, that's…" She shakes her head. "I don't know what to say except I think it's an amazing idea."

"I want to make a difference." And I think that's what my abuelo and Jamie would want, too. They wouldn't want me to waste my life wallowing in sadness and self-destructive despair. They'd want me to *live*. To be a positive force in this world…and use what I've learned from their loss to leave a mark, even if it took so much heartache to get here. "The only thing is," I say after a beat, "I know my dad and the board will never go for it if I can't make the program profitable in some way to Hallazgo, and while I have some ideas on how to do that, I'm not a numbers guy. I can use a calculator like the best of them, but this is going to take something special, like a math genius, to make this proposal foolproof."

Blondie's lips press into a coy little smirk. "Did you have someone in mind?"

I beam, and she bursts into the most hard-on-inducing giggle fit when I roll her onto her back and tickle her.

"What do you say, Blondie?" I ask, punctuating the words with open-mouthed kisses to her neck, collarbone, and chest. Resting my chin between her ample breasts, I peek up at her with a smile full of so much affection and love it seems to spill out of me. "Want to change the world together?"

She considers me with a pensive hum. "Like Batman and Robin?"

"I mean, I'm definitely Bruce Wayne in this situation with the handsome looks and butt loads of money, but you"—I drag my lips along her sternum, then rise until I'm hovering over her—"are certainly no Robin."

She arches a brow. "Yeah? Who am I, then?"

"Superman," I answer. "Obviously."

"Superman?" she parrots.

"Mmhmm. You have that whole Clark Kent thing going on with those glasses. It's *very* sexy."

Her face scrunches up in confusion, and she wrinkles her nose, jostling said glasses. "I thought Clark Kent was the nerd, and Superman was the sexy one?"

"Oh, he is," I say, brushing a rogue curl from her forehead. "But lucky for you, I dig nerds. Speaking of"—I sit up, looking around the general vicinity—"where's that cute 'I love pi' T-shirt of yours? I've had *way* too many sex dreams about it, and I want to see if the dream lives up to reality."

She giggles again. "You're incorrigible," she scolds, shifting upright and pushing me back against the sofa to straddle me.

I shrug and lean back to admire the view, my fingers languidly caressing the sides of her naked body. "I don't know what that means, but I'll take your word for it. Now, kiss me, Blondie. I'm dying over here."

Although she rolls her eyes, she obliges.

CHAPTER

TWENTY-SEVEN

✦ *Lexi* ✦

**Pi is a paradox: irrational yet unavoidable.
Kind of like falling in love with
someone you once thought you hated.**

DECEMBER

The next month is a whirlwind. Between classes and studying for finals before Christmas break, almost every available moment is spent with Damian working on his proposal. Some nights, we chip away at it in his dorm room, sprawled side by side on his bed like two research goblins—him on his laptop scouring public data, industry reports, and economic papers, and me half buried in spreadsheets and numbers—only breaking to occasionally frisk each other or caffeinate. I alternate between perfecting an affordability formula—one that doesn't just look at a person's income, but takes into account variables like debt, existing medical expenses, dependents, and cost-of-living adjustments to determine what they can *actually* afford—and a price elasticity model that balances affordability for patients with long-term sustainability for the company, ensuring that Hallazgo remains profitable while allowing the initiative to grow and help the people who need it.

A few nights into our collaboration, I realized that Damian was watching me work, his eyes focused on the way I moved through the numbers with ease. When I met his gaze, I saw something in it—a sort of unbridled curiosity, like he was trying to figure me out. At first, I dismissed it, chalking his reaction up to the usual skepticism people always show when they witness me solving complex equations so quickly. But then I glimpsed that look on his face again—the question in his eyes, like he wanted to understand—and without him saying a word, I found myself explaining the way my brain works. I told him how numbers and formulas aren't just numbers to me—they're colors and physical shapes in the world, like math-based art only I can see.

And that's when it occurred to me…Damian wasn't surprised by my answer. He didn't ask follow-up questions or even blink at my explanation. He merely smiled as I spoke and nodded, as if he already understood on some level, and I was just filling in the blanks.

His reaction to my synesthesia was not what I expected…or anticipated, not with the memory of my father still so clear in my head. Of him walking away. I hadn't realized until then how much I'd been holding onto my fear of people not understanding me, of them judging me for something I can't change or control. Something that just makes me…me. But Damian didn't react the way I feared. He just accepted me without condition or hesitation… the way I wish my father had.

And I think it was in that moment that I truly grasped that not all men are like my father. That Damian isn't like my father. Because instead of the frustration and confusion my dad often exhibited when I was a child—not just that he couldn't understand me, but that he couldn't even be bothered to try—I saw an unfiltered awe in Damian's eyes, quiet but genuine. He looked at me like I was something not just wholly unique but *special*. Someone to be cherished. And for the first time since this agreement began, I really allowed myself to believe he wouldn't ever walk away.

As the days and nights blur together, with each of us immersed in our own dedicated corner of the project, it becomes clear that the hard part isn't the math; it's the constant hunt for the right data to back it all up. Fortunately, a lot of information is accessible online—industry pricing and sales data, studies and surveys on patient affordability and existing patient assistance programs, copay and deductible trends, as well as insurance denial claim rates specifically related to the drugs Hallazgo produces. We even scour crowdfunding sites like GoFundMe for real-world examples of people struggling with healthcare costs, which fuels our motivation when we see just how widespread the problem really is in our country.

But despite what we're able to find, what we *don't* have is access to Hallazgo's financial department or internal data—not until Damian actually starts his employment there, which is still several months away, assuming it happens at all—so the best we can do is construct a theoretical framework of what the program might look like using what information we can glean from those publicly available reports, financial disclosures, census data, and studies, as well as the insider information Damian is able to persuade out of industry professionals who agree to meet with him because of his name.

And a *lot* of people agree to meet with him, eager for the chance at a partnership with the industry-leading Hallazgo brand, which has traditionally focused on high-margin specialty drugs and exclusive insurance agreements over exploring its corporate social responsibility, showing us plenty of untapped potential is out there if the company were to branch out. When Damian first asked me to help him with the proposal, I underestimated just how much he had already planned and considered. For someone who's made a habit of only coasting when it comes to his schoolwork, I'm taken aback by how clever he is, and beyond impressed when it becomes clear he knows a lot more about this industry than I had expected. He wasn't joking when he said he had ideas for ways to make the program profitable and appealing to the company's board of directors, and with every research university department head and hospital executive who shows an interest in what we're setting out to achieve, the more I believe this can actually work and become something real. Something *good*.

And each time I glance at Damian while we're working, those dark eyes set on his laptop screen or on the dozens of medical and economic journals scattered around him, I find I love him a little bit more—not just for what he's done for me and my mom, but for what he's attempting to accomplish now. The kind of man he's aiming to become. More than anything, I love him for taking this risk, for reaching for something. For chasing the dream he holds onto so tightly, even if there's the risk his father might reject it. What matters is that he's *trying*, that he *cares*, which means way more to me than any amount of money.

During these weeks of research, I glimpse a side of Damian I haven't seen before, and I quickly find that Ambitious Damian is the sexiest version of

Damian by far. He's intelligent and calculating in a way that's often masked by his sarcasm and general demeanor, and getting this chance to see him—really *see* him—opens a floodgate inside me that I don't know how to close.

Some days, I feel like I could go mad with how badly I want him. Other days, I don't bother resisting. I simply lay down whatever I'm working on, push his laptop aside, climb into his lap, and show him just how much his drive and determination turn me on.

When we aren't cooped up in Damian's dorm, we relocate to the library, or on the days when Gina has work, we come back to my house in-between classes and in the evenings, so I can keep an eye on Mom. Following her collapse last month, she was released from the hospital after twenty-four hours without needing a transfusion or any further complications, but the fear that it could happen again lingers like a bad taste in my mouth; I refuse to take any chances by leaving her alone for too long.

Luckily, Mom doesn't seem to mind. In fact, I think she even likes Damian despite learning about the bet. I'm sure it helps that I told her about his family drama, so she knows there's a rebellious aspect to his past behavior. Plus, he's a perfect gentleman in her presence, the epitome of charm. He's polite, attentive, and even cooks us dinner most evenings (I hadn't been aware he *could* cook, although I guess I'm not really surprised after meeting his abuela, who is an absolute mastermind in the kitchen). And I can tell she respects what he's doing—that she has an emotional stake in what he's setting out to accomplish with the initiative. I suppose it's hard to dislike someone who is actively trying to financially help people with chronic and terminal illnesses, especially when one of those people is you. And I know she feels grateful to him for paying her hospital bill, even if she keeps insisting that we need to stop taking his money.

Still, the more time he spends at my house, the more I'm convinced it isn't anything *he* does that sways my mom's mind in his favor so much as her seeing me happy.

And I *am* happy. I'm freaking ecstatic, and it took feeling this elation to realize just how *not* happy I was before. I wasn't unhappy, per say—there were plenty of good and meaningful things in my life—but in a lot of ways, I was just surviving the day to day, like Damian was, treading water with no land in sight. But now, I've finally found my way to solid ground, and with every step onto the shore, I'm leaving behind the endless, exhausting pull of the tide.

It's terrifying, knowing how easily and suddenly life could snatch this away, but in those moments of fear, I remember what Ronnie said to me at the hospital—how I shouldn't let this second chance slip away just because I'm scared. And in those moments, I cling even tighter.

While I'm thrilled my mom approves of Damian, Gina is another story. She was already firmly in his corner after what happened at the hospital in November, but now, she's positively smitten—so much so, I'm starting to worry she might do something truly cringeworthy, like start an online fan club. To my horror, Damian is just as obsessed with my aunt. Because of her work schedule, we don't see her often, but when we do, Damian always cries out, "Where the hell have you been, loca?" and then they immediately begin chattering like two pre-teen girls discussing their latest celebrity crush. They're *so* engrossed in each other during these talks that I'm fairly certain I could burst into flame right next to them and they wouldn't notice. But despite my internal grumblings, I secretly love it—love seeing how welcoming my family has been with him.

In fact, Damian grew on my mom and aunt so quickly that he even scored himself an invite to Thanksgiving, which we celebrated a week late to give my mom a chance to recoup after being in hospital. Ronnie and Andie were there as well, and that evening, surrounded by all the people I care about, my heart felt near to bursting. I even witnessed something that some would dare to call a miracle: Ronnie and Damian not only speaking civilly to each other but *laughing*. About something having to do with *Twilight*, (Damian's go-to conversation starter) but still. I thought I'd sooner see Hell freeze over than witness the two of them getting along, and it made me wonder if there isn't something to Damian's vampire obsession after all—if it has some secret magical power that somehow brings people together.

When I said as much to him that night, he barked out a laugh and pulled me into a crushing hug, chuckling into my hair.

"It isn't *Twilight*," he murmured before kissing the top of my head. "It's you."

Those two words have stuck with me since, and I see them echoed in every glance Damian's thrown my way these last few weeks, in every smile he flashes. I *feel* it in the way he holds my hand now as I try not to squirm under the intrigued gazes of the people around us, bedecked in sharp suits and dresses, each of them assessing the unfamiliar blonde on the arm of the Navarro heir. We don't go on many public dates anymore—not because we're hiding, but because we don't need to. Now that this thing between us has become something real, there's nothing to prove.

Still, stepping into his world like this, surrounded by people who recognize him but not me, reminds me of how different our lives really are. The atrium of the Hallazgo conference building is breathtaking—a towering space of glass and steel, with polished marble floors reflecting the warm glow of the chandeliers overhead and the moonlight filtering in through the vaulted skylight. The gentle notes of a string quartet curl around us and intermingle with the surrounding conversations like smoke, and a massive Christmas tree stands near the entrance, its twinkling lights casting shifting patterns across the floor-to-ceiling windows that reveal the snow-dusted paths and manicured gardens outside. Even the air smells expensive, tinged with champagne, pine, and whatever cologne the men in their tailored suits are wearing. I've done a lot out of my comfort zone these last few months, but attending the Hallazgo Christmas party might just take the cake.

"You look beautiful," Damian murmurs, lifting my hand and kissing my knuckles when he notices me fidgeting for the umpteenth time this evening. I have my contacts in, so I can't reach for my glasses, and my fingers are restless without something to grab at. "I'm so glad I picked out that dress. It fits you like a glove."

I glance down at the dress in question, the ruched red mini with the long sleeves and high collar—the neck further accentuated by my hair, which is swept into an elegant updo—that Damian bought for me at that designer boutique near Warwick. That day he took me shopping feels like a lifetime ago, and it's crazy to look at where we started when this agreement first began and where we've ended up. It's crazy to look at this gorgeous man beside me and know that he's mine. Damian is impeccably dressed himself, his black suit cut to perfection, the dark silk of his red tie catching the dim light overhead. The overall effect is effortless, polished, and completely unfair, especially with the way his sharp jaw and messy waves make him look both put together and roguishly disheveled at the same time.

He looks me up and down with a feral grin, then leans in close to whisper in my ear, "I can't wait to peel it off you later."

I flush at his purred words, which only make me squirm more. When Damian suggested I wear this dress tonight, I hadn't been sure about it. It's modest at the top, but it shows a *lot* of leg, and I was worried I would stick out like a sore thumb in a sea of cocktail dresses and chic floor-length evening wear. But I've spotted enough other short dresses this evening to not feel too out of place, and I can't deny that I like the way Damian looks at me when I'm wearing it.

Honestly, I think I could have worn an old potato sack, and people would still look at me the way they're staring at me now—with that same sense of curious examination. And they *are* curious; they want to know how a girl who came from nothing, armed with only a high IQ, managed to tame the unruly Damian Navarro.

"Damian," a gruff male voice calls, and our gazes turn in sync to lock onto one of those very people sauntering toward us. The man who approaches is older—mid to late fifties if I had to hazard a guess—with neatly styled hair and a close-cropped beard that are both more salt than pepper. When he's an arm's length away, he holds out his hand. "I didn't think we'd see you this evening, but I'm pleased to find I was wrong."

Though Damian offers the older man a polite smile and graciously takes his hand, he stiffens—just a little. Just enough that only I seem to notice. "Mr. Cunningham. Merry Christmas."

Mr. Cunningham—a Hallazgo board member, I presume—glances between us, his gaze catching on mine. "Merry Christmas to you both. And this is…?"

Damian's hand loops around me, settling on my hip with a silent possessiveness that's surprisingly exhilarating and *hot*. This man isn't a threat to me—I can tell as much by his kind hazel eyes—or to the place Damian has in my heart. And Damian isn't the kind of guy who gets easily provoked, despite that one instance last month when I suspect he might have punched someone in the face (fingers crossed, it was Mason). But that isn't what this is about. His arm around my waist isn't a show of ownership or jealousy; it's a quiet reassurance, a reminder that we are solid. That no one's scrutiny—not the board's, not the public's, not even his parents'—can shake us or what we have.

"Alexandria Dornan," I say with an easy smile, shaking Mr. Cunningham's proffered hand.

"Ah. The genius, I presume?" he asks, the fascination clear in his eyes. Someone has been reading the tabloids, it seems.

"That's the one," Damian confirms with a grin that's somehow both cool and detached and yet, full of so much heat it scorches my insides.

Mr. Cunningham nods. "Very good. Well, I'll let you young folk mingle. It was good seeing you, Damian. I hope our paths cross more frequently in the future."

The tension in Damian's shoulders only eases when Mr. Cunningham strolls away.

"Oh, you hated that, didn't you?" I whisper.

Damian shoots me a sidelong glance. "Oof, I hope it wasn't that obvious to him."

I chuckle. "I doubt it. I just know you." And I could see how his polite veneer was masking an obvious disdain.

"You do," he agrees with a dopey grin, using the arm around my waist to pull me in so he can press a soft kiss to my lips.

"He seemed happy to see you, though," I note when we separate a moment later. "That's a good sign, right?"

A thoughtful crease forms between his brows. "As far as my dad's board of directors go, Mr. Cunningham actually isn't all that bad. If any of them are going to be forgiving, and more importantly, be onside with our proposal, it would likely be hi—" Damian breaks off mid-sentence, his eyes enlarging. "Shit, incoming," he mutters.

I follow his distracted gaze to his mother, who now crosses the room toward us, clad in a midnight blue evening gown, a flute glass in one hand.

My stomach twists at the sight of her. I haven't seen either of Damian's parents since that trip to Guadalajara, and though Lenore was kind enough to me, I can't forget the look of concern in her eyes when she questioned me, or the careful hope that had replaced it when we said our goodbyes.

It's been seven weeks since then—seven weeks in which she could have changed her opinion of me. Will I find that same apprehension in her eyes again? That doubt?

Or will I find something new?

To my relief, a genial grin splits her face as she approaches us. "Damian," she says, punctuating his name with a kiss on the cheek. Then she turns and takes my hand. "Lexi. It's wonderful to see you again. You both look lovely."

I flush at the compliment and pray she doesn't look too closely at how high my hemline is. "Mrs. Navarro."

She clicks her tongue. "Lenore, please," she corrects me, and the warm smile that follows immediately sets me at ease. "I hope you two are enjoying yourselves?"

"Immensely," Damian deadpans.

I bite my lip as Lenore gives her son an admonishing look, but then an amused smirk creeps across her face, washing the tension away.

"I'm sure this is all a bit boring for you both," she muses, glancing around the crowded room at the other partygoers—at the Hallazgo employees and their plus-ones—some exchanging pleasantries in small groups, while others sit at their assigned tables, partaking of unfathomably overpriced champagne. With a sigh, she turns to face us again. "This scene is hardly popping, is it?"

Damian chokes on a startled breath. "*Popping*? Mother, please don't try to be cool."

She ignores him, reaching out and touching a hand to his shoulder. "I know, why don't you take Lexi on a tour of the grounds? Show her what we have to offer here."

I peek over at Damian, who looks torn between asking Lenore if she's suffering some kind of mental break and happily accepting the chance to escape this dull, so-called party unscathed.

"Uh, okay," he says after a beat of hesitation. Unlatching his arm from my waist, he holds it out for me to take. "Shall we?"

I nod, threading my arm through his, and we're just about to leave when Lenore's voice stalls him in his tracks.

"Damian, I'm—" She falters, swallowing hard, then gives a slight jerk of her head. "*We're*…glad you came."

Damian responds with a kind smile, though the other half of the "we" she's referring to is nowhere in sight, likely off entertaining his guests (or the board) instead of acknowledging the effort his son is making, not just by being here, but over the last few months in general. Even without saying a word, I can see that Damian feels his father's absence, even if he struggles to physically be around him. One glance at his expressionless face is enough to tell me how empty it makes his mother's sentiment…and how much he worries about what that absence might ultimately mean for his future—not just in his family, but at Hallazgo.

But Damian doesn't voice those worries, even though I know they're there, buried just under the surface. Not to me. Not to his mother. There's a fleeting moment where I think he *might* say something—acknowledge the weight of her words, the absence of his father, the complicated mess of it all. But he just stands there, expression unreadable, his jaw tight, eyes fixed on the space she left behind when she finally walks away.

The evening air nips at the exposed skin of my legs, and I huddle deeper into my coat as Damian guides me along the pedestrian path away from the conference hall, where the Christmas party is still in full swing, the snow crunching under our heels. I can smell the threat of another impending flurry in the frigid breeze that assaults my nose, but since snow never lasts long in Newport due to our proximity to the ocean and the high salt content in the air, I try to appreciate these moments for the short time they last, letting the cold sting my cheeks, breathing in the crisp night, and reveling in the silence and fresh clarity the winter chill brings to my mind.

"So, anything in particular you want to see?" Damian asks, gesturing to the buildings flanking each side of the path.

I'm not sure what I expected when Damian invited me to his family's company Christmas party—someplace domineering and impersonal, I suppose. Certainly not this beautiful campus with its sleek, glass-fronted buildings, well-groomed greenery, and pathways that are lined with embedded lights in the stone to safely guide those who walk them at night. I anticipated something colder, more sterile, but there's an unexpected warmth to it all, like it was designed not only to be worked at but lived in. Like whoever planned this place wanted it to feel like a home to its employees.

"Just…point things out to me as we go," I suggest, nestling closer into the warm embrace of his arm, which he wraps around my shoulders, pulling me in tight against his thick woolen peacoat.

His mouth twitches into a lopsided smile as he points to a building on our left up ahead. "All right. So, over there is the main lab building. That's where the magic happens."

"Ah, yes. The birthplace of overpriced prescription pills," I muse. "Truly inspiring."

Damian chuckles under his breath before shifting my attention to a single-story complex on our right. "That one over there is my favorite building on campus. The cafeteria. Swear on my life, they have the best pizza I've ever tasted."

I let out a playful tut. "Typical man. Always led by his stomach."

His eyes veer to mine as his lips pull into a mischievous grin. "Well, that and my—"

"Solar panels?" I interrupt, pointing to a large facility ahead, the roof tiled with flat, reflective tiles that shine in the brief glimpses of moonlight that peek between the clouds.

Damian nods, a wistful look crossing his face. "Hallazgo is actually pretty big on renewable energy," he explains. "It was one of my abuelo's last initiatives before he passed." His expression turns sardonic then, his tone biting. "Our medication might not be affordable for the masses, but we're at least doing our part to save the planet while gouging their wallets."

Clearing his throat, he points to another building on our right. "That's the R&D building. It's where all the smartest people employed by Hallazgo argue over who forgot to refill the coffee machine. Oh, and you know, do some science. And in that general direction"—his hand swings to the left—"there's a parking garage. Very exciting, I know, but honestly, it's where the real drama happens. Someone took my dad's spot once and didn't live to tell the tale."

I snort out a laugh. "Let me guess, they were 'reassigned' to the basement lab with the mutant rats?"

"Mutant, *man-eating* rats, no less," Damian corrects me.

He matches my smile, and for a moment, we're both silent as I take it all in.

"When I think of pharmaceuticals and healthcare, I think…sterile. Cold."

Like the endless, empty hallways of hospitals, the hum of machines. The waiting rooms where the air always feels too thin. "But this is all so…nice."

Damian gives me a considering look, like he knows exactly what I'm thinking…because he's felt the same cold chill of dread. Endured the same suffocating quiet.

Retracting his arm from my shoulders, he holds out his hand. "Well, if you think the buildings are nice, you'll love this. Come on."

Our fingers interlace as Damian leads me along the winding footpath around a small hill crested with a large oak tree, bringing us face to face with a breathtaking sight on the other side of the knoll. Unlike the pruned shrubs, flower beds, and potted plants that decorate the rest of the grounds, this area feels almost wild by comparison—not neglected but as if it's been allowed to grow freely. To thrive in a way the meticulously maintained landscapes surrounding it haven't.

A wooden pergola covered in climbing vines and bright flowers dominates the center of the garden, adding vibrant bursts of warmth to contrast the cold colorlessness of the snow. But what catches my eye the most are the marigolds, which shouldn't still be in bloom given the low temperatures in New England at this time of year, their golden petals glowing against the backdrop of night like small orbs of sunlight in an uncharacteristic refusal to bow to the cold.

The garden seems to defy the season. Even the plants that are dormant hold onto their strength, standing tall and proud, unfazed by the frost on their leaves. And the air feels different here, too—frigid still but more alive, as if this one space has found a way to survive in spite of the winter chill.

The contrast between the harshness of the climate and the quiet persistence of life in this small corner of the campus is almost magical.

"This…" I turn in a slow circle, staring in awe at the rainbow of plant life around me. "Is it weird this reminds me of your abuela's house?"

Her home had felt magical, too, with the same luscious colors and beauty. The marigolds especially remind me of that brief trip to Mexico—of the warmth, the brightness, the feeling of something vibrant and alive, even in the face of change. They're a flower tied to remembrance, to honoring the past, but here, they feel like something more. A sign that, even in the cold, even when everything else is still, life finds a way to push forward.

And maybe I can, too.

"She and my abuelo planted this garden together," Damian says, a fond, faraway look in his eye as the memory pulls him in. "Just the two of them with their own bare hands. It was one of the first things they did when they purchased this land because my abuelo wanted someplace special just for my abuela—a sanctuary of sorts, dedicated to her for all the sacrifices she made as well, and to thank her for taking the journey here with him. Someplace that would feel like home—like Guadalajara—to remind them of their roots and all they'd gone through together to get here. The rest of Hallazgo was built around it when they expanded."

"It's beautiful," I breathe, my voice filled with wonder, but I'm not only talking about the garden. What Damian describes—the devotion and love his grandparents shared—is awe-inspiring. It's the sort of love you see in movies and read about in novels, the kind of love I never would have envisioned myself ever coming close to finding. Until now.

Until *him*.

"It's my favorite place at Hallazgo," he whispers, his breath heavy with longing and fear. Longing for the grandfather he lost. Fear that this dream he's finally embraced could be snatched away before it has a chance to become something real.

I squeeze his hand. "They must have really been in love. You can almost feel it." And I mean that. It's as if Damian's abuela left a piece of herself here, always persisting in those stubborn marigolds.

He sniffs. "They were. Let's sit down for a bit."

Damian leads me under the pergola, and gently tugs me down beside him onto the lone bench beneath it. The wood is cool against the exposed backs of my thighs, sending a shiver crawling over my skin, but the beauty of this place—of this moment—eclipses any discomfort, pushing it to the back of my mind.

I glance at Damian, drawn to the way the golden glow of a nearby lamppost flickers over his face, illuminating the sharp angles of his jaw and the warm honey in his eyes. He meets my gaze, his lips curving into a smile—charming, devious, utterly devastating. The kind of smile that promises trouble. The kind that makes my pulse stutter and my breath catch before I even know what he's thinking.

"So, I got you something. For Christmas."

My heart kicks against my rib cage—a reflex, sudden and instinctive. Surprises unsettle me. The not knowing, the expectation, the possibility of reacting the wrong way. I don't hate them, exactly, but they make me nervous.

"I got you something, too," I say, shifting awkwardly on the bench, "but I didn't bring it with me."

That mirthful smile deepens, and he arches a brow. "Oh, color me intrigued. What is it?" he asks. "I don't mind spoilers."

Since the start of December, I debated whether I should get Damian something for Christmas. I wasn't sure if it was too early for gifts—too soon in our relationship to take that step. But then, when mindlessly browsing the internet the other week while in peak procrastination mode, I saw it: the perfect present.

Although I had been looking forward to seeing his face when he opens it, I can't resist telling him—not when he's staring at me so eagerly. I'm as bad at keeping secrets as I am at lying.

"A *Twilight* T-shirt," I answer proudly, "with the words, 'This is the skin of a killer, Bella,' and Robert Pattinson's face covered in rhinestones."

Damian's jaw seems to unhinge from his whole damn head as he gasps, "Magnificent."

I shrug. "I felt you needed a nerdy T-shirt of your own."

He cackles then, throwing his head back and laughing so loudly it echoes in the quiet of night around us. "Absolutely. Oh, my god, I can't wait to see it." His eyes lock on my face again as he snaps the fingers of the hand not currently entwined in mine. "And then we can wear our nerdy T-shirts together. Adorable."

I don't know why, but the mental picture of that makes me blush. Maybe it's because Damian has fucked me seven ways from Sunday in several of my own nerdy T-shirts, or maybe it's the way he owns his interests so shamelessly, ready to proclaim them to the world without a single care for what anyone thinks of him.

His confidence isn't just attractive, it's *intoxicating*, and it triggers something primal within me. Something that makes me contemplate risking frostbite to straddle him right here on this bench.

"You better not be shitting me about that T-shirt," he warns, his eyes narrowing into skeptical slits, "because I'm very excited about it."

"I promise, I'm not shitting you," I assure him. "I can give it to you when you bring me home."

His face softens, and that broad smile returns. "Excellent. I can't wait to wear it. But in the meantime…" Keeping his eyes on mine, he reaches inside his coat pocket. "Let's focus on something *you* can wear."

When he retracts his hand a few seconds later, I notice he's holding a small rectangular box fastened shut with a sparkly red and green ribbon.

"Here," he says, his cheeks flushing pink under the lamp light as he offers it to me, and I can hear my heartbeat in my ears as I slowly reach out my own hand to take it.

I can't hide the trembling of my fingers as I untie the ribbon, or the faltering cadence of my breaths as I anticipate what I'll find inside. My mouth is dry as I pop off the lid and place it on the bench seat beside me.

Neatly folded black tissue paper greets me from inside the uncovered box, and when I peel it back, a slim golden object lies in wait on a bed of red satin.

Holding my breath, I gently pluck the cylindrical object free and hold it up to the light. As I shift my wrist, turning the strange cylinder to examine it, I note that it resembles a pill, but it's much larger, roughly the length and girth of my thumb. It even has the indent around the middle where a pill would snap in half, but this clearly wasn't meant to be swallowed.

"Is this…a *butt plug*?" I practically screech. I round a furious glower on Damian. "I swear to god, if by wear it, you mean shove it up my—"

"The gift is inside it!" he blurts out defensively, and I can tell he's trying his hardest to bite back a laugh. "Though, I would *love* to hear what you think about butt plugs at a later date. For now, however…" His fingers find mine, guiding them until I'm holding the small golden container in both of my hands. "It unscrews."

A quiet click pierces the air between us, the sound so soft I barely catch it, and I peer down at the pill that isn't really a pill as it separates into two halves. When I pull them fully apart, that's when I register the difference in weight. Resting the empty top half down on the bench, I extend my right hand and tip the not-empty bottom section upright, a gasp parting my lips when a golden necklace tumbles out onto my waiting palm.

There are two chains: the shorter one is in a Figaro style while the other, only slightly longer, is a continuous rope dotted with dainty gold-encrusted pearls. Both chains are thin, delicate, but it's the pendants affixed to them that hold my gaze—the bold, golden pi symbol and the single green gemstone suspended above it.

"An emerald?" I breathe, the question burning my throat. Or maybe it's the impending onslaught of tears I'm feeling. "Any significance there?"

"Your eyes," he says as if it's the most obvious answer in the world, and there's a ghost of a smile on his lips I've never seen before. A smile that seems to radiate not just with like…but with love. "The emerald," he clarifies. "It reminded me of your eyes. May I?"

He jerks his chin to the necklace still held aloft in my hand, and I nod, turning my back to him so he can help me put it on. His fingertips skim my shoulders, then the back of my neck, as he fastens the single clasp where the two chains join at my nape. And as the pendants settle against my chest, I gaze down in wonder, silently vowing to never take it off.

A shudder races through me when Damian kisses the spot just behind my left ear. "Do you like it?" he whispers, and I give a shaky nod, my entire body trembling.

"I…I love it," I murmur, shifting on the bench to face him again. "Thank you." But those words feel insufficient. They don't say enough. They don't express how much this gift truly means to me. How much *he* has come to mean to me.

They don't tell him what I really want to say.

I love you, I think, wishing I had the courage to say it aloud.

"Feliz Navidad, pi lover," Damian croons, smiling up at me as he bends down to kiss the back of my hand.

Suddenly, I'm transported back to that day in Touro Park—the day that started everything—and all at once, the pill box makes sense. I want to laugh. I want to comment on how far we've come since that fateful day when he misread my email address as *pill* lover instead of *pi*, and I was convinced the universe was playing an elaborate joke on me. But I can't. Because I realize now it wasn't messing with me at all.

It was bringing me exactly what I needed. I just didn't know it yet.

So, although I want to, I don't laugh. Instead, I just stare at him—at this frustrating, sarcastic, sexy, unexpectedly ambitious man I love—and my heart is racing so quickly I am breathless when I whisper back, "Merry Christmas, fuckboy."

CHAPTER
TWENTY-EIGHT
✦ *Damian* ✦

Después de la risa, viene el llanto - After laughing comes crying

**Translation: What goes up must come down.
And I am a plane that was always destined to crash.**

JANUARY

The new year starts with a bang. After spending Christmas in Guadalajara with my abuela, I ring in New Years with Blondie, her friends, Gina, and her mom at the Dornans' house. It was probably the most low-key New Years I've ever experienced—we sat around their living room wearing party hats and drinking bubbly, talking and laughing long after the clocks had ticked past midnight—and I cherished every minute of it. I think that night was the first time in my life I really felt like I belonged anywhere. Like I actually had real friends.

My abuela has always done her best to make me feel loved, and she does a bang-up job of it, but I would be lying if I said that New Years celebration wasn't also the first time I truly felt like part of a family since my abuelo died. Part of something that isn't fundamentally broken.

It's like that saying: la familia no siempre es de sangre, sino de corazón. Family isn't always by blood, but by heart. And this is definitely the family I choose.

Blondie's friends have warmed up to me, and her mom and aunt have embraced me like a second child. Nothing about their affection feels conditional; they know the worst of what I've done and accepted me in spite of it—something I can't exactly say about my parents. In the story of my life, I am a hostage on a pirate ship, one wrong word away from walking the plank, but with Blondie and her family, there is no ship. They are the land in the distance, the haven promising refuge from the ravenous sea that would otherwise swallow me. They are my sanctuary. They are home.

Blondie is my home.

I don't think I moved my arms from around her that entire night. We sat on the floor against the sofa, her back to my chest, the chiming sound of her laughter rumbling through me like a shock wave. It was fucking euphoric seeing her like that—in a place of safety and comfort, surrounded by people she could be herself with, and knowing I got to be a part of it. There were fleeting moments when I felt like an impostor, like I had stolen something that didn't belong to me. Moments when I was certain I didn't and *couldn't* ever deserve this happiness. Moments when I believed I didn't deserve her. But then I would catch a glimpse of the necklace I gave her for Christmas around her neck, and those doubts and worries would wash away, like the ebbing of an ocean tide. Sure, I might have chosen Blondie, but seeing that necklace on her told me that, flaws and all, Blondie has chosen me, too.

Every day since then has felt like the extension of a dream I don't want to wake up from. Maybe because this all feels too good to be true, like waiting for the other shoe to drop. Maybe because I can sense something on the horizon of this happiness—something that is steadily creeping closer, getting ready to destroy it.

That something takes the form of a text from my dad that arrives halfway through my first week back at school after the Christmas break, effectively jerking me awake and pulling me from the safety and comfort of the dream I had so desperately hoped would become my new reality.

Because dreams can't exist without nightmares to counter them. And the feeling clenching my gut as I stare down at my phone screen tells me that's exactly what I'm about to walk into.

Mein Führer

I need you to come home. Immediately.

My parents live in a waterfront New England shingle-style mansion in Jamestown, a twenty-minute hop across the bridge from Newport. There's a lot of generational wealth in the area, and since old money types value their privacy, my parents fit right in with their stuck-up noses and pompous demeanors. Plus, it's removed from the tourists (a bonus, according to my mother) while still being only a short drive from Hallazgo and the local amenities.

The house itself is luxurious, its design heavily influenced by the coast it overlooks. The exterior is painted in the same grayish-blue hues of a stormy ocean, the color accented by the cobblestone first-story walls and the crisp white trim that highlights the sharp edges and clean lines of the property. Ivy creeps intentionally across select parts of the stone, carefully planted for effect, and well-maintained shrubs sit under the windows, their frost-tipped leaves unmoving in the still, frigid air, pristine and obedient in every way.

Unlike me.

Before my abuelo passed and my abuela moved away, my grandparents lived in a charming older house in Newport—still nice, still large, still technically a mansion, but nothing like the showy property my parents own. Their home had history—creaky floors, lots of wood, and the kind of charm and warmth that could only come from a place that had been truly lived in, not that unlike my abuela's current home. A lot of people were surprised by how understated the house was, but my grandparents never needed some self-indulgent designer mansion to prove anything. They had a yacht—the *Lucia*—for their adventures, and that was where the real luxury was. The house, on the other hand, was a representation of their life together—full of love. And I felt it every time I walked through their door.

I don't have that same experience here.

It's a weird feeling entering the code for the gate at the end of the sweeping circular driveway that curves in front of the house. I haven't come back here more than a handful of times over the last four years; I stay at school when possible, which is most of the time, even opting to sign up for one or two classes over the summer period so I have an excuse to remain in the housing on campus, and I always spend holidays with my abuela. I know she would welcome me down in Guadalajara for the extended breaks, but she has her own life, and I don't want to cramp her style. And honestly…maybe I was always a bit scared that, if I stayed too long, I wouldn't want to leave out of fear of losing her like I lost my abuelo. Like I lost Jamie. Or maybe I feared staying would only accelerate that inevitability.

Whatever the reason, these last four years, I made it a point to never go home unless absolutely necessary—like after we returned from Guadalajara in November to fetch the Renesmobile. It's not like my parents miss me, and for the rare occasion when they actually request my presence, they just summon me to Fernando's, where bad news pairs well with good wine. And since bad news is the only kind they ever seem to have, I can only assume there wasn't enough time for their usual theatrics if they felt the need to call me here.

Whatever this is about, it couldn't wait. Or what they're going to say is so bad they don't want to risk an audience.

It's an even weirder feeling approaching the house, a thin layer of melting snow crunching under my shoes, and pushing open my parents' front door. *My* front door, I suppose, though this place hasn't felt like a home to me since Jamie died.

The entry hall is eerily silent as I walk inside. While the late afternoon sunlight flooding in through the windows gives the interior a light and airy vibe, filling me with a false sense of ease, that misleading comfort doesn't last. Dread pokes at me as I inch farther into the foyer, peering into the empty rooms I pass.

"I'm home," I call out.

Nothing. I don't even see or hear the housekeeper, Mrs. Jones.

I take another step. "Hello?"

Turning in place, I cut through the living room on my right and round a corner, passing through the adjoining hallway until the coastal-inspired gourmet kitchen—my mother's pride and joy of the house, even though she can't cook to save her life—slides into my eyeline.

"Oh, *there* you guys are," I say when I spot my parents. I skirt around the marble-topped island and approach the brightly-lit breakfast nook overlooking the harbor outside where they sit in silence at the round mahogany table.

"Didn't you hear me calling? I—"

My gut twists when I notice the condemning look they shoot my way. The silence they have yet to break.

"Wait." My pulse kicks up a notch as that feeling of foreboding tightens in my chest, and I stop in my tracks, glancing between their solemn faces. "Why do you both look like you're about to stage an intervention?"

My father, whose hands are folded on the table, unclasps his fingers to pull out the empty chair beside him. "Sit down."

Sit down. *Period.* No Damian. No hijo. Just those two conclusive, damning words.

Swallowing hard, I step forward and slide into the seat, anticipating what I'm now certain is coming—the moment one of them will speak, and the happiness I've let shroud me these last few weeks will be torn away without mercy.

My world is about to come crashing down around me, I know it. And yet…neither one of them seems eager to say as much. I wish they would. I wish they would just fucking say it and get this over with.

My palms are sweaty as I clasp my hands under the table. "Mom?" I prod, glancing at my mother, but she averts her gaze. However, the disappointment that ekes out and spreads across her face is impossible to miss.

It's my father who finally breaks the silence.

"Earlier, Mr. Harrison called us after noticing some concerning transactions in your account while reviewing the family's finances." His dark eyes pin me in place, his mouth turned down into a harsh frown that borders on a grimace. "Perhaps you care to explain?"

I blink at him. The tone of his text had me convinced this was about something else, some final straw I wasn't even aware I had pulled, and that this would be the day they yanked the rug, and their connection and remaining love—assuming they still feel any toward me at all—out from under my feet. I had been certain they were going to announce their intent to cut me off, and maybe they are, maybe that *is* what this is about. But if so, I can safely say I have no fucking clue what I've done to deserve it. Transactions? What transactions? I don't know of any big expenditures I've made except—

My skin pales, and all the blood rushing through me turns cold. Suddenly, the urgency—why they called me to the house instead of their usual mindfuckery at Fernando's—makes sense.

Fuck. Fucking *fuck*. They know about the cash I've been sending to Blondie. They must; that's the only possible thing my dad could be referring to when he says "transactions." It's not like I've spent any differently than I normally do—aside from that day at The Couture Room and when I took Blondie and her friends out on the *Lucia*. And, of course, there was the necklace I got her for Christmas. But other than that? For someone with a fuck ton of money to burn, I'm surprisingly non-spendy. Generally. For the most part.

But my monthly payments to Blondie? Those would definitely stand out in a haystack of otherwise unconcerning expenditures, and what's worse, it never occurred to me, in all my staggering idiocy, that my parents would eventually notice them.

And it was pretty much a guarantee they would. Mr. Harrison is our family accountant—he manages all the Navarro finances, including those for Hallazgo—and as it's the start of the new year, we've officially entered tax season…which means, *of course*, he'd be looking at all our accounts to be certain everything is in order and take note of every last fucking penny. A completely minor detail that didn't cross my dumbass mind when I started sending those monthly sums to Blondie.

God, I can only imagine how this looks; they probably think I knocked her up. I would ask myself what I was thinking, but the truth is, I wasn't thinking at all. And I sure as shit wasn't considering the potential IRS implications. I don't even know how much you can legally gift to someone, or if our agreement would be classed as some form of employment. I've never had cause to worry about such things, and I've certainly never paid much attention to our finances or to what happens behind the scenes to keep the Navarro name in good standing. And it's not like my parents have ever asked me about my spending before; they never had reason to.

Until now. Until I started doing something completely out of the norm— or rather, out of *my* norm. Shit, no wonder it caught Mr. Harrison's eye; that guy is a fucking hawk on a bad day.

I can't believe I was ignorant enough to think the money would go unnoticed. That five figures a month would easily fly under the radar in this family just because we're worth billions. But then, I guess it's true what they say: the rich don't get rich by giving their money away.

On some level, part of me is convinced this whole agreement with Blondie was always destined to fail. That I would always fall victim to my parent's ultimatum.

I just never anticipated it would be my own stupidity that would cause my downfall.

"I…" I try to speak, but my mouth and tongue are as dry as sandpaper, and I don't even know *what* to say. Nothing comes to mind that won't implicate me further.

"Is that Dornan girl blackmailing you?" my mother asks.

My eyes flit to hers, narrowing on her face, which is taut, like a wire on the verge of snapping. She holds my gaze as I resist the urge to bark out a humorless laugh.

Only a few weeks ago, she was smiling at Blondie and telling her how "wonderful" it was to see her. And now?

Funny how quickly Blondie went from Lexi to "that Dornan girl."

"*No*," I retort, my tone dancing on the edge somewhere between scathing and pleading. "You have it all wrong. This is entirely on me, not Lexi. She hasn't done *anything*."

My father scoffs. "Except extort tens of thousands of dollars from us," he grumbles.

Forget accidental pregnancies, my parents think we've crossed into full-blown felony territory. Of course, they would assume the worst. Although, after years of immaturity and immoral behavior on my part, I suppose I can't really blame them. I've set a precedent, and considering Blondie's connection to the bet last spring, it's to be expected they would jump to conclusions that I did something else shitty that might possibly result in blackmail. That's a fair assumption to make about me.

But what I won't stand for is them thinking poorly of Blondie.

I round on my dad, my upper lip curled back in a sneer. "She didn't *extort* it. I gave it to her."

"Yes, and who gave *you* that money?" he challenges, pushing to his feet, his cheeks ruddy with anger. "You don't support yourself, you don't pay your own bills, and yet, you're out here throwing money around that doesn't even belong to you. We aren't your personal piggy bank! And we did not consent for you to freely hand out what is ours."

It takes all my self-control not to shout back, even as the rage flares within me at the insults and insinuations hurled against my girlfriend. I can handle the words thrown at me. My dad isn't wrong, after all—it isn't my money. I am not financially independent. Not yet, anyway. But they're acting like I gave away millions of dollars, like we're on the verge of financial ruin, when the reality didn't even put a dent in their net worth. They're still in the one percent. They're still among the wealthiest people in the world, even though the level of wealth our family has accumulated is far from ethical.

They're acting like two fucking dragons who have just discovered they're missing a few measly gold coins.

"I didn't just give it away," I growl, reaching for the only justification I have. "It was payment for services rendered."

"Services?" my mother repeats, her voice a high-pitched squawk of distress. "What kind of 'services'?"

"Yes, payment for *what*, exactly?" my father presses.

Resigning myself, I blow out a sigh through my nose, the last of that happiness I've been clinging to drifting away. I try to think of Blondie's face, to hold onto it for a moment longer, but it's as if someone has overturned the table where the puzzle that is us—that is our story—has been assembled, and the pieces have scattered all over the place.

"To pretend to be my girlfriend," I admit, the words like ash in my mouth. It feels weird to say it out loud, maybe because she *is* my girlfriend now. Because the lie has become something real.

The agreement had transformed—we had put the lie behind us—but it seems I have no choice but to face it. To take responsibility…just like my parents wanted.

"After we met at Fernando's at the start of September," I begin to explain, "I put out an anonymous ad on Craigslist, which Lexi answered. The deal was that she would pretend to be my girlfriend until graduation to help me show you I was capable of commitment. Of being a grown up. Of—" I hesitate, a lump rising in my throat that threatens to choke me into silence. I force it down, but when I speak again, my voice is shaking. "To prove I'm Hallazgo material. In return, I agreed to pay her fifteen thousand dollars a month."

"Oh, Damian," my mother whispers beside me, her expression crumpling behind her hands, which she cups to her mouth as if to hold a sob at bay.

My insides twist at the look on her face, at not just the shock that shines in her eyes, but the heartbreak, clear as day, beyond it. Maybe she didn't think I was capable of stooping so low. Or maybe she really was rooting for me, rooting for *us*—me and Blondie. Either way, whatever glint of hope I saw in her eyes during that trip to Guadalajara is gone, extinguished like a flame in the rain. All that's left now is disappointment. It's the most emotion I've seen her show since Jamie died.

A guilt that's knife-sharp slides between my ribs.

"So, it was all a lie," my father mutters. Closing his eyes, he pushes out a loud breath and shakes his head. "I knew something had to be wrong with that girl for her to date you after what you pulled with that bet."

My restraint snaps like an overstretched elastic.

"There's nothing *wrong* with Lexi!" As the shout explodes from my chest, I shoot to my feet so I'm on equal footing with my dad, and slam a hand down hard on the table, startling my parents, who gape at me with matching scandalized looks that would be comical if I wasn't so pissed off. A quiet voice in the back of my head warns me to keep my shit together, that lashing out won't accomplish a damn thing, but a louder voice is pressing me to defend Blondie—to clear her name and try to make my asshole parents see reason. The words spill out of me like water from an overturned glass. "Her mom has cancer, and their insurance recently stopped covering her chemo meds. She was *desperate*. What would you have done if it was Jamie, and the only hurdle that had been in the way of him surviving was money?" That question makes both my parents flinch, but I don't back down. "Don't fucking judge her," I bite out. "At least she's doing whatever it takes to give her mom the best chance to beat this."

It's a low blow, using my brother's death against them this way, especially after everything my abuela told me about my dad and the terrible decision he was forced to make. I know that. But that doesn't make it any less true. Because I know if the outcome hadn't been a foregone conclusion, if it had instead been a simple matter of money standing between Jamie's death and his survival, my parents would have moved the fucking earth to ensure the latter. So, how can they possibly judge her for making that choice when they've been in Blondie's shoes?

For several tense seconds, my parents are quiet. My mother's expression wilts like a dead flower, which only drives that knife of guilt in deeper. I never wanted to cause her—cause *either* of them—distress with this ploy. Shit, they were never even supposed to find out this whole thing with Blondie was fake, especially now that I have no intention of ending it. As for everything else—all the pranks and bad behavior of the last four years— none of that was *meant* to hurt them, but to open their eyes to my pain. To make them actually *see* me. To make them acknowledge the shared trauma we went through and how no one will fucking talk about it.

It's on the tip of my tongue to say that—to unleash all the years of pent- up resentment and anger. To make them realize how this put-together facade they've enforced has only done me harm and hasn't given me space to process my pain. How I've spent these last four years alone with my grief because they refused to join me in it. Because they slammed the door on it and threw away the key so no one else would see the reality of what our family has endured.

I consider explaining how Blondie and I started off as a lie but then became something real to appease them. How I have been changed by her and become someone that I can almost be proud of. Someone I think they would've been proud of, too, if they weren't so focused on the destructive path that led me here.

I even contemplate telling them about the proposal if only to show them what I'm capable of. That I *can* be Hallazgo material if they'll just let me try.

I want to say all that…but I don't. Because the look in my father's dark eyes—so like my own and yet, so distant—is enough for me to know there's no point. His mind is made up. Nothing I say now will change it. My words will only fall on deaf ears.

"You have clarified her side of the story, but what of yours?" he finally says, and the finality in his tone sends a terrified shiver racing over my skin, leaving goosebumps in its wake. It isn't a question—not really. He doesn't want me to offer him an answer or an explanation. He just wants to make it clear how much he thinks I've failed him. Failed our family.

Failed my abuelo.

"What excuse do you possibly have for yourself that isn't just another lie?" he continues. "If the media had caught wind of this, it would have been a disaster. Do you know how this looks?" He catches himself as his voice starts to rise, reeling his temper back in. And as it fades, he seems to deflate, collapsing back in his chair as if weighed down by his ever present disappointment of me. "We were foolish to think you had matured, that you had outgrown your selfish, childish tendencies." He waves a dismissive hand before dropping his palm to the table with a thud. "But here we are. I guess we were wrong."

Neither of my parents look at me again after that, and their silence is all the indication I need to know the conversation is over. Three strikes, and I'm officially out of the game. I don't bother saying anything either as I turn and storm out of the kitchen.

As I make my way to the front door on unsteady legs, I cycle through each of the five stages of grief, hurtling quickly toward a dazed acceptance. The one outcome I had been hoping to evade through my agreement with Blondie is now unavoidable. My parents will cut me off and disown me after this. I am doomed.

But she isn't, a small voice in my head calls out from the void. *Not yet.*

My hands shake as I reach into my pocket and pull out my phone. There might not be much I can do for Blondie after today, but I can at least do this one last thing for her while I still have time. While I still have money to do something with. Tapping open my cash app, I select her contact, type in the max amount it will let me send, and hit the button to transfer, letting out a breath of relief when the success notification takes over my screen.

Whatever happens now, I can rest easy knowing Blondie will be fine. Her mom will be fine. At least, for a little while longer.

I barely process the walk from the front door to my car, and no sooner do I slide into the driver's seat and turn on the ignition than Blondie's name pops up on the console, alerting me to her incoming call.

Though I hit the answer button, I can't seem to find the strength to speak. "Damian?"

My hand clutches the gear stick, but I don't shift it into drive or lift my foot from the brake. I just stare out the windshield at this house I once called home, certain this will be the last time I see it.

"Hello?" Blondie prompts when my silence persists.

My voice is like gravel when I finally force myself to respond. "I'm here."

"I just saw the transfer," she hedges. "What's going on? Why did you send me all that extra money?"

A moment passes. Then another. My pulse is drumming in my ears, in my throat, in my head, and my breaths seem to echo around me, punched from my constricting lungs. The sound of each exhalation is deafening in the confined space of the car, and my vision is blurring.

Is this what a heart attack feels like? A panic attack? Whatever it is, I feel like I'm dying.

"I just wanted to make sure you and your mom are taken care of," I manage, trying to blink the haze from my eyes. I only register the distortion as tears when one breaks free and slides down my cheek.

"What is that supposed to mean?" Blondie asks, and I hear it then—the worry and doubt in her voice.

"They know," I rasp, mimicking the words she said to me that night in Grape Expectations. The same words but with very different results. That tightening in my chest intensifies to the point my lungs are almost completely strangled of breath. I slam my eyes shut and inhale through my nose, then exhale through my mouth, repeating that process until I'm calm enough to elaborate. "My parents just confronted me about all the money I've been sending you. Their accountant picked up on it when he was doing our taxes."

Although it's soft, I catch Blondie's sharp gasp. "I… What does this—"

"I don't know how much longer I'll have access to my account," I cut in. "I wish I could send you more, but that's the limit—"

"Wait, stop for a minute," Blondie begs, and she must hear the ratcheting panic in my voice because she hurriedly adds, "Just…take a breath. We can fix this, okay? We can talk to your parents together. We'll explain everything."

I shake my head, even though she can't see it. "There's nothing to fix, Dornan," I whisper. "It's too late. The damage is done."

All the work we put into the proposal, all the energy and time we invested has been for nothing. It's over. My dad might not have said it out loud, but I knew he was thinking it, and he was right. I've failed my abuelo. I've failed

Jamie. I've failed Blondie.

Most of all, I've failed myself.

"Then let's call your abuela," Blondie suggests, her growing agitation mirroring mine. "She'll understand. She—"

"You don't get it." I let out a harsh, cynical laugh. "I can't come back from this. Not with them."

Her quiet whine of distress rakes over my skin like nails. "Don't do this. Don't give up. I can only imagine how scared you are, but you don't have to face this alone. You *aren't* alone. You know that, right?"

Blondie's words seem to extend from the speaker and reach through my chest to touch something inside me. Something dark and twisted that's been shoved deep down.

"I should be," I breathe as the harsh reality of the absolute clusterfuck I've wrought on myself—on both of us—finally sinks in. Who is Damian Navarro without his family's money? Nobody, that's who. Just a worthless, useless nobody. "I ruin everything I touch. I can't even uphold my end of our agreement anymore—"

"Fuck the agreement, Damian!" Blondie counters as that tightening in my chest becomes so overwhelming I struggle to focus. Her words are dampened by the growing beat of my pulse in my ears and my head. "I'm not talking about that, I'm talking about *you*. Just…come over and we'll work it out."

Clamping my eyes shut, I press my forehead to the cold steering wheel. "I can't. I…" Swallowing past the dryness in my throat, I force myself upright. "I need to think."

I need to figure out what the fuck I'm going to do.

As if sensing what's coming, Blondie says, "Damian, don't shut me out—" but I hit the end call button, put the car into gear, and drive.

CHAPTER
TWENTY-NINE

✦ *Lexi* ✦

Sometimes, the hardest equations to solve
are the ones that involve people.

Over two days pass without a word from Damian. His phone goes to voicemail every time I call him, and he's MIA on campus; he isn't going to his classes, and he's not at his dorm—I waited outside both and even cornered a few of his classmates, who confirmed it.

I'm at a loss for where else to look. I'm sure he's hiding somewhere, licking his wounds, too ashamed and heartbroken to surface, and while part of me wants to be mad at him for ghosting me again, I know he's only doing it because he's hurting, not because of anything I've done. Because something so important to him is about to be ripped away. Perhaps, on some level, he's embarrassed to face me after all the work we both put into the proposal, but that's the least of my concerns right now. All I care about is finding him, so I can be there for him the way he was there for me with my mom. If nothing else, I wish he would tell me he's okay.

Ronnie and Andie joined in on the hunt, and once we exhausted every available option, we decided it was time to rip a page out of Damian's book. When Damian and I first made our agreement, he had flirted my address out of Meredith, one of the older ladies working in the administration office at Conwick. I might not be a handsome smooth-talking billionaire, but I *do* have Ronnie, who could make even the most heterosexual person second-guess their preferences.

Unfortunately, Meredith turned out to be a much more crafty adversary than we were prepared for, completely immune to Ronnie's charms. Fortunately, Andie noticed something Ronnie and I didn't—the abundance of eighties paraphernalia decorating Meredith's desk space. Using that as her opening, Andie jumped in, stating that I needed Damian's home address so I could go have my John Cusack boombox moment (a reference that was entirely lost on me and her cousin). In response, Meredith's gaze had softened, and smiling at me, she scribbled the address on a Post-It, handed it to me, and muttered with a wink, "You go get your man, girl."

Which is how I ended up here: at the domineering gate to the Navarros' Jamestown home on a Saturday afternoon, a Conwick tote bag tucked under one arm, and the Post-It clutched tight in my hand.

Swallowing, I scrunch up the small square of paper and jam the wad inside my coat pocket, then lift a finger to the intercom button on the keypad mounted on the stone gatepost.

A melodic chime, not unlike a doorbell, rings softly from the speaker. Licking my lips, I adjust my glasses before moving my fingers to the necklace Damian gave me, pinching the pi symbol for courage as I stare up into the camera staring down from its perch on the pillar. One moment passes. Then two. Then three.

I shuffle my feet, preparing myself for defeat, when a woman's voice emits from the intercom, freezing me in my tracks just as I'm about to turn and leave. "Yes?"

That one word is too curt for me to discern if the person speaking to me is Lenore. I hedge my bets, assuming not.

"Um, hi." I swallow again, clearing my throat. "I'd like to speak to Mr. and Mrs. Navarro. Please."

"We don't accept cold callers," the voice retorts. "If this is about charity—"

"It isn't," I interrupt. Though, I suppose that's not entirely true since I'm relying on the Navarros being charitable enough to actually see me. "My name is Alexandria Dornan. I'm Damian's girlfriend."

There's a pregnant pause, and then a loud buzz shatters the silence, and the gate begins to slowly swing inward. Goosebumps rise across every inch of my skin as I readjust my grip on the strap of my bag, and follow the long drive to the Navarros' front door where an older woman with graying hair waits for me at the threshold. Her expression is unreadable as she leads me inside, and gestures down a corridor on my right.

"The second door on the left," is all she says before she turns and walks away.

With a shaking breath, I creep down the silent passage, my eyes drifting along the sculpted cornices and paneled walls, which strangely lack any photographs of the Navarro family together.

And, more notably, any pictures of Damian's brother.

A shudder runs through me at how empty and hollow the house feels. No wonder Damian felt the need to act out all these years. It's as if his parents are pretending Jamie never existed, erasing every trace of him, as if refusing to acknowledge the tragedy could somehow make it disappear.

My stomach twists as another thought occurs to me.

Will they erase Damian, too?

I clench my fingers into fists to keep from touching my glasses when I turn into the second room on the left as the housekeeper instructed. The room I step into is bright, with a plush carpet that matches the cream-colored walls, and a three-piece sofa set arranged around a cobalt blue ottoman coffee table. Mr. and Mrs. Navarro sit on opposite ends of the sofa, each sipping out of intricately detailed mugs with gold handles that probably cost a fortune. Two matching pots—along with a small creamer pitcher and sugar bowl—are on a wooden tray on the ottoman.

"Miss Dornan," Hector says by way of greeting when I enter the room. The lingering look he gives me borders on a glare, and though Lenore's expression is less harsh than her husband's, it lacks all the warmth I saw in it at the Hallazgo Christmas party.

Neither of them stand to greet me, and I hazard a silent guess that they don't plan on offering me a coffee or tea from the tray. Not that I expect them to. This isn't a social call, and they sure as hell don't look happy to see me.

"I…apologize for showing up like this at your home," I stammer, "but it's imperative I speak with you."

Hector arches a brow. "About the money you took from us?"

I flinch at the bite in his voice, though I'm not entirely surprised by it.

From what little I gleaned from my brief call with Damian, his parents didn't take the discovery of our agreement very well. And while I can't blame them for being mad that we lied, or that Damian sent me large sums of money that, in all fairness, was likely theirs, I am *fuming* that it's all they seem to be focused on instead of the deeper issue at play here.

My face tenses into a glower as I hold Hector's gaze. "About your *son*."

With a sigh, he sets his mug down on the tray, and gestures for me to sit in one of the chairs. "Have a seat."

I opt for the armchair nearest the door, though I don't remove my bag or coat. I won't be staying long.

"Firstly," I begin, sitting ram-rod straight on the edge of the seat, "I am sorry for deceiving you regarding my relationship status with Damian. It was never my intention to hurt anyone. I just wanted to help my mom."

I hear Lenore's soft intake of breath, but when I look over at her, she dips her eyes to her cup. Hector, on the other hand, holds my gaze.

"Damian told us about her condition," he says, his voice gruff but not entirely unkind. "You have our sympathy. But it doesn't excuse the deceit."

"No, it doesn't. You're right," I agree. "You know, I actually struggled with it a lot at first. The lie," I clarify. "But then I thought, anyone who would go to such lengths to impress their parents must have a good reason." Although Hector scoffs, I press on, undeterred. "Damian just wanted to get his life back on track. The way he went about it was…problematic, but I think he didn't know how else to do it. And honestly, I'm glad it played out the way it did because I don't think we would've ever gotten to know each other otherwise, and that would be a far bigger shame than the two of you finding out we lied."

"You said something along the same lines on the plane to Guadalajara," Hector points out, and though it isn't a question, I can hear the interrogating note in his voice.

I lift my chin a little to show I'm not afraid of him. He can test me all he wants. My anxiety might be scratching under my skin, but I've never met an exam I didn't ace, and I came prepared for anything.

"And I meant it," I retort, not caring about niceties or sounding polite. I only care about them hearing what I have to say. "The only lie I told you during that trip was that your son and I were dating. Which, coincidentally enough, kind of stopped being a lie that same weekend."

Lenore's head snaps up. "Are you saying that you and Damian are *actually* dating now?"

She doesn't sound like someone confirming something she's already heard, but rather like she's learning this news for the first time. She sounds shocked, as if the idea of me and Damian having a real relationship is completely beyond the realm of reason.

I slow-blink in confusion. "Did he not tell you that?"

It's Hector who answers. "He didn't say much at all…except that none of this is your fault."

There's a skeptical edge to his voice, but it's soft, contemplative almost, as if he's wrestling with the two possibilities before him and is unsure which one is the truth. Though, the longer I study his stern face, the more I realize that's not because he wants to give *me* the benefit of the doubt…but because he's done giving it to his son.

Any trust—any belief and faith—he had in Damian is shattered, like a dropped glass as it collides with the ground. Seeing that finality in his gaze seems enough to tear my soul in two. I can't allow things to end like this. I won't. So, if they won't listen to Damian—if he isn't willing or able to stand up for himself…

Then *I* need to stand up for him.

"You know, I hated Damian when we first made our agreement. Literally *hated* him." I huff out a laugh, earning a pained look from his mother. "But then I got to know him. To *see* him." *And then I found I didn't really hate him at all.* I shake my head, looking again at his father. "I know he's done some things that have been…difficult for you to overcome as a family, but surely, you know why."

When neither of them answers, I peer down at my hands, which I clamp together in my lap until the knuckles are bleached of color to keep my anxiety at bay and to distract my fingers. My breath is shaky when I force myself to say, "I won't pretend to understand what it's like to lose a child, but I do understand how it feels to have a family member who's fighting cancer. If I'm honest, I don't think either of you see just how broken Damian is over losing his brother. He is deeply hurting, and I can't help thinking that, maybe, it was more important for you to show the outside world that everything was okay than to actually acknowledge it wasn't."

My eyes dart up, locking on Hector's again. "He blames you…for Jamie." My tone is brusque, and he flinches as if I just struck him across the face. My chest constricts at his wounded expression, but if he's going to hear me—*really* hear me—blunt honesty is the only way forward. And he needs to hear this. For Damian. "You realize that, right?" I press. "In his mind, you chose Hallazgo over saving his brother's life."

Hector's knuckles turn milk white as well as he tightens his grip on his mug. I expect him to challenge me. To say this is none of my business and to get the hell out of his house.

But he doesn't.

"It was more complicated than that," he protests, his voice strained.

I give a small, sympathetic nod. "I'm sure. But grief doesn't care about complicated. My dad abandoned me when I was little, and yet, I still miss the bastard for reasons I can't even begin to comprehend. There are days I still wish he would come home, even though I think he's a deadbeat waste of air. Damian's grief is like that," I explain, exchanging a brief glance with Lenore. "It's confused. And he acts out because he feels suffocated by this public perception of *fine* you're constantly forcing on him. Because you've made your love conditional on him fitting into this perfect image you've built to keep your world from crumbling." I exhale a tremulous breath, but push on before I lose my nerve. "You couldn't control Jamie dying, but you *can* control Damian. Or at least, you tried to. But he acted out because he doesn't need to be controlled. He *needs* you to acknowledge his pain. And yours."

Hector does react with rage now, his features contorting as he perceives my words as an insult rather than the harsh truth they are. "You have been engaging in this charade with our son since…when? September?" he barks. "And *you* presume to know him better after less than five months than his own parents who raised him?"

"With all due respect, sir, yes," I fire back, my own fury rising in direct competition with his. "Because, unlike you, he's not afraid to be honest with me. You're so caught up in the fact he lied that you aren't even bothering to look at why he did it."

He snorts. "Because he was clearly afraid of losing the free ride our family's wealth has afforded him."

Jesus, is that really what Damian's parents think of him? If so, they don't know him at all.

"Because he was afraid of losing Hallazgo." At the confused look on his parents' faces, I slide the strap of my bag off my shoulder and reach inside, pulling out the thick folder I had safely tucked within. "It's not quite finished," I say as I extend it to Hector, "but if I can't convince you, maybe this can."

His dark brow wrinkles as he reaches out a hand to take the folder from me. "What is this?"

I lick my lips, trying my best to ignore the frantic way my heart is racing. *Here goes nothing.*

"A proposal," I answer, "for a program that would cover medication and treatment costs for patients struggling with chronic illnesses and terminal diseases like cancer, through partnerships with hospitals, pharmacies, and research universities." I pause for a beat—just long enough for my words to sink in. "I have spent every single day of the last two months watching Damian work on this. He has devoted countless hours to researching, speaking to relevant industry contacts, whatever it takes to make this proposal foolproof."

Shock wipes the anger clean off Hector's face, and he stares at me for a tense moment before finally opening the folder. My eyes flick to Lenore as he flips through the pages, but she doesn't say a word, though she has put down her mug and scooted closer to her husband.

I stay silent as Hector carefully scans the proposal—as both their gazes trail the calculations and explanations within. And with every second that passes without them speaking, the more Lenore's eyes seem to tear up.

"He did all this…?" she whispers with a hesitant glance at me.

My own anger softens a little at her pleading expression.

"Yes. Aside from the calculations with the affordability and sustainability models. The math is mine, but the ideas were all him. He was determined to find a balance—a way to help people, to ensure no one else has to lose their Jamies, while taking steps to make the initiative profitable. And a lot of people have already expressed an interest in partnerships if Hallazgo were to launch it, which would assist with funding, and the majority of the associated costs would qualify as charitable contributions, making the program not only socially impactful but also financially sustainable."

A tear slides down Lenore's cheek, which she hurriedly wipes away.

Hector's gaze remains fixed on the folder. "These calculations…"

"I know what I've done is different from many traditional affordability models," I say, feeling suddenly self-conscious, which is *insane* since math is my thing, and I know I made those figures my bitch. But then, having my work scrutinized like this, by the father of the man I love—where so much is hinging on his reaction—is a position I've never been in before. I guess it only makes sense I'd be nervous. "Most of them focus primarily on income levels, but I wanted to account for real-world financial behaviors. By incorporating both the debt-to-income ratio and cost-of-living adjustments, I've analyzed how patients might prioritize treatments. That was something Damian really pushed for—to understand how the average person struggles with more than just their medical bills, so we can find a way to avoid patients having to choose between potential financial ruin and their health. It's a game theory approach, illustrating how different price points would affect patient decision-making, especially when it comes to continuing or abandoning treatments due to cost. The goal wasn't just to make medication more affordable, but to determine the threshold where more people could access the care they need without compromising Hallazgo's bottom line. And that can be done by leveraging subsidies, cost-sharing agreements with hospitals, grants, and discounted medication prices through pharmacy partnerships. As well as those charitable write-offs I mentioned."

Hector looks up at me then. "Since you don't have access to Hallazgo's financials, how did you determine sustainability?" It doesn't escape my notice that the rough edge to his voice is gone. Now, all I hear is a genuine curiosity.

I roll my teeth over my bottom lip. "I built risk assessment models based on publicly available industry data, historical market trends, and real-world case studies—everything from insurance claim denials to crowdfunding campaigns for medical expenses. I even ran predictive simulations to test different economic scenarios, ensuring the program remained viable even if market conditions fluctuated."

He blinks. "You…ran simulations," he echoes, the words drawn out and laced with bemusement.

I nod. "Several. I had to be sure the numbers held up. If Hallazgo moves forward with this initiative, it won't just be a PR stunt or some superficial corporate social responsibility effort. It'll be a financially sound strategy that expands market share while *actually* helping people."

With a sharp breath, Hector sinks back into the sofa cushions, as though the weight of what I've just told him has knocked all the air from his lungs. It's the first real crack I've seen in his carefully controlled demeanor. The first real hint that he's *really* listening. Beside him, Lenore sits frozen with one hand hovering over her open mouth as if she's about to say something but can't quite find the words.

Relief barrels through me. Numbers might help me make sense of the world, but I don't need a math formula to tell me I've gotten their attention.

"I have to say, this is highly impressive, Miss Dornan," Hector says, his tone stunned. "I'd expect this kind of work from a seasoned industry expert, not someone still in college."

It's nothing I haven't heard before—from teachers, professors, admissions scouts. Hell, I was invited to join Mensa in elementary school after achieving a perfect score on my RICAS exam (which led to my official IQ test), though I declined due to the membership costs since money was really tight at the time. But coming from Damian's father, those words hold more weight than I'm prepared for.

But this isn't about me.

"I'm not looking for your admiration or praise. I may have run the numbers, but everything else that's in this proposal—the vision, the commitment to making a real impact—that's all Damian. He's been the driving force behind this project. He's not just viewing Hallazgo as a business, but as a platform on which to build something meaningful. Something that can change lives… like *your* father wanted."

Hector blanches at the mention of his father. Or perhaps, at the realization that he doesn't know his child as well as he thought.

"I only helped to make it something tangible using *his* ideas," I continue. "Something that you might actually take seriously."

And he has. He *is*. I can see it written all over his face. And I know that even if he rejects the proposal, he can't reject the hard work and dedication Damian has put into it. Or the compassion and ambition it was born from.

Having said everything I wanted to say, I hoist my bag strap over my shoulder again and rise, standing to leave. Neither of them attempt to stop me, and maybe it's their silence, maybe it's my lingering resentment of how they've treated their son, but when I reach the living room door, I throw out one last sentiment.

One final food for thought.

"You know, for someone who you think only cares about money, Damian sure is determined to try to use yours for good."

Then, with their stunned expressions seared into my mind, I turn and walk out of the room without looking back.

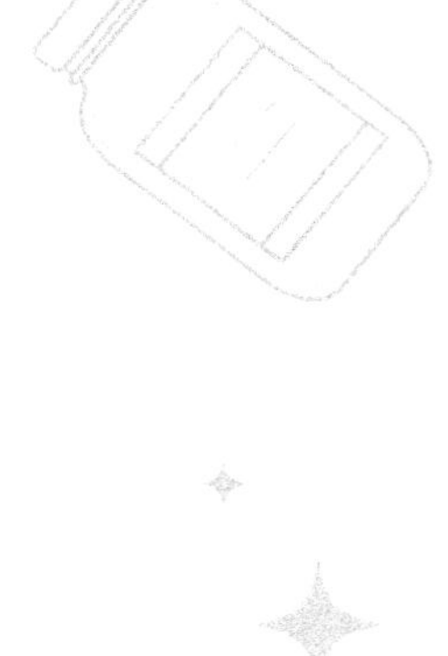

CHAPTER
THIRTY

✦ *Damian* ✦

**No hay mal que dure cien años - There is no evil
that lasts a hundred years**

**Translation: Bad times don't last forever.
And it feels like things are finally starting to look up.**

Sunlight beams in through the cabin windows, searing my eyelids and wrenching me from sleep. This morning has clearly chosen violence, but I guess it's my own damn fault for forgetting to lower the blinds in here last night.

Sighing, I push up onto my elbows, and look out through the glass panes at the bright cerulean blue sky beyond. After the shitshow with my parents on Wednesday, I couldn't bring myself to go back to campus, so I came here instead—to the *Lucia*, where I could hide away from the outside world for a while, and lament how completely I've blown up my life.

This is my fault, I know that. My parents might have had a hand in pushing me to this point through sheer emotional neglect, but the choices I've made are what put the nails in my coffin, so I really have no one but myself to blame for whatever comes next. I've tried to think what that may be—shit, with nothing to do the last three and a bit days *except* think about it, you'd assume I'd have a plan or even a slight inkling of an idea. But I don't. It's as if, one moment, I was reading the completed novel of my life, and then the words were suddenly wiped from the page. Now, I'm just left with a cliffhanger and no way to access the subsequent chapters to find out what's going to happen, good or bad.

I can't stay on the *Lucia* forever—my parents will eventually realize where I am, and it's not really stocked for permanent residence—but what else can I do? I can't go to my abuela's. I don't want to pull her into my mess or force her into a position where she has to choose between me and my dad, her only child. That wouldn't be fair. But I can't go home, and I can't bring myself to go back to school; partly because I don't know how much longer I'll be enrolled there before my tuition payments are cancelled, but also because the thought of being there makes me feel too exposed, too easily within my parents' reach, even if they've made no sign or show of wanting to see or talk to me again. They haven't tried to call me, and I've been too much of a coward to check my accounts—to see if they've followed through on their threat in September to cut me off. If they have, I'll be even more stuck than I already am. Homeless. Floating out to sea, like a raft with no paddle, helpless as I'm carried aimlessly by waves I can't control. Every second I spend in this weird limbo seems to only pull me farther from the shore of the life I was settling into, and all I can do now is wait for the tide to either swallow me or leave me stranded in this new, unfamiliar reality.

There's always Blondie's house—I know her mom and aunt would take me in without question—but I can't put that burden on them, and the truth is, I came here not only because of my parents and to avoid returning to school…but because I'm most afraid of facing *her*. Of seeing Blondie and her mom, and knowing there's nothing more I can do to help them. I don't want to run away from Blondie, from what we have, from what we could be, but I'm fucking terrified of letting her down. And right now, I feel like that's all I'm doing—like I'm failing everyone in my life, both past and present. I'm sure she would tell me I'm being stupid—that I've already done plenty, especially with the fifty grand I sent her on Wednesday to see them through however many months of meds that will cover on top of what she already has from me, but still… It's the future that scares me, the unknown.

The not knowing if I've done enough.

Flinging back the heavy gray blanket, I climb out of bed and plod to the kitchen, which is thankfully stocked with nonperishables, so there's at least something to eat, even if that something is boxed pasta at ten a.m. on a Sunday. I'm just about to heat the jarred sauce I found in one of the cupboards in a saucepan on the stove when my phone buzzes on the marble counter beside me.

I hesitate for a second before flipping it over to glance down at the screen, expecting another text or call from Blondie—she's tried roughly thirty times over the last three days, and it breaks my heart to ignore them. To ignore *her*, even if I'm not in the right headspace to talk. Not until I figure out what I'm doing.

Instead, I find a message from my mother.

Madre

Please meet us for lunch at noon at Fernando's. I know it's been a tense few days but we need to talk.

My stomach curdles at the mention of the restaurant which serves as the backdrop for so many of my worst memories, and at the unspoken expectation weighing on those final four words.

We need to talk.

Talk about what? Their intent to disown me? To strip me of the Navarro name? Well, newsflash: I'm already aware. No need to spell it out for me or rub salt in the open wound.

I turn off the burner and slump down onto the stool at the breakfast bar, scowling down at my phone, reading and rereading the message. My mom doesn't usually text me. At least, not about the serious stuff. That's always left to my dad, the enforcer of rules, the executor of discipline and unrelenting disappointment.

I shouldn't go. I should stay here where I'm safe and sheltered from their scrutiny and judgment. I should make a clean break. And yet…there's a voice inside me that wonders if there's still a chance, however small, that I can change their minds. Our relationship might be too broken to fix, but Hallazgo—I don't want to let go of that. I don't want to let go of my abuelo's dream. *My* dream. And I don't want to just throw away everything Blondie and I have worked so hard on.

I slowly rise from the bar stool, resolved. If this is the only opportunity I'll have to fight for what I want for my life…

Then I have to take it.

It's exactly twelve o'clock when I yank open the door to Fernando's, my palms slick with sweat. Coming here feels like a one-way ticket to heartache, but I have to do this. I owe it to my abuelo and Jamie to not give up without at least trying.

My pulse is a rapid cacophony of anticipation and fear as I step into the large sunlit dining room, the familiar sounds of the arpa jarocha in the corner doing little to settle my nerves, which rake along my insides like nails scratching at the underside of my skin. I swallow when my eyes land on my parents, sitting in their favorite spot by the window overlooking the marina, though their demeanors lack the usual dismissive sense of calm I'm accustomed to.

My father is tapping one finger against the bright white tablecloth, his eyes cast on the gleaming water outside, while my mother is chewing her thumbnail—literally *chewing* on it, destroying her three-hundred dollar manicure. If my manner-obsessed maternal grandparents were here to see this, they'd have a conniption.

My mom's eyes catch on mine as I cross the room toward them, and her gasp is audible as she anxiously pats my father's shoulder to get his attention. "There he is," I hear her say, like someone eagerly awaiting the chance to meet their favorite celebrity, before she then jumps to her feet with a nervous smile.

"Come," she breathes when I'm within earshot, hastily pulling out the chair between theirs. The only other free seat at the round table is in the same position on the opposite side, and I can't help feeling that was intentional so I can't put any breathing space between me and them. Specifically, between me and my dad. "Sit." Her eyes are imploring, so I do as she asks and plop down on the seat.

Everything I plan to say to defend myself—to make them listen to me just *once*—evaporates on my tongue when my father announces, "Your girlfriend came by the house yesterday."

The cogs in my brain screech to a grinding halt as I try (and fail) to process what he's said. So much for pleading my case, I guess.

"Lexi?" I ask.

I wince at the mocking voice in my head that shouts, *Well done, genius. Who else would he be talking about?*

As if reading my thoughts, my dad arches a brow and quips, "Do you have *another* girlfriend that we're unaware of?"

I practically choke on the breath that escapes me. "What?" I splutter. "No, I—"

"She's rather outspoken, isn't she?" he muses, ignoring me in favor of the fork he now twists between his forefinger and thumb. "Not afraid to speak her mind."

Is that an insult or a compliment? I wonder. With him, it could honestly be either.

I watch my dad carefully, feeling completely bamboozled, and as my mouth snaps shut, I frown at him, torn over what to say. To do. Did Blondie offend him? Should I apologize on her behalf?

Do I even care?

Fuck that, I decide. I'm not apologizing for shit, and I learned my lesson about doing *anything* on behalf of my girl. Besides, the only thing I'm sorry about is that I wasn't there to hear it. I can only imagine what she must have said for them to feel the need to summon me today.

"No, she definitely isn't," I murmur.

Ronnie once told me she loves how Blondie doesn't ever sugarcoat things. Honestly, it's what I love most about her, too.

My father lets out a thoughtful hum. "We spoke about you, and she had quite a strong opinion on the matter. She gave us a rather impassioned speech, actually."

I snort. "Yeah, she's not really known for holding her punches."

Figuratively *or* literally.

He nods. "I gathered as much." Clearing his throat, Dad sets down the fork, then his hand disappears under the table as he reaches for something on the empty chair to his left. When it emerges from beneath the tablecloth a few seconds later, my heart nearly stops. "She also showed us this."

My eyes lock on the black folder clutched in his hand—or rather, on the title page peeking through the transparent cover sleeve—and I have to will myself to believe what I'm seeing. It's the proposal. *My* proposal. But how? Blondie and I haven't even finished compiling all the data we need to complete it, so how the hell is it here? And *with my dad*? Not to mention like *this*—like a real, honest-to-god, professional document that someone like my eternally unimpressed father might actually take seriously?

I'm lost for words. Blondie did this. She not only organized all our research, but she printed it, bound it, and undoubtedly went beyond the limits of her comfort zone to present it to my parents. For *me*. To fight when I couldn't find the strength or courage to fight for myself.

My eyes burn as my father sets the folder on the table before him, but he doesn't move to open it. He just gingerly places his palms flat on top of the cover and stares down at the backs of his hands, his usually stern expression unreadable.

His voice is quiet when he continues. "I spent the afternoon combing through this after she left yesterday, and I have to say…" He pauses, drawing in a deep breath. "This is tremendous, hijo."

I blink, momentarily lost for words. At first, all I'm aware of is the fact that he just called me hijo again. That endearment, that familiarity, was so notably lacking in our previous conversation, and hearing it again eases some of that fear, that anxiety, that's been eating away at me these last few days. But then something else grabs my attention, and my focus becomes singular—wholly consumed by one particular thing he just said. Something far more surprising.

My dad just *complimented* me.

"You…read my proposal?" I manage past the lump of shock in my throat.

Meeting my gaze, Dad gives me a small, solemn nod. "I did."

"We *both* did," Mom adds before reaching across the table to take my hand. As her fingers wrap around mine, her eyes shine with an emotion I don't recognize, and for a moment, I wonder if I'm being trolled. Or if I've somehow stepped into an alternate timeline where a benevolent alien race has abducted my parents and replaced them with more emotionally available doppelgängers. "And it's a great idea, Damian."

"The last few years, all we wanted was to see some initiative from you, but this?" A startled grunt escapes me when Dad lifts one hand and claps it against my back. "When you begin at Hallazgo this summer, I want you leading the team that—"

"Wait," I interrupt, needing a second to process. I tug my hand out from under my mother's, and lean away from my father's touch, casting a wary glance between them, uncertain. "You still want me to come work for Hallazgo? I'm not…cut off?"

Mom's face instantly crumples at the strained vulnerability in my voice. "No. *No*, forget the ultimatum. Forget the vote," she says to me, her tone thick with tears. "That was a mistake—"

"We don't want to lose another son."

I stiffen at my father's gruff baritone, my eyes moving in a sluggish crawl as they shift back to his, my reactions slowed by the lightning strike of shock jolting through me. Beside me, my mother is equally still.

Dad's gaze is unwavering, and I register the slight bob of his Adam's apple as he rasps, "We don't want to lose *you*, hijo."

All the emotions I've bottled up these last four years threaten to spill out at his words. This is so fucked up. I feel like I'm living in Upside Down Land where the ground is above me, and I'm standing on nothing but sky, free-falling into an endless abyss.

They don't want to *lose* me? After everything, what new mindfuckery is this?

I let out a derisive snort as I gesture to the dining room around me. "Then why ask me to meet you *here* of all places?" Frustration hitches my tone up an octave.

Out of the corner of my eye, I catch Mom shaking her head.

"What are you talking about?" she asks.

I round on her, scowling. "You two only ever ask me to meet you here when you have bad news. Wednesday's fun little hoedown at home being the one recent exception." I scoff.

Her mouth pops open as she brings a hand to her chest and clutches the string of pearls around her neck. "Have we really done that?" she whispers, aghast.

I'm about to answer her when my father chokes out a humorless laugh. "I suppose we have." When I turn to look at him again, his head is lowered, propped up by his hand, his fingers pressing into his eyelids. "Truthfully, I've always chosen this place for the difficult conversations because I used to come here with your abuelo. Being here helps me feel closer to him. And I needed that support to know how to be a good father to you." He looks up at me then, his expression miserable. "Something I have clearly failed at."

I…don't know what to say. That is the most self-aware thing my father has ever admitted out loud—at least to me.

Straightening, he clears his throat again. "Miss Dornan enlightened us about a few things that we were unaware—" He winces, shakes his head, then quickly says, "No, that we were *willfully* ignoring. I don't blame you for being angry with me. *I'm* angry with me, hijo. Not just for what happened to Jamie, but for disregarding what *you* obviously needed in the aftermath."

My chest seems to cave in around my heart, crushing it. This isn't like him. We don't talk about this. We don't talk about Jamie. We don't ever talk about what happened.

But then…that was always the problem.

"That choice…" It's only when he sniffs that I notice the sheen of tears in his eyes. "The guilt that's followed me since is something I'll live with every day for the rest of my life, but what I *can't* live with is knowing that I have failed both my children." My eyes widen as he turns in his chair to face me, his hands clenched into trembling fists in his lap. "It was foolish of me—of *both* of us," he adds with a nod toward my mother, "to think that if we never talked about Jamie then, somehow, our grief would just go away. It was foolish of me not to see how much you were hurting, for focusing on what you were doing and not the why behind it. For not seeing that you were acting out from a place of pain. And for that, I'm so incredibly sorry."

Tears burn mercilessly at the corners of my eyes and at the back of my throat. I don't dare to speak. One word and I know the floodgate will break.

"I'm not a perfect man," Dad whispers now, his voice barely audible, "but I want to be a better one. I want to be a better father. I don't want this rift between us to be irreconcilable. I know I can be stubborn, but I'm not above owning my mistakes. And it would be a mistake not to tell you how *proud* I am of you. Of *this*." He raises his left hand and rests it on the table again, on top of my proposal. "If your abuelo was here…he'd be so proud of you, too, Damian."

Proud. That's a word I never thought I'd hear out of my father's mouth—not in relation to me, anyway. And even though I realize now it's something I've wanted him to say for far longer than I'm even aware of, and it's totally *not* the appropriate response to this situation, I snort.

"Wow, Lexi must've *really* gotten to you," I say because years of unresolved grief and a penchant for sarcasm have both completely warped my knee-jerk reactions.

To my immense bemusement, my dad's face splits into a grin. "She's a very impressive young woman. I can see why you like her."

I more than like her, I think, but I don't tell him that. It's not for my parents to hear. Not yet. Not before I muster up the nerve to tell Blondie.

On my other side, my mother gently nudges my shoulder.

"Perhaps you could convince her to come work at Hallazgo," she says with a coy smile, and when I catch my father nodding at her, I know this isn't just some off-the-cuff suggestion, but something they have both seriously talked about and considered. "With a mind like that, she'd be a real asset."

I stare at each of them in turn, my eyes swinging back and forth between their expectant faces like a pendulum. Blondie…come work at Hallazgo? With me? Not that I haven't fantasized about that—about spending our days together. About what our future would look like. But this? Even this is beyond my wildest fantasies.

What is even happening? These people can't be my parents.

Seriously…doppelgängers. They *have* to be.

"Lexi still has two years left at Conwick," is all I can think to say, and just like that, the dream fizzles away. "There's no way she could come work at Hallazgo right now."

My father shrugs. "If it won't interfere with her studies or scholarship requirements, she can always come on board part-time as a private consultant to help implement the program until she graduates, after which time we can offer her a full-time position."

I gape at him, my mouth hanging slightly ajar. "A private consultant? Seriously?"

"Just a few hours a week to go over the numbers with the rest of the team, ensure everything is in order," he explains, as casually as if we're discussing what to have for lunch. "And under our specialized contract for high-level consultants, she would be eligible for certain benefits in exchange for her expertise, such as stock options…and access to Hallazgo's health insurance plan."

His words strike me like a fist to my sternum, and I push out a loud, whooshing breath. Is he saying what I *think* he's saying?

"But it's her mom who's sick, not Lexi," I breathe, my voice strangled. From what I learned while researching for the proposal, and from what Blondie told me since opening up to me about her mom's cancer and their family's financial struggles, healthcare insurance only tends to cover spouses and dependents. Which means any insurance she might obtain through employment wouldn't pay for her mom's treatments or meds, leaving them right back at square one. Sure, they might be better off with a salary from Hallazgo, but those costs add up, and it might still not be enough.

As if he can hear my frantic thoughts, my dad says, "Our status as a private company gives us flexibility with our coverage. Our insurance plan has a QOL clause, so we can cover not just our employees but their immediate family members, even extending to parents. Which means her mother would qualify."

My breaths, the blood pumping through my veins—it all seems to freeze.

This feels way too good to be true…but could it be? I don't have access to the financial inner workings at Hallazgo, and I never had cause to ask about their insurance plan, so I genuinely wouldn't know. But if it is…

"So, you're saying her treatment…" I falter, licking my lips, trying to gather my thoughts. "Her medications—"

"It would all be paid for," my father assures me.

A sudden warmth barrels through my body, and I instantly recognize it as comfort. Happiness. *Hope.* What my dad's offering…it could erase Blondie's money problems. It could help her mom and see them through the financial side of her illness so they only have to focus on her getting better.

It's more than I could imagine. More than *I* can do for her. And I'm eager to reach out with both hands and grab onto that offer before it slips away.

I don't even realize a tear has slipped down my cheek until I feel my mom's hand on my shoulder. I meet her gaze, but she says nothing—just offers me a barely-there smile.

It's my dad who breaks the silence.

"It was your abuelo's primary ethos when starting this company that Hallazgo assist its employees in times of crisis, especially in relation to any family-related health challenges. 'A company is only as strong as the people who built it. Take care of them, and they'll give you everything they've got in return.' That's what he always used to say, and that mindset is what helped Hallazgo to prosper."

I remember my abuelo saying that, too, but I was too young in the years before he died to truly understand what he meant, or just how far he was willing to go to follow through on those words. From what my abuela told me, there was so much my abuelo wanted to accomplish with Hallazgo, but couldn't thanks to bureaucratic roadblocks within the healthcare system. So, it soothes my grief-stricken heart to know he was at least able to do this—to take care of the people who helped him lay the foundation and build the company into what it is now.

My father's voice drowns to a hum in my ears, but when I hear Blondie's name, my attention snaps back to him. "We want to support Lexi, and this will allow us to do that in a way that can be classed as legitimate compensation…and *won't* have the IRS scrutinizing our finances." Despite the severity of his tone, his words lack heat, and I swear I even catch a glint of amusement in his eyes. The slight upward tilt at the left corner of his mouth a moment later confirms it.

"That's…really generous, Dad." With so little to be grateful for these past few years, it feels foreign to show gratitude now, especially to my father, who I have blamed for so much of the bad in my life. But I will…because it *is* generous and I *am* grateful, and I would humble myself before even my worst enemy if they were willing to help my Blondie.

"Lexi is important to you, which means she's important to us," my mom says, giving my shoulder a squeeze. I have to resist the urge to laugh. Guess Blondie is no longer "that Dornan girl" and is back in my mom's good graces again. Who would've thought all it would take was a little verbal spanking from my fearless girlfriend.

"And selfishly," my father adds, and I suppress a groan because I know what's coming, "I see an opportunity here, and it would be senseless not to bring on her talent when we have the chance."

My dad is and always has been an opportunist, but for once, I can't disagree. Blondie *is* remarkable, and he would be an idiot not to snatch her up before the rest of the world realizes what she has to offer.

"I… Thank you," I say, and I mean it. "I'll talk to her about it, and let you know what she says."

"Excellent." Dad smiles again, and it takes all the self-restraint I have to stop myself from alerting the press. Wow, that's two in one day. He slaps the cover of my proposal. "As for this, when do you think you can have it completed?"

My heart leaps in my chest, but I try my best to tamp down my excitement. I don't want to get my hopes up. "When do you need it?"

He pivots in his seat, and folds his hands on top of the table, reverting to business mode. "I'd like to take it before the board as soon as possible. And I want you there with me."

What?

"Damian?" Mom prompts when I don't respond.

I should say something, right? I mean, they're literally offering me everything I want—not just the chance to work for Hallazgo, but to truly build something that matters, like my abuelo wanted. And better yet, to do it with Blondie.

So, why does that suddenly not feel like enough?

Because it isn't, my conscience whispers, and my heart squeezes, reminding me that there's something close to it that's still unresolved.

"I have something to say. Something I need to make clear."

My parents both look at me, confused. I swallow, staring down at my hands, which I fold together in my lap.

"What you're offering…I want it. I do," I tell them. "But if I'm going to come work at Hallazgo, I have some conditions."

"*If?*" my mom practically screeches. Her hand slips from my shoulder, and I glance up as she peers over at my father, her face lined with concern. "What are you—"

"It's fine," Dad interrupts, his tone surprisingly cordial as he holds up a hand. "Let him speak, Lenore."

I exhale a shaky breath.

Be brave. Be bold. Be fearless, I say to pump myself up, once again quoting my mother's favorite decorative sofa cushions. Damn, maybe inspirational homeware is really onto something. That shit has become ingrained in my brain.

"Working on this proposal," I begin, measuring every word, "hearing that you want me involved, I—" I shake my head. "It's everything I want…but I realize now it's not enough." I meet my father's gaze. "I know you're afraid of making any decisions that could negatively impact Hallazgo, but you can't keep running from progress, not after what happened with Jamie. I want to head up this initiative, but if I come on board, if I do it, it's with the condition that Hallazgo pushes for change in the medical field, and invests in experimental treatments and drug development. Pediatric cancers in particular are vastly underfunded, you know this…but they don't have to be. I want us to work with universities, contribute to research in not just pediatric oncology but also in stem cell therapy, gene therapy, CAR-T cell therapy, tissue engineering…so that all the other Jamies out there have that potentially life-saving option when every other choice is exhausted."

Dad opens his mouth to respond, but I cut him off before he can speak, heading off his protest. "I don't care about the board's opinion," I tell him, because I don't, and if I'm going to work at the company, he needs to know I won't be intimidated or pushed around by some old farts who don't have the same emotional and personal stake in this business as I do. "Hallazgo is *my* legacy as much as it is yours, and I want it to be known not just for its success from an economic standpoint but for the impact it has. And to do that, we need to be willing to push boundaries. So, you can convince the board or I will. But this *has* to happen. It's the only way forward." Unclenching my hands, I reach out and tap a finger against the cover of the proposal. "If you want *this*, if you want *me* to be part of Hallazgo…then *that's* the only future I see."

My parents are silent for so long I start to wonder if I've broken them… or if I've irrevocably blown things up again. Are they going to retract their offer—not just for me to work at Hallazgo, but everything they said they'd do for Blondie? I hope not, but they've both always been so hard to read, especially my dad. And this might be the one point he's not willing or able to budge on.

After what feels like an eternity, my father blows out a loud breath. "Perhaps, I have been a coward—placed too much weight on protecting your abuelo's legacy instead of fostering it like he always wanted. Maybe this is how we move forward."

Astonishment ripples through me at his soft-spoken admission. He scrubs a hand across his face, and though the other remains on my proposal, when he looks at me, I know he's not thinking about Hallazgo or even all the good I know we can accomplish if he'll only give us the chance to try. I know he's thinking about us as a family. About how we're going to finally find our way out of our grief. Together.

My throat tightens at the thought. "For Jamie," I whisper.

To my right, I hear the quiet break of my mother's composure, the stifled sound of her sob—it's the first time I've witnessed her cry since my brother's death—but I cling to my father's gaze, willing him to meet me halfway. His own is unblinking.

I don't even notice I'm holding my breath until he extends one hand. "For the future."

And as I stare down at it, as I slide my hand into his, returning the smile he offers me, I realize it's not just an offer of peace, but an offer of partnership. A chance to build something great…and to finally take that first long-overdue step toward healing.

Love isn't a formula. It's the solution.

My entire body is still buzzing with the adrenaline rush from my confrontation with Damian's parents yesterday. A year ago—hell, even five months ago, when I made the agreement with Damian, and really pushed myself to the limits of my comfort zone—I never could have imagined doing something so brazen, putting myself out there like that and being so unabashedly bold. But then…five months ago, I wasn't in love.

I guess it really is like Maya Angelou said: in the flush of love's light, we dare to be brave.

Love. God, it's weird to admit it, but it would be weirder to deny what it is. And what I feel for Damian *is* love. And I suppose that love *has* made me brave, but on the flip side, it's also made me scared. Because now that it's real, it's become something I can lose. And I don't want to lose Damian.

I wish I knew where he was. I wish I knew if what I said to his parents made the slightest impact or difference. But I don't know either of those things, and the not knowing is driving me insane.

I considered focusing all this pent-up energy and worry on the proposal, on shrinking the gap between its current state and what it needs to be fully fleshed out and completed, but ultimately concluded there's little point until we know if Damian's dad will actually support the initiative. He might have seemed impressed by the work Damian and I both put into the idea, but holding a venture in high esteem and actually backing it are two different things.

So, to distract myself (and to avoid wearing a hole in my carpet from the pacing I would be doing at home), I decided to head to the library to see if CASS—Conwick's Academic Support Services—needed an extra hand. Wednesdays might be my scheduled tutoring night, but there's usually more demand than CASS can accommodate, so they never turn down a spare tutor or two if anyone is feeling benevolent enough to offer up their night willingly, especially when that night falls on a Sunday.

Unfortunately, it doesn't provide *quite* the distraction I'd hoped for, and—to the disgruntlement of a junior sorority girl named Shannon, who begged for my help with her combinatorics homework—I keep catching myself staring off into space more often than not.

"I really don't get this whole factorial thing," she grumbles beside me, but I barely register her complaint. All I can think about is Damian. Where is he now? Has he spoken to his parents since yesterday?

Has he spoken to them at all?

"Lexi?"

I jolt at the touch of Shannon's hand on my arm, and whip my head around to face her. "W-what?" I stammer.

She purses her lips. "Factorials? I don't understand them."

"Oh, right."

I blink at her, then shift my gaze to the open textbook sandwiched on the table between us. As my eyes crawl over the page, I give my head a small shake to clear it.

Get it together, Lexi. I know you're worried, but there's nothing more you can do.

"Okay, um…let's break it down." Closing the textbook, I push it across the table and reach for my notebook, opening it to a fresh page. "So, a factorial is just the result of multiplying all the numbers starting from one up to a specific number. Let's say five." I write the number five at the top of the page and underline it twice. "For five factorial, you multiply five by each of the numbers that comes before it, so five times four times three times two times one." My pencil scratches against the paper as I speak, so Shannon can follow along. "It helps us count how many different ways we can arrange things when they're all unique."

Shannon's brow wrinkles a little, but it doesn't look like I've completely lost her, so I carry on.

"For example, if we had five distinct letters, there would be five factorial ways to arrange them. But what if some of those letters were the same? Take the word MATHEMATICS." I scribble the word a few lines down. "There are eleven letters, but among those eleven letters, there are two Ms"—I underline both—"two As"—I underline these next—"and two Ts"—I underline them last—"so swapping those identical letters around doesn't create a new, distinct arrangement. That's where dividing by the factorials comes in, so we can account for that repetition and eliminate those duplicate combinations from being counted multiple times. In this case, eleven factorial is the total number of possible arrangements if all the letters in the word MATHEMATICS were different. But since we have repeats with the Ms, As, and Ts, we divide by two factorial for each letter—the number of times those letters repeat—to avoid overcounting."

I pause for a moment to let this all sink in, then ask, "If you wanted to work out the factorial for MATHEMATICS on the assumption that all the letters are different, how would you do that?"

The column of Shannon's throat shifts when she swallows, the sound audible in the stark quiet of the library. "Umm…multiply eleven by ten by nine by eight, and so on?" she answers, her tone uncertain.

I nod encouragingly. "Correct. And what does that give you?" Shannon blanches at the question as if I just asked her to do something impossible, like prove the Riemann Hypothesis. I flash her a quick, reassuring smile. "It's okay, you can use your calculator."

With a soft, "Phew," she turns from me and reaches into her bag. By the time her hand resurfaces a few seconds later, her calculator clutched between her manicured fingers, I've already worked out the answer in my head, the blocks of color building in front of me like my own personal rainbow wall that only I can see. But I don't say as much. I know math doesn't come easy to everyone, and I don't want to make her feel stupid.

"39,916,800," Shannon says timidly after a moment, her tone lilting at the end in question despite the numbers on the screen before her.

I give her another affirmative smile. "Well done. Now, remember what I said about the repeats. Next, you want to divide by the duplicate factorials. How many sets of those do we have?"

Shannon's gaze follows the movement of my pencil when I tap it against the word MATHEMATICS written in my notebook. Her face lights up with confidence.

"Oh, I know this! Three. One for the Ms, one for the As, and one for the Ts."

I nod again. "Right. So, if we have two of each of these letters, that means it's two factorial for M, two factorial for A, and two factorial for T, which gives us…?" I trail off, prompting her to answer.

She scrunches her face, considering. "Six?"

"If we add them, we won't actually be accounting for all the possible arrangements," I explain, "so instead, think of it as three separate groups of duplicates rather than how many letters are repeating. And since we're dividing the total number of ways to arrange the letters by the number of repeats for each group, we don't add them together, we…"

"Multiply them?" Shannon guesses. "So, we have eight?"

I snap my fingers. "Bingo. So, now, you're left with a fraction with the eleven factorial on top and the duplicate factorials on the bottom, and it's just a matter of simple division."

Shannon gives me a skeptical look and scoffs. "Simple. Right," she deadpans.

My own expression is patient as I gesture to her calculator, which she picks up again with a sigh.

"Okay, so, thirty-nine million, blah, blah, blah, divided by eight is…" Her fingernails clack against the buttons as she enters each number. "4,989,600." Her eyes slide to mine for confirmation.

"Yup. And that's your answer," I tell her.

Her mouth pops open as she looks down at her calculator before glancing back up at me in surprise. "That's…actually not that hard."

"Nope," I agree. "It isn't."

I'm about to come up with another example for Shannon to try when something tickles my senses, coaxing me to raise my head. My eyes lift at that silent, inner command, instantly snagging on a tall, dark-haired figure at the opposite end of the atrium near the library entrance. And as my heart stumbles in my chest at the sight, it occurs to me that I really *do* have a built-in fuckboy detector because that familiar figure now meeting my gaze across the room is Damian.

No other thoughts seem to penetrate my brain other than a staccato *he's here, he's here*. He smiles at me, and my relief is so palpable I can taste it, but I've barely had time to process his presence when he jerks his chin in the direction of the library stacks.

Math section, he mouths before disappearing from view behind a bookcase.

It takes more self-restraint than I knew myself capable of to not jump out of my seat and go running to him like the female love interest in a romcom movie. Instead, heart hammering against my rib cage, I turn to Shannon and say, "Think you can try a few problems on your own? I'll be right back."

My voice is surprisingly calm as I speak, and she gives me an unbothered nod as I slide my chair back and stand, keeping my pace steady as I head in the direction of the mathematics section.

Damian is already there waiting for me, shoulder propped against the bookcase so he's leaning at an angle, his feet effortlessly crossed at the ankle. His eyes are downcast, fixed on the open book in his hands.

"Isn't math supposed to be a universal language?" he asks without looking up, sensing my presence as easily as I seem to sense his, like we are two parallel lines drawn so closely together we might as well be one. He snorts, his brow creasing in consternation. "I feel like I'm trying to decode an alien dialect."

Straightening, he snaps the book shut, and slides it back onto the shelf. Then those dark eyes are locking on mine, and those plush lips I am dying to kiss are twisting into a lopsided grin.

"Hi, Blondie," he murmurs, smiling at me, and hearing those two words—that familiar endearment I've never told him I adore—is enough to break my composure.

I stumble forward a step. "Are you…okay?" I ask, hoping that easy smile isn't disguising something much darker behind it. Something that might be breaking him. "I hadn't heard from you, and I—" My voice catches, and I swallow to push down the lump of emotion building in my throat.

Damian's lips hitch at the corners, his grin turning rakish. "Were you worried about me, Dornan?" His already molten eyes darken with amusement.

My face contorts into a scowl. "Of course, I was worried about you, you *idiot*. You sent me fifty grand out of the blue, and then vanished. I couldn't find you. You weren't answering my calls. Do you have *any* idea how—"

Before I can say another word, his arms are encircling me, pulling me to his chest, and his lips are at my ear, whispering, "I'm sorry," over and over, his voice so low only I can hear it. I shiver from the touch of his warm breath on my neck as my hands instinctively hook around his waist and splay against his back, holding him to me as much as my trembling fingers will allow.

We stay that way for a moment, me clinging to him like I really am a freaking spider monkey, my face pressed into his shirt, inhaling his scent, while he smooths his hand over my hair and repeatedly apologizes. I want to tell him he doesn't need to be sorry—that I understand why he shut me out—but I'm just so glad he's here and in my arms that I can't find the words.

"It just felt like my whole world was imploding, and I was so afraid of letting you down," he eventually says when I finally pull back to look at him, though he doesn't meet my gaze. "Of fucking up things with you like I fucked up everything else."

Lifting my hands to cup his face, I swipe my thumbs across the soft skin of his cheekbones. "Hey, you haven't fucked this up, okay?" I tilt my head toward him just a little so he's forced to look at me. "It's fine," I assure him. "*We're* fine." I pause, hesitating out of fear of the answer, before once again asking, "Are *you*?"

Damian considers that for a moment, then lets out a shaky breath through his nose. "Things looked a bit dicey there for a minute, but it's all good now. It's great, actually."

My hands falter against his cheeks. "Great?" I parrot, arching a brow.

His lips twitch into another smile. "Yeah. All thanks to you."

I start to protest. He's giving me way too much credit. Sure, I said my piece to his parents, but it was *his* idea, *his* proposal that made them actually listen. Before I can get any comprehensible words out to tell him so, he takes my hands in his, pulling them away from his face. He then brings them down into the narrow space between us where he interlocks our fingers together.

"I wouldn't have had the guts to do what you did," he says in a tremulous voice, "and I…" He shakes his head with a disbelieving laugh. "Honestly, I don't deserve you at all, but I'm not going to question it. Not if it means I get to keep you."

My pulse skitters under my skin as hope blooms in my chest. "Does this mean—"

Damian is already nodding before I can finish the question. "My dad wants me to start work at Hallazgo this summer."

My heart is thundering so loudly in my ears I struggle to hear his next words. But I see them on his lips. I feel every syllable punctuated in the kisses he plants on each of my knuckles.

"What?" I'm suddenly breathless.

"He wants me to head up the program," Damian clarifies. "He said we'll go in front of the board as soon as the proposal is finished."

This revelation makes me feel weightless, like the slightest breeze might knock me over or blow me away. I can barely think straight past the happiness barreling through me. "Oh, my god, Damian," I manage when my head stops spinning. "That's incredible."

"There's more," he adds, his smile deepening as he divulges every detail of his meeting with his parents earlier today. He tells me about his dad's apology, about how they finally talked about Jamie and their shared grief as a family, and about his conditions for going to work for Hallazgo. That last part in particular has my eyes stinging with tears because I know how hard it must have been for him to stand up to his dad. To stand up not only for himself but for Jamie. The fact he was willing to sacrifice something he wants to ensure he does right by his brother's memory says more about his character than any initiative ever could.

"I didn't know your brother or your abuelo, but I'm certain they'd be proud of you. *I'm* proud of you," I whisper.

"Of *us*," Damian corrects me. I'm about to wave him off, to tell him my part was easy, and to not minimize just how much of the proposal was down to him—down to the fierce, compassionate heart he's kept guarded from the world for far too long—when he says, "I didn't do this alone, Dornan. And because of that, I'd like to make you an offer."

That takes me by surprise. "An offer?"

A prickle of unease raises the hair on the back of my neck.

What kind of offer?

"So, *apparently*, large transfers like what we've been doing the last few months raise all kinds of red flags about money laundering or whatever, so we can't do that anymore."

My stomach plummets into my shoes. I'm not sure what shocks me more: his point-blank delivery or that I now have to face the one thing I've been actively *not* thinking about because I was afraid of this very outcome. I've been purposely avoiding the money issue—what I'd do to help Mom once the current money runs out now that Damian's parents know about our agreement. I figured it couldn't continue—that they wouldn't allow him to keep sending me those payments—but I couldn't bring myself to think about it beyond that, keeping my current focus only on my concern for Damian.

But now that I know he's safe and okay, that anxiety comes rushing back in, like water flooding my lungs, suffocating my breaths. The fifty grand Damian sent me a few days ago will see us through for an additional few months, sure, but with no definite end to Mom's treatment in sight, I can't be certain it'll be enough to cover us long-term, especially if the worst should happen and she ends up in the hospital again—god forbid, for an extended period next time. If that does happen, what then? How the hell am I going to come up with the money?

Are we really going to get so close to the finish line only to fail at the end of the race?

"*But*," Damian interjects, and I'm so relieved there's a "but" that I nearly sink to my knees. He holds me steady, one hand moving to my back again as the other reaches up to tuck a loose curl behind my ear. "How about coming to work for Hallazgo?"

This time, it's my heart that sinks. Because while his offer is a lifeline, it's also impossible. "I'm only a sophomore, Damian," I remind him. "My mom would kill me if I dropped out of school."

"You won't have to drop out," he assures me, but I raise a skeptical brow. "It would be part-time until you graduate. Your hours will be flexible, and completely revolve around your studies so your scholarship and grades won't be affected. And your scholarship is merit-based, right? So, there's zero risk of any money you earn jeopardizing it."

I blink at him in surprise. Is he being serious?

Could I actually do that?

"Doing what?"

Damian looks as giddy as a kid on Christmas morning when he answers. "Private consultant. Basically, you'd be our numbers guy, which, let's be real, we both know you'd spank the shit out of that job. And if you accept, you'd be covered by our insurance, and by extension, so would your mom. Before you ask"—he holds up a hand when I open my mouth to interrupt— "*yes*, I know insurance doesn't usually cover non-dependents, but my dad assured me Hallazgo has this quality of life clause in their plan that covers all immediate family members, even extending to parents." His hands move to my arms now, rubbing up and down my sleeves as if he knows that the anxiety writhing inside me needs soothing. "You won't have to worry about her treatments or meds anymore, Dornan. It will all be covered. I promise."

I promise.

The tears I've been holding back break through at these words, and I clamp a hand over my mouth to muffle my cries, the pent-up stress of the last few days—hell, most of the last two years—finally boiling over. Damian wraps his arms around me once more, and pulls me close again, hugging me tightly, the pressure of his embrace a needed anchor for my overstimulated senses, grounding me.

This all feels too good to be true, and on some level, I'm afraid to believe it, but standing here in his arms, safe and secure, I know I would trust anything he tells me. And I *do* trust him, just as much as I trust that the feeling filling my heart to the brim is love.

I love you. I love you. I love you. That same thought loops in my head, but every time I reach for the words to say it aloud, they evade me. So, instead, I just hold him tighter, trying my best to imprint the emotions overwhelming me into his skin so he might be able to feel them.

"It's a good salary," Damian murmurs in my ear when my sobs finally start to ebb. "Like, *really* good. And you'll have stock options. You'd have all the money for cosplay you could possibly want," he jokes. "Hey, maybe we can use some of that cash to invest in a few things for the bedroom—"

Choking on a wet laugh, I push away from him and playfully swat at his chest. "If you suggest *Twilight* role play, I'm breaking up with you."

Damian gives his chin a thoughtful scratch. "I *was* going to say a sex swing, but your idea is much better."

Snorting, I glance down at my feet to hide my flush when my eyes catch on my watch. I've been back here for over ten minutes. Shannon is going to think I walked out on her, or that I died under an avalanche of library books.

"Crap, I need to get back," I mutter, wiping my wet cheeks with the heels of my hands.

Damian presses a thumb to my chin, catching a stray tear I miss. "Math waits for no one," he says with a shrug, then his grin turns devilish. "How soon can you be done here? I am *dying* to have my way with you."

Heat curls in the lowest depths of my stomach, and spreads through me until I feel it everywhere. If my cheeks weren't red before, I guarantee they are now.

I swallow hard, pressing my thighs together. "Give me five," I rasp.

When we make it back to Damian's dorm, it's like that drunken night in September all over again. Being separated the last handful of days after nearly five months of almost daily interaction has amped our mutual longing up to eleven, and we collide in the hallway in a desperate clash of tongues and roaming hands before we even reach his room, unable to stop ourselves from touching each other. When we finally tumble through his door a few moments later, our clothes are quickly discarded.

His lips find my neck as he backs me toward the bed, one hand cupping my breasts as the other moves to grip my ass, his fingertips skimming dangerously close to the building heat between my legs. Then his hands are on my face, and he's trailing his lips over my mouth, my cheeks, my forehead, only pausing before each kiss to sprinkle me with compliments that have me blushing.

"You're brilliant."

"You're funny."

"You're incredible."

"God, you're so beautiful," he whispers last in my ear, and goosebumps pimple my skin at the astonished way he murmurs those words, like he almost can't believe I'm his when *I'm* the one who can't believe he's mine.

I moan when our mouths meet again, his tongue slipping past my lips, and I melt in his arms as his kiss consumes me, body and soul. Every light skim of his fingertips against my bare flesh leaves a trail of electric fire in its wake, his touch lighting me up from the inside out until I'm burning with an overwhelming need for relief, like a sun on the brink of a supernova.

For all the similarities this moment holds to the one-night stand that caused our lives to intersect again, there's something different about it. Something softer. More intimate. I guess because, as hard as we tried to keep emotion out of our agreement, it ultimately found its way in anyway, transforming this thing between us into something we both urgently needed, even if neither of us was aware of it at the time. Maybe fate is real like Ronnie believes, and everything that's happened was necessary so we could find our way here—to this place where two people who seem wrong for each other end up being exactly right. A perfect solution to a seemingly impossible equation.

And Damian *is* perfect for me. I see that so clearly now that all I feel in that once empty space between us is that desperate love squirming inside me. It begs for me to let it loose. To scream the truth from the top of my lungs.

To tell him.

The words take shape in my mouth, but I can't bring myself to stop kissing Damian long enough to say them, and my ability to form coherent thoughts becomes fully non-functional the instant his hand dips between my legs. I gasp at the delicate slide of his finger against my clit, my knees buckling slightly.

The backs of my thighs bump into the foot of the bed, and Damian carefully guides me down onto the bedspread, blanketing my body with his. For a moment, he just hovers over me, staring down into my eyes with a want I've never known before with a guy. I might have dated Parker for two years in high school, but we were never like this. We never had *this*—this fiery need for each other that seems to transcend logical thought. We were similar and had certain things in common, like our academic achievements, but our connection never seemed to go further than that. He certainly never had my heart. Not really.

Not like Damian does.

I realize that if there was ever a moment to tell him I love him, it would be now. I ready myself to say it, to shout it like my heart is demanding, but before I can utter a word, Damian is bending down and kissing me again. And perhaps I am weak, too hungry, too mesmerized by his lips, but I don't dare to stop him, reveling in his touch. His kiss this time is slow, like he's making it a point to memorize every angle and inch of my mouth and the way it molds to his. As if he's trying to memorize *me*.

We explore one another like that for a while, our hands worshiping each other's bodies with a tenderness that has my heart thudding so rapidly I can hardly breathe. With a stilted gasp, I arch my back, and my pebbled nipples brush against the naked skin of his torso. Damian ducks his head in response, drawing one of my breasts into his mouth, and when I moan long and low, his palm trails down my thigh, gently hitching my leg up.

When I feel him at my entrance, he pulls back just enough to look me in the eye—a silent request for my permission—but I don't hesitate. My hands reach down to cup the firm curve of his ass, and holding his gaze, I pull him toward me, guiding him in.

Damian and I have had sex more times than I can count since that trip to Guadalajara, but this…*this* feels different somehow. Like something more.

Like making love.

Damian's mouth finds my neck again as his hands steer mine above my head and press them into the rumpled blanket, our fingers interlocking. I lick my lips as he peppers kisses up to my ear.

"I'm so lucky to have you," he breathes, his voice edged with emotion.

A tear slips free from my eye, and he brushes it away from my cheek before kissing me deeply again. From then on, his mouth never once leaves mine, not even when our pace increases and we're both gasping, on the brink of climax. When we crash over the edge, we go together, and when we reach the other side, it's with our lips connected, and with more love in my heart than I know what to do with.

Afterward, he holds me, my back to his chest, and it isn't long until I hear the quiet sound of his breaths evening out, telling me he's fallen asleep. As the lure of sleep starts to make my own eyes droop, something occurs to me, and shaking myself awake, I carefully slide out of bed, moving slowly so I don't disturb him. He's had a trying week, and right now, he just needs to rest, assured that everything is okay.

It takes me a minute to locate my jeans in the dark, but when I do, I tug my phone free from my pocket, tiptoe back to the bed, and climb beneath the covers again, curling up next to Damian under the welcome weight of his arm. Once I'm settled, and I'm certain he's still asleep, I click on my phone screen and find Ronnie's number. Then, positioning the camera so the flash won't wake him up, I snap a picture of Damian's arm wrapped around me, and send it to Ronnie along with a simple caption.

Me

I didn't let it slip away

When I drift off a few minutes later, it's with a smile on my face.

CHAPTER
THIRTY-TWO

✦ *Damian* ✦

I wake up the next morning feeling like a new man, sated, mentally at ease (a welcome development), and above all, *happy*. Truly, honestly, so beyond fucking happy for the first time since Jamie was alive. It's like I've been given a new lease on life overnight, like I have something to live for now. A purpose. And what makes it even better is knowing Blondie will be a part of it, beside me every step of the way.

Now that all the drama with my parents is settled, and Blondie and I are stepping into our winning era, there's just one last thing to do. A bucket list set us down this path, and so it only seems fitting that a bucket list is how I mark the start of the next chapter. Except, this time, there's only one item on my list. One box I want to check.

1. Tell Blondie I love her.

She might be my girlfriend now, but I plan on locking this shit down eventually, and besides, this confession is long overdue. After last night, especially, it feels like something heavy and unspoken between us. Something that needs to be brought out into the open.

No time like the present, I encourage myself.

With a quick mental pep talk, I draw in a deep breath, shaking off the lingering haze of sleep, then roll over, ready to pull Blondie into my arms and make damn sure she knows how I feel.

"You know, I could get used to—" I start to say, but my hand finds only air where her body should be.

My eyes blink open, and for a long, confused moment, I stare at the empty bed beside me. The blankets and pillow are rumpled, molded by the frame of her figure from where she fell asleep, but my gorgeous golden goddess herself is nowhere to be seen.

"Dornan?" I call, sitting up and scanning my surroundings as much as I can from the vantage point of my mattress, but I don't get a response.

I blindly reach for my phone on my bedside table to see if she called or left a message, and to check the time, but it's not there. "Shit," I mutter, remembering it was in my coat pocket when we tumbled in here last night, so it's probably somewhere on the floor.

That's what you get for not investing in a clock, my conscience scoffs, but I ignore it, glancing instead at my wrist. Luckily, my smart watch still has some juice in it, though another expletive slips past my lips when I register the time.

It's already nine-thirty, and seeing as it's a Monday, and Blondie has a terrifying, masochistic tendency to choose morning classes, she must be in a lecture right now. Adorable, math-loving nerd that she is, she doesn't like to skip, not unless she's taking her mom to chemo, so I'm not at all surprised she left. Still, part of me wishes she had woken me up to say goodbye, while on the flip side, I completely understand why she didn't. I *am* a master of temptation, after all, and she likely feared she wouldn't have had the strength to leave me if I had urged her back into bed. And I probably would have, though I like to think I would have ultimately taken the high road, and convinced her to go to class, even if Damian Jr. would've been very displeased with that decision.

As for me, I *had* been planning on returning to my own classes today after missing most of last week, but it's definitely too late to get to my Laws & Patents lecture and have any hope of slipping in unnoticed. Welp, looks like

I'll be skipping again. Oh, well. One more day off won't hurt anyone. It's early enough in the semester to not really matter, and after the events of this past weekend, I'm sure my parents will understand.

I bark out a laugh. That's one sentence I never thought I'd say to myself, but then…I also never really believed I would ever allow myself to fall in love. And yet, here I am—loved up and obsessed with my girl like my boy Eddie in *Twilight* and, even more shockingly, on somewhat good terms with my parents again. If it was still December, I'd call it a Christmas miracle.

While I now don't have anywhere I have to be until this afternoon, I'm too jittery to lie in bed any longer—not when there are confessions of love that need professing to a certain grouchy genius. So, I kick off the blanket, ready to jump in the shower and start my day, when my gaze catches on the bedside table—not the one I usually use, but the table on Blondie's side of the bed. On it, folded in half, is a white piece of paper with the words SOLVE ME written in black pen.

Curious, I scoot across the mattress, and grab the note Blondie left me as I swing my legs over the edge of the bed, but when I unfold it, I'm only met with confusion.

"The fuck?" I mutter, taking in the complex equation scribbled along the top of the page. I don't even know what kind of math this is supposed to be, but it's like something out of a nightmare, and I have no clue how I'm meant to solve it. There are fractions, square roots, those little numbers floating above other larger numbers that I can't remember the name of. Shit, there are so many letters written down, it's like half the alphabet is involved. I took some foundational math classes for my biotech minor my first two years at Conwick, but I'm rusty at best, and besides, my focus is more on the patents, business strategy, and entrepreneurship side of things rather than the science end of pharmaceuticals, so I don't have much need for math. My future work at Hallazgo certainly won't involve solving for x. Or in this case, i. Or u. Or e.

My eyes start to cross the longer I stare at the equation, willing it to solve itself. Blondie has either massively overestimated my ability to do math, or she's really testing me.

An idea pings into my brain, and with the paper in hand, I run into the kitchen where I last left my computer. I don't even realize I'm still naked until I slide bare-assed onto the cold seat, but my need to decode Blondie's message is stronger than my need for boxer briefs, even if Damian Jr. and his two friends are shivering in disapproval.

Opening the laptop, I pull up the browser, and I'm about to type the equation into Google to get the internet to solve it for me when my fingers freeze over the keyboard. How the *hell* do you type this? I definitely don't see a square root option among the symbols printed above the numbers you access by using the shift key, and fuck knows how you type in the tiny digits whose name still eludes me.

"Fuck it," I mutter, closing my laptop.

I give myself five minutes. That's it. Five minutes to shower, brush my teeth, put on clothes, and make myself presentable to the world before I'm racing out of my room with the note clutched in my fist. The tutoring sessions at the library tend to primarily be in the evenings, but CASS is open all day to students, so surely, someone must be around who can help me make sense of this.

I glare down at the page in my hand as I quicken my pace, frowning.

Yeah. Universal language, my ass.

I'm yanking open the door to the library less than ten minutes later, and I don't pause to catch my breath before throwing myself at the CASS reception desk. The man sitting there—another senior, possibly, though I don't recognize him—gives me a startled look when I blurt out, "Hi, sorry, are you a tutor here? Math, specifically."

He blinks blue eyes at me behind large, rounded glasses that remind me of Blondie. "Well, I'm *technically* the academic support coordinator," he says, "but I do also tutor on occasion. Is there something you need help with?"

I whip out the folded page, and slam it down on the desk in front of him. "Yeah, this. I have no idea how to solve it."

The man seems surprised, but adjusts his glasses and reaches for the slip of paper. I don't miss the way his gaze lingers on the words SOLVE ME, or the way his brows draw together when he unfolds it. Fuck. Maybe he doesn't know how to do it? His eyes skim back and forth for a moment before snapping up to look at me again. "Is this homework or something?" he asks.

"Or something," I mutter, unsure what else to tell him.

He shrugs. "All right, go get a chair and come sit down, and we'll take a look."

Relief surges through me as I run to the nearest table and grab a chair like I'm being timed, and if I don't do it quick enough I'll be eliminated from the most intense game of musical chairs to ever exist. The guy at the CASS desk watches me with raised brows, his expression bemused, but he makes no comment when I plop the seat down beside him.

"Okay," he begins, flattening and attempting to smooth out the paper, which I had crumpled a bit on the journey here. When it's the best it's going to get, he grabs a pencil and taps it against the first fraction in the equation. "So, in this part, the natural logarithm and the exponential function are inverses of each other. In other words, applying the logarithm to an exponential function essentially cancels out the exponential, leaving you with the exponent itself, which in this case is $2i$. Following so far?"

I stare blankly down at the page with a newfound appreciation for Blondie's wonderful brain. Is this the kind of math she had to do for our proposal? Math she was doing effortlessly in her head in a matter of *seconds*? If so, she's not just a genius, she's a fucking wizard. Meanwhile, I wouldn't be surprised if I looked up and found little cartoon question marks bobbing over my head.

"Uh…sure," I manage after a moment, but to absolutely no one's surprise, I don't sound convincing.

My dude gives me a dubious look, but I nod for him to continue.

Clearing his throat, he looks back down at the page. "Now, over here, since the cosine of zero is one, this part simplifies to two because we're adding this one to it here." He taps the equation with the end of his pencil where it says + 1 next to what I'm guessing is the cosine he mentioned.

I bob my head. "Okay, that kind of makes sense." I think.

"Then the square root of $9u$ squared over here is $3u$, so if we rewrite the equation…" Underneath Blondie's handwriting, he scribbles a new set of numbers and letters across the wrinkled paper, then leans back and points his hands at the page, making a *ta-da* gesture. "See? Not so scary looking anymore. And now that we've gotten rid of the logarithm, the square root, and the cosine, we're just working with basic algebra."

This is supposed to be basic? I muse, but I don't bother to say that out loud.

"So, let's start with simplifying this first fraction. We can combine the terms that have the same variables, and once we do that, what do you notice about the numerator and denominator?"

I glare down at the page as if it has personally wronged me. Fucking hell, I hated fractions in school. What's the rule with them again? Something about common denominators? No, that doesn't apply here. This is just a single fraction…

I frown, certain steam must be coming out of my ears from how hard the wheels in my brain are turning. I swear, Blondie is lucky I love her because if this had come from anyone else, I would've thrown it in the trash before I even left my room.

Think, Damian. Do it for Dornan. What do you see?

I narrow my eyes at the equation.

"They both have a two?" I guess.

The man gives me an encouraging smile. "Right! So, we can cancel that two out, leaving us with $i + u$ for the first fraction. Then for this next fraction, we want to isolate it on one side, then use common denominators to simplify."

Common denominators! I knew I remembered something from math! Thankfully, though, my guy doesn't ask me to do any of the calculations myself, determined to hold my hand through it, which I'm incredibly grateful for. Still, I follow along intently, attempting to understand just in case I glean something from the numbers that will give me a clue as to what Blondie is trying to tell me.

"Now, we multiply everything by four to get rid of the fractions, and then you rearrange to combine like variables until you're at a point where you can solve for i," he explains, rewriting an even more simplified version of the equation underneath the others. "Once we do that, we…"

It takes me a second to realize the man has gone silent, and I peek over at him, sucking in a deep, calming breath to quash the unease in my chest. Is he going to say the equation's impossible? Or that it means nothing and Blondie was just fucking with me?

I'm about to prod him when he huffs out a laugh. "Oh, I see what they did there. Cute."

Cute?

"What?" I ask, confused.

The man scrawls something at the bottom of the page, then turns to look at me, placing his pencil down. "Who gave this to you?" he asks.

I hesitate, somewhat perturbed by the amused smirk on his lips. Why does he want to know? Did Blondie just come up with the solution for world hunger using math or something? Spilled some big government secret? Does the simplified equation resemble a dick?

"My girlfriend…why?" I drag out the words.

Mr. Academic Coordinator lets out another soft laugh. "It looks like she's trying to tell you something."

No shit, Sherlock, I nearly say. *The question is, what?*

But that question is answered when he turns the page toward me, revealing the final version of the equation.

$$i < 3u$$

"*i* is less than *3u?*" I say, and it's only when the words slip out of my mouth that I realize what it's really saying. When positioned next to each other, the less-than symbol and the three resemble a heart. It isn't just math. It's a message.

I love you.

My pulse trips. Blondie loves me. She *loves* me. And she's telling me the way she knows how to convey it best, in a way that's comfortable and safe for her.

With numbers. With something she easily understands.

My breath catches as I jump up from the chair. "Thanks, man. I owe you one."

I hear a flustered, "No problem," as I give the guy an appreciative slap on the shoulder, then I'm pocketing the paper and pencil, and sprinting for the exit, off to find my girl.

And finally tell her I love her, too.

Curious stares follow me as I race across campus, my ears only catching bits of the confused mutterings that accompany them, but I don't pay attention to any of it. My focus is singular.

i <3u

Blondie will be out of class by now, and though we usually meet for coffee at Izzy's, we didn't make plans for today, and seeing as she spent the night with me, it's likely she's heading home now to get changed and to check on her mom. I hope she is at least, since that's where my feet carry me as I put Conwick's campus behind me, and bolt through Newport's streets like a man possessed.

Blondie's neighborhood is only a few blocks away, and when I veer onto her road, relief and elation nearly bowl me over when I spot her walking on the sidewalk toward her house. Easing my pace to avoid alerting her to my presence just yet, I pull the paper and the pencil I swiped out of my pocket.

I only speed up again when she's about to turn onto the short path leading up to her porch, breaking into a jog.

"Dornan!"

Her steps falter at the sound of my voice, and her gaze whips over her shoulder, those green eyes piercing beneath furrowed brows, which pop up when she spots me, reaching for her hairline with bewildered surprise. She turns to face me fully, her mouth puckering with probably several unasked questions as she takes me in.

"What are you—Did you run all the way here?" she asks, no doubt noting the slight bead of perspiration dotting my forehead. I've suddenly never been more grateful that I make it a point to keep fit, and actually have the stamina to run for a couple of blocks without breaking much of a sweat. Otherwise, I would be a disgusting mess right now, and what kind of aesthetic would that set for this moment?

I slow to a stop a few feet away from where she stands watching me, and hold up the folded piece of paper. "I solved it."

Her eyes widen, fixing on my upraised hand.

A torturous silence stretches between us, and the only movement I notice her make is the subtle shift of her delicate throat when she swallows.

"And here I thought you couldn't do math," she rasps, her voice barely above a whisper.

I shrug. "I got a bit of help." Drawing in a steadying breath, I take a step forward and extend my hand.

Her cheeks—which have turned a striking pink—twitch with an aborted smile as she hesitantly reaches out to take the paper from me. It doesn't escape my notice that her fingers are trembling.

"So…is it right?" I hedge as she unfolds the note.

Blondie swallows again, more loudly this time, when her eyes lock on the simplified equation. She lifts a shaking hand to her glasses, and my stomach sinks a little when I recognize her telltale sign of anxiety. I didn't get the answer wrong—the ridiculously gorgeous stain of red spreading across her face makes me damn sure of that—which can only mean she's worried about my reaction. Perhaps she thinks it's too soon, that we're moving too quickly, and regrets telling me how she feels. Maybe she thought I wouldn't solve it for another decade or two. Or more likely—given what she said to me at Grape Expectations that night she got drunk all those weeks ago—she's worried that I won't reciprocate. Not yet, at least.

I nearly laugh at the thought. How could I *not* love her? This brilliant, stubborn, fierce but soft-hearted, unapologetically blunt, beautifully chaotic gem of a woman who matches my weird and makes my world make sense just by simply existing in it. Even if I went back to the start of senior year without any memory of the last five months, I would fall in love with her all over again.

Because we're inevitable. She is the exception to every rule I ever set for myself, the balm to my grief, the life-saving breath to my drowning lungs. And she has converted me, not only to love—to the raw vulnerability it takes to really let another person in—but away from my longstanding loyalty to Team Jacob, which is saying something. Because Blondie is the Bella to my Edward.

And we're not just inevitable, we're eternal.

"Turn it over."

When Blondie peers up at me, I jerk my chin toward the note clutched in her hand, and as she slowly shifts the paper in her grip, I catch a fleeting glimpse of the message I wrote on the back when I first turned onto her street.

A confession of my own, unspoken but from the heart. Just like hers.

I love you too

Her breath catches.

"Are you sure?" Her gaze lifts to meet mine, uncertain.

I snort out a laugh. "Not quite the reaction I was expecting."

Her eyes flit away. "It's just…past experiences have told me that I'm not always easy to love." Her tone is guarded, and I know in this moment, she's thinking not only of her asshole dad, who abandoned her instead of telling her every day how absolutely fucking remarkable she is, or of the jerk-off she dated in high school, who dumped her because she stayed in Newport, but of *me*—of how easily I ghosted her my junior year after making her think I liked her. A mistake I sure as hell don't ever plan on repeating.

"Well, that's where you're wrong, Blondie," I chide, bridging the remaining distance between us. I take her chin in my hand, forcing her to look up at me. "Because loving you is the easiest thing I've ever done."

As she stares at me, I silently plead, *Hear me. Believe me.*

And when our lips collide, I know she does.

Me + Damian = Happily Ever After?

MAY

onwick's annual commencement ceremony is held at Brenton Square—a spacious historic green on campus with a large, adjoining hall—so the school can host graduation outdoors on the quad while having someplace nearby to divert the students and their guests indoors if it rains or once the formalities are over, where a veritable feast of champagne and overpriced canapés awaits.

To the joy of everyone present, the sun is shining brightly overhead—there isn't a cloud in the sky—and the air is mild, perfect weather for such an important and meaningful day. It feels kismet, a concept I wouldn't normally give any weight to (much to the disgruntlement of Ronnie) but which seems appropriate in this instance. In a lot of ways, it's like the universe is smiling down on us.

I sit in the front row of the audience waiting for the commencement to begin (a perk of being here as a guest of the Navarros, who have sway at Conwick), sandwiched between Damian's parents and his abuela on my right, and my mom and Gina—who Damian also invited—to my left. Even Xolo is here, sitting by my feet with his sweet face propped on my knee, tail wagging happily, because the Navarros donate a shit ton of money to our school, and no one in the administration was about to risk alienating such a wealthy family by telling Lucia she couldn't bring her dog.

I give his head a gentle pat just as my phone buzzes in my jacket pocket. His head tilts at the sound, and he watches me curiously as I tug it free. When I tap the screen, I find a new text in my group chat with Ronnie and Andie.

Ronnie

Tell D congrats from us xx

A grin tugs at my lips. For someone who once hated Damian, possibly even more than I did, Ronnie has really warmed up to him recently. They went from reluctant acquaintances to frenemies to actual *friends* in only a matter of months, bonding over their shared interest in cringey movies and, of course, their mutual love for me. The only reason she isn't here today is because her and Andie flew home to California a few days ago for Andie's younger sister Sammy's birthday. Knowing Ronnie like I do, I'm sure she's feeling guilty about missing Damian's big day, but she's here in spirit with us, and that's all that matters.

Grinning at my phone, I tap out:

Me

Will do. Tell Sammy happy birthday from me xo

I shoot off the text, then turn off the device and shove it back into my pocket just as the ceremony is about to begin.

The procession files onto the quad in a uniform sea of deep purple gowns and caps, the rich hue only interrupted by the spots of varying color displayed by the tassels denoting every student's individual focus of study. I spot Damian among the herd of graduating seniors, a sandy brown tassel signifying his business major swinging gleefully by the side of his face. As if sensing my lingering gaze, he turns his own toward the audience, and when he catches my eye, he gives me a wave.

Just past where the graduates sit, a large white stage has been erected on the quad specifically for today's ceremony, and all the teachers at Conwick and the university administrators are in attendance with the exception of one: my Applied Discrete Mathematics professor last semester and advisor, Professor Bensen. Just over a month after school started up again following the Christmas break, it was discovered that he was the one who had sold my name to the tabloids in exchange for a whopping one hundred grand—which he apparently needed to pay off some pretty hefty gambling debts—after seeing the photographs of Damian and me together online. Whether he noticed Damian crashing his class that one time in September remains unknown, and we'll probably never know, not that it matters. The violation was the same regardless, and when the university found out, he was fired.

At the time of my name being released in the media, I never really stopped to wonder about the who or why behind the leak, probably because it always felt like an inevitability—a matter of *when* rather than *if*. Damian never thought of it either; his focus was strictly on damage control and swinging the story in our favor. But when news broke of Professor Bensen's involvement, I saw a side of Damian I hope to never see again. The terror in him. The worry. Obviously, I was disappointed Professor Bensen would sell out a student, though I couldn't help empathizing with him considering my own desperate actions when I needed money. Damian, however, viewed it from an entirely different angle. All he could see was yet another male parental figure in my life letting me down, and it took weeks of assuring him I was okay—that I hadn't lost my faith in humanity or my trust in men. That this betrayal wouldn't break me.

And it hasn't—it won't—because there is too much good in my life now to allow any of it to be tainted by the bad. Good like this beautiful day and the milestone we're celebrating.

After the opening remarks and guest speakers, the ceremony moves on to the conferring of degrees, and when Damian ascends the stairs to the stage, the audience erupts into cheers, with our row being the loudest by far. Beside me, Lucia shouts something in Spanish, Xolo barking in agreement, while on their right, Damian's mother is weeping, and his father looks on with an approving smile. To my left, my aunt whistles like she's at a sporting event, and my mom claps with so much enthusiasm and energy, it brings tears to my eyes.

As of last month—in large part thanks to my new job at Hallazgo and the incredible benefits that come with it—Mom officially went into remission to the surprise of everyone, including her doctors. With every passing day, she's looked better and better, healthier and more alive than I've seen her in the last two years. It's scary to think things might not have turned out this way if it wasn't for Damian—if Andie hadn't jokingly pulled up Craigslist on my laptop to cheer me up, and I hadn't taken a chance on his ad. But I try to not focus on the *what ifs* these days and instead stay here in the present, in these moments of immeasurable happiness where my heart is so full with love and optimism (a new one for me) that all those fears that bogged me down for so many years now feel like a distant thing of the past. Like they belong to someone else and not to Present or Future Lexi.

And Present Lexi is a big fan of her current life. *And* of her smoking hot boyfriend, who is waving at his loved ones from the stage with one hand while holding up his diploma with the other. A smile pulls at my cheeks that stretches so wide my face begins to hurt, but I'm so freaking proud of him, I couldn't care less about my discomfort. He meets my gaze once more as he makes his way down the stairs and back to his seat, and just before he sits again, he sets the leather-bound folder containing his diploma on the chair, and holds his hands up high so I can see them over the blanket of graduation caps. He then brings his fingers together, his left hand forming a less-than symbol with his pointer finger and thumb while the first few fingers of his right hand form a rough approximation of the number three—our private way of saying, "I love you."

Blushing, I hold my hands up and make the gesture back.

The rest of the ceremony passes in a blur, and once the president of Conwick makes his closing remarks, everyone around me seems to spring from their chairs with excitement. In front of me, clusters of graduates hug each other, while behind me, the attending family members and friends all funnel forward in a herd, rushing off to track down their children so they can tell them how proud of them they are.

As we make our way through the busy throng to find Damian, Lucia holds onto my arm, gushing about how much she's looking forward to our extended visit to Guadalajara before her grandson begins working full-time at Hallazgo. Although Damian doesn't technically step into his role as Innovation Project Lead until early next month, he's been spending most of his free time making good on those connections he formed with hospitals, pharmacies, and research universities when we were working on the proposal, establishing the partnerships that will make The Jamie Initiative come to life, and give it the outside backing it will need to thrive and accomplish its mission.

As for me, Hector brought me on board straightaway so I could start benefiting from the company's health insurance—a move my mom and I were both immensely grateful for, and which I repaid in kind by returning the money I received from Damian minus what I had already spent on the insurance deductible and January's prescription, with a promise to repay the difference, clearing my Mom's conscience (and mine). Now, a few hours a week around my classes and tutoring, I've been working in the finance department until I transition into my official role as Financial Sustainability Analyst, which will align with when Damian joins the company, so we can work together to get the program up and running.

And thankfully, we'll be able to do that with the full support of Hallazgo behind us. After we finished the proposal in early February, Damian and his father went before the board to pitch the idea, and not only were the directors in favor of the initiative, but they agreed to Damian's conditions regarding his eventual employment—no vote needed, just as his mom promised. As a result, Hallazgo has publicly changed its stance on experimental treatments and drug development, and will now be working closely with research universities to develop therapy regiments and other life-saving interventions for diseases like cancer. That day was the first time I ever saw Damian cry, and it was all I could do to hold him, and to remind him in quiet, repeated whispers that he's made his abuelo and Jamie proud.

That he's made *me* proud.

And he's continued to make me proud every day since. Sometimes, it's crazy to think my Damian is the same guy who ghosted me freshman year, but then, I think I needed to hate him so I could eventually love him as much as I do now. Because if we could find a way to overcome that kind of hate and animosity, then we can overcome anything.

"Dornan!"

I follow the sound of Damian's voice calling to me through the crowd, and smile again when I spot him. Holding my gaze, he pushes his way through the other graduates to come meet us, but is intercepted by Xolo, who had been trotting along at my heels and immediately ran past me and Lucia when he noticed my boyfriend.

"Buen perrito," I hear Damian coo as he squats down to give the yapping dog a scratch behind the ears. Xolo whines, demanding his full attention, but Damian stands again when we approach.

"Ay, mi niño," Lucia cries, releasing my arm to step forward and cup Damian's face in her hands. "Estoy tan orgullosa de ti." Patting his cheek, she adds in a soothing voice, "Your abuelito would be so proud of you, too."

"Thanks, abuelita," he whispers, dwarfing her tiny figure as he pulls her in for a hug.

Behind us, I hear Damian's mom let out a quiet, hiccuping sob.

"Aw, come on, Mom," he mutters. "Don't cry."

Lenore waves her manicured fingers at her face in a feeble attempt to dry her tears. "I can't help it. I'm just so proud of you," she says, her voice wavering.

"We both are," Hector adds as Damian steps forward to wrap a consoling arm around his mom's shoulders. He meets his father's eyes as the older man holds out his hand. "Well done, mijo."

One of the most unexpected developments to come out of these last several months (which is setting a high bar since *everything* since September has been pretty unexpected) is the shift in Damian's relationship with his parents. Things aren't perfect—there's a lot of residual trauma they still need to process, but they're trying, and they're openly acknowledging their emotions. They've even been going to family therapy once a week to have a third-party mediator help them work through their shared grief surrounding Jamie's passing, and have unpacked some deeper, generational issues and expectations that were making it difficult for them to establish healthy boundaries. It's given Damian a safe space to open up to his parents, and most importantly, they're *listening*. No more ultimatums, no more threats. Just three people doing their best to repair something that was broken.

Damian takes his father's outstretched hand, and they shake, exchanging a smile that would have seemed impossible only six months ago. Releasing his son, Hector gives Damian a fond pat on the back, then inclines his head toward me before leading his wife and mother away to Brenton Hall for refreshments so my family and I can have a moment to congratulate Damian, too. Xolo whines again, not wanting to leave just yet, but reluctantly follows when beckoned.

"Congratulations, Damian," Mom gushes once the Navarros have left us, giving him a tight, motherly hug.

"Thanks, Carol," he says, squeezing her back. When they pull apart, he glances between her and my aunt. "Thank you both for coming."

"Are you kidding?" Gina scoffs, playfully nudging his shoulder. "Like we'd miss this. You're family now, kid."

The smile that lights up Damian's face is so bright it's like staring directly into the sun. I bask in his happiness, feeling it warm me from the inside out.

After a few more words of congratulations, and a quick confirmation that Damian is still coming to our house for dinner tomorrow before we fly to Guadalajara with Lucia the following morning, my mom and aunt say their goodbyes.

Then we're alone, just the two of us, like we were at the beginning when this thing between us first started.

"So, today's the day," I say with a casual step toward Damian, my hands clasped behind my back. "The deadline of our agreement, and the official end of our fake relationship."

"So, it is," he notes, face comically serious.

Lifting a hand, I tap the pad of my pointer finger to my bottom lip. "I feel like we should mark the occasion. What do you think—should we stage a fake break-up, or would you rather make an Instagram post informing the masses? That worked last time. Or maybe we should just call TMZ so they can hear it directly from the horse's mouth?"

Damian waves a dismissive hand. "Nah. We'd only confuse people. Besides, did you forget already? If so, you wound me, Blondie."

I arch a brow. "Forget what?" I ask innocently.

"That you agreed to date me for real," he reminds me, snaking an arm around my waist, and pulling me close to his chest. "Don't think I'm letting go of you that easily."

With a delicate sniff, I mutter in a coy voice, "I remember. So, what do you suggest we do instead?"

He shrugs. "Well, we could always just make a new agreement. One without a deadline this time, of course."

"Oh? And what would this new agreement entail?"

The humor fades from his face as his piercing eyes lock on mine. "That we take it one day at a time. No lies, no faking. Just unfiltered honesty, and facing everything life throws at us, both the good and the bad…together."

His words aren't just a promise, they're a vow. One that threatens to set my soul on fire with hope.

A smile curls my lips as I loop my arms around his neck. "Together. I like the sound of that."

My stomach flutters as he leans in and kisses me, and in this moment, despite the cacophony of laughter and shouts of "Congratulations!" surrounding us on all sides, it's as if we're the only two people in the world.

Damian shifts one arm from my back, and I peek open my eyes to find him holding his phone at an angle above us.

"What are you doing?" I murmur against his lips.

"Marking the occasion," he breathes, sending a shiver rippling through me as he kisses me deeply again. I'm so lost in it I barely hear the click of the camera.

Afterward, I watch as he opens up Instagram and posts the picture he just took of us kissing with him in his graduation gown and cap, a scene of chaotic celebration erupting behind us. Underneath the photo, in the caption area, are two simple words.

#Dexi forever 🖤

And I know we will be.

THE END

Today's math lesson: glitter ≠ lube.

"Is that…*body glitter?*"

I reach out and swipe my fingertip across Damian's left pectoral, then pull back my hand, rubbing the silver residue that transfers from his skin to mine between the pad of my pointer finger and thumb.

Yup, that is definitely glitter.

Ignoring me, he lifts his chin and stares down at me with hooded eyes, his gaze borderline predatory. "This is the skin of a killer, Dornan." He pauses, his lips curling into a menacing smile. "And I am about to *murder* your pussy."

I snort out a laugh. "I feel like I just walked onto the set of a badly written porno."

Damian's left cheek twitches. "Are there any *well* written pornos?" he counters.

I consider that for a moment then shrug. "Fair point."

"Anyway"—he shakes out his arms and resumes his previous position with his chest puffed out and chin raised—"come on, get back into character." When I don't immediately comply, he frowns. "You promised," he reminds me, his voice a low whine.

With a defeated sigh, I roll my eyes. "You better enjoy this while it lasts, Navarro. Because I'm never doing it again."

He arches a dubious brow. "You say that now…"

I hold up a hand. "Listen, the only way I'm roleplaying *Twilight* again is if

I get to be Charlie and *you* dress as Carlisle."

That brings Damian up short. His face scrunches, and I just know he's trying to picture how my suggestion would play out. "What...? How would...?" He juts out his lower lip in confusion, then his eyes bug wide as the realization suddenly hits. "*Butt* stuff?" His gaze darkens, and he takes a step toward me, dipping his head, wiggling his brows suggestively at me. "You know, you never did tell me your opinion on butt plugs."

"Wouldn't you like to know?" I croon. "Besides, who said *I'd* be the one wearing the plug? Pegging is a thing, and Charlie is totally a top."

Damian recoils a bit at my words. "I consider myself to be an adventurous person, Blondie. But that might be a touch *too* adventurous for me." He pauses, as if reconsidering, then adds, "Let's file that one as a maybe. I'm willing to try anything if it's with you. But for now"—he straightens again and takes a step back, resuming his previous position—"I believe we were in the middle of some morally questionable vampire seduction."

I sigh. "Okay, here we go." Clearing my throat, I search deep inside for my inner Bella—well, the horny, pornstar version of her, at least—and try not to die of embarrassment as I say, "You're impossibly fast. And *huge*." I inch toward Damian, who watches me with hungry eyes as I reach out a hand and gently rub his dick through his jeans. "Your length is rock hard," I coo in a sultry voice that has his pupils dilating. "I know what you are."

"Say it," he demands in a husky voice. "Out loud."

The correct response here is "Vampire." I remember it from the movie, and Damian even made me a script so I would know my lines because he was determined to tick this mortifying experience off his new sex bucket list, which consists of all the dirty things he wants to do with me. And *to* me. Not with other girls. Not because of a bet. Just a list of things for us to try as we explore our relationship. Together.

But of course, that's not what I say because I cannot take this seriously.

"A...sex addict?" I answer, trying hard not to laugh.

Damian glowers at me. "Okay, you are officially terrible at this."

"Who wouldn't be?" I counter. "Also, this wig is *really* itchy, you know." As if to prove my point, I poke a finger under the wig cap and scratch my nail against my scalp an inch or so above my ear, sighing at the instant relief.

Damian rubs a hand along his chin, assessing me with narrowed eyes. "Yeah, I have to say, you as a brunette isn't really doing it for me. Show me those gorgeous blonde curls, baby."

I grin up at him as he helps me pry off the wig, my cheeks flushing at the look on his face when the brunette locks fall away and my real hair pops back into view. "Maybe you're more of a Rosalie guy?" I suggest, but he just shakes his head.

"I'm more of a *you* guy."

Those words, and the undeniable love behind them, do more for me than any role play ever could. Rising onto my toes, I throw my arms around Damian's neck, and when I kiss him, he eagerly kisses me back, his tongue sliding along the seam of my lips, begging me to open.

I let him in with a moan as his hands follow a calculated trail along my torso and waist—explorers in the familiar land of my body—his fingers touching me everywhere except where I need them until I'm squirming and desperate. The heat building in my core is an ache demanding gratification, but while I would happily take him inside me right this moment to alleviate that hunger, that *need*, I also want to savor this. Savor *him*. I might not be able to fulfill his *Twilight* fantasy with a straight face, but I can at least show him just how much I want him.

How much I *love* him.

Breaking our kiss, I slowly drop to my knees, my hands sliding down his defined torso until my fingers reach his belt. Damian lets out a stilted breath, throwing his head back when I unbuckle his pants and rub him again through his briefs. Smirking up at him, I tug his jeans and underwear down to release his cock, and when it springs free, ready for action, I—

"Oh, my god, Damian, did you put glitter on your *dick*?"

Sitting back on my heels, I slap a hand over my mouth to muffle my outburst of laughter.

Damian blinks, glancing between my face to his raging erection, which stands at attention, ready and waiting, pre-cum leaking from the tip.

"I was being authentic!" he retorts, gesturing to his cock, which almost looks like it's crying because I refuse to touch it. "If Edward glitters in the sun, then surely, it stands to reason his dick would glitter, too?"

I shake my head. "You are unhinged. I am *not* fucking a bedazzled penis." At Damian's dejected expression, I say, "That shit has yeast infection written all over it."

His face falls—out of disappointment more than embarrassment, I'm sure, since Damian doesn't have a shred of humility or a single self-conscious bone in his body—but he doesn't argue.

With a beleaguered sigh, I climb to my feet, and when I slide my hand in his, he looks at me like an injured puppy. "Come on," I mutter, giving his arm a gentle tug. "I'll help you wash it off."

He perks up at that, a tentative smile creeping onto his lips. "Sexy shower time?" he asks, hopeful.

I peer back at him over my shoulder as I lead him toward the bathroom and shrug. "Well, that depends."

"On?" he prompts, narrowing skeptical eyes at me.

I pause and give him a quick, assessing once-over. "On how easily this all comes off. Seriously, you look like you got glitter-bombed."

It takes twenty minutes, two sponges, and a full bottle of body wash, but after some rigorous scrubbing, Damian is finally glitter-free.

"What do you think?" he asks, spinning in a slow circle for me to examine him fully. The water from the shower head rains down on us where we stand in his ridiculously large wet-room style shower, and I bite my lip as the rivulets run down his gorgeous muscled body. "Am I clean enough for you?"

I make a show of checking him everywhere before sliding my hands across his torso. "You look pretty clean to me."

Damian brushes my wet hair from my face as he pulls me in for a deep, electrifying kiss that sends a thrilling buzz through my veins. I could spend my hours—my *days*—this way, just kissing Damian, just feeling the soft, pressing touch of his lips against mine. But right now, there are other things I want to feel on my lips.

Pulling away, I peer down at his cock, which gently brushes against the meeting point of my thighs, and biting my lip again, I sink down to the shower floor, taking him in hand. His length is rock hard and throbs beneath my touch, and I can feel the warmth of his pre-cum as I swipe my thumb over the tip in the second before it mixes with the water and washes away.

Damian groans, and spurred by that sound, I bend forward and wrap my lips around him, swirling my tongue around the head for a moment, then drawing him in deeper as I trail my hands along the curve of his ass. He bucks when I hollow my cheeks out and pull back, sucking along the full length of him, his fingers knotting in my hair as if to restrain himself—to fight off the undeniable urge to thrust into my mouth.

I tighten my grip on his ass, pulling him even closer, giving him my unspoken permission, and as we both pick up speed, I hear his breaths growing ragged above me.

"Fuck, Dornan. That mouth of yours…" He moans again before urgently tapping me on the shoulder.

I pull off his cock with an audible pop, and sit back on my heels to look up at him.

"Come here," he beckons, gesturing for me to stand. Offering me a hand, he helps me back onto my feet, and for a few seconds after, he just stares at me, grazing his thumb across my swollen bottom lip. "As incredible as that felt, I don't want to come unless it's inside you."

I let out a gasp at his words, that heat in my core now on the verge of a nuclear meltdown.

"Can I?" he whispers, bringing his lips to my ear, his hot breath on my wet skin making me shiver. "Can I fuck you, Blondie?"

When I nod, his hand slides between my legs, and I arch my back as his finger swipes through my wet folds and begins to circle my entrance.

"Damian…" I rasp, breathless, completely consumed and already so far gone just from the lightest touch of his hand. It's a wonder all the times I've had him inside me didn't kill me or cause me to spontaneously combust.

"Always so wet for me, aren't you?" he murmurs. His finger plunges inside me, his palm slapping against my clit, but just as I start to feel the fire of my impending release, his hand disappears. "Look at me," he whispers.

When I meet his gaze, he leans in to kiss me again, one arm curling around my waist as he carefully guides me over to the wall. When my back crowds against the tile, his arm retracts, hooking instead under my knee and pulling it up to my chest. His other hand dips between my legs, rubbing my aching bud, but then—just like his hand before—it's gone again before I can come. I'm about to complain, to urge him to keep going, when I feel the blunt head of his cock and immediately bite back any protests.

I cry out as he slides into me, his length hitting all the right places at this angle, stroking my nerves like the strings of a guitar until I am the physical embodiment of a song known only to us. He pulls in and out so slowly I could die, his rhythm a punishing descent into carnal madness. It's only when I beg him to fuck me that he picks up the pace.

That fire grows inside me with each slide of his cock slamming home, eventually igniting into an inferno. It devours me—this hunger, this need, this desire for him and only him that burns through every part of my body until it feels destructive. Life-destroying. But maybe that's the point. In some ways, Damian *did* destroy my life—shattered the walls I'd carefully built around my heart—but he's also the one who fixed it. He taught me there's strength in vulnerability, that love isn't something to fight or run from, but a truth to embrace. He is the answer to the equation I could never quite solve—the missing piece that makes everything fall into place. And together, we are better, stronger, more *whole* than we ever were apart.

Before, we were lost, wandering the endless abyss of our individual griefs and the traumas we were refusing to face. But together, we aren't lost. Not anymore.

In each other, we are found.

"I love you," I whisper against his lips, my core tightening as the fire fully consumes me.

Damian's eyes snap to mine at those words—words I've only ever put in writing or in our secret hand signal but never said aloud—and when he meets my gaze, a hoarse shout explodes from his lips that rivals my own cry of ecstasy. His pistoning hips falter as his body shudders against me.

I blink, chest heaving under the hot spray of the water as I take in his wrecked expression.

A light giggle escapes me. "Wow, did my profession of love just make you come?"

Damian exhales a soft laugh. "What can I say? Knowing you love me was already the best feeling in the entire world…but *hearing* it?" He lowers his head to my shoulder and shakes it before straightening again to look at me. "For what it's worth…I love you, too."

His hand curves around my cheek as he dips his head to kiss me again, and for a long while, we stay this way—just kissing in the shower with him still inside me until his flagging erection hardens once more, and we do it all over again.

His movements are firm and sure, grounding me in a way I never truly understood I needed before him. Before *us*. And somewhere in the mix of our breathless moans, those three beautiful words slip out again—spoken plainly, without hesitation or fanfare.

When we both come for a second time, he pulls me into the warm embrace of his arms, and that touch, this moment, it isn't just the comfort of being held—of being *loved*—but the quiet certainty that we're building something we can both stand on.

And that the ground beneath us is unshakeable.

"Sorry I messed up your *Twilight* fantasy," I say a few minutes later when we're back in his bedroom and toweling ourselves dry for bed.

Damian waves a dismissive hand at me. "It's okay. We'll just move onto the next thing on our list, which is…" He makes a show of thinking long and hard, as if he's mentally ticking off the options. After a moment, his pointer finger pings upward, his eyes springing wide, and it's as if I can literally hear the light bulb turning on in his head. "Library role play!" He looks me up and down with a mischievous grin. "You'd make one very sexy librarian, Dornan. And I've been a very bad boy, not returning my books on time."

I snort as I carefully pluck out my contacts and put on my glasses. "We got lucky the last two times, and something tells me third time is *not* the charm. If we try to have sex in the library again, we will end up arrested."

That devious smile widens. "And it would be totally worth it."

My own smile falters a little. Damian pushes me to try new things, to test my comfort zone, and I truly love him for it. On top of our sex bucket list, we have multiple others—foods to eat, places to go, non-sexual things to try.

And our life together so far has been adventurous, especially in the bedroom. But while I definitely enjoy it, there are times—like now—when I can't help wondering if he needs it. The excitement. The escapism.

If me on my own isn't quite enough.

"Hey." Damian walks over to me and presses his palm to my cheek, his dark eyes roving over my face with concern. "You know I'm just teasing about all that, right?" And then, as if he can read my mind, he adds, "If there's ever anything you don't want to try, all you have to do is say the word. I don't need any of it—role play, kink, whatever. What we just did? Just you and me stripped back without all that? It was fucking phenomenal. It's enough. *You're* enough. You're *more* than enough. Whatever you want is what I want. Always."

My heart stumbles at his words—at the ardent earnestness behind them. How could I *not* love him when he's always putting me first? When he's never asking to meet me halfway, but always overshooting that middle point so I never have to go beyond what I'm comfortable with?

How could I *not* love him when he so selflessly loves me?

And yet, heat flares across my cheeks as I bite down on the inside of my bottom lip. "Are you…sure?" I ask, hating how self-conscious I sound.

Though I've managed to put a lot of my abandonment issues behind me since we got together (or rather, in a taped-up box in the back of my closet I plan to never open again), they still rear their ugly head from time to time. But then, trauma is like that. We might heal, but I'm not sure it ever truly leaves us. Still, it bothers me—how needy I feel in these rare moments when I seek his verbal reassurance, but they also serve to remind me that I am worthy of love. That me as I am is enough. And best of all, Damian never fails to deliver exactly what I need.

"Yeah," he promises, looping his arms around my waist and tugging me close to his chest. He flashes a lopsided smile before bending down to kiss me on the tip of my nose. "The fantasy is fun and all, but honestly? My reality…" He inches to the side, kissing me on the cheek. "*You…*" he says next, his mouth brushing the corner of mine. "It's far better than the dream. I wouldn't change it for anything."

And when our lips meet again, and he kisses me so fully my heart skips, I know I wouldn't either.

WANT TO FEEL *ALL* THE VIBES?

I made a playlist for this book—aka the emotional rollercoaster you just survived—complete with all the songs that inspired this story and that I often found myself listening to while writing. So, if you're not ready to say goodbye to Lexi and Damian just yet, this one's for you.

Scan the code below & hit play.

Because your ears deserve a happy ending, too.

As an author, I believe we always put a little piece of ourselves into everything we write. Sometimes, that piece we put in is subconscious; in those instances, we aren't actively aware we are doing it. Other times, like with *The Girlfriend Agreement*, we invest so much of ourselves into the story that it becomes something deeply personal—a reflection of our own experiences, almost like looking in a mirror.

Before you ask, no, I did *not* fall in love with a billionaire hottie heir to a pharmaceutical company. But I do know what it's like to live with crippling anxiety and a cocktail of neurospicy ingredients rattling around in my brain. And I do know what it's like to live with a family member battling cancer.

Writing this story was therapeutic for me in a lot of ways. It allowed me to inject a tiny piece of how I experience the world into not just Lexi's character but Damian's—particularly his battle with grief. My mom was diagnosed with cancer when I was young. I can't remember the exact age I was, but I was in middle school—a time that was already particularly difficult since I was on the cusp of puberty and dealing with a degenerative bone condition that was causing me immense daily pain. Though, nothing hurt me as much as the way my family handled my mom's cancer. I remember how my parents didn't really ever tell me what was going on, even as the years progressed and my mom got sicker, and the anger I felt at being left out of the loop and only realizing just how bad things were when it was already too late.

Unlike Lexi's family, mine was in the unique position that we could afford my mom's cancer treatments. Like Damian's family, that ability to afford those costs ultimately didn't matter. My mom passed away in 2011, just four months shy of my wedding. She only met my husband once, and as I was living in the UK by that time, I couldn't get back to see her before she died due to extenuating circumstances. Not being there is a guilt I will live with every day—a different kind of guilt to what Damian's parents endure in this story in regard to Jamie, but the helplessness we both felt is the same. That kind of guilt never leaves you.

While the issue of healthcare affordability is a major focus in this story, the funding of medical research—particularly for underfunded cancers—also plays a crucial role in Damian's character arc, influencing his decision to push for investment in experimental treatments by the end of the book. Chronic lymphocytic leukemia (the cancer Lexi's mom, Carol, has) is relatively well-funded in terms of cancer research. Unfortunately, the same cannot be said for pediatric cancers—especially pediatric brain cancer, which claimed the life of Damian's younger brother, Jamie.

Brain cancer, including pediatric glioblastoma, is the most underfunded cancer in the U.S., with only 4% of the National Cancer Institute's (NCI) federal research budget allocated to all pediatric cancers combined. That means children facing these diagnoses are often left with limited treatment options, and families like Damian's are forced to navigate an impossible reality with few viable solutions. This is why research funding is so vital. It isn't just important—it's *necessary* to give these children a fighting chance.

While familial loss is a large theme in *The Girlfriend Agreement*, I was adamant that Lexi's mom go into remission at the end of the story— to experience that happy ending Jamie never got to have. That my own mom never got to have. But Lexi's experience with the struggle to afford medical treatment isn't unique to this book. As of 2024, a staggering 45% of Americans face challenges affording healthcare, including prescription medications, some of which are vital for their well-being. There are some people out there actively working to combat the U.S. healthcare crisis— Mark Cuban (whose CostPlus company was the main inspiration for the initiative Damian and Lexi propose for Hallazgo) is a fantastic example of someone using their wealth for good to tackle this issue—but the majority of people facing terminal and chronic illnesses like the Dornans are often burdened with the choice between potential financial ruin and what could very well be their survival.

That's why it was so important to me that Lexi and Damian's story didn't have an isolated happy ending where things only worked out for them, or even, by extension, their families. I wanted to do something to fix a system that is so tragically broken, even if that fix only exists in fiction. And I wanted to give Damian the closure and redemption arc he deserved. Because I *have* been Damian. I *have* been self-destructive and angry and drowning in so much guilt it sometimes felt like I would never resurface. Ultimately, I wanted this book to be a story of hope.

To the industry professionals (especially my girl Rebecca, who is an absolute MVP), thank you for answering my endless questions and helping me to understand the intricacies of the U.S. healthcare system and the confusing clusterfuck that is medical insurance. Without your expertise, I'm not sure I could have convincingly written this book. I hope I did it justice. And for any parts I might have gotten wrong, let's just agree to brush it off as creative license for the sake of writing a compelling story.

To Alisha, Heidi, Lindsey, and Rebecca (again), thank you for enduring long phone calls and text conversations with me on what felt like a near daily basis and giving me all the reassurances I needed to know this story wasn't an absolute dumpster fire. Heidi, I love our video calls so much. You are just a gem and literal sunshine in human form. Thank you for brightening my days and being my family by choice. Alisha, I want to take a moment to give you an extra shout-out as well because I drain down on you more than anyone else, and I need you to know how much I appreciate you. Like, so freaking much. You have genuinely become my dearest friend in the world, and I love you so much for always being there for me and never getting fed up when I'm having (yet another) writing-induced panic attack. I hope you know that every single *Twilight* joke in this book was for you. You will always be the Alice to my Bella.

To Angi and Kiara, a huge thank you for double-checking the Spanish used throughout this story, and for being so gracious and patient with me when I got it wrong (and for helping me correct it). I have the greatest respect for Mexican culture and sincerely hope I've captured its essence with the care and authenticity it deserves.

To my husband and daughter, who are so supportive and always give me the space and encouragement I need when it comes to my writing. I know I can turn into an absolute feral rage goblin sometimes when I get overstimulated, and I love and adore you both for putting up with me and always loving me back. Also, Daniel, thank you for feeding me. I would probably die of starvation without you. Or poor dietary choices.

To everyone out there who has also faced familial loss or is in a position similar to Lexi's: I am sending you the biggest hug. There aren't really any words I can say that will ease your pain, but I hope you have found your way to healing. Just know: I see you.

Lastly, to you: the reader. Thank you so much for reading *The Girlfriend Agreement*. I hope this story has resonated with you in some way and that you'll stick around for book two, *The Boyfriend Vendetta*, featuring our favorite spunky redhead. I promise that one will be on the lighter side (and may or may not feature Ronnie writing some truly deranged Timothée Chalamet fan fiction). Your support has meant more to me than I can put into words, so from the bottom of my heart, thank you.

ABOUT THE AUTHOR

ROWAN CROFT is an American-born romcom enthusiast now thriving in picturesque Cornwall after finding her own happily ever after in the UK. When she's not chasing caffeine-fuelled inspiration, she's busy in the publishing world as a graphic designer, diving into a good book, or simply enjoying day-to-day life alongside her hunky British husband, bubbly daughter, and Milo, her delightfully moody Jack Russell.

She writes the kind of romance she loves to read—full of quick-witted banter, undeniable chemistry, and just the right amount of chaos. For her, there's nothing better than a love story that keeps you laughing, swooning, and maybe yelling at the characters to just kiss already.

Find her online at:
www.authorrowancroft.com

9 781914 483318